ANDREW HUNTER MURRAY

The
Last
Day

arrow books

1 3 5 7 9 10 8 6 4 2

Arrow Books
20 Vauxhall Bridge Road
London SW1V 2SA

Arrow Books is part of the Penguin Random House group of companies
whose addresses can be found at global.penguinrandomhouse.com

 Penguin
Random House
UK

First published in Great Britain by Hutchinson in 2020
First published by Arrow Books in 2021

www.penguin.co.uk

A CIP catalogue record for this book is available from the British Library.

ISBN 9781787463615

Typeset in 11.11/16.3 pt Times New Roman by
Integra Software Services Pvt. Ltd, Pondicherry

Printed and bound in Great Britain by Clays Ltd, Elcograf S.p.A.

The authorised representative in the EEA is Penguin Random House Ireland,
Morrison Chambers, 32 Nassau Street, Dublin D02 YH68.

'I looked up into the air, and I saw that it was greatly disturbed. I looked up to the vault of the sky, and I saw it standing still; and the birds of the sky were at rest. I looked back to the earth and saw a bowl laid out for some workers who were reclining to eat. Their hands were in the bowl, but those who were chewing were not chewing; and those who were taking something from the bowl were not lifting it up; and those who were bringing their hands to their mouths were not bringing them to their mouths. Everyone was looking up. And I saw a flock of sheep being herded, but they were standing still. And the shepherd raised his hand to strike them, but his hand remained in the air. I looked down at the torrential stream, and I saw some goats whose mouths were over the water, but they were not drinking. Then suddenly everything returned to its normal course.'

The Book of James

Prologue

June

Two thirty a.m., and no signal yet.

The American was waiting in his cramped little room; waiting for a pulse that would tell him London was calling.

The whole building was boiling hot tonight. The air conditioners had broken down again, and here he was, the last one left at his station, fiddling with transmitters just to pass the time before the call came through. He would have to sleep in the office. No chance of getting home before he'd have to turn around and come back.

He sipped his coffee, now only as warm as the air around him, and re-read the briefing document he'd received earlier today, the one that gave him and his department two months' notice.

Eventually, fifteen minutes later, it came, the trademark rhythm of pulses that told him who was on the line.

'Are you there?' The voice was British, hurried and coughing.

'Thank Christ. You're two hours late.'

'I'm sorry. I thought I was being watched. I had to wait. But I've got news. Good news. There's something big on its way.'

'What kind of something?'

'Supposedly some evidence that could change the whole balance of power. That's what my contact says. And he should know.'

The American sighed. He'd heard stories like this a dozen times before. They were never true; the contact always fell through at the last minute, or the secret documents turned out to be the junk from someone's bottom drawer, a mishmash of garbled data that gave nothing away. A 'top-level contact' was generally some middle-ranking officer in the grip of a midlife crisis, wondering what life was like on the other side. But he was professional, so he asked the questions he should.

'Any details? Where's this information from?'

'Someone I used to know very well. He's qualified, though. More than qualified. He's got something for us and he's finally ready to hand it over.'

'And has he said what he wants from us in return?'

'He doesn't want anything. He says he's got nothing left to gain or lose. He says he wants to make amends – his words.'

The American thought of his family for a second: of the hot little house they shared with two other families, too crowded, and of the suffering land stretching for miles around him, the wilting crops. His children were thinner this year than they had been last year. They were lucky even to be here, when so many others were not; it felt irrational and ungracious to expect that things would ever be better. But calls like this one made it so much harder not to feel hope.

'What's your opinion?' he said.

The voice at the other end of the line was earnest. 'I think he's telling the truth.'

He looked at the briefing document on his desk, the one telling him he and his colleagues had just sixty days until the world changed for ever, and in spite of the heat, he shivered.

'I hope you're right,' he said. 'We don't have much time.'

August

The ship of the dead, that was how it had begun. She remembered that later.

This one looked like it had been drifting for decades. It hung low in the water, its former use impossible to tell: the paint on the hull was almost all gone, the lumps of iron scattered on the deck rusted beyond recognition. Even the barnacles around the waterline had shrivelled and died. On the railing, a pair of gulls that had never seen a human stared out like absurd sentries.

That was how they found it on their arrival.

Their own boat was smaller, faster, pummelling across the water; the drone of its outboard motor was the loudest noise for miles in any direction. There were seven of them inside. They wore bright orange overalls, and at their sides they carried masks with huge eyes and grotesque blunt snouts.

They docked on to the larger vessel, levered a ladder up, and six of the seven climbed onto the deck, leaving a guard behind. Hopper's colleagues all wore black boots; she wore faded white trainers. Her colleagues all carried rifles on their backs. She did not.

The condition of the ship – not a ship after all; maybe an old fishing boat, she decided – was even worse up close. The deck's planks had shrunk in the heat of the sun; the railing was missing in erratic sections. The wheelhouse door was slack on its hinges, and creaked back and forth in the breeze. And there was a faint sour smell, stronger around the cracks where the hatch led down to the hold below.

Two of her colleagues climbed the steps to examine the wheelhouse; two more crossed the deck in a slow loop, testing the rails. And she and the final soldier walked to the hatch in the middle of the deck. It was padlocked shut, but eventually they prised it open, donned their masks and clambered down, fumbling for torches as they went. The odour grew stronger as Hopper descended, even through her mask. She was beginning to feel the usual distress, her breathing quickening.

The boat's hold was no bigger than a shipping container. It was dark: apart from their torches, the only slivers of light came from between the shrunken planks of the deck above. At the back of the low-roofed chamber a few hooks hung from the ceiling, and bundled nets dangled from them, unfilled.

At the front of the hold was a huge pile of empty food tins, a dozen mattresses, and, on top of those, thirty human bodies, rotten almost beyond recognition. Above them, the gaps in the deck striped the scene with floating motes of dust, and the strips of light swayed to and fro with the wallowing of the boat.

Her colleague turned, uninterested, and started searching the back of the hold. Hopper shone her torch onto the bodies and forced herself towards them, eventually so close she could nudge the rags aside to better see the skeletons. Mostly men, from the shape of the pelvises: a few women, and, resting in the starboard corner a little way apart from the others, two smaller bodies, their sex impossible to tell. She could feel the familiar fingers of panic encircling her throat, and reminded herself: *stay calm, stay calm*. Appear calm.

The bones filling the rags were dark, not shining like bones supposedly did. Not clean. Most of the skulls still bore patches of stringy hair. She knelt and rested the beam of her torch on the smallest body; down the line of the arms, onto the tattered fabric wrapping the torso, back up to the skull. Its second teeth had not come through yet. On the floor beside it was a little amulet: a primitive spiral of metal, pierced by a string.

A minute later, her colleague appeared beside her and gestured: he had found a cache of unopened tins. They loaded them into his blue canvas sack and moved to the stairs. As he climbed, Hopper darted suddenly back to the smallest body and plucked the amulet from the floor.

Back on deck, all six clambered back down the ladder to the smaller boat. One of the soldiers attached a lump to the larger boat's side, just below the waterline, and jammed a short stick into it. As the engine coughed into life, he tore off a strip from the edge of the stick, and it began to fizz and smoke, bubbling under the water.

A minute or two after their departure, the fuse had burnt down, and there was a dull thud as the hull was breached.

Five minutes later, the boat was noticeably lower in the water. Ten minutes after that, it was gone.

She was the only one in the smaller boat who had turned back to observe the process. Above them, the pale sun gleamed down upon the ocean from its spot near the horizon, as, at this latitude, it did every hour of the day.

The *Rig Rocket* gathered pace. It was a sturdy little thing: used for maintenance, training, towing jobs, anything. It wasn't always available unless there was an urgent need. As Schwimmer and his soldiers operated it, it tended to stay where it was until the iceberg alarms went off.

This morning, they had sounded at 5.07. They spat a thick, wailing blast, painfully loud, designed to ensure the listener could not stay in bed without discomfort. Hopper woke with shock whenever they sounded, even after three years on the rig. Still, she was fortunate – as a scientific officer, she had a room of her own. The squaddies were in rooms of four.

They were almost at full speed now. She looked around: Harv was at the engine, his long hair practically horizontal in the wind, his arm taut on the rudder. He caught her eye and winked. He had been calmer than her back in the hull. She had nearly fled on seeing the bodies; had nearly run back up to the deck out of that cool, foul air. Harv's presence, massive and calming, had kept her there, although she had been grateful of the mask. She could taste bile in her throat even now. Her mother would have been in a boat like that.

Harv would be more used to bodies than her, of course, although she doubted even he had seen any for a while. No soldiers had died on the rig in her three years there, with the exception of Drax after his accident, and one foolish twenty-year-old, Lambert, who had ventured on deck during a storm and had been swept away. Once the weather had cleared they'd gone out and looked for her, driving in ever-increasing circles until Schwimmer decided enough petrol had been wasted. A week later, her beret had been discovered, improbably snagged on the iron palisade where the rig met the sea.

It was bitter this morning. Every time Harv gunned the engine, they sped up, and the cold was fresh again. Hopper looked across at the pale, glum soldiers on either side of the boat's narrow aisle. Leeson looked wretched, hunched over the little craft's hard orange rim.

He was only nineteen, Leeson. He'd arrived just a few months before and was clearly hating every minute. It could be a lot worse, she found herself thinking. He could be stuck in the Bread-basket, or patrolling the Highlands, or making hunting sweeps in the Kent marshes. At least here there were three meals a day and no chance of actual combat. Leeson didn't know his luck: berths on rigs were rare.

The Last Day

Hopper twisted left in her seat, looking at their wake. Out here, in the North Atlantic, the sun hung low in the sky, lingering a few thumbs' breadths above the horizon. A morning sun, a powerful yellow smear too diffused by the atmosphere to provide real warmth yet too bright to persuade oneself it was ever night. On the rig, it was always just after dawn.

The boat with its heaped dead wasn't the only thing upsetting her, she knew that. She was still thinking about the letter she'd received a few weeks ago, dated a month before even that, thin yellow paper covered in a faint wavering scrawl.

Ellen, please do not destroy this letter without reading it. It will cause you pain even to hear from me, I know. But a great deal more depends on it than you could guess. There is not long.

Harv had done well finding the tins, she told herself, although she'd be much happier if he didn't tell her when they were being prised open and cooked, as he had done the last time a boat had yielded anything. This was as close as they would get to the old world – eating fruit harvested decades ago, grown in sunlight few now remembered.

She would eat what they had found today, of course – she wasn't principled enough to turn down extra calories – but she already knew she would spend the whole meal wondering about it. When had the food in those tins been picked, processed, canned? When had the cans been bought or looted, when had they been taken out of storage and packed behind the panel in the boat's hold to fend off starvation?

Most of all, why hadn't they been opened, and how had those poor people died? She guessed disease over violence, hence the lock on the hatch. Wherever the boat was from – South America, maybe southern Europe – there could be a whole zoo of conditions that showed no symptoms until the crew was at sea, making their way across the Atlantic with no doctors and little medicine. Maybe the crew had taken the lifeboats and abandoned their passengers?

She wondered which of them had been last to die, then told herself to stop. Whatever pitiful scene had played itself out in that boat, it was over now. Anyway, if the vessel had come from the other side of the Atlantic, the children in the hold were probably older than she was. All the boats from America had set out a long time ago.

There was the letter again, worming its way to the front of her mind, right behind her eyes. The phrases had repeated themselves; even two weeks after reading it, she could remember every word.

There is more that you never knew at the time of your studies – a great deal more. It is imperative that I tell you, and you alone, what it is. I am near the end of my life now. I can do you no further harm. But you can prevent a far greater evil being done. Please. You must read this. There is not long.

Forget it, she told herself. Forget it, forget it.

Boats were rarer than they had been, of course, but there were still thousands out there, an enormous fleet whose only admiral was blind luck. By now most of them had drifted into the dead zone at the centre of the Atlantic and were becalmed in an armada fifty miles across, an archipelago of rust destined to do nothing more than rot and sink piece by piece. She had read once that before the Slow, a hundred thousand ships were on the sea at any one time. It sounded impossible.

Ships weren't really a threat these days; there weren't enough people left in the countries that would have sent them. Icebergs were far more common. More dangerous, too: boats were no problem unless they were big, but even a small iceberg could be disastrous.

Still, they had the twenty-mile ring set up around the rig. Thanks to Harv's electrical talents, whenever the ring broke, it notified the rig by radio which section was affected, to give them a bearing. Then they sent out the *Rig Rocket* to scout. If it was an iceberg, they'd dispatch the bigger boat, *Gertie*, to tow it onto a new course. But they were expected to deal with smaller vessels themselves.

Hopper's job on iceberg trips was to calculate the direction of travel and the prevailing currents at the surface, and recommend how much force to apply and in which direction to avoid a collision. It was satisfying to perform a task with a tangible result, but it was a child's job, and a distraction from her real work.

Her real work. And there he was again, the man who had first taught her all about what she was doing now. She could hear the words of his letter in his voice, apologetic and low, as it had been the last time she'd seen him.

I have done you great harm. I know that. But I also know exactly how I must atone. You are the only person who can help. I trust nobody else.

The rig was in sight now. The reactor towers were always visible first, and the wisps of steam from the heating system, little puffs issuing from chimneys designed for greater use. There it was, the closest thing she had to a home: an icy stack of radiation-riddled metal, parked in the freezing sea.

On opening, the rig had been heralded as a pioneer. Today it sat, abortive and decrepit, two hundred miles off the south-west coast of England: the first of a new species and the last of its kind. She knew from conversation with Harv that its reactors still produced enough energy to keep itself going, with some left over for the mainland. As soon as that slight functionality fell away, it would be abandoned, unlamented, like so much else in this rotting world.

And the final lines in the letter, that entreaty. Not for forgiveness, but for – oh, who knew what else? Some useless attempt to apologise, most likely, dangled with the bait of a secret. Hopper had no interest in secrets any more.

Please contact me discreetly at the address above. Ellen, do not attempt to come any closer. The risks to you are substantial. But contact me. Please. I have something you must see.

And then nothing but the shaky signature: *Edward Thorne*.

She had burnt the letter. She had taken pleasure in holding it at just the right angle so its beginning had burnt last. The last words visible were *Ellen, please do not destroy this letter*, then *Ellen, please do not* and finally just *Ellen*. She had deliberately refused to learn the address he had included, in case her resolve weakened later. She had sent no reply.

They were closer to the rig now. The whole thing was visible above the waves, sorrowful and weather-beaten. It looked like a titanic iron crown: the last remnants of some huge drowned king.

The Last Day

The four legs were scurfed with rust, the anchor chains around them buffeted by spray and clanking in the North Atlantic breeze. At its base, the rig had turned green, furred with plant life that stuck doggedly to it, as though aware there was no better home for hundreds of miles.

Hopper unclipped her water tin from her side, poured some into her mouth, stared out to sea in case of an unexpected whale.

And then, as the boat coasted towards the rig, she looked back at it, and saw for the first time the large black helicopter squatting like a bluebottle on the deck.

3

Now, thirty years after it all ended, the Slow seemed the most natural thing in the world. It felt quaint to imagine people reacting to it with shock.

Hopper knew she was one of the last 'before' children: born four years before the planet's rotation finally stopped. She was a rarity. There had been plenty born since, of course, but the birth rate had plummeted in those final years. The world had paused, waiting for the cataclysm, and those children already young had been treated like royalty – fed well, spoiled whenever possible, as if in premature apology for a ruined planet their parents could not mend.

But during those years, new children were perceived at best as an extravagance, at worst as a cruelty. Why bring a child into a world winding itself down? The chaos and shortages at the end of the Slow had kept the planet's libido in check. Many pregnancies had been brought to an end, prematurely and inexactly.

The imprecision of timekeeping towards the final sunrise meant no child was formally identified as the last one to know the old world: the world of dawns, sunsets, cool, clear evenings. Even if some great clock had been stopped exactly with the planet's spin, and the hospitals of the world scoured for the final birth, it would have been a pointless endeavour. Whoever the child was, the odds were it was now dead.

Hopper's generation, consequently, was smaller than those on either side. Things were better now, on the mainland: more babies, more families, more weddings. In the old days there had been whole magazines devoted to weddings. Hopper had seen one in her father's house, annotated in her mother's beautiful handwriting – asterisks here, flower arrangements ringed else-where. It was hard, now, imagining having that much paper to waste. As she thought of her mother, she felt the customary stab of pain: dulled by time, still unbearable.

Regeneration. A new factory each month, she read in the bul-letins. Each week more farmland under the harrow, each year more schools, more roads, more food. Two years ago, a new railway line. The Great British Resurgence was well under way. Sometimes, from a rust-bitten rig frozen in a permanent autumn morning, it was hard to perceive. But the dispatches remained optimistic.

They weren't strictly true, of course. Everyone knew there were patches of the country where governmental control was more honoured in the breach than the observance: up north, in the huge new grain belt across Scotland, in lots of places outside the big cities. There were riots, wearily suppressed; every so often the corpse of some blameless agricultural inspector might be left in a public square with a sign asking for collection by the authorities. None of this was officially acknowledged, of course, but it was remarkable how much could be known despite never appearing in either newspaper.

And now, appearing from nowhere, a helicopter. Its body was thick, squat, the glass bubble on its front resembling an insect's eye.

The rig had a helipad, but this was the first time it had been used in Hopper's time here. Fuel was scarce, and was used for important governmental work only. The soldiers had spotted the aircraft too, nudging each other and gesturing. Hopper felt an unaccountable hostility towards it.

For a moment she wondered whether they were coming for Harv, because of the sirens thing. Then she managed to laugh at herself. Last month, Harv had managed to discover that Schwimmer's birthday was coming up soon. So on the day, as the soldiers had lined up on deck for morning inspection – just as Schwimmer was about to open his mouth – Harv had triggered the rig's sirens to play a strained electronic 'Happy Birthday', off key and wailing. Hopper had laughed as she watched from the mess: the soldiers singing, Schwimmer's face purpling as anger and amusement fought it out within him.

As Schwimmer's adjutant, Harv could have been punished severely, but he had talked the CO round. That was Harv. Always charming.

If the government could spare enough helicopter fuel to fly out and talk to Harv over something like that, England must be a more peaceful and better-governed place than she had imagined.

The *Rig Rocket* had almost passed beneath the iron entryway, into the dock where it met the water. Just as it did, a figure appeared by the helicopter – in dark clothes, with the smudge of a white band on its arm.

The boat puttered to a stop, coasting into the little bay, and the soldiers jumped out and started hauling it up the slipway. Hopper climbed onto the platform and watched them.

What merited a helicopter? A change of commander? The new one would surely just come out on the supply boat. A medical emergency? It would have to be something really bad, and she'd heard nothing of that. Then again, she realised with a lurch, they could have come because of the letter.

Harv spoke in her ear, startling her. 'You'll find out soon enough.'

'Find out what?'

'Who's come to play.'

She took a breath. 'I'm sure it's nothing.'

He grinned. 'Suit yourself.'

The soldiers removed their orange overalls, hanging them in the gunmetal lockers lining the bay. Hers and Harv's would have to be cleaned. She ditched hers, and the salvaged food tins, in the makeshift decontamination box – really just an equipment crate lined with lead plates, a home-made skull and crossbones glued on the top in fluorescent fabric. If the tins didn't show any radiation, they would be cleaned and eaten. If they did, they'd be jettisoned, strapped to a waste container so they could poison the seabed instead of the rig.

The troops finished their work, numbered off and left through the metal hatch. The steel door clanged shut after them. She and Harv were left alone in the bay, the water bobbing black and tarry in the central square. The slap of the sea against the outer walls made her shiver.

'I hate those ones.' She still felt nauseous, remembering the sickly swaying of the fishing boat, angry with herself for revealing her weakness even as she said it.

'The boats? Nobody likes them, El. You'd be a bit sick to like 'em.' Harv's deep voice still carried a touch of an accent: he'd grown up in Boston at first, one parent English and one American. He'd moved here as a child, just before it all started, had been one of the last lucky ones unquestioningly granted full citizenship. Knowing him as well as she did, she sometimes noticed him burying his American side, trimming his vowels, determined to show enough loyalty that nobody could question his nationality based on his voice.

'Where do you think they were all from?'

'Best not to think about them. They probably haven't been in a position to worry about anything for a while now.'

'You can't tell me you like sinking them.'

'I'd rather be sunk than float around for ever. Come on.'

Hopper followed Harv through the door, to the staircase up to the deck. They hadn't had that many bodies for a while. The last two boats had been almost unoccupied. But the one before that, a South American ferry three months ago, had been much fuller. She still dreamt about it at least once a week.

'What do you think it is?' She couldn't help asking. They had found out Thorne had written to her. They must have done. But how? And why was it important enough to send someone all the way out here from the mainland?

'What, the helicopter? Probably just some jobsworth mainlander checking we're not eating too many chickpeas, or making sure our blankets are the regulation thickness. Won't be anything serious.'

He turned and smiled, showing his teeth. Harv had a tooth missing – knocked out by a club in a fight up near the borders, he had said. He was handsome, but Hopper sensed he was proud to have acquired some obvious mark of conflict in his appearance.

She thought. 'Supply run?'

'Helicopters that size can hardly bring anything. It won't be that unless the last supply boat forgot the tin opener.'

'Medical evac?'

Harv shrugged. 'Everyone was healthy last night as far as I know. And Donaghy has every medicine he could possibly need for the next quarter, assuming all we get is syphilis and headaches. So: news, is my money. Either way, the chopper's one of ours.'

'How do you know?'

'I recognised it. British model.'

'Maybe the Scandis have invaded and we're the final refuge of the British Empire.'

He snorted at that. They lapsed into silence, Harv's heavy boots clumping up the iron steps, her trainers squeaking. The rig was several floors deep. Parts of the power station were non-operational these days: half of it was off limits, full of old machinery useful only to be cannibalised for parts. On her day off, Hopper sometimes went walking through the corridors to see how long she could go without bumping into anyone else. Her record was two and a quarter hours.

They reached the top of the stairs. Harv leant into the door, and the cold air came rushing in. It was never freezing out on deck – it must have been grim in the hours of darkness, before the Stop – but it was usually chilly enough that coming back in was a relief. Hopper knew; she ran laps of the deck for an hour each morning.

Across the rig's platform was the long, curved roof of the mess hall and rec rooms, designed to give residents a view of the ocean. They walked over, passing the helicopter. Leaning on the railings, facing the sea, was the figure Hopper had glimpsed from the boat: a man, with bleached hair cropped close to his skull. He looked like a motorcyclist – leather jacket, black trousers, high boots. He ignored them, staring out to sea, a cigarette burning unattended in his hand.

As they approached the mess hall, Hopper saw, through the doors, Schwimmer's bald patch, facing away. He was sitting at one of the long steel benches, and twisted at their approach.

Harv saluted. Schwimmer saluted back, murmuring, 'At ease,' as he did so, before adding, 'Good morning, Dr Hopper.'

'Good morning, Colonel.'

'Captain. Report?'

'Yes, sir. Intercepted it about 0645. Small boat. We all went aboard, except for Drachmann, who kept watch. On boarding we noted . . .'

As Harv continued, Hopper took in the rest of the room, her eyes adjusting to the gloom after the brightness of the deck. Two figures sat facing Schwimmer on the other side of the table. A man, still in his overcoat, and a woman.

The woman was imposing – apparently taller than the man, although perhaps she just had better posture. She was in her middle forties, Hopper guessed, and looked like a Hollywood siren gone somewhat to seed. Her dark brown hair, tinged with red, was curled elaborately, and her mouth was bright with thick red lipstick, with a slight, built-in curl of satisfaction at the sides.

The man was a few years older. He was gaunt, his hair greasy and receding, just starting to grey. His complexion was grey too, except round the jawline, where a blunt razor had left the skin angry and reddened. His shirt collar pinched his neck, making a vein bulge out a little. He looked tired and uninterested.

Before the pair, on the long steel bench, rested two cups of the rig's appalling coffee. 'Neptune's piss', Harv called it. No steam rising from the cups; they must have been here a while. She tuned back in to Harv's voice.

' … ready whenever Fraser wants to step down and decontaminate, sir.'

'Thank you, Captain. That'll be all.'

'Sir.'

Another salute, and Harv vanished back through the door to the deck. Hopper watched his figure as he moved, and turned back only to realise she'd missed something Schwimmer had said.

'I'm sorry, sir?'

Schwimmer was too urbane to note her inattention. 'I was just saying, it's fortunate you joined Captain McCrum, Doctor. You have visitors. From London.' There was a ghost of mockery in the last drawled word – *fancy, these Londoners coming to see you*. He gestured to the table, as the woman stood and offered a hand. Hopper took it.

'Good morning, Dr Hopper. I'm Ruth Warwick. I'm from the Home Office. I thought I might wake you, but evidently you were up even earlier this morning than we were.' She smiled suddenly, a smile of bright, flat artificiality that left her face as quickly as it had arrived. She did not introduce her colleague.

She turned to Schwimmer. 'As discussed, Colonel, might we speak to Dr Hopper in private for a few minutes?'

She sounded well educated. Hopper thought she knew the type. Private school, then straight into the military as an extension of boarding school, rather than wasting three years at one of the few universities still going. A few years in the army, then a turn to the civilian, with a faint regret for simpler times and a residual love of receiving orders. Not much family, Hopper reckoned. She wore a wedding ring, though, a thick gold band too masculine-looking even for her large hand.

Schwimmer nodded. 'Of course. If you need anything, I'll be in the office.' *Office*. That was clearly intended to make the room – a six-by-nine-foot steel box overflowing with pointless paperwork – sound more impressive than what it was, which was somewhere for Schwimmer to sit apart from the troops in the evenings. Schwimmer never had been especially good with people, for which Hopper liked him. He nodded at her, wearing his familiar crumpled-neutral expression, then turned and left them.

After the door shut behind him, silence filled the canteen for a few seconds. Hopper stood across the table from the two visitors, feeling like she'd been called to the headmistress's study again, remembering the sympathetic secretary who'd sat in the outer office. Miss Vernon, that was it. She wondered where Miss Vernon was these days. Almost certainly dead.

Please. I have something you must see. The words from the letter returned to her without prompting.

'Have a seat, Dr Hopper. Thank you so much for sparing us the time.' Now Schwimmer was gone, Warwick spoke informally, with a warm, well-cushioned timbre to her voice.

Hopper sat, feeling the cold of the steel slats through her thin trousers. 'This must be important, if you've come all this way. Which part of the Home Office are you from?'

'Technically, Security. But Inspector Blake and I' – she gestured to her colleague – 'are not here on security business. Dr Hopper, you're the chief scientific officer here, yes?'

'Chief is a rather grand word. I'm the only one.'

'Very remote lifestyle you lead. Quite a self-imposed hermitage. The commanding officer was telling us you spend your time lassoing icebergs.'

'Only when requested.'

'What do you spend the rest of your time on?'

'Measuring currents, water composition, temperature, salinity. Testing for DNA in the water, to see if there are any fish we don't know about.'

'You're an observer, then. Not a doer. Seems a rather abstruse path to follow when there are people to feed.'

Hopper shrugged. She did not want to explain her work to this woman any further than was necessary.

Warwick carried on. 'But I suppose it affects the land, is that right? The water flow and so on?'

'What's this about, please? I'm sure you didn't come this far for a job satisfaction survey.'

Warwick raised her hands in mock supplication. 'Forgive me. We appreciate how busy you are. You studied at Oxford, did you not?'

Hopper's muscles bunched involuntarily. She'd been right. They'd come because of the letter. 'Many years ago. Yes.'

'You knew Edward Thorne, is that correct?'

'I ... yes, I did.' Warwick remained silent. 'Not very well. He taught me for a year.'

'He seems to recall that you were friends.'

'He taught me. I wouldn't say we were friends.' There it was, the first lie of the meeting. Or her first, at any rate.

'Well, I'm afraid I have some bad news. He's seriously unwell. He's in hospital at the moment. We visited to see if there was anything we can do for him, and he asked to speak to you. We're here to ask if you're willing to come and see him. Any days you take will of course not be deducted from your annual leave.'

'That's what you've spent your helicopter fuel on?' She could feel herself growing angry, now the shock was past. Angry with Thorne for getting her into this, and angry at these strangers crashing into her new life and trying to drag her back to London.

'He was one of the most important men in the country for many years, Dr Hopper. We wouldn't deny him a favour in his final days.' Somewhere in there she detected another lie. Convincingly told, but a lie nonetheless. 'And the British government can still manage to get a helicopter airborne. Just about.' Warwick chuckled at her own witticism. The man by her side did not.

They hadn't had a helicopter spare last year, Hopper remembered, when that boy Drax had lost a foot in an accident in the loading bay. They had radioed the mainland for a medical evac, and received only excuses. Drax had worsened. In the end, Donaghy had administered an injection to carry him off. They'd wrapped his body in a cheap plastic sheet and thrown him over the side. Warwick kept talking.

'I'm sure you think our sudden arrival a little overdramatic, but Dr Thorne's case is urgent, and important to us.'

'I wasn't aware Thorne's reputation had recovered so far,' Hopper said. 'When I last saw him, he was being sacked from Oxford as a liability. And he was only there after being sacked by the prime minister.'

Warwick ignored her and spoke a fraction louder. 'You're also overdue for leave. You didn't return to London on the last boat.'

'There isn't much compelling me to return.' So they'd looked through her personnel file for her leave history.

'You really should. Progress all the time.' There was that smile again.

'Why didn't you phone ahead?'

'Well, Miss Hopper ...'

'Doctor.'

'Forgive me, *Doctor* Hopper. Dr Thorne only mentioned he wanted to see you last night, which is when we decided we'd come and collect you ourselves. And his life is drawing rapidly to a close.' The man, Blake, had not taken his eyes off Hopper since she had sat down, and a muscle in his face flickered as his colleague spoke.

'I'm busy here. I was under the impression our work was supported by government.'

'Of course it is. But Dr Thorne expressed a strong interest in seeing you.' Warwick shrugged. 'Many people would treat it as an honour.'

'I don't.' Hopper felt the woman's surprise, quickly masked. 'My work won't allow me to visit him, and frankly, I don't know why he would want to see me anyway. I can hardly believe I made much of an impact on his life.'

Warwick shrugged. 'We can't compel you to come, of course.'

'No. He, of all people, will understand that work comes first.'

Warwick sighed and spread her hands. 'We did our best.' Her tone brightened. 'Your position here is up for renewal next year, isn't it?' She sifted the papers in front of her and studied one. Hopper recognised her upside down employment contract as Warwick continued. 'It would seem wiser to take a few days from your work now than to run the risk of losing a permanent place. If what you're doing here is so very important.'

So they did want her back in England, badly enough to threaten her job. And her work was about the only thing that still mattered to her. Hopper sat back.

'How soon could I return here?'

Warwick looked relieved. 'There's a maintenance boat coming out in a week. That's wonderful news, Dr Hopper. Do you have anywhere to stay in London?' She had already assumed Hopper's acquiescence.

'Yes.' Another lie. She'd think of somewhere.

'Good.' Warwick looked at her colleague and nodded. 'We'll leave as soon as you're ready.'

'I'll have to finish a few things here, hand over some notes to my colleagues.'

'I thought you were the only scientific officer here.'

'There are experiments they can keep running in my absence.'

'How soon will that be dealt with?'

'A few hours.'

Warwick looked at her watch, a dainty timepiece dwarfed by her large wrist. '*Could* you get it done by ten o'clock? Time really is of the essence.' Her tone had shifted again, to that of a hostess determined to accommodate a difficult house guest.

'All right.'

'I'm sure Dr Thorne will be very grateful you've made the effort.' There, again, a smile where there had been none, and then nothing at all.

Harv was lingering in the doorway, his arms above the frame, a little crescent of his torso showing below his shirt.

'How long will you be gone?'

'I don't know. A week, maybe.'

'It'll be boring without you here, Hop. I'll miss you.'

She couldn't help smiling, despite the lump in her throat. 'Yeah. I tried to explain that to the grim civil servants, but they seemed to think some things are more important than how entertained you are.'

'Very disappointing when people take that attitude.' He stood there, balancing on the thin metal rim of the frame, wedging the door open with his foot as he watched her pack.

A lot of people mistook Harv for a tough man, because of his size. She supposed he must be tough, really; he was comfortably over six foot, and broad with it. Even so, she had never seen him actually in a fight, so all she had to go on was his conversation. He was funnier than his looks suggested, and more thoughtful. His hair was long, dense and black, barring one grey forelock.

For her first year on the rig, they had hardly spoken. She had hardly spoken to anyone, in fact: she was not long out of her marriage, out of everything, in an emotional state she could have stayed in for good without distress. The troops, and the crew of the power station, had shown no interest in acquiring new friends. They were perfectly happy not to know anything more about her than her surname.

Then, one meal, she and Harv had found something in common. It was nothing really – a book they'd both read – but it had been enough.

She hadn't intended it, certainly hadn't planned it, but about a year ago they'd drifted together one night, after a party the soldiers had thrown, some birthday or something. They'd got through a couple of bottles of the home-made alcohol the squaddies distilled. It was appalling stuff, the bottles inadequately cleaned, the sour alcohol fighting to drown out the tang of metal, but it had had its effect on them both and they'd ended up in bed.

She had avoided him for a long time after that. But since another such party a few months ago, they had slept together perhaps a dozen more times. Her desire for some bare minimum of intimacy, emotional and physical, occasionally overpowered her desire to keep apart from everyone, Harv included. And Harv was alive to her need for solitude. He never imposed his own demands, simply adjusted to hers, and was willing to talk only when she wanted it. He was her closest – her only – friend on the rig.

She turned back from the wardrobe to her small canvas bag, throwing a few more shirts in.

'So, let me get this straight. Edward Thorne himself, great national hero et cetera, and your old college tutor, writes you this mysterious letter. Now he's dying …'

'Apparently.'

'And he wants to see you.'

'That's what they said.'

'Did they say why?'

She thought of the letter she'd burnt, of the urgent words. 'I don't know, Harv. I have no idea. I hardly knew him.'

'Really?'

'Really. I don't know him, I'm not interested in seeing him, and I hate London. And I don't like this woman either.' Warwick's comment was still playing in her ear: *You're an observer, then. Not a doer*. It rankled all the more for her suspicion that it was true.

Harv shrugged. 'But you're going anyway.'

'Guess so.' She didn't want to tell him any more.

He shifted, levering the door further open with his foot, unoffended by her terseness. 'You all right after this morning? The boat?'

'Not really.' She kept thinking of the two smaller bodies hunched together, how the sinking would have ruined that tableau, jumbling the remains beyond sense until the bone worms had their way with them. But she didn't want him to see how much it had affected her, so she kept folding.

'Where did it come from, would you estimate?' He was clearly trying to move her away from the upsetting scene on to a question of fact. She was grateful for it.

'One of the Americas, most likely. Although I couldn't tell you which one.'

Given where they'd located the ship, it was almost impossible to tell where it had sailed from. The old current system had collapsed, of course, and the dominant new current that kept Britain and western Europe cool flowed from the north, several hundred miles east. But the counter-current that would have brought the fishing boat towards them was fed from enough other sources that it could have come from anywhere west or southwest of here. She listened back to herself and laughed.

'Some fucking ocean scientist I am. Got it narrowed down to two full continents for you. That specific enough?'

He shrugged. 'You'll work it out. If anyone will, you will.'

'I've got a lot of it worked out, Harv. It just doesn't seem to be making much difference to anyone.'

'Don't talk like that. It's important work you're doing.'

For a second she disliked him for attempting to cheer her up; wanted only to be alone, savouring the feeling of failure and the sensation that none of her work would make a difference in the end. Then she mastered herself. She'd been slipping into that mindset a lot lately.

'Thanks. Anyway, you'd better go. Haven't you got soldiering to be doing? Underlings to shout at?'

Harv grinned again. 'Oh, sure. It's all go here.' He crossed the room and hugged her tight. 'Take care of yourself in London. Seriously. And call any time if you want to talk.'

She hugged him back for a second, then disengaged. 'I will. Back in a week.'

The door clanged shut behind him. She turned to pack the rest of her few things, her smile fading, and as she did, caught a glimpse of herself in the scale-pocked mirror above the sink.

She was thirty-four years old; had spent nearly fifteen of those years as a scientist. Life on the rig was starting to make her weather-beaten; her work was probably leaving its mark too. Her career, at first gilded, had been marked by a decade of sheer difficulty, and a fog of official indifference. No children, no parents, no close connections, barring a semi-relationship with a soldier. Apart from her brief and ill-starred marriage, her whole adult life had been spent fleeing intimacy, and was now approaching its perfect expression: life in a cell on a floating rig, barely tethered to the sea.

And now Thorne, the man who had driven her here, had returned to her life as he was dying. The man whose work had built the rotten state she had escaped. She realised she had repeated to Harv her own lie to Warwick. What had she said again? Ah, yes. *I hardly knew him.*

5

As Hopper packed, her eye fell on the little globe she'd kept, one of the presents David had given her on their wedding day as a joke, and she couldn't help her thoughts turning to the whole Slow again.

When the earth had finally stopped turning, thirty years ago, there had been no single moment of epiphany, no final report of the time and date. The exact moment of the Stop was lost in the chaos of events. It took a fortnight for most people to realise the sun's new place in the sky was its final home.

It was hardly unexpected. The initial discovery that the earth's orbit had started winding down had come almost a decade earlier. The Stop was merely the final confirmation that the earth and the sun were now in almost perfect lockstep, as the moon was with the earth.

The first day of slowing had been five years before Hopper was born, but she'd read several histories. It had come in late May 2020.

That day, shortly before noon, a series of catastrophic, inexplicable failures in GPS occurred across the planet. Online maps crumpled. Satellites missed messages from the ground, were reduced to multimillion-dollar ornaments barrelling across the sky, winking down in sly acknowledgement of some big cosmic joke. Defence systems bucked in ways baffling and unnerving to their operators.

The failures threw cities, ports, flights into gridlock. Shipping deliveries were suddenly disarrayed; planes circled helpless above the world's airports.

Charges were levelled against a broad and incompatible range of suspects: the Russians, the Chinese, the North Koreans, anti-Western hackers, anti-development Westerners, Apple, Google, Davos, Goldman Sachs. None of the explanations accounted for the fact that every country in the world had been affected by the disaster.

The next day, an underground laboratory beneath the forests of Germany – home to a device called a ring laser gyroscope, which measured the planet's spin – confirmed the earth had added 0.144 seconds from the 86,400 making up a day. The planet's GPS systems, so brilliant and exact, had collapsed in the face of even this tiny imprecision.

The next day, the planet had gained twice as much again. The following day, three times as much as that.

The problems of the first day were patched. The internet still worked, after all; the filigree of undersea cables wrapping the planet remained unharmed. Paper maps were dug out of storage. Sailors began using old navigational tools once again. The world assumed the problem would be solved, that the sextants could be discarded before long. This was a glitch.

And yet it kept happening, the deceleration increasing just a little each day.

The search for a cause in the heavens had begun immediately. It had long been known that the earth's rotation was slowed down fractionally by the friction of the moon's pull, and the loss of momentum as the earth's oceans crashed into its continents. The rate of slow had been tiny, milliseconds per century. But it was real: so it followed that a change thousands of times larger must be caused by something in the skies. The world's observatories adjusted their focus, looking for any near-earth objects that might explain the deceleration.

Countless theories were proposed and tested – the Milky Way's spin slowing down, a black hole, the region of the galaxy the planet was passing through. One by one, they were junked. The search was made harder by the very symptoms under investigation: the slow of the planet's spin had thrown all celestial calculations out of kilter. One astronomer compared the hunt to going fishing by sticking one's head into the ocean with a torch in one's mouth.

For months, nothing was found. There seemed to be no scapegoat. The anger turned temporarily inwards – a few anti-science marches took place, a few observatories were torched – but by that point, most people were transferring their attention to other problems.

Eventually, the cause was discovered. A white dwarf star, a rare celestial creature the size of earth but two hundred thousand times as dense, loosed from its own star system by a supernova explosion, now free to barrel through space disrupting everything in its path. It was travelling at two thousand kilometres a second through this part of the Milky Way, its trajectory and enormous gravity dragging the earth slowly backwards, its path as perfect as if it had been designed by some malign heavenly committee. It was already millions of kilometres away by the time it was spotted, speeding from the wreckage, its damage done.

Hopper often wondered what might have happened had they found the rogue star in time – whether they would have made some hopeless attempt to blow it out of the sky, to cancel the end of the world. It didn't matter now.

The final flare of interest in the heavens had come with the uncertainty over whether the earth would stop spinning completely – meaning it would experience one day and night each year as it circled the sun – or whether it would simply drift into lockstep, as the moon was with the earth, always showing the sun the same face.

There had been a final flourish of international cooperation when it seemed the world might end up with six-month days and nights – promises of food supplies shipped back and forth, a grand new planetary bargain, a dawning era of global collaboration as never seen before. And then it had become clear that the alternative was far likelier. The new barriers of daylight and darkness were being established in perpetuity.

The Last Day

Overnight, alliances that had lasted centuries collapsed. The relationships shared at half a planet's distance, the web of connections promoting ideology above latitude: all came to an abrupt stop. Geography became the only factor affecting a nation's prospects. Australia's national interests were now diametrically opposed to those of Britain. Pakistan and India were shocked into rapprochement.

Different nations adjusted to the news at different speeds. The two Koreas reached a fragile accord just six months before they were plunged into darkness for the last time, and weeks before the governments of both nations ceased to function. There were no tearful reunions, no hauling-down of flags. By the time of the Stop, plenty of nations had stopped hauling flags up in the first place.

Three years before the Stop, the internet had slowly shut down. The servers around the world were no longer maintained; the undersea cables ground to a sludgy halt. Then mobile phones had stopped working. Televisions had flickered and frozen. Mankind was being rapidly catapulted back through all the advances of the previous century. Diseases had resurfaced, too: smallpox, freshly thawed from the Siberian permafrost, and others less baroque but no less fatal.

The satellite network ringing the earth had collapsed amid the chaos: another totemic achievement of mankind abandoned, superseded by the need to feed a population. Some had smashed into each other, reduced to thousands of lethal shards of debris. Perhaps a few were still in their old orbits, useless hunks of metal these days, passing overhead a dozen times a day, frying and freezing alternately.

There was no prospect of escape: the technologists who had predicted fleeing the earth for more habitable zones had been wrong to a man. There was no time to do anything but mothball the International Space Station, no secret fund to strike out for a new planet as this one collapsed.

Around the edges of the continental plates, the planet's fragile skin had ruptured in response to this insult from the heavens. Earthquakes shook and re-shook the planet as it slowed. Fissures and weals broke out across the earth's face; volcanic eruptions darkened the skies across thousands of miles. The world was swept with gales across its surface as the air currents wrapping the planet collapsed. Gravity had stayed functioning, despite some people's fears: the planet was still the same mass, still exerted gravitational force. But the final years of slowing had been torment.

The last night had lasted six months in Britain: half an old year of madness, and mayhem, and near-starvation in the dark. And then, agonisingly slowly, the sun had crawled back into the sky as the planet cruised to a stop, the boundaries of day and night locked for ever.

The dawning of the last day, they'd called it. The year was 2029.

Now, thirty years on, here the planet hung in space, making one lazy revolution for each orbit around the sun. Thanks to the tilt of its axis, there was a slight variation in its exact position, so a slender ring of borderlands varied between total darkness and a fractional glimpse of the light.

Even so, for the vast majority of the world, the situation was fixed. Enjoying the constant light of the sun: Europe, half of Russia, much of Africa, the Middle East, the eastern edge of North America and the top of South America. The centre of that zone: meltingly hot, full of ash and the remains of cities. On the very edge, in the cool area bisecting the Indian subcontinent, Eurasia and the Americas: sunlight so weak no human life could survive. Between the two, a slim band where one could still raise a crop, still pretend one lived in a country.

And on the other side: darkness.

6

She'd only been in a helicopter twice before – once visiting her father in Scotland, and once travelling to a scientific summit in Copenhagen. She had argued against it as wasteful that time, but she'd been overruled. It had been considered important to show the Scandis and the Russians that Britain could still get around by helicopter if necessary.

Inside, she faced the two of them. Warwick was looking out over the sea with apparent interest. The man, Blake, had fallen asleep almost immediately, his greyish skin puckered where his headphones dug into it.

The water passed beneath them. By the rig it had been darker, lying in thick, churning ridges. Here it was choppier, bluer, lighter. As they flew, the sun's altitude was changing fraction by fraction – imperceptible now, but by the time they

42

arrived, it would be noticeably higher. The only way to experience a proper dawn or a sunset these days would be to travel Coldside to Warmside in a jet. But the days of jets were long gone.

Aged seventeen, Hopper had thought she remembered real sunsets. Later, she had realised those memories were of nothing more than watching them on film. Or she was misremembering those of her very earliest years. Towards the end of the Slow, the sunsets had been languorous and other-worldly, breathtakingly beautiful. The last one had taken a month.

Then, of course, had come the collapse, and a few years after that, the turbulent Reconstitution. And the earth had rolled around the sun in its new orbit for just over thirty years.

This fortress built by Nature for herself ... The phrase came to her unbidden. *Against infection and the hand of war.*

That bloody speech. She – her whole class – had been compelled to learn it. It had been painted in the school hall as a mural, the unicorn and lion flanking it miscoloured, the curly script rendering it near-illegible. And yet, after prayers each week, they had read it en masse. Even now she could see the light streaming through the windows at the end of the hall, the headmistress conducting them like an orchestra. There were others flanking it – *Henry V* on the English, or *Measure for Measure* on death – but the *Richard II* had been supreme.

They never learnt the final lines of the speech. Part of her had been unsurprised when she eventually looked it up. This sceptred isle, she discovered, had *made a shameful conquest of itself.* The teachers had declined to teach them that.

And now, ahead of them, there it was. Britain, one of the world's last hopes, the great slaver nation; warm and stagnant in the sun's constant light. 'The luck of the British', they'd called it. On the Warmside, far enough in to raise crops but far enough out to still be habitable. The Goldilocks zone. Not like those poor bastards in southern Europe. 'Locust-fuckers', they had called the southern Europeans, back when there were still enough of them to insult. And here, the Highlands suddenly a new agricultural powerhouse. The sheer dumb luck of it.

They would miss Ireland, Warwick had explained before take-off, and would pass over the mouth of the River Severn instead. Ireland was very successful these days, she had added, with what Hopper considered unwarranted pride.

One thing they hadn't missed, could not miss, was the beginning of the TDZ.

The Tidal Defence Zone was the ring of coastline around the country, two miles out from shore. Some of it was afloat; the vast majority was not. Even here, just a hundred metres off the coast, Hopper saw the occasional tip of white fracturing the surface of the sea. Below the water, heaps of metal lurked – the ships of the last century, scuttled to drag down any that approached today. Britain had locked itself in while the rest of the world fell apart.

Bristol's coastal defences were by no means the most impressive part of the ring of jetsam imprisoning the country – safeguarding it, as Davenport and his ministers would say, from foreign invasion. The real achievement was the longest chain of the TDZ, south of the mainland: the Channel Barrier. The great asset of the British, the great crime, perpetrated in the name of security.

The Last Day

The English Channel – slightly shrunken these days, but still nineteen miles wide at its narrowest – was studded along almost its whole southern length with teeth of submerged scrap. Thirty years ago, in the year of the Stop, the government had begun sinking any ships they could acquire, starting in the shallowest waters. Around those, mines had been planted, concrete poured, huge floating defences and platforms set up: anything to make the crossing impossible for deep-draught ships.

The navy had sunk the container ships first. They were longer, and there were thousands of them. They had been easy to garner. The people who had populated those ships would now be either dead or in the Breadbasket, unless they were among the few brought to the mainland as possessing Special Skills.

The sinkings had not been comprehensive: not until twenty-four years ago, at the time of the second collapse, the Hotzone collapse, when Davenport had finished the job he had started six years before. At that second phase – after he had taken office – the initial sinkings had grown and grown, had become a huge midden of rust, stretching the length of the Channel. The only crossings surviving today were those left for the navy, and those for the huge grain ferries from the Breadbasket and the Fishing Fleet.

Hopper thought of the most recent sinkings, the topmost layers of the vast pile of rotten metal clogging the gates to the rest of the world, and remembered how many had been sunk with their crews and passengers still aboard. And her stomach turned at the reminder of how she had learnt that fact.

Here, outside the Severn, were three old warships still barely afloat, interceptors once intended to scoop up the rare boats from South America or South Africa that had made it through the TDZ and transport their desperate passengers to the Breadbasket. And here, inside the rusted fangs under the water, was the government's first investment, the huge anti-flood defences, once gleaming, now green and furred, abandoned for decades. The water was lower these days. The concrete fortifications showed their foundations like an elderly mouthful of teeth, the gums receding and decayed, part of a face no longer bothering to conceal its decline.

Beyond these last defences lay Bristol. It looked washed out in the sunshine, the elegant buildings by the former shoreline crumbling and dowdy, their decay visible even from this height. The streets looked busier than she recalled, though, and she thought there were new buildings too. Perhaps things really were improving.

The flood damage was now a distant memory, at any rate. The SS *Great Britain* still sat at anchor in its original spot. The areas flooded at the time of the Stop had been cleared, and ten thousand homes built on the new plain; brick, too, a step up from canvas or corrugated iron. The brick factories in the Midlands were building the Britain of tomorrow. Hopper shook her head. Half the words in her head these days were from some propaganda report.

Bath was visible a few miles away, the thin railway line running between the two cities like a bracelet linking two jewels. She'd been there on holiday with David before they married, remembered with a pang how boyishly he had enthused about its buildings. It was still largely intact – the beneficiary of a rare City

Preservation Order – still the same rich honey colour, its rooftops darker, the spires still poking blindly into the sky. Some miles south of here were the beginnings of the American Zone. Hopper kept looking out, hungry for more.

A voice crackled in her ear, making her jump. 'Look any different?' Opposite her, Warwick was watching her, smiling. Without opening his eyes, the man, Blake, raised his hand and flicked a switch on his headphones, presumably muting them both, before pushing himself further into his seat and folding his arms.

Hopper felt an irrational irritation at the question, at Warwick's unwitting intrusion into a private memory. 'I don't know. This is the first time I've seen it from the air.'

Warwick shrugged. 'I thought you might have noticed. As a scientist, I mean. The soil around the city has improved hugely in the last few years. It's a real success story.'

Hopper nodded, unsure what she was supposed to do with this information.

Warwick spoke again. 'Progress, Doctor. Progress every year, on land and at sea.' She gazed out at it, looking maternal. So that was it. Warwick must be a true believer in the whole Davenport project.

Bristol and Bath were behind them now. The land was beautiful from up here; a patchwork of browns, greens, yellows, the occasional river threading its way across the land back in the direction they'd come from. Warwick started reading some paperwork, and her colleague slept on. Half a century ago, they might have been bored commuters on a train. Maybe this was a normal day for them.

Below them now was a huge expanse of concrete, studded at regular intervals with shapes Hopper recognised only vaguely as planes. It wasn't much of a waste really. Planes were only useful if there was somewhere worth going, and right now, Britain was one of perhaps twenty habitable places left on the planet.

Hopper closed her own eyes, and the face of Edward Thorne appeared to her: coolly observant, intelligent and sorrowful, writing his letter to her over and over. Other faces arrived: her brother, her mother, David. The green lawns at school, and the barbed wire marking the edge of the grounds.

She must have slept. The next thing to disturb her was a burst of static in her ears, then the pilot's voice:

'Outskirts of London in ten minutes.'

She opened her eyes. For a moment she was disoriented, staring at the thin wall of the helicopter without thoughts. Then her gaze shifted to the back of the pilot's head, and the events of the morning returned: the slippery ladder back down to the *Rig Rocket*, the spiral amulet still in her pocket now, the heaped corpses on the boat.

Warwick and her colleague were in conference, their heads almost touching over a paper. They were making occasional notes with a pencil and speaking – on a private channel, she guessed, as she could hear nothing they were saying. Beneath them the landscape was a mess of greens and browns.

And then she looked ahead. As far as she could see on either side, the city stretched out. It was overwhelmingly big, the sclerotic heart of the new British Empire. London.

From up here, at least, the outskirts had lost a little of the depressed quality she recalled from three years ago. The houses were still dilapidated, occasionally smeared with the telltale blackening of a fire. And the gardens were predominantly soil still, studded with buttons of green.

And yet even here there were signs of improvement. New houses, brighter rooftops. A few of the gardens had lawns, even. Hopper felt a little bump of hope.

London's population was a third lower than before the Slow; it hadn't been possible to support ten million with the first erratic harvests after the Stop. Then the Breadbasket had been set up in what remained of Europe, of course, and there had been more food. Perhaps it was true – perhaps the city was recovering. Below her, she saw a string of vehicles: enormous water tankers, making their way into town from the purification plants further up the Thames.

A flash of light from the ground caught her eye. As she looked for exactly where it had come from, there came another, a brief gleam that could have been a reflection from a mirror. She pressed the button at the side of her headset.

'What are those lights down there?'

Warwick looked down and pressed at her own headset.

'Some suburbers enjoy loosing off fireworks at anyone flying overhead. Just bored kids, mostly. The odds of anyone hitting us from down there are negligible.' Blake, Hopper noted, had not looked up from his paper at the conversation.

'Bored kids?'

Warwick smiled. 'Nobody's managed to bring down a helicopter for several years, Dr Hopper. I think we'll get through all right.'

Hopper looked at the pilot. He had not visibly reacted to the flashes, and stayed in his seat, occasionally adjusting the instruments before him. But she could see the tendons in his neck standing taut as they flew on.

They were approaching the Roadblock now, the barrier between central London and the rest of the country. Viewed from above, it might almost not be there. The only thing that made it visible was the shadows cast by the buildings of the shanty town that had sprung up outside it.

London had been designated the first of the key defence zones, soon after Davenport had taken over. And so: the Roadblock. A ragged line of soldiers at first, soon supplemented by rows of concrete blocks, mushrooming in erratic patterns to halt truck and car bombs. And then, eventually, proper brick huts, and extra concrete emplacements, and all the paranoid paraphernalia of a state in retreat from its own people. It was easy to get out these days; harder to get in.

They were coming in fast, south of the river. Hopper had lived around here for a year when she and David were going out, remembered the tiny stairwell, saw him curled up in her little armchair with a book. Battersea Power Station, its single remaining tower leaning at a crazy angle; and on the right, the Houses of Parliament, the high tidemark from the old floods visible even from the air.

They were descending – towards Green Park, she guessed. She was right. They sank towards it across Westminster, and as the ground loomed up, Hopper felt a needle of excitement in spite of this unsettling morning and the people who had forced it on her. London: the place she had come after university and built whatever life she could, and just as rapidly thrown it away.

The helipad was visible now, two soldiers waving them down with paddles. Once they had landed, Blake heaved himself out of the seat, smoothing his greasy hair as he went. Warwick followed. Hopper moved last.

It was always strange, walking on dry land after the rig. Hopper missed the slight instability as she stared out at the park, surprised at the lush green surrounding her. She looked at her watch: only three hours since she'd left her cell.

London smelt of tar. She had forgotten that. The same pollution, she guessed, the same industrial works belching out poison as when she had left. The air was thick with it: a warm oiliness pervading the air, almost visible, a thick yellow blanket lying on the city. It made its way everywhere: into the pores, into the deepest recesses of the lungs, between clothing and skin, creeping thick and hot, industrial and intimate. After thirty seconds she felt suffused with it and waited for her nose to adjust. But London didn't let you acclimatise: every time she moved, the tar reasserted itself.

Thirty metres from the pad was a little hut; beyond that, a car park. Warwick spoke again. 'Step this way, Dr Hopper. A few little checks to go through.'

'Worried about what I'm bringing with me?'

Warwick smiled. 'There's no harm in safety, Doctor.'

Inside the hut, Hopper's name was taken by an elderly, moustachioed customs official in a uniform of faded blue, very worn at the collar and lapels.

'Passport?'

Her passport – a battered clump of papers bearing the right stamps and a few official seals – was matched with her records on an ancient desktop computer. Her bag was placed on the table and searched, and Hopper given a stare of impersonal but practised disdain.

Anyone entering the country was supposed to be checked for foreign pathogens, but as she'd been on a British rig, she was allowed to forgo this extra kink of bureaucracy. Eventually the official handed back her passport, reluctant, as though only a lack of evidence compelled him to release her on this occasion. She stepped out of the hut at its other end, the red asphalt spongy underfoot.

'We've booked a car for you.' Warwick was already waiting, tapping at a phone. Cars and cellular phones. More special treatment.

'Thank you. Where do I go?'

'Oh, don't worry. We're coming with you.'

Hopper wondered if this was their whole job, escorting unwilling ex-protégés to meet dying saviours of the country. As though she'd overheard her, Warwick spoke.

'It's a very unusual day for us too, Dr Hopper.' Again the slight crinkle at the corners of the mouth, switched off after half a second as if to save power.

Hopper said nothing, but Warwick continued undeterred. 'Normally, of course, it's desk work for me. I suppose they thought we needed the trip.' She nodded at her colleague standing ten yards away, surveying the field, his hollow cheeks reddened by the sun.

The sudden possibility that they might be a couple occurred to Hopper. For some reason she found the idea illogically grotesque.

Warwick took out cigarettes, and offered Hopper one. Funny, really; surrounded by tar-soaked air, and the first thing she did was light up.

Cigarette still in hand, Warwick strode off to find the car, and Hopper stood and smoked for a minute, staring at the rest of Green Park outside the helicopter area. They had landed on the northern side, facing the old buildings of Piccadilly. At this distance, they were beautiful.

In fact, in this light, it was almost impossible to see anything wrong with London. Outside the helicopter landing zone, there were flower beds, and beige-suited gardeners carrying out their tasks. Beige for gardeners, she remembered; blue for street teams, black for police.

Here, you could kid yourself the Slow had never happened. The plants had clearly been selected to provide maximum cheerfulness for minimum water usage. She wondered whether Green Park was the final park being maintained – the rest ripped up and converted to crops, to shanty towns for the displaced, to nothing.

Beyond the park, London was quiet. A few cars made their way along Piccadilly, infrequently enough that each engine could be distinguished from the others by sound alone. Hopper smoked and stared until Warwick returned, saying: 'The car's here, if you're ready.'

At the park's entrance, an aged black sedan waited, augmented with blue government licence plates. As long as cars were black and had blue plates, they qualified as government-issue. The make and model didn't matter any more.

'Only five minutes away, really, but it's worth driving,' Warwick said brightly. Behind the wheel was the same young man who had piloted the helicopter. Warwick ducked ahead and opened the door for Hopper before moving around to her own side.

As the car moved off, Hopper noticed across the road a pair of blue-coated cadets scouring the wall. They were working their way inwards, removing some red paint. All that remained of the daubed message was the words *ON WHICH THE SUN*, the scarlet letters dripping to the pavement as they rubbed and scrubbed away.

With the roads as empty as they were it took barely five minutes. They were heading to the site of the old Middlesex Hospital. The car swung right out of Green Park, the crunch of gravel beneath its wheels replaced by the low burr of tarmac, and proceeded sedately east along Piccadilly. Warwick sat beside her, staring out of her own window, giving Hopper room to look around.

On the right was St James's Church, still functioning – thriving, in fact, with extra pews sprouting into the old marketplace. As they passed, Hopper heard a choir inside, enthusiastically singing what sounded like 'We Plough the Fields and Scatter'.

The resurgence of the English Church had been extraordinary. In the years before the Stop, the government had struggled with the nation's lack of employment. There had been protests every day, and riots at the weekend. The long nights had played host to murders marked by the tang of ritual, sprouting like mushrooms in the darkness.

And then, somehow, amid this chaos, the established church had surged back, casting aside its old array of shop-worn mumbled comforts. It had offered people meaning, struggle, the prospect of another life. Attendance had soared. There hadn't been this many bishops per head of population since the four-teenth century.

Not even the rig was immune to religion, crewed as it was by soldiers raised on the mainland. On Sundays, the chaplain, Brandt, led prayers on deck for those who wanted it. Almost all the troops joined in with enthusiasm, and the services were occa-sionally surveyed by an amused, faintly embarrassed Schwimmer. Once, in an unguarded moment as they watched, he'd muttered to Hopper, 'I always knew the Lord intended to divide the people of the earth into the damned and the saved. I don't think anyone expected he would do it with a fucking ruler.'

They were nearly at the end of Oxford Street now. Just before they turned left, Hopper saw the charred lower half of Centre Point up ahead – they had been talking about demolishing it three years ago, and clearly they were talking still. They moved up Rathbone Place and into the grounds of the New Middlesex.

Another reception desk; another bored guard-cum-reception-ist. An orderly – a gentle young man, huge and stooping – swiped a keycard and led them through the double doors at the end of the entrance hall.

They walked for a minute or so along corridors studded with beech doors. Rooms, not wards: Warwick had been telling the truth about Thorne being treated well. A few of the doors were open, the beds interrupted by withered shapes. As Hopper looked into one room, a blue-shirted orderly was turning a figure on the mattress, and her eyes met those of the hairless, toothless creature on the bed for one desperate second before her movement carried her past.

Up a few flights, they stopped outside a windowless door. Warwick spoke, curtly. 'We'll wait out here.' Then she and her colleague sank onto one of the benches lining the corridor wall.

Her mouth suddenly dry, her hands flexing, Hopper turned, and entered.

The room she entered was light, warm, and protected from the corridor's smell of floor cleaner by a large bouquet of flowers standing on a table at the end of the bed. In the corner, a television mounted on the wall babbled quietly, showing whatever cheap soap Albion Television had commissioned.

And in the bed lay Edward Thorne, former saviour of England, now reduced to almost his simplest components: breath, and sight, and digestion, and little more.

7

She had arrived in Oxford for the first time in 2043, and had stayed throughout that year; the absence of a family home had made it more convenient to stay during the holidays. Only the college's inability to provide accommodation over the summer months had forced her out. She had spent two months back in London, spending her inheritance on cheap lodgings and wasting whatever money she saved on endless half-filled cigarettes.

And now, a year after her first arrival, she was back, a second-year student, not knowing why, wondering whether she would be allowed to stay until the end of the term, whether she even wanted to.

The college's central lawn was still unnaturally green: artificial, Hopper had learnt soon after arriving. Only the very wealthiest colleges could afford lawns both green and real. Most had one expensive artificial lawn for show and left the real ones yellow and sparse.

She was sitting overlooking the main lawn with her friend Kat, another second-year undergraduate, a chemist. In the flower bed behind them, a blackbird hopped about, searching for grubs among the unpromising dirt. Kat spoke first.

'Harlow's not coming back this year.'

'Why not?'

'His wife had a stroke in the break, so they're moving to Norfolk. He's got family there.'

Harlow had been their last tutor; a disappointed man. His life had been marred by three things: a marriage undistinguished by love, a research career that had never quite caught light, and a frail child, cosseted from the sunshine by Harlow's wife. He had worn the badges of these defeats heavily, and frequently reiterated the setbacks of their discipline with far more zeal than he did its successes. Hopper sometimes thought he was determined to make failures of his students so his own career might take on a less unexceptional light by comparison.

She felt a drop of water on her arm. The clouds above weren't heavy enough to really rain. Poor Harlow.

'Apparently his replacement is someone impressive.'

Hopper felt a needle of interest. 'Who?'

'He's called Thorne. *Apparently* ...' never wholly immune to the prospect of drama, Kat dragged on her cigarette before continuing, 'apparently he's some ex-government bigwig who got sacked, nobody knows why. He only got the job here because he's pals with the warden.'

Two days later, at the first dinner of term, a lean, scarecrow-like man of about sixty sat at the Warden's right hand, talking to his other neighbour during the unpleasant fish starters, then angling his chair left and conferring closely with the Warden for the rest of the meal. Their heads almost touched as they spoke.

Hopper was near the top of the hall, giving her ample opportunity to observe the pair. The warden: expounding, gesturing, animated, doubtless proposing some new pet theory of hers about the Reconstitution. The new arrival: pushing food around his plate, but always listening, interjecting, occasionally pointing his fork for emphasis. He looked tired.

The hall was half empty, even on the first night of term. All the colleges were half empty these days, even in Oxford. Most other universities had been closed down, their grounds requisitioned, rooms used as barracks, playing fields converted to crop use. The universities had been one of Davenport's first compulsory land reclamations, and it had been popular. Davenport had attended Oxford, so it was one of the few that had stayed open.

After the meal, the top table decamped to the senior common room, the largest of the warren of little chambers below the dining hall. Hopper's college was not a wealthy one: it lingered an unfashionable distance north of the city centre, its buildings a peculiar mishmash of the arch Victorian and the lumpen mid-twentieth-century extension. It was an awkward newcomer, lingering in the doorway of a long-established party. She rather liked that.

A few gilt-framed paintings hung on the room's walls, their sheen only drawing attention to the low ceilings, the faded fabric of the cushions, the cheap pine doors replacing older, sturdier wood. Heavy curtains shut out almost all the sun, creating an artificial evening.

Hopper accepted a drink from the waiter, took up a position by the wall, and surveyed the little crowd of dons and students. Her friends had promised they'd be in the White Horse around now. She would go after one free glass of the warden's wine, maybe some of her fruit.

No, she would leave now. This was too dull. She turned to go, then turned back, trying to find a surface to put her glass down on; and in a moment, the crowds parted and the warden's dining companion stood before her.

'Miss Hopper, is it?'

'Yes.' He didn't reply immediately, and she felt herself pulled into the gap by his silence. 'I'm just starting my second year. Earth sciences. I don't think we've met.'

He nodded. 'Forgive me – Caroline said I should introduce myself.' He gestured across the room to where the warden was lecturing two of her favourite history students. 'I'm Edward Thorne. I'm joining your department this year. I believe I'll be teaching you.'

'Pleasure to meet you, Dr Thorne.' She stuck out her hand, regretting the gesture almost immediately, feeling gauche. He took it.

'And you. Please call me Edward. I'm not very used to formality.' For the moment, she gave up looking for a sideboard to ditch her drink on.

'So, what brings you to Oxford?' she asked, remembering Kat's remark about him being sacked.

'Just a whim. The desire for change. One gets stagnant after too long in the same place. We all do.'

'So you came to Oxford? Nothing changes here. Half the world's on fire and this place is still going.' She smiled. He smiled back, and she could not help noticing how much it changed his face. For an instant, he looked friendly and conspiratorial, almost roguish.

He nodded. 'Perhaps change isn't the word, then. But it'll be a bit of variety for me. You're enjoying your studies?'

'Not hugely. I'm not sure many people teaching here know what they're doing.'

He arched his eyebrows. She was as surprised as him. She hadn't intended to say it.

'What a worrying prospect. Perhaps we can talk about it over the next few days?'

'I doubt you'll be able to do much about it. The authorities have suggested I leave if things don't improve by the end of this term.'

'Well, as I'm teaching you, I would hope I'm exactly the right person to do something about it.' He smiled, gently sardonic. 'Have you consulted your family about your concerns?'

'No.'

'Do you have a family?'

'Only a brother. My aunt was looking after us. She died two years ago.'

'I'm sorry to hear that. Do you mind if I ask how?'

'Just illness. Nothing sudden.' But it had been sudden. Hopper's aunt had been bitten by an insect, and even after the wound had turned black, she had smiled, and gritted her teeth. After three days sweating in an inadequate bed with no proper medicine, tangling the blankets around her thin limbs, she had died. The large house she had lived in had been in a requisition zone, and Hopper and her brother had received a small percentage of the value.

'And you were living with her?'

'Yes.' She saw a little wrestle between curiosity and tact in his countenance. Tact won. She decided to tell him anyway.

'She looked after me on and off for a few years, whenever I wasn't at school. My father died when I was sixteen. He did infrastructure.'

'I see.'

Her father had been a connector, one of the government officers tasked with getting resources to remote communities between cities. It had been dangerous work, travelling the countryside in those years. But he had gone, and come back, and gone again. Until eventually, on one trip, his phalanx of supply vehicles – tankers of water, trucks of rations, inexperienced military escort – had been torn apart by men with guns who took everything they had and left two survivors from a party of fifty.

Thorne pursed his lips. 'And your mother?'

'Six years before that. I was ten.' He nodded; again Hopper felt drawn in. 'She was a doctor. She was working in Europe. Didn't make it back.'

'I see.'

It had been nine years ago, in the middle of the second collapse – the wholesale flight of the populations living in the Hotzone, the part of the planet closest to the sun. The governments of those countries had kept going for a while: farming indoors with huge hydroponics, using the glut of solar power suddenly available, digging into the earth to house their populations. One day – not quite a day, but all had crumbled over the course of a single month – the entire region had failed, in a great chain of riotous collapse. Millions had died in the heat. The burnt region had cleared, barring a few unhinged individuals who still lived there today, clad in armour and digging ever-deeper tunnels.

The long retreat had been a column of individuals, tens of millions, walking step after step in inadequate shoes, with inadequate shade. Hopper's mother had been a doctor trying to help the straggling convoys making their way north to Europe, to give them medicines as they moved, to heal them once they reached France. It had been an impossible task. It would have been impossible even to bury the bodies by the road. Hopper and her brother had visited her briefly, when there was nobody else to look after them. She still remembered it now.

'How did she die?'

'We're not sure. But we know she made it back as far as the French coast. She had passage booked on a civilian transport. That was just as the second round of sinkings started. She thought the ship she had found was safe. Nobody had told her it wasn't.' She was surprised at herself for telling him. She usually found it much easier to fabricate parents still living.

'I'm so, so sorry.'

'I still have a brother. Others have lost a lot more.'

'It's not a competition. You don't have to have lost more than others to feel pain. And nobody should lose their mother like that.' For just a second, a look of intense emotion passed across his features, fleeting but unmistakable, and she felt a sudden extraordinary sympathy with him, one she had not felt for years. Since her aunt had died, she had been close to almost nobody; her brother was wrapped in his own studies, and she had no other family remaining. There was only her work, and she was on the brink of abandoning that, to go she knew not where.

She felt relieved when they were interrupted by a little barked shout.

'Teddy!'

The warden was moving towards them through the crowd, a sycophantic undergraduate hanging feebly in her wake. Hopper finished her glass, putting it down on the sideboard. 'Nice to meet you, anyway. Sorry it'll be brief.'

'I hope you make it to our first session before you leave.'

She had had no intention of going to any more tutorials. But that moment of sympathy was still jarring within her, and she found herself saying, 'It's in a couple of days. I imagine I'll still be here. Which are you teaching, geography or biology?'

'On paper, geography.' He smiled again. 'But really, it's almost all politics.'

The figure in the bed looked almost nothing like the man Hopper remembered. He looked nearer ninety than seventy-five. His hair had thinned drastically, and the fringe around the back of his head, formerly brown, was now the colour of dirty snow. His arms, thin and sun-mottled, rested above the sheets, and the lines around his face had slackened. He was still tall – under the sheets his legs filled most of the bed, but they looked as thin as drainpipes. For a second she pitied him.

He was asleep. The bed sheets covered him up to the chest – a little patch of exposed skin there made him look terribly vulnerable. He lay half upright, propped by three enormous pillows. His chest rose and fell, fractionally and irregularly, and from his arm a tube ran to a drip stand.

She moved to the bed, to the cane chair beside it, and edged it round so she could sit next to him. Not quietly enough. He opened his eyes, and turned his head.

'Ellen.' His voice was faltering, effortful.

'Hello, Edward.' Hopper had been determined to stay cool, but clearly she had not yet recovered from her surprise at his appearance. She could hear the tremor in her voice. Thorne spoke again:

'I didn't know I was ... as bad as all that.'

'I was just surprised. You look fine.'

'You never were a good liar.' He waved a hand as she started to demur once more. 'I can appreciate ... I've looked healthier.'

'Have you been told what it is?'

'The sun.' Skin cancer, then, or perhaps skin and another variety, she thought. Rates of the disease had rocketed, despite the campaign and sunblock distribution. It had probably progressed fast. A lot of drugs weren't available these days; many were mouldering in long-dead factories on the other side of the earth, at the other end of cauterised supply chains. So many foreign scientists, pharmacists, manufacturers had been imported towards the end in an attempt to keep the industry working: not enough.

'I'm sorry to hear that.' But her voice was flat, and she wouldn't have believed herself if she'd heard it in that tone.

He shrugged. 'There are worse fates.' He shifted a little in bed, wincing as he did so, and coughed into a shaking hand. 'How's your ... work?'

'It's fine.'

'Life in the middle of the sea, they told me. Just what ... you always wanted.'

'Yes. Just what I wanted.' She tried to think of something to say. There was nobody else in his life she knew of. She couldn't very well ask about his plans. All she could focus on was a little red mark on his pillow, a small bruise among the whiteness. Why was she here?

'Is there anything I can do to help?'

He shook his head. 'Nothing. Only myself to blame.'

'I suppose so.' Feeling as phoney as Warwick, she tried a smile.

There was another silence. He was staring not at her now, but at the foot of the bed. 'A very long time since we last spoke.'

'Fifteen years.' She remembered his office at university: remembered leaving it for the last time, after she'd learnt the truth about him. Her skin was burning at the memory.

'You must be … angry with me.'

'We all had to make choices. You made yours.' She felt furious suddenly, furious that her rage was now directed at this powerless, wizened creature too weak even to look at her.

'I would be angry too.'

She took a breath, swallowed hard. 'You were the reason I stayed on at university, Edward. Your example. Your work. I think you probably knew that. I thought you had been fighting these people. And then I found out you were one of them. So I had to leave.' How many times had she imagined this moment, rehearsed telling him what she thought of him? None of the sentences she had thought of, prepared, were coming out now. It was too much, all at once, too garbled. He twisted away, looking out of the window.

'Edward.' His head swivelled back to her. 'Why did you send for me? Why …' She paused, looking at the door to the corridor, and lowering her voice. 'Why did you write to me?'

He breathed, effortfully, and twitched his eyes towards the door for a second. Hopper thought she understood his meaning: *be careful*. He spoke. 'I wanted … to apologise.'

'Everyone you need to apologise to is dead.'

He shook his head. 'I do need to. I'm so sorry.' She saw a tear on his cheek. She looked at the little mark on the pillow. 'You always wanted the truth. I remembered that about you, from the first day we met. Only the truth. That's what I remembered about you, all these years. And I didn't offer it.'

He shook his head, the tendons sticking out from his receding flesh. She could see the toll it was taking on him. He was tiring himself out. How long had he been in here?

He reached for the water at his side. She lifted it to his lips and he took a sip. A little spilt down his front. He drank again, and she put the cup back.

'Edward …'

'I'm so sorry. And not just to you. For all of it.'

Christ. This was too much. She felt a tightness in her throat. Her eyes prickled.

He swallowed, moved his lips soundlessly for a second, carried on. 'Ellen. There is … something else.'

She leant closer. 'Something you wanted me to see?'

'I can't tell you here. That's why they brought you. They want it too.' His eyes widened, and he gestured with his head towards the door. Was he paranoid?

'You can tell me later. You're tired.'

'No. There's no time.' He sucked air into his lungs, and she heard the rattle as he coughed.

'Edward, I'm going to fetch a doctor.' She started to get up.

He reached out a hand to her, clutched her arm with surprising strength. 'I asked for weeks, Ellen, and they only just brought you. Weeks.' He pulled at her, brought her ear down level with his mouth, and strained upwards. She smelt his aroma, of old age, and decay, mingled with the sickly scent of the flowers. His voice was hardy audible. 'They brought you here thinking I would tell you everything, so they could listen. They are listening now.'

His hand was digging into her arm. 'Edward, stop. I'm going to get you some help.'

But he had pulled her down to his level again, and was whispering, almost inaudible even to her, '*My . . . house.*' Then his head veered away, and he said, louder, 'But I'm too clever for that. I haven't told you anything. Nothing at all. Nothing. Nothing.'

He stared at her, eyes wide open, dragging small breaths into his lungs, and his head fell back onto the pillow, mouthing that final word over and over.

9

The time had fuzzed. When anyone spoke to her, the words took a little while to arrive. She kept noticing small things. A shaving cut on the doctor's face. A fly, crawling jerkily across a window. The rhythm of the sprinklers in the garden outside.

Nearly two hours had passed since Edward Thorne had died.

The doctors had gone in, spent twenty minutes in the room. Then the bed had been taken out and wheeled quickly away. After another hour, the bed had been brought back, still full, but without urgency.

There was a clock ticking somewhere, but she couldn't see it, and she was not inclined to move her head to find it.

She was in a little waiting area at the end of the corridor, by the window. The London sun was even warmer than she remembered. No wonder the crops were growing so fast these days.

Triple harvests in a year, they apparently got. Sometimes quadruple. The Breadbasket lands, the old Low Countries and northern France, where they sent prisoners to grow food, must be working overtime.

Warwick had stayed; her colleague Blake had gone. After a brief, muttered conference, he had folded his coat over his arm and left. Warwick seemed content to let Hopper sit. Why she was still here, she didn't know.

And now a doctor appeared in front of her. He was young and tired; young enough to be born post-Stop, she guessed. He was speaking; Thorne's body was ready for her to say farewell, if she wanted to. He led her into the room, saying more words, and left her alone with it.

It was just her in here; her, and the body on the bed. It was less unsettling this time, now she knew to expect an old, old man. He had been tidied up; his eyes had been closed, his arms placed by his sides under the covers. Much tidier than the bodies on the boat.

At the foot of the bed – she hadn't seen before – were his medical papers. She looked around to check there was nobody watching through the glass porthole in the door, and pulled the little sheaf from the plastic holster. The front page was the basics – address, contact information, age – then came prescriptions, progress, responsiveness to treatment. And at the back, in fresh ink, the details of death.

My house, he had said.

She took the chart, ripped away the front page, folded it into four, and crammed it into her pocket. They wouldn't notice the absence. He was dead; it could do them no good.

She looked once more at the thing on the bed, shivered, and stepped away, back out into the green-lined corridor with its clean, empty smell.

She and Warwick were at the door, passing a tower of leaflets: nutrition deficiency, euthanasia guidance, the ubiquitous Sun Defence logo reminding the public of the risks to their skin.

Weeks, Thorne had said he'd been in hospital. Had he really been trying to contact her all that time?

Back in the car, Warwick turned to her.

'Where to?'

She hadn't really thought about it until now. 'My brother's home, please. Brixton.'

As the car began to move, she spoke again. 'Actually, sorry, could you let me out by St Martin's? I should ring ahead.'

There was no response from the driver, but he turned in the right direction as they swung out of the car park. She should have walked; it wasn't far. Now she was trapped in the car for one last interview with Warwick.

'Well, I must say, you've had quite a day, Dr Hopper. I expect your brother will be glad to see you, whether you're staying for the funeral or not.'

Hopper nodded mechanically. She had no intention of letting Warwick know anything else about her brother, nor about herself.

The route down through Soho was grubbier than Green Park. Soho Square wasn't maintained. The only people present were a few exhausted-looking wretches scattered on the grass. On the right, eroded beyond recognition, the statue of Charles II, an unfashionably merry king presiding over an unfashionable part of town. The rest of the royals had disappeared.

Beyond that, south through the heart of the district, there was nothing but half-open shops and a few grimy cafés. A few open doorways made their services luridly known, the bright orange swirls notifying passers-by of sold sex in shuttered upstairs rooms.

They moved on to the Charing Cross Road and down. It was livelier here, the streets busier; as they approached Charing Cross, they passed a guided bus heading the other way. The tours were popular: it was a treat for out-of-towners to see London. There had been visitors from the American Zone too, until life there had started to become really hard. The numbers of defectors had spiked, and the border had been closed.

Outside St Martin-in-the-Fields, the car pulled over. Hopper turned to Warwick to say goodbye, but was pre-empted by another warm, bland smile.

'Dr Hopper, I'm so glad we could help today. Please do contact me if there's anything more we can do.' A card had appeared in her hand, and she pressed it into Hopper's.

'Thank you.'

The car glided off towards Whitehall. Hopper walked up the church steps, threw down her bag, and sat, looking out at Trafalgar Square.

A feeling of profound disorientation swept over her. Here she was in the middle of London; eight hours ago she had been in the North Atlantic, staring at a boat full of bodies and thinking of her mother.

She pulled from her pocket the page she had stolen – taken – from Thorne's records, and found his address. He had lived somewhere in North 3. Hampstead.

Why not, after all? She could go to see her brother afterwards. On a whim, she found a bus, an elderly twin-decker, heading in the right direction, and boarded.

The bus was full of tired passengers, most dressed for work, the paleness of exhaustion showing through their reddened skins. They didn't seem like they were running one of the last great nations of the earth.

The few not formally dressed were more obviously poor. The mother, awkwardly moving her rickety pram on three original wheels and one replacement; the sleeping man in a ragged jacket and no shirt, who managed to keep the seat next to him clear as the bus filled, until finally an angular, owlish civil servant perched beside him, as far out as he could.

She must have drifted off to sleep; the next thing she heard was the word 'Hampstead', shouted from the front, and she jerked upright, grabbed her bag, and pushed through the little throng around the doors to leave.

As the bus pulled away, quiet descended, broken only by the ceaseless chirping of the crickets. There was a little shop across the road. The shopkeeper looked Korean, and as she picked a packet of gum from the half-empty shelves, and pointed to the address on her purloined sheet for directions, she idly wondered whether his family had arrived before or after the Stop.

The street Thorne lived on – had lived on – was luxurious. It was lined with tall red-brick houses, set back from the road behind a phalanx of hedges. The trees studding the pavement were hardy southern European strains, the sort now supplanting traditional English varieties across the country.

Another sign of affluence: the road was fully lined with cars, beautiful makes that hadn't been manufactured for thirty years. Private cars were rare even in wealthy areas like this one – moving ones, anyway. Apart from the lightweight Tin Tigers made in the Birmingham factories, the few cars in operation ran on parts canni-balised from other machines. Passing a distinguished bottle-green old Bentley, she looked inside and noticed it had no seats.

As she walked down the road, looking at the house numbers she passed, she read the sheet she had taken:

Patient name: Edward Joshua Thorne
Patient address: 74 Harlesden Road, North 3
Date of birth: 02/05/1983
Date of admission: 09/06/2059
Age of patient: 76
Reason for admission: Melanoma (SIV)
Course of treatment:

… followed by a list of drug names and doctors' signatures. Hopper noticed the size of the doses unevenly but inexorably increasing down the page.

68, 70 … She could see it now. There was a gap in the neigh-bour's garden, and Thorne's home jutted out in front of the house before it. It was four storeys tall like its neighbours, dark red brick, lined with creeping plants. Poking out of the roof was a round brick turret, surmounted by heavy slate.

And then, from behind the hedge, she saw a man waiting outside the house; uniformed in the shiny beetle-black of the police. Hopper's initial instinct was to turn and walk away, until she realised how that might look. Her next instinct was to walk by, and yet instead she stopped and looked past him, up at the high windows of Thorne's house.

She spoke first. 'Good afternoon. Excuse me.' She made as if to move past him, through the gate, until the officer drew a little closer to it, blocking her way.

'Do you live here, madam?'

He had the gun by his side, the standard belt of pacifiers: canisters of gas, electric baton, black carbon handcuffs. But he was young – perhaps twenty-five – and gangly. A livid red rash lined his neck above the tidemark of his collar. If his collar was too small, his jacket was a little large for him, and looked heavy in the heat.

'I ... No, I'm on my way to see Dr Thorne.'

'I'm afraid that's not possible, madam. We can't let anyone in. Even if you were Mr Thorne himself.'

'Why not?'

'I'm afraid I can't say.'

She spoke as persuasively as she could manage. 'Please. Dr Thorne and I are good friends. What's happened? Is he all right?'

He looked at the house, back to her, softened slightly. The crickets in the garden continued their monotonous vigil. 'We were called out this afternoon. There's been a burglary.'

Another little hinge in the day, another moment Hopper had not been expecting, but one that fitted into the whole pattern of unpleasant surprises from the moment she had seen the helicopter on the rig.

Her face must have betrayed her surprise. The policeman looked at her with a little curiosity. 'Are you … family of Mr Thorne?' She could feel him assessing – was she a girlfriend, a mistress?

'*Dr* Thorne. No. I just …' If she mentioned the hospital, he would know she was lying about wanting to visit him. 'I'm just coming by to visit him. We're friends.' The officer kept his face blank, clearly drawing his own conclusions. 'Was he … in?'

'No, nobody was in. Lucky we were called really. A neighbour phoned and reported a couple of strangers making their way into the property.'

'Do you know who they were?'

'Not yet, madam. We've only just finished making the premises safe. Once that's done we'll start gathering evidence.'

'Can I go in to drop something off?'

He shook his head. 'I'm afraid not. If you have something you want to give to Dr Thorne, I'd happily pass it over once we've finished here.'

She tried to come up with a mental inventory of the things in her bag that could conceivably be classed as presents for Thorne, and gave up.

'No, that's fine. I'll see him another time.'

A crackle of static came from the radio on the policeman's arm.

'I can pass a message on, of course. What's your name, madam?'

After a brief hesitation, she answered: 'Jessica Hayward.'

Where had that come from? Jessica Hayward was a girl she'd been at school with, now living a life of uninterrupted domesticity in Suffolk, married to a civil servant in Solar.

'Well, I'll let him know that you called, when he returns, Miss Hayward.'

She wished he wouldn't use the name. It made him likelier to remember it.

'That's not necessary. I'll contact him myself. Thank you.'

She took one more look at the house, then shouldered her bag and turned the way she had come. As she walked, she resisted the urge to turn and check whether the officer was watching her.

On the other side of the road, the next house along from Thorne's had a large bay window on the first floor. At the edge of her eye, she saw a tall figure there, momentarily silhouetted in the sunlight, looking out at the street.

10

Hopper made her way back to the main road, starting to sweat under the weight of her bag, but the pain in her shoulder wasn't enough to distract her from the wings of panic fluttering in her throat. She looked around her, then made her way back to the shop by the bus stop, asked the shopkeeper if he had a phone. He waved aside her offer of money and ushered her into a back room, where an yellowed Bakelite phone sat on a desk, half swamped by old receipts and other shop junk.

She picked up the phone. A buzz, then a click.

'Hello … South 4, please. Hopper. I think it's 493 … Yes, that's the one. Thank you.' For a few seconds she sat in the chair, her gaze roving from the half-full ashtray on the desk to the cheerful tins of mustard powder on the shelf opposite. She heard another click.

'Hello?'

'Mark? It's me.' And then, because it had been a few years: 'Ellie.'

'Ellie?' Her brother sounded astonished. 'Why are you in north London? I thought you were on the rig?'

'I had to come back. Just got in this morning.'

'Why?'

'Do you remember Edward Thorne? My old tutor?'

'Of course I remember Thorne. What's happened? Has he died or something?'

'Well … yes.'

'Oh, Christ. Sorry, Ellie. I didn't mean to … I was being flippant.'

'It's fine. I just came from the hospital.'

'Are you all right?'

She breathed deeply. 'Yes. I'm fine. Just a very long day.'

'Do you want to come for dinner?'

'I'd … Only if it's not too much trouble. Yes, I'd love to.'

'Of course it isn't any trouble. Will you stay the night?'

'I can't prey on your hospitality like that.'

'Of course you can. What are you going to do, go to Bristol and wait for a boat straight back to the rig?'

She sighed, and considered her few options. This was the best. 'Well … I'd love to stay, yes.'

'When can you be here?'

'About an hour, I think. I'll get a bus to you.'

'I'll tell Laura. See you soon.'

Another click and the line died.

She thanked the shopkeeper, bought a couple of unnecessary packets of cigarettes to repay him for the use of the phone, and stepped back into the street, waiting for a bus heading south. The sun's light was dimmed by clouds, too light to promise rain. It was nearly eight in the evening.

It took two cigarettes for the bus to arrive. She climbed to the top deck, unoccupied except for a pair of children squabbling on the front bench and their wan mother. Hopper moved to the back.

The policeman seemed not to have known Thorne was dead. Or, if he had known, he'd been under instruction not to pass the information on. And now, if anyone asked whether Thorne had had any visitors, the young man on the door would say a woman answering her description had come by, with some absurd story about a present.

Occupied by these reflections, Hopper made her way to South 4, formerly known as Brixton.

The streets were heaving as she got off the bus. The old Underground station had once been the town's meeting point; after the network had atrophied, the centre of gravity had shifted upwards, to the green outside the old cinema. The whole circus of human life was there: traders offering shirts too good to be new and too cheap to be honestly acquired; grocers shouting about new cultivars; touts offering tickets to the latest classical performance at the Electra. Funny how it was called the Electra, when the only

reason it hosted so much classical music was the sporadic elec-
tricity shortages.

Now – just after seven in the evening, comfortably before
curfew – activity was at its peak. The station and its surroundings
were heaving with salesmen, lingerers, shysters, beggars, crooks.
They were trading, gambling, cheating, cursing and gossiping,
all fuelled by tots of rum sold by a rackety man with a wooden
cart. A colossal pink-necked hawker, completely bald and clad
in a huge speckled smock, was offering anyone in earshot the
chance to see a show.

The smell of spices lingered in the air, coming from the row
of little shacks huddling around the walls of the old cinema. So
many jostled beside each other that even London's stink of tar
was drowned out and the scents merged into one, a single enormous aroma of a hundred foods.

At the end of the green closest to the old Underground station
were two more police – slightly more thuggish, these, with shiny
black carapaces of body armour instead of the dark suit worn by
the young officer outside Thorne's home.

There were rumours the government had repaired the key
lines on the Underground a few years before and that it now ran
trains once again, but only for the benefit of the security services,
letting them transport officers, shields, batons, tear gas across the
city in minutes.

Hopper didn't believe it. The network required too much
technology, most of it foreign-built. Redeveloping it would
have taken decades. She preferred the alternative theory: that
the tunnels were still waterlogged after the great floods of the

Stop, and that blind cavefish and crocodiles now made the Tube their home.

She moved through the crowd, self-conscious. There were more people in this small square than on the whole rig. One patch of pavement was lined with men seated against the wall in various poses of agony. Several were missing limbs. Many held crude signs in faulty English. Some had children seated by them; gaunt creatures, perching by their fathers' sides like little crows, their frames shrunken inside too-large coats, their shoes improvised from card or rags. On seeing Hopper's well-cut jacket as she passed, her clean trainers, one man said, in a thick middle-European accent, 'Please. Berlin. Please.'

Before long others had joined him, and the children approached her too. She walked faster, feeling awkward, making her way through the crowds. Eventually she escaped between two of the stalls onto a little patch of green shaded by trees, a place for couples to linger in semi-darkness. Another memory struck her, of being here with David. She dismissed it, and set off for her brother's home.

Colville Crescent was the place: as genteel as it sounded, an elegant bow of bricks. No throngs here, no street-side card games; just a curved progression of suffering poplars and Victorian houses. Halfway along it was the pleasant, white-painted home of Mark Hopper, security specialist to the British government, southern region. She noticed his neighbours had had new shutters installed since her last visit. A street of people still dedicated to self-improvement, even after everything.

Mark opened the door almost as soon as she rang – he must have been lingering in the front room to pre-empt Laura. He hugged her awkwardly, not giving her a chance to put her bag down, then stood back and looked at her.

'Hi, sis.'

'Hello, Mark.'

He took the bag from her, then absent-mindedly wedged it between the hall table and a pushchair, and straightened up. 'Sorry to hear about Thorne.'

'Thanks. It's …' She stopped. The length of the day caught up with her, and impulsively she hugged him again, less awkwardly this time. They stayed like that for a few seconds, then she patted him for release.

'You must be starving.'

Apart from a snatched breakfast before leaving the rig, she had not eaten all day. 'Yes. Oh God, yes.'

'Great. Well, we're ready. The kids have already had theirs and gone to bed, so it'll just be us.'

'Have you waited? You shouldn't have done.' Laura would be annoyed. Hopper didn't quite care.

'It's all right. Meant I got a bit more work done.'

'I feel like I'm imposing.'

'No imposition.'

As he turned to stow her coat in a hall cupboard, she glanced at her brother. His face was pale, and there were dark circles under his eyes. When he had looked away from her, his face had dropped, but as he looked back, he smiled again.

'How's Laura?'

'Great, thanks. She's just back through here.' He spoke as if to remind her: *whatever you're thinking, keep it to yourself.*

'And you?'

'Oh, not bad.' He had already started walking towards the back of the house. 'Every day a new adventure. Please do come through.'

Hopper followed. He was so formal sometimes. Even during their childhood he had treated her with perfect manners, as though she was a house guest arrived in his home two years late. He had got out of cars to open doors for her, and signed birthday cards *best regards*. For years she had suspected he disliked her, then she had seen him with a girlfriend, and realised: this was his way with almost everyone.

The house's basement was beautiful: a kitchen-cum-dining-room running from the front to the back, with windows bowing onto the garden. The room had been fitted with the clever blinds they had these days, which used reflectors to create the impression of darkness outside. The air was cool, too – air-conditioned – and the dining table flanked by shelves of new-looking books. Mark must be doing well in his work.

Laura was in the front half of the room, the kitchen, with its iron-barred windows to the street above. She turned as Hopper entered, a serving dish in her hands, and put it back on the stove. As they hugged, Hopper wondered idly if she had been waiting to pick it up just as she came in, to show exactly how much trouble was being taken on her behalf.

'Hello, Ellie. You well?'

'Not bad, thank you. A long day.'

'I'm sure. Well, make yourself at home.'

She and Laura had never really enjoyed each other's company. One of the few times they had spent any time together alone had been a weekend away shortly before Mark and Laura's wedding. They had stayed in a Cotswolds hotel, a converted Georgian house run by an elderly couple. The place had been beautiful but the mood unpropitious; the owners' only child had been badly injured in some training exercise during his conscription. They were now caring for him, a man of forty, and gaily attempting to appear unconcerned about the future despite their frailty.

Mark had been summoned away to attend to some crisis in London. She and Laura had argued on the first night, and spent the rest of the weekend avoiding each other's company when possible. Really it had been less an argument than the establishment of a strong difference of outlook: Laura was as keen to build and protect homes as Hopper was to flee them.

At least there was no false bonhomie between them. They were comfortable not knowing each other's inmost lives, and they tolerated their occasional contact with each other due to their common love of Mark. And that was something, at least. Laura really did love him. Their marriage was one of the strongest Hopper had ever seen.

Mark had always shied away from addressing the gulf between his wife and his sister. Like a planet circled by two moons on opposite sides, he was aware only of the one in his field of view, and on the rare occasions when the two appeared in the same vista, he was surprised but not unduly bothered.

'Please, come and sit down. Glass of wine?'

'Thanks.'

She sat at the dining table, picking up the bottle as Mark went to fetch another glass. *Norfolk Estate*, the label read. Norfolk was good for wine these days. It was definitely better than the brackish Cornish stuff. Those grapes suffered the currents of the Atlantic passing nearby and gave every glassful a tang of what the makers called 'ocean bouquet' but everyone else recognised quite clearly as brine.

She stood as Laura approached the table with a casserole dish. 'Can I help?'

'It's all right. Only one or two more things to come. Sit.' Laura had clearly intended to sound less peremptory than she did, adding, 'I mean, if you'd like.'

Only once they were seated and the food – a gamey mixture of some unidentified bird, plus vegetables ('from the garden') – had been dished out did Mark turn to Laura and say, 'Ellie's had a bit of bad news. Her old tutor, Edward Thorne, died this afternoon.'

'How sad. Was he ill?'

'Yes. But I didn't know about it until today. A couple of his colleagues turned up at the rig' – had they been his colleagues? She didn't know – 'and called me back to see him, at his request.'

'Were you close?'

'No. We hadn't been in contact for years.'

'Then what did he want to see you for?' As before, the tone of Laura's voice sharpened the question a little too far.

Hopper smiled, not meaning it. 'I think he just wanted to speak to one of his students again.' The slight lie made her flush a little. *That's not why he wanted to see you*, she thought. 'How are the children?'

Laura spoke. 'They're fine. Jenny was four last week, so we threw her a little party. Tom's still obsessed with the army, of course. Marching up and down the park.' Her whole face softened when she talked about her children.

'And how's your work?'

'Fine, thanks. Nothing much to write home about. Mark's the one who's really been up against it lately.'

Mark's work was something in Security – he had never told her exactly what, beyond the vague catch-all answer of counter-terror. From the amount he'd told her, he could either be cleaning the place or running it. Laura had finished her national service and retrained in solar – organising new installations and grid management. Today she spent her days administering power generation for a swathe of the south-east, although admittedly from a comfortable office in Whitehall.

'I'm sorry to hear that, Mark. Sounds stressful.'

Laura spoke again. 'It's been really excessive actually. Lot of late nights. Something big brewing with the Americans, isn't that right?'

'Oh, there's always something.' Mark glanced at Laura as he smiled. Clearly he'd told her a few details too many. She nodded slightly, as if understanding the cue, and he changed the subject. 'Ellie, do you know how long you'll be staying in town?'

'There's a boat going back to the rig in a few days. I'll be on it.'

'Well, stay with us until then, obviously.' This, clearly, had been rehearsed too. There was no way Mark would have made the offer without consulting his wife first.

Hopper took a mouthful of wine. 'Thank you. I'd love to.'

'Here we go.'

Standing at the sideboard, Mark rubbed his face with his free hand as he poured the whisky. Laura had gone to bed soon after supper, and Hopper felt more relaxed already. It was luxuriously dim in the living room – darker than the rig was, even with its huge industrial shutters.

He turned, handed Hopper her glass, sat.

'You really are welcome to stay.' He looked at her along the sofa. 'I mean it. Stay for a month if you like.'

'I meant it too. I'd love to.' Well, that was a stretch, but it beat private lodgings, and she and Mark never saw each other these days. In their photos on the mantelpiece, his children were unrecognisably big. 'I'm sure you'll get tired of me before then.'

'Ha.' He rubbed his eyes again. 'Sorry for shutting off a bit about my work. It's just a ... a healthy habit to be in.'

'Mark, it's all right. I'm not offended by secrets.'

'Thanks.' He looked relieved.

'Anyway, I know what you government types are like. You're not the first civil servant I've met today.'

'What do you mean?'

'The two who came to pick me up from the rig. A real double act. Warwick was the woman's name.'

'Warwick?' There was a note of recognition in his voice, suppressed so quickly that a casual listener might have missed it.

'Yeah. Ruth Warwick. Woman in her mid forties, very dressed up. Man maybe a bit older, looked a bit of a bruiser. Blake, his name was. She was chatty and he said practically nothing. Why, do you know them?'

Mark shook his head. 'I'm thinking of someone else. I'd be surprised if I did, but sometimes people switch departments.'

'Well, they were memorable, at least.' The conversation lulled after that. Eventually she bade him goodnight, and hauled her bag upstairs.

The guest room was perfectly laid out, the bed sheets disconcertingly smooth after the rough linen of the rig. The last thought that occurred to her before she slept was that, despite the nature of his work, she knew very well that her brother avoided lying whenever he could, for the simple reason that he wasn't very good at it.

She dreamt she was with her mother, somewhere she could not name, in a chamber that was rocking to and fro. She was being told to look in a mirror. As she turned she saw, staring back at her, a skull, its sockets empty and its jaw missing, moss clinging to one cheekbone, and a little spiral amulet around its neck; and the mirror would not smash, no matter how she beat it with her cool white hands.

11

Hopper woke slowly, drifting up through layers of half-consciousness and dream until eventually she was staring at the ceiling, disoriented. And then, in one shift, the shapes around her resolved themselves into the familiarity of the spare room. It was after nine. The house felt still beneath her.

She busied herself pulling clothes out of her bag, shoved the old ones into the bottom of it. She put nothing into the cabinets or wardrobe. Even on the rig, she had lived out of her trunk for two months after her arrival. The comforting thought that it would be easier to make a hasty departure if one's cases were already half packed always outweighed the temporary comfort to be found in a home. In her experience, you inevitably had to leave sooner or later.

After her mother's death, her childhood had been a noisy mess of departures – she and Mark moving around the country with her father's work. His work had been the constant presence in their lives.

Widowed with two children after thirteen years of marriage, their father had thrown himself fully into his job. His compulsive labour had been a retreat of sorts – from a world that had taken his wife from him – but when Hopper looked at it now, it seemed like an advance too, a concerted effort to reshape the world in the hope that it might one day be more stable for her and her brother.

Whatever the cause, her abiding memory of her father was of the side of his face as he stared intently at screens or documents or talked on the phone. He had seldom been unkind, but it would be deluded to claim he had not been neglectful.

The second half of their childhood, with no mother and a workaholic father, had acted on the siblings in very different ways. Where Hopper resisted close relationships, Mark had thirsted for the stability denied to them as children. From the age of sixteen he had almost constantly had a girlfriend. Whenever a relationship ended, he would begin a new one within the month.

It would be impolite to suggest that Laura had simply been his girlfriend at the time he was first ready to marry, but not inaccurate. Hopper wondered sometimes if Laura knew she thought this, and disliked her for it. But perhaps Laura simply thought of her sister-in-law as an unnecessarily chaotic element in an already disordered world.

Downstairs, there was a note in the kitchen, pinned under a cereal bowl:

Ellie – have gone to work. Laura's had to go into town after dropping the kids at school. Here's a spare key – we'll be eating around eight. You're welcome to join us, obviously. Regards, Mark

Regards, indeed. She picked a biro from the pot and drew two thick lines under her brother's note, then wrote a brief reply:

I'll be out most of the day, but sure I'll be back tonight. If not, I'll ring. Which raised the question: out where?

She could feel thoughts of Thorne at the gates of her brain, and realised she felt suddenly hostile to the whole mad story. Now she had slept, yesterday seemed like a fantastical storm that had swept her up and deposited her hundreds of miles from home. All she wanted to do was get back out of Britain. In a few days she could return to the rig and resume what passed for her life, studying the currents; free of responsibility, floating on the surface of things. There was no purpose in thinking about Thorne. None at all.

Before leaving the house, she stopped in the hall, picked up the phone, and rang the rig. That was another effect of the Slow that still surprised some older people – the curdling of the world's time zones. Here in London, it was ten in the morning. Out at the rig, the sun was twenty degrees lower in the sky, but it would be ten o'clock there too.

As the Slow had begun, there had been a spell of adjustment, as the old system – the twenty-four-hour clock, the world crazy-paved with time zones – frayed. The earliest months had been easy. As seconds were added to the duration of the planet's spin, so they were added to the length of each day. A body had been set up to establish the precise rate of deceleration – in Germany, one of the old European states – and the information was communicated to the world's nations.

The empty time between days had been called Dead Air. At the end of each day, the planet's televisions and radios hung suspended for a little while, until the next day. Midnight lasted twenty seconds, then thirty, then a full minute. Some countries displayed a message from the authorities; others left only static.

Each night the Dead Air lasted a few seconds longer. Soon, the gap stretched to ten minutes, then twenty. Gradually people would wake earlier, and stare silently at their clocks, as day and light lurched further away from each other.

Fifteen months into the Slow, the Eurotunnel crash had occurred. Britain had been adjusting its timetables daily; France had saved up the difference and made the change each week. Nobody had noticed the thirty-second discrepancy that built up towards the end of each week. The gap had contributed to a crash between a British passenger train and a French freight train that left eight hundred dead. The smash had unseated the government, led to the tunnel being sealed off, and added to the 'Britain Alone' myth on which the current administration had so heavily relied.

Her reflections were cut off by the operator. 'Number, please.'

She gave the number for the rig, then looked outside while the operator connected the call. It was overcast; thin clouds stretched across a light grey sky, the sun bright behind them. Still no rain today, probably. The weather was as dry on the rig: the back-up desalinators they kept would be working overtime.

Harv picked up the phone. He would be sitting in Schwimmer's office, on duty. His voice was distant, but the shade of Boston in his voice was so familiar that a little thrill of recognition went through her.

'Hello, Hop. How are you?'

'Fine, thanks.'

'What happened with the tutor? Thorne, right?'

'He died.'

'Ah, shit. Were you close?' Everyone seemed to want to know that.

'Not especially.'

A pause. 'Sorry to hear it anyway. Did you get a chance to talk to him?'

'Not much. He seemed ... I don't know. Paranoid, somehow.'

'Being Richard Davenport's former best pal will do that to a man.'

'Yeah. Anyway, it's over now.'

'How's London?'

'More or less the same. Bit cleaner.'

'Anything else?'

'Well ... yes, actually.' She told him, briefly, about her visit to Thorne's house. At the end of it, he stayed silent until she prompted him. 'What do you think?'

'The burglary? I don't know, Hop. Sounds like a coincidence. Maybe it was because the house was empty.'

'It had been empty all the time he was in hospital. How would anyone know to break in the day he died?'

'I don't know.' He changed the subject. 'So are you coming back?'

'I'll stay today, visit the department, then try to hop on the next supply ship. Unless they give me a helicopter back.'

'As you deserve. We miss you.'

'No you don't.'

'Well, I don't, but Schwimmer's inconsolable.'

'Obviously.'

'Hey, Hop.' He paused again. 'When you come back, I'd like to talk.'

'About what?'

'About us, I guess. I've missed you. It'd be nice to … oh, I don't know.'

'To what? Make it official?' She smiled.

'Yeah. If you want to put it that way, yeah.'

'You absolute cheese.' And then, a little concerned not to hurt his feelings, and secretly aware that the prospect rather pleased her: 'Sure, Harv. I think I might like that.'

She could hear the grin in his voice as he signed off. 'Catch you in a few, Hop. Take it easy.' A click, then the smooth purr of the empty line. She hung up.

The government office that employed her to sit in the rig and study the currents was a tall concrete building south of Holborn.

Her colleagues were surprised to see her; her superiors, grey and rumpled, could summon little interest in an update on her research. Work on the ocean was unfashionable; it escaped the cachet awarded to those who could squeeze an extra rotation out of a field of crops each year. Her old office was occupied by a new face, a young graduate looking into soil depletion in the north-east.

When she got back to the lobby, the heavy wooden door to the street had been closed, and several people were waiting inside on the long benches, apparently without aim. But she did not notice these signs, and as she heaved the door open just enough to slip through, she heard a voice behind her, raised in protest, saying something urgent. But by then it was too late, she was through, and as it thudded shut behind her, she heard a click from the lock.

In the street outside, her eyes first registered only a wall of movement. Along the middle of the road, a phalanx of people, perhaps ten across, was half walking, half marching towards the river. They were in approximate rows, which occasionally shimmered into the impression of order, before one individual sloucher slowed the whole group down and the column fractured again.

There were no apparent restrictions on membership: she spotted a grey-haired man who must have been seventy, two girls of eleven or twelve, and all ages between the two. They were every shape, every height, every colour of skin. Their clothes were in poor condition, loosely orbiting a rough uniform of off-white shirts and trousers; many did not fit. Some had shoes; others had feet crudely bandaged. A few walked barefoot on the hot tarmac.

Up and down the edges of the column, mounted soldiers in black, fitted with helmets and truncheons, rode at a gentle trot, and every hundred yards another soldier slouched behind the wheel of an armoured car. The crowd walked without speaking; barring the shuffle of their feet, and the noise of the horses' hooves, the street was almost silent. The doors and shutters lining the road were also shut.

On the pavements, a few spectators were observing the crowd. Hopper approached one, a rat-like man in late middle age who wore a flat cap and a long coat, tattered at the edges.

'Excuse me.'

'What you want, miss?' He barely glanced at her before his eyes returned to the scene.

'Who are these people?'

'They're being shipped to the Breadbasket. Off to grow your dinner.'

'Prisoners?'

He nodded, snorting heavily through his nose. 'Yeah. They bring them all here, march them through. Happens every month.'

'But where are they from?'

'They're criminals.' She saw the satisfaction with which he said it, and he repeated it, louder, as though hoping the exhausted bodies passing by might register it. '*Criminals*. Pris'ners, foreigners, es-cay-pees. Don't you worry, they deserve it, I can guarantee you that. They deserve everything they get.'

She remembered now. The ceremony was called the Winnow. It was another of Davenport's little bits of street theatre, designed to keep people quiescent by reminding them what waited for anyone who committed a serious enough crime. She had never actually seen it before. The route through town must have changed in her absence.

'Why do they march them through here?'

'To show other crooks what's coming to them.'

'It's horrible.'

He grinned. 'You don't like it, you can join them. The foreigners all cheated their own people to get here. Left their families behind, most of them. And without them working away, you don't get your food, miss. You don't look like you refuse your bread.' He nodded, before a thought struck him. 'Why don't you know about it? Where you from?'

'I've been living on one of the rigs, out at sea. British rigs. I'm not an escapee.'

'Better you're not. Not like these people. Scum. Not even got any shoes, some of them. And they steal. Scum.' After half a minute of silence, he shuffled slowly away down the line, glancing back at her with suspicion, before stopping to continue his vigil. She noticed his own shoes were falling apart, the tops and bottoms crudely bound by packing tape.

Further down the street, the crowd swept left around the Aldwych, towards the riverbank. Maybe some old cruise ship converted into a prison hulk would take them across the Channel from here, straight to northern Europe's farmland.

Or perhaps the riverside destination was another bit of theatre, and they would be loaded into lorries and taken the more sensible route down to the Newhaven crossing. Once it would have been Calais, before the port had been blown up. More government-as-performance from Davenport; another ritual hauling-up of the national drawbridge.

The crowd had developed a knot, about thirty metres up from where she was. Two figures had fallen out of the line. She stepped off the pavement towards them. As she did, she saw another figure approaching, one of the police horses. Hopper arrived first.

A child, a boy, had slumped to the ground. He must have been about fifteen; he was long-faced, short-haired, wearing a grey shirt several sizes too big for his skinny frame. The shirt was cinched in at the waist by a belt with an improvised hole. The skin on his face was burnt and peeling.

The other figure was an older woman – Hopper assumed his mother – who was quietly urging him back into the line. But she was even slighter than him and he was determined not to be moved. He was saying, loudly, 'I can't. I can't. I can't,' again and again. He had a yellow crust at the corner of his mouth.

Hopper addressed the older woman. 'What's the matter with him?'

'He doesn't have medicine. He needs it. He's not had it three days.' She sounded like she was from the Midlands.

'What medicine?'

'Pills for his heart. Help me lift him.'

'Get back into the line, please.' The soldier on the horse had arrived and dismounted.

Hopper ignored the command. 'He's ill. Where's your medical station? Where's the doctor for this group?'

'We have medical facilities on the transport ship, madam. We'll look after him there.' The soldier's tone was flat. He barely bothered to varnish the lie. She saw, fifty metres down the road, another rider, alert in his saddle, waiting.

'He needs treatment now. There's a hospital nearby, up on Holborn. He should be transported now.'

'This is a matter for us to deal with, madam.' A second horseman, equidistant on the other side, had also arrived. The eyes of the passing crowd were all averted.

'I just want to get him some water. He won't make it to the ship without that. Look at him.' The boy's lips were cracked and his eyes were unfocused. She turned to him, leaning over him for a second, and there was a brief burst of intense pain in the back of her head.

She hardly felt herself being picked up, dragged to one side and dropped in a shaded patch at the side of the road. She did not see the young man shoved into a stumbling walk with his mother, did not hear the horses' hooves slowly receding on the hot tarmac, sensed nothing of the gentle breeze on her neck as she lay sprawled on the pavement, her body twisted inelegantly.

The first thing Hopper smelt was the tar again: strong, suddenly, prodding at her nose. Then she felt the warm, hard ground under her. Her throat was burning and dry. There was a throbbing at the back of her head, which pulsed in time with the noises she was hearing.

Someone was speaking to her.

'Do you hear me? Can you open your eyes?'

She opened her eyes slowly. Too bright. She closed them again. Waves of pain were passing through her skull. She felt sick. No, wait – she was going to be sick. She leant over, nauseous. Eventually she managed to speak.

'What time is it?'

The man standing at her side was young, wearing a suit, looked smart.

'It's noon.' She had been unconscious for an hour. He spoke again. 'What's your name?'

'Where am I?'

'Kingsway.' She pushed herself upright and looked around. She was barely a hundred metres from the entrance to her department. She had been placed in a tiny patch of shade in the lee of a skeletal kiosk. What a curious little delicacy to show someone you'd just beaten. 'What happened to you?'

Hopper struggled to remember. 'There was a column, prisoners ... Someone was struggling.'

'So you intervened?'

'I was just trying to get him water.'

'I don't know if you know this, but traditionally the Samaritan helps the guy who's been beaten up. He doesn't get himself beaten up in the process. Here. Drink this.'

'Very funny.' Still, she took the canteen he offered, drank from it. Her wrist hurt from the way she'd fallen, and her jaw too, but as she touched it now, she could feel no break in her skin, though there was a lump on the back of her head.

'You shouldn't interrupt a Winnow. There's nothing to be done about them.'

'I hadn't seen one before.'

'How could you miss them?'

'I'm not from here. I live on one of the Atlantic rigs.'

'And you chose to come back? Jesus. Get out while you can.'

He kept talking to her, making suggestions, asking if he could help, but that was the last of his comments she really focused on. She stood eventually, politely declined his offers, and made her way to a café by the old Holborn. She sat, muzzy-headed, and tried to work out what to do, discreetly tidying herself in the partial plate-glass reflection and smoking a trembling cigarette.

For a few minutes, she nearly went straight home. She would phone Warwick and arrange her transport on the next ship available. She could stay on the rig, studying the currents and the paths of the few whales left, and let this episode fade from her memory. She could still do it. This was her last chance.

And then she recalled the face of the boy in the shambling column. And the policeman outside Thorne's burgled house, and her brother's lie about Warwick. And Thorne's words to her as he lay in bed. *You always wanted the truth. Only the truth.* And she realised he had been right.

It was almost one when Hopper reached her destination. The day had warmed up: first in patches of sun, then in a long, unbroken stretch of cloudless heat. The bus east had limped along despite the quiet of the roads, then had broken down wholly, disgorging its passengers onto the pavement between stops.

When the next bus had eventually turned up, its driver, grease-lined and sweating, had taken them with ill grace, squinting at their tickets through dirty green-tinted spectacles, complaining that the cheap ink had smudged the date of purchase. He had probably just been trying to save his precious petrol, but it had been tiring and degrading.

Still, it was worth it to be here, in the canteen of *The Times*. These days the paper was housed in an old factory in east London, a mile north of Shoreditch. It had been here ever since the great clearing-out of the riverbanks at the time of the floods. The area was an outskirt, yet still within the central zone; a useful *terrain vague* for unfashionable industries.

The *Times* building itself resembled a vast shipwreck stranded on a dried-up sea. Scattered around it at ground level were smaller buildings like lifeboats, and at its edges, the barnacles of unofficial extensions and lean-tos of corrugated iron. The old factory's name was still picked out in brickwork at one end of the main building: *PLOMLEY'S DOG BISCUITS*.

At the gate, Hopper had been inspected by a suspicious steward, and eventually collected and deposited in the canteen by a cheerful young woman. There she had waited, nervously, for the only man she thought could help her, and who had the least reason for wanting to see her again.

'So. Are you going to tell me what happened to make you look like that?' David Gamble sat down, sliding her tea and a sandwich across the table. She had ignored all his questions on first seeing him, trying to conquer the crippling personal awkwardness of it and trying to remember: *this is more important than feelings*.

'No.' While he had been buying the food, she had tried to discreetly comb the knots out of her hair, feeling the growing lump at the back of her head. 'Just fell over. You know me. Clumsy clumsy.'

'Sure?'

'Sure.'

'As you like.' He had always been easy in conversation. 'So, what brings you here?'

'Do I need a reason to come and see my ex-husband?' She spoke with a lightness she didn't feel.

'I suppose not. You were bound to turn up eventually. Crawling back, that sort of thing. You're only human. Sugar?'

'No thanks.' Sugar these days was unpleasant stuff: beet derived, murky in colour, and with a faint tang of grit at the bottom of a cup, as though two separate consignments had been mistakenly married. She often wondered if there was a load of grit somewhere with an unexpectedly sweet savour.

'OK.' David served himself a liberal dose, watching the two spoonfuls slowly disintegrate as he stirred. He looked around at the busy café with some satisfaction.

He had hardly changed in four years. Hair as thick as straw, and almost as light; pink cheeks; the same amused eyes, blue flecked with grey. He looked nearly as young as he had at their last meeting, apart from a few more lines around the eyes, and a few grey hairs creeping in at his temples. It had been a shock seeing him so unaltered.

'Looks like you're doing well.'

'I'm only bloody news editor.' He produced a little printed business card, as swiftly as if he'd been holding it ready since her arrival. 'Impressed?'

She smiled, already well into her sandwich. 'Very.'

'Good. That's exactly what I wanted to hear. Well, the whole place is doing all right. And recently refurbished. Did I ever tell you about our presses? Original 1930s, resurrected wonders from the great days of print?'

'I dimly remember you mentioning it once or twice.'

He grinned. 'Sorry.'

'How've you been keeping, though? Really?'

'All right. Not very much to do except work.'

'How's Pamela? She finally give you those children you always wanted?' Hopper was trying to lighten the mood, to confront the awkwardness head-on. As soon as she had spoken, though, she realised her mistake. A deeper spot of colour appeared in David's cheeks, and he looked down and nudged the sugar bowl with his knuckles.

'Pamela and I are ... ah ... no longer together.'

'Oh God. Sorry, David. I didn't mean anything by that. I mean, I didn't mean to ... you know. Sorry.'

'Forget it. You weren't to know. How about you? Any rig sweethearts?'

'Not really.'

He grinned. She decided to steer towards safer ground.

'What's on the agenda today?'

'Big report on NTB.'

She must have looked blank, because he smiled and said, 'I forget you've been out of town. NTB equals New Tower Bridge.' She remembered now. Davenport had been photographed at the sinking of the first pile, dwarfing a ceremonial spade with his fists.

'Is it in trouble?'

'How dare you, Ellie. It's a significant national project with the PM's personal backing, and as such is going fabulously. Keep up.'

'I see. What else is going on?'

He looked at her for a second, then leant across the table, lowering his voice as he did so. 'You wouldn't believe some of the stuff we're not printing, El. Chaos outside London. Army running low on people, weapons, you name it. Patchy, everywhere. As soon as one blotch of civil disobedience settles down, another bit of the country goes bright red.'

'Seriously?'

He nodded. 'And that's not all. Everything in short supply. Right now Britain's manufacturing base is making an enormous surplus of bullshit and not much else. It's just as well we still know how to make Scotch tape. Once we lose that, we're fucked.'

'Is any of this getting into the paper?'

'Of course not. But most civil servants sound like they've had two hours' sleep for the last month. Davenport needs a victory pretty soon. If he doesn't get it, that might be it for him.'

'Do you think he'll get it?'

'Actually, I do. There are rumours. Just rumours, of course.' He breathed deeply, as if appalled by what he was about to say. 'But the word is he might be getting what he wants out of the Americans at long last.'

'What's that?'

'Ellie, where have you been? The one thing he's always wanted is the nukes.'

'Oh. Right. I knew about those. But what would he even do with nuclear weapons?'

'No one seems sure. But the fact that they've been in American hands for thirty years is the one thing that's been keeping him in check. This would let him restore control over the whole country – everywhere within their effective range, I guess. If he had them, he could invade the Scandis tomorrow, or wherever he wanted.'

'Christ.'

'Like I say, it's just a rumour. Here's hoping it's not true.'

Someone passed close by them. David leant back and ostentatiously changed the subject.

'Still living in the rig, then? Still trying to nail down the currents?'

'Yeah, still the rig. You?'

'Still the old place. Not many changes.' The 'old place' was the home she and David had shared in Queensway, until she had left. 'Very quiet these days' – he smiled – 'but I'm not there much. Mostly just a place to not get enough sleep.'

'How are your colleagues?'

He nodded to himself, staring around the café. 'Good, thanks.' He looked again and added, quietly, 'Just as much trouble.'

She kept her voice as low as his. 'Still don't know who's working for you?'

'Oh, they all work for us. It's just that half of them have a second job. Just the kind of industriousness Davenport likes, really.'

It was an open secret that the government maintained a presence at the newspaper. If the printers looked like going on strike, even if editorial conferences became heated – whatever the news, it would make its way back to Whitehall.

After the bulk of newspapers had been closed down – just as the state of emergency began, one year before the Stop – *The Times* had been allowed to keep operating, under an arrangement known as 'strategic supervision'. The editor at the time had been close to the government; the board had proved acquiescent. Any journalists who seriously objected had been released from their duties.

The paper had lived for three decades in a curious state of limbo; neither an official organ of propaganda nor a newspaper in the former sense of the word. There was one other national paper, observed as closely as David's, and the state radio station.

'That must be difficult for you.'

David sighed. 'It's even worse these days. Even when we know who the moles are, there's nothing we can do about it. If we fire them, we'll be shut down. Effectively, we're totally free to print whatever we want, as long as we don't, and the government will happily accommodate fractionally negative stories because they're proof they don't tell us what to write. If I wasn't so cheerful, I'd tell you how difficult and depressing the whole thing is.'

'David Gamble, I believe you're disaffected. I never thought it could happen.'

'Me? Far from it. I'm here ...' he shrugged, 'at the prime minister's pleasure. And what a pleasure it is.' But she sensed his exhaustion.

He sipped his coffee, and brightened up. 'Anyway, you didn't come to see me because you were worried about life at *The Times*. If you did, they're not working you nearly hard enough on that giant Meccano set you live on.'

Hopper told him briefly the reason for her visit: the letter, and the summons, and the hospital, and the burglary.

'Edward Thorne?' David leant back in his chair. 'Didn't you tell me once he taught you?'

'Yes.' That was all she had told David when they'd met in London after university, when she'd been trying to rebuild her life. She'd turned the whole thing into a little anecdote: *Thorne, the great minister, teaching me. Amazing, huh?* Maybe if she'd confronted it head-on, told him the truth, it wouldn't have eaten away at her, pushing her away from the world, from David. Too late now. 'Do you know anything about him?'

'Not much off the top of my head. Think he had a scientific background at first. Crop stuff, genetics. Matey with Davenport for years before the Stop. Was running half the country soon after it. Almost everything internal went across his desk while the PM ran the military side of things. Then he had some sort of catastrophic falling-out with Davenport and was moved upcountry, or retired or something – after a stint teaching you, of course. I'd assumed he was already dead.'

'That's "not much"?'

He shook his head, smiling. 'He was pretty big news in his day. But I don't understand what he could have had to tell you. He'd been out of government for fifteen years.' Not *he's been*, but *he'd been*. Thorne had slipped effortlessly into the past tense, unnoticed.

'Do you have anything extra? On paper, I mean?'

'Course we do. Want me to look him up?'

'Yes please.'

'All right then. I have to go to the archive, though. Come and see it. It's rather fun.'

He got up at her nod, and she followed him across the café, watching him greet a few colleagues as he went.

News editor. He'd always wanted that. When they'd first met, he'd been a court correspondent. Eventually he'd been shunted sideways onto the home affairs brief, where he'd become more biddable and started his rise through the paper's ranks. He had more gravitas these days, a heaviness that sat strangely alongside the boyish glee she remembered.

During their marriage, as he had grown more senior, his ambition had overwhelmed the things in him she had found admirable. The court reporter, always pushing a little further than he should, had slowly become the editor, hedging, making little cuts, keeping everyone safe. He carried that seriousness now, for all his jokes and indiscretions.

And, of course, he had wanted a child she had no desire to bring into the world. That had been it, in the end.

She had loved him. But his desire for a family – something he had not had in the ten years since his parents' deaths, and wanted keenly – had stood between them. She had felt entirely unequal to the responsibility. After just four years, the ship of their marriage had been foundering. And when, late on, she had become pregnant, then quickly miscarried, that had become another secret keeping them apart. She had never told him.

They moved up the stairs at the back of the café, and through drab corridors variously lined in dark wood or painted brown to look like it. Every so often they skirted the edges of larger open-plan offices, where journalists sat typing or murmuring into their phones.

They went up three flights, over the great clanking factory floor, then back down again. Eventually, in a low vaulted basement, they passed through a swing door to the archive, a drab space with a counter. Behind it, metal shelves thick with cardboard stretched out until they were lost in gloom.

'Good afternoon, Mr Gamble.'

The woman behind the desk was in her mid forties, sallow, and wore an expression of blank resistance to the world – an expression cast off for a broad simper on one side of her face as soon as she saw David. She took her large tear-shaped reading glasses off immediately and smiled again, before giving Hopper an unfriendly glance.

David spoke. 'Good afternoon ... Sarah.' Hopper could hear the little snag of memory in his voice, and realised he had read the archivist's name from the plastic label she wore. 'How's your health?'

'Oh, not at all good, Mr Gamble. Very bad.'

'I'm sorry to hear that.'

'But all the better for seeing you.'

He smiled. 'They should prescribe me in hospitals, eh?' He gestured at Hopper. 'This is my cousin. She's visiting me.'

A little of the hostility went out of Sarah's manner. 'What can we do for you today, Mr Gamble?'

'I'd like a personal file, please. Total sweep.'

'Name?'

'Thorne, Edward.'

'Of course, Mr Gamble.'

When she had disappeared, Hopper said, a little louder than she'd intended: 'You nearly didn't remember her name.'

David put a finger to his lips, before pointing at the desk, and whispered, 'You know me too well.'

Not any more, Hopper thought.

Eventually, Sarah returned, and handed him a slim green folder, with the same lopsided smile. 'There you are, Mr Gamble.'

'Thank you. I'll have it back within the day.' He signed a chit for it with a little flourish and grinned at Sarah again. Not for the first time, Hopper reflected on David's curious popularity with women. He was so enthusiastic, that was part of it. In the full glare of his attention, one felt wholly cared for, at the centre of things.

They made their way back out, David clutching the folder under his arm.

Outside the archive room, back in the stairwell, he said, 'Sorry to shush you. But it's a bit, ah, porous in there. Half the reason anyone gets caught out in this place is because they forget a name. Remarkable the extent to which minor, unintended slights can reflect on you later.'

'Why was I your cousin?'

'I suspect Sarah has a bit of a crush on me ...'

'Yes, I'd say so.'

' ... and if she thinks you're my cousin, she's less likely to gossip about it.'

'Right.'

'And I thought it would be funny.' David smiled, and Hopper felt a pleasant tremor of déjà vu in that moment of conspiracy. 'Here we go, then. Your old chum Thorne. Let's see what we can't find.'

He opened the folder and picked out a docket at the front. 'Ah. Thought it felt light.' The file held only a few pieces of paper. The latest entry on the docket was dated two months before, and read simply: *Int. Sec. Removal.*

'I'm afraid it looks like we've been beaten to it.'

'Int. Sec.?'

He grimaced. 'Internal Security. It's the memory hole.'

'I know. My brother works for Security, remember?'

'Well don't mention it to him, for God's sake.'

'You're saying Internal Security have deleted everything the paper's ever run on Thorne?'

'No. But as good as. Firstly, a new all-paper search would take weeks. And secondly, every time you institute a search that big, it crosses the Internal Security desk, so they would know I'd been sniffing around. So ...' He shrugged. 'There you go.'

'Is there another copy, anywhere, of everything you've run on him?'

He looked at her quizzically. 'What are you getting into, Ellie? Stuff they've removed is stuff we almost certainly wouldn't be allowed to repeat. Are you sure looking into this is a good idea?'

'Yes.' She hadn't considered it until now, and her voice sounded uncertain. She stiffened it. 'Yes. I am. Can you get another copy of this file, without a new search?'

'We can't.'

'Would that woman, Sarah, help?'

'No. Sarah and her little lot are right in the pocket of Internal Security, which is why I'm so extremely friendly to them.'

'Do you have anything else?'

'No.' He pulled at his lip and stared at the ground. For a second he looked as though he was counting. 'Unless ...'

'Yes?' She was impatient now.

'Sometimes the editors commission an obituary. Those get stored separately.'

'So do you have one on Thorne?'

'Maybe.' David's brow unfurrowed, and he gave her a side-long look. 'Come and meet Harry.'

13

'Harry' was on the top floor of the building, which was accessed by a lift. The lift itself was one of the old ones – small, noisy, the buttons ringed by grease – but it was still a rare treat. Most lifts on the rig didn't work.

They emerged onto a corridor of ill-tended carpets, smelling of must. Thirty yards along, they reached a dark wooden door on which *OBITUARIES* was hand-painted in a small gold crescent. David pointed at it and smiled. He knocked, listened to a muffled response from within, and entered.

Inside the room were two desks, each a mountain of yellowing papers studded with books. The whole right-hand wall was lined with filing cabinets, themselves piled high with more paper. The lowered blinds were inadequate against the sun outside. An old radio in the corner was playing a bright piano concerto.

The Last Day

The man behind the larger of the two desks was perhaps sixty: tall, florid, overweight, with a thick moustache. Hopper was reminded of a walrus. He was engrossed in a document, leaning back on his chair, and halfway through a cavernous yawn. At the second desk was a man in his twenties, with dark hair and a pouting mouth, who glanced at them incuriously before returning to his book.

David spoke first. 'Good afternoon, Harry.'

The older man finished his yawn and looked across from the document he was reading.

'Gamble! What a nice surprise. Come to beg for your old job back? Every chance you'll be replacing Charlie here. Great things, Charlie's destined for.' He gestured with his pen. Charlie did not acknowledge the joke.

'I wish. Afraid they're keeping me pretty busy downstairs.'

'Nobody remembers Obituaries,' Harry muttered. His accent was Scottish.

'This is a friend of mine, just taking a tour.'

'Come to see the most important bit of the whole paper, eh?' Harry laughed, and almost immediately started coughing. He whipped a handkerchief out of his pocket and hacked into it. The young man flashed him an unpleasant look, noticed only by Hopper.

Harry hauled himself out of his chair, and moved around. Hopper saw he was wearing carpet slippers beneath his tweed suit. She shook his proffered hand. 'Nice to meet you.'

'And you. Harry Markham. This is where we do it. Get 'em in each morning after conference, then me and Charlie here write them up. If you're looking for a proper tour, I haven't the time, I'm afraid.'

David spoke next. 'Actually, Harry, there was something specific we were hoping to ask about. It wouldn't take long.'

'I don't have long. We're preparing a big job on Henriksen.'

Hopper had heard the news a few days ago. Henriksen had been a junior defence minister, killed by a bomb as he opened a new factory in Birmingham.

'Ah, yes. A great loss to the nation.' It was impossible to tell sometimes whether David was joking or not.

Harry shook his head. 'Do they have any idea who did it yet?'

'No fucking clue. Anglian nationalists, Cornish separatists, Scots ultras wanting to clear southerners out of the Highlands ... could be anyone.'

Harry grunted. 'Anyway. What was it you wanted?'

'Well, it's a little complicated, Harry, to tell you the truth.' David let his eyes stray to the younger man, hunched over his book with a pencil behind his ear.

Harry followed his look, and nodded. 'Charlie, could you go and check on the day's post, please?'

After a few seconds' pause, Charlie levered himself sullenly from his seat and sloped out of the room, without making eye contact with any of them. They heard his footsteps along the creaking floorboards outside, and then the lift grille slamming shut behind him.

Harry cackled. 'Little shit. Caught him going through my desk the other day. Doesn't mean he's Security, of course. Could just be a journalist. Anyway, it pays to get him out of the way if we're going to talk about something important.'

Hopper looked at the book Charlie had been reading, a thick pencil wedged to mark his place. *HENRIKSEN: A Study in Courage*. It was as thick as a brick and had a picture of the minister as a young military officer on the front of it, looking heroic. 'Are you sure it's all right just to get rid of him like that?'

'Yes. By the time he's editor, I'll be well under. So, Davey. What are you here for?'

'Do you have anything on a man called Edward Thorne?'

'Thorne? Why, is he dead?'

'Afraid so.'

'Ridiculous. He's only a few years older than me.'

'Still.' David wobbled his head side to side equivocally. Every so often he did something that reminded Hopper of their marriage. 'Do you have anything on him?'

'I can't remember. He fell out of favour, as far as I recall.' Harry must have seen Hopper's disappointed expression. 'Don't worry. If we have, we'll have kept it. Rule one: never throw anything away. We'd look pretty stupid if he was suddenly man of the month again and we'd chucked our first obit away.'

David spoke again. 'Thanks, Harry. I knew you'd have something. Can you run us off a copy?'

'In two shakes.' He walked over to the filing cabinet in the corner, and unlocked it. He pulled out a file and a sheaf of papers, and took them over to the copying machine in the corner, a hulking monstrosity with a huge domed lid. As it began working, he turned back to them. 'This won't be everything, you understand. Have our little friends swiped the rest?'

'Looks like it.'

'This fucking place. Well, you've got our draft obit in here, a few of my notes, a few of the bigger stories from when he was really well known, about twenty years ago now. A bit thin, but better than nothing.' He pulled the replicated papers from the copier and handed them to David, who shoved them into the folder from downstairs and wedged them under one arm.

'Thank you.'

'Thanks, Harry.'

The older man waved his hand. 'Forget it. I'll trade your thanks in if you can help me get rid of this lad.' He jerked a thumb at the second desk. 'It's him or me, although I have a funny feeling it's going to be me some time soon. What's it all about, Gamble? Thorne, I mean.'

'We're just doing a bit of background research on him.'

Harry snorted. 'Like shite.'

'Let's put it like this,' said David. 'There's a chance you won't get to run your obituary on him. At least this way your research won't be going to waste.'

'I suppose not.' Harry gestured vaguely and started back to his desk, before turning. 'Next time, it'll be me asking you a favour, Davey.'

'I'm sure it will.'

David nodded at Hopper, and they turned and left the older man there, already ensconced behind his desk again. The lift was making its way back up the building as they approached it, a nasty squeal coming from some unloved metal within. Charlie shouldered his way out as the door opened, not bothering to open the grille fully, and passed them without looking up, a few yellow envelopes in his hands.

In the lift, going back down, David looked at her.

'Quite a character, eh? He remembers newspapers before they were ...' he gestured around the miserable lift, 'like this.'

'Are you enjoying it, David? Honestly?'

'Just a job, isn't it? I'm simply happy to be here.' David handed her the file on Thorne, which she jammed into her bag.

'Sure. That's probably why you risked your job getting me information you couldn't print.'

'Very funny.'

They reached the ground floor. He hauled at the grille, and they walked out into the lobby.

She patted her satchel with the file in it. 'Don't you want to see what's in here?'

He shook his head. 'Tell me if you find anything decent. But for the moment, it'd be safest if I showed my cousin off the premises and went back to work.'

He walked her out of the building and across the deserted car park. All the paint marking the spaces had long since washed away, and clumps of knotweed were pushing through the cracking concrete as if to insist: *we are here, we are here to replace you.*

They arrived at the outer gatehouse, and David stopped. 'Will I see you again before you head back to the rig?'

'I don't think so. I'm only here a few days.'

'Pity. You could have come for dinner.' There it was again, a sense that he was leaving something unsaid. 'Of course, whatever you're looking at, it could be related to the Americans. If it is, let me know.' Then he turned and walked across the concrete, back to the building and his office.

14

The Americans. Some eight million of them lived on the south coast, in a zone made habitable by the final spending spree of the US government. The last remnants of the New World.

During the middle phase of the Slow, the only matter worth thinking about was the question of where the planet would come to its final stop. For a short while the world's researchers and scientists had devoted themselves almost entirely to working out which half of the planet might have a chance of survival.

The question was finally answered after six years. In Anglo-American terms, at least, the Old World would outlive the New. In the USA, a slim crescent of New England would remain just about lit by a weak sun. The rest of America would not. Even that land on the east coast would be so close to sunset it would be impossible to farm or keep livestock alive. One's shadow would be a hundred feet long.

As soon as these facts were known, the great migration had begun, the vast tide of humanity sweeping from the nations due to be swallowed by darkness towards those forecast to end in the light. More than expected had stayed put. The days and nights had lasted three weeks at the time, and many could not bring themselves to move from their own side – where it was currently light – into darkness halfway round the world, in the promise of eventual sun. Others could not abandon their own countries, their own infirm.

Even so, perhaps a billion people had moved. One of the chief nations making the shift – certainly the most organised – was America. In its final act of reinvention, the richest nation on earth had ensured the country's core would survive.

The policy of the United States of America had been one of 'managed withdrawal'. The idea was simple: to sequester a small number of people, a few per cent only, and move them wholesale to selected locations in the prospective warm zone.

It should never have worked. The project would not – could not – be kept secret. Those due to be left behind should have rioted, should have easily torn down the fences the protected millions were being kept behind. Luckily for the authorities, crop failures across the country had rendered much of the population incapable of effective riot. So the ships were loaded, and the ships came. And once the huge, stately containers had been emptied of passengers, they had been sunk in the Channel and helped keep the desperate flotilla from other nations out.

The millions who came from America brought with them a great deal needed for their survival – whole factories, even some of the new hydroponic works devoted to growing food without soil, so suddenly vital. They guarded the three or four southern counties they had been granted with great zeal.

It had been a matter of unwarranted pride to Britain that the United States of America had chosen Britain as the site for their last sanctuary. In fact, Britain had not been the Americans' only harbour. Smaller groups had been sent to France, to West Africa, even one to the Middle East. They had all failed. The Middle East camp had not been heard of since the second collapse, several years after the Stop. The West African mission had ended fractiously: the last sounds heard before the feeds cut out were heavy gunfire and garbled requests for help. And the remains of the French mission had been salvaged six years in as the continent fell apart, and brought over piecemeal from a little harbour not far from Dunkirk.

Even at the height of Britain's self-delusion over its new-found significance, the price it exacted for its land had been substantial. The remnants of the American navy were placed under British control. Any ships too badly damaged had been scuttled and added to the grim, treacherous shoals sealing the country in. Today, Britain's navy was the last serious blue-water force in the world. The New World had come back, humbled, to live with the Old.

The Americans' chief asset – the only thing, Hopper thought, that stopped Davenport invading the southern counties tomorrow – was their enormous stockpile of nuclear weapons, shipped over with great care, complete with the capacity to launch them. But they had never had a Breadbasket of their own, no great storehouse of supplies to keep them going through lean years on the mainland, and the rumours that their crops had failed for a couple of years in a row had made it even as far as the rig. They must be completely desperate if they really were considering handing the weapons over now.

And what remained of the American continent? The sunlit edge of the country – the metropolitan fringes of New England, the huge towers of New York – was frozen, waist-deep in snow. Out there, the sun was barely visible above the horizon. For some years after the Stop, there had been idle talk of gangs of survivors roaming the east coast, but even the most implausible rumours had petered out twenty years ago.

And beyond that, in the regions facing out towards the universe rather than in towards the sun ... nothing except thousands of miles of frozen fields and mountains and plains, interrupted by cities and towns populated by the dead.

The bus Hopper had boarded outside *The Times* jerked to a halt. They had reached the chicanes at the eastern end of Oxford Street, established fifteen years ago after a spate of truck bombings. Once they'd been installed, the threat had shifted elsewhere almost overnight, but nobody had removed the chicanes.

She pressed the button to stop the bus. Here would do. Thinking about the Coldside – as it was referred to on the rare occasions anyone mentioned it – upset her more than it used to. For children growing up today it had almost no meaning beyond a vague and imagined realm of freezing darkness. It had been cut from their mind's eye, the earth slowly becoming half a sphere. And anyone her age or older knew how the Coldside had been treated by the sunlit world, and never mentioned it at all.

These days she frequently found herself thinking of the millions – why sugar it, the billions – still in Asia, Australasia, the Americas, frozen in their homes and on the roads, facing the cold, dead starlight, their bodies frosted, perhaps hardly decayed at all, as though they might get up and move again if only exposed to the light of the sun. A colossal army of the dead, conscripted and condemned by the blind whim of the planet's slow.

They were posed, in her imagination, halfway through a normal day: behind supermarket tills, their stiff hands still gripping the levers of cranes and fruit machines, waiting at kitchen counters by kettles full of ice. Sometimes she considered the likelier alternative – that they were congregated on roads, clustered at harbours where the darkness had overtaken them, huddled in the last places the lights had failed: community halls, gymnasiums. Anywhere the night might be staved off for a few hours more.

Hopper never told anyone about these thoughts. She had no desire to discuss them, even though her mind was drawn there almost every day by some morbid gravity she didn't understand. The living planet's attention was focused on the damage it had suffered rather than that inflicted on others. Still, she wondered how often her colleagues woke from dreams about skeins of ice spreading across their skin, about frosted gates shutting them out in the cold, about crawling through darkness towards a steel wall specially designed to poison them.

That had been tried, she'd heard: the purposeful irradiation of the land barrier to the Coldside by the remnants of the Chinese government, a limited nuclear release to defend themselves from their own people and from the huge numbers moving north from South-East Asia. Britain's government had relied on the cold sea, on its cliffs and its guns.

Hopper looked around her as she left the bus. She was only fifteen minutes from the gardens on the Embankment: it would be quiet there. As she walked south, she stayed off Kingsway. The crowd moved around her: unhappy burnt faces, hurried and unaccommodating.

Up ahead, in the centre of the pavement, was a Ranter. He was tall, broad-chested and shirtless, his dark skin flaking about his face. He wore tattered trousers, no shoes, and his tangled beard ran with sweat as he berated the air. His chest was raw with sunburn.

The pedestrians had simply made a space around him, keeping their distance while simultaneously not acknowledging what it was they were avoiding. So he stood and shouted as they moved past him on either side.

She couldn't hear the words he was bellowing. 'Blood' was one, and 'Christ' another, but beyond that, the pitch and ferocity of his words blocked any sense. The police tended to leave Ranters alone as more trouble than they were worth, and only intervened if they started damaging property or passers-by.

Supposedly, many remained in control of their senses. The ranting – which took the form of shouting, crying, begging for a curative 'scourge' – was designed as a performance. God had given up listening, so mankind must speak louder: only through performative self-harm could He be encouraged to turn His attention once again on the earth. The whole idea made her feel sick.

Thirty years ago, the Ranters had commanded substantial numbers. In the chaos after the Stop, many of them had banded together and taken to the streets in unison, chanting and sobbing and urging the Lord to pay notice to their unworthy flesh. That was the time when the police were just one of many gangs, and the army another.

Once, out with her aunt, Hopper had seen a cluster of them suspended from a lamp post. On the ground, knots of people had gathered to observe the sight, looking like patrons at an art gallery. On a wall behind them, the words *RANTERS BE WARNED* had been painted in dark brown matter.

These days almost nobody adhered to the original faith – just these few men, and occasionally women, ignoring everyone ignoring them, and scarring themselves in the street.

Here were the Embankment Gardens. The old watergate was still standing. But it had been half submerged in the huge flood after the Stop, and in the years since, nobody had cleaned the thick scurf from the bottom half of the pillars. Across the gardens, Cleopatra's Needle was pinioned in place by broad metal pipes, held up like a thief on the cross. The chipped sphinxes on either side stared at it, appalled.

She found a bench, and pulled the papers David had given her from her bag.

The first sheet contained a list of names and addresses.

The second was Thorne's obituary. It had been typed on one of the old typewriters and bore the initials HM at the top – for Harry Markham, she guessed. It had been written seventeen years ago – two years before whatever event had driven Thorne out of government. She began to read: *Edward Thorne, one of the architects of the post-Slow world and principal planners of the new Britain, has died.*

His career had been gilded almost from the first. He'd been born in 1983, an only child, to two physicist parents, a gifted student from a young age. He had attended both Oxford and Cambridge, and visited MIT for post-doctoral work in the then rapidly developing field of bioengineering. He had developed crops that would flourish in constant light, that didn't need cold soil to prompt their growth. It was as though he'd predicted the Slow years before it came to pass.

A black-and-white photo of Thorne was clipped to the second page. Tall and long-faced, he was lounging against a gatepost wearing a pale suit, in the process of adjusting his cuffs. His quizzical look at the photographer had survived. By his side was a young woman in a dress of sharp slanting blocks.

She read on. His scientific career had been truncated when, at twenty-five, he had temporarily abandoned research altogether and applied to Sandhurst to train as an officer. A year later he had been commissioned into the Royal Lancers, from where he began the first of several tours of duty – Afghanistan, Iraq, North Africa. He kept writing, observing, even publishing under a pseudonym.

It was during this period that he had met the man who would become his closest friend. Richard Davenport had joined the army out of school and was nearly a decade younger than Thorne, but the two had become inseparable. Thorne had been the best man at Davenport's first wedding; Davenport had saved Thorne's life when he was shot in Kandahar.

Invalided out of the army, Thorne had returned to his scientific career, working on agriculture. A few years later, the Slow had begun. And when the Slow had curdled into the Stop and the country was perilously close to collapse, when the widely respected General Richard Davenport had begun his rise first to authority and then to power, he had recruited Edward Thorne as his adviser.

Davenport's own ascendancy was here recounted, although there could be few people unfamiliar with it by now. Hopper skimmed it, and finding she knew the whole story, lifted her gaze and stared over to where the Thames lapped at the concrete embankment.

The politicians had promoted Davenport from a mere general to minister for security as the Slow was drawing to its close. It had been Davenport who had closed the country's gates. But he had resisted the first calls to replace the sclerotic ministers who preceded him, whetting the country's appetite for his eventual takeover. His real affirmation of power had begun six years after the Stop.

By then, the Americans in the southern counties were struggling to survive. The second collapse – that of the nations nearest the Hotzone, baking in the sun – was under way and threatening to overwhelm Britain's borders, or so the government claimed. The emergency administration was impotent, seized up.

The breakdown of law and order had reached its worst point. The only real power in the land had been Davenport's civil defence units, almost indistinguishable from the army, its ranks swollen by his conscription drive.

Eventually, with the utmost reluctance, Davenport had consented to serve in the office of Supreme Commander, appropriating a title from the old NATO as his own. He had initiated the Reconstitution. He had seized control of food supplies, and helped stabilise the American Zone with aid packages. Most importantly of all, he had pulled up the national drawbridge.

He had been responsible for the very first sinkings, the boats from the Coldside immediately after the Stop, but his next drive had been far larger. And he had established the Breadbasket, imposing order on the old Europe with a simple push just as the continent fell apart. First the border had moved two hundred yards into France, then half a mile, then ten miles. Today Davenport governed more of continental Europe than any Englishman since the Hundred Years War.

It had worked. Food supplies had improved. Water supplies had grown cleaner. The cholera epidemic had slowed and eventually stopped. Britain had reindustrialised. And at some point in the process, Davenport had become prime minister. When the worst of the crisis had abated, there seemed no sense in returning to the emergency government, and the appetite for elections was nil, so he had carried on.

The obituary was followed by another photo, of the two men. Thorne must have been in his early fifties. He had a neat little beard; the suit was darker, the eyes more lined but his hair still dark brown. Davenport was in uniform. The pair were standing on the deck of some vessel, perhaps one of the new ships from the Liverpool yards.

When this photo was taken, Thorne had been one of the most important men in the country. And then, after nine years of working as the right hand of the prime minister – theoretically his chief scientific adviser, in practice his deputy – he had left government so abruptly even the newspapers had covered the story.

Not with much scrutiny, though. The clipping in the file that dealt with this development gave no hint about why it had happened. It merely observed, with careful blandness, that Thorne had 'chosen to leave government to teach at Oxford', and gave the details of the appointment.

Hopper turned back to the list of names and addresses at the front. From the look of it, they were mostly Thorne's former colleagues – almost all dead or retired now, a handful still in post. They were accompanied by little ticks and crosses at the side, and further squiggles: *background only, friends said, wife hostile*.

One name stuck out, ringed with thick dark ink and marked with a double tick. *Private secretary. Graham Chandler.* An address accompanied the name. Camberwell. Well within the central zone.

Hopper looked at her watch. She could probably be there by three.

15

'Yes?'

He had barked the word out as she entered. He was facing the door, sitting at his desk, already half immured in paperwork.

'Miss Hopper. How nice to see you. Take a seat.'

A week had passed since their conversation in the common room, and now here she was, sitting in an armchair in one of Edward Thorne's rooms. The walls were covered in old prints, the bookcases so full they spilled onto the floor, sprawling heaps sitting like foothills before a sheer cliff face of paper. It was warm today: a single large fan stirred the air listlessly. He picked up a piece of paper from his desk.

'The warden sent me this. Your first year; no work completed worth speaking of.'

'No.' Hopper looked onto the quad. One of the gardeners was laboriously pulling a roller along the artificial lawn.

'And she tells me you raised no objections when she suggested you leave. My plan for the term not enough to pique your interest, I take it?'

'This is something I've been considering for a while. It's nothing to do with you, Dr Thorne.'

'Edward, please. Nor with your achievements before you came here.' He gestured at the papers in front of him. 'You're clearly bright. Could you tell me why you wish to leave?'

She shrugged. 'I don't see the point in staying.'

He pushed the paper aside, came out from behind his desk and sat in the other of the two armchairs, wincing a little as he did.

She continued. 'And I don't need you to tell me how stupid I'm being. Or that I have potential. I've been told that shit before. *Edward.*' He had long, bony hands, she noticed. The joints of the fingers were so long she wondered how he formed a fist.

'Do you have something else to do?'

'No.' This was true, at least. Someone with less inbuilt perversity might have wanted to remain in the final institution in her life that resembled a home. Without knowing why, she felt pleased by the prospect. 'I'll think of something.'

'Do you have no desire to finish your studies?'

'As I said, I don't see the point.'

'Why do you say that?'

'Everything's falling apart. Europe has collapsed. People are starving even here, and all we're doing is fending off the remains of the world, hoping we can keep ourselves going for

… how long? And people sit here studying Western civilisation like there's going to be a Western civilisation in fifty years. Christ.'

His tone was amiable, reasonable. 'You think it's time to roll over, then?'

She looked at him, smiling and genial, and pitied him for his optimism. 'There's no point preserving ourselves if this is the life we can look forward to.'

Thorne picked at his fingernails, looking back at her. 'You think a decline in the world's quality of life means that life should come to an end, is that it?'

'Not necessarily, but—'

'But these conditions are extraordinary. And what would you say if I was to tell you I knew – knew, mind you – conditions would improve?'

'I'd say you were lying. Or a fool.'

He did not react to the insult. 'Let me tell you one thing, Miss Hopper. Early in my career – years before the Slow began – I was sent as a peacekeeping soldier to a famine in East Africa. Things were dreadful. Worse, if you can believe it, than they are here and now. Far worse. People were eating bark, boiling grass. Some ate the earth.' He paused, looking down at his lap. 'Some ate each other.

'But we developed new strains of crops, hardier ones, proofed against disease. And we were able to avert the next famine. And the one after that.' His voice hardened. 'And the next time the crops might have failed, they grew instead. And we saw people alive – children, alive, running, playing – where without the intervention of clever men and women like yourself, there would only have been graves.'

She wanted to laugh. 'You can say anything you like about the world before the Slow. Things were different then. The world was a paradise almost everywhere. When there were problems, plenty of people went to help. There's nothing like that now.'

'There's never going to be enough to help everyone, Miss Hopper. If you want a world free of suffering, you'll be looking a long time. It's your decision. But that's life these days. A series of horrible decisions. Including, perhaps, whether you're going to disengage totally, or whether you're going to help.'

He stopped, then spoke again, gently. 'It sounds like your parents were a couple of the people helping. Your mother a doctor, you said. And your father working in aid.'

Hopper's throat tightened. She should never have told him about them. He carried on, mild, as if unaware of the effect he was having. 'Are you worried about not matching up to their example, perhaps?'

'No. That's not it.' She was furious. 'You have no idea about them.'

'As you prefer. But don't let their goodness stop you from doing the work you're meant to. You could be brilliant, Ellen. If you allow yourself to be.'

They sat in silence for a minute – her wrestling with her feelings, him looking down as if waiting for her to master herself – before he spoke again, his tone lighter.

'Was there something in particular about last year's course you found inadequate?'

She felt a little calmer. 'Well, I mean, lots of things, but … yes.'

'Name it.'

She had thought it so many times, sitting listening to Harlow preaching his doctrine of decline, it would have been perverse not to say anything now someone was actually asking. She took a breath. 'There's almost nothing in the main earth science syllabus about the state of the oceans. It's all soil, land reclamation, farm fertility, crop supply, distribution. It's so stupid.'

'Go on.'

'We know what the old system was like: currents generated by the wind, the tides, and differences in density. We know the system kept the atmosphere and the ocean near this country warmer, kept areas at this latitude free of ice and snow. We know the old conveyor belt, the deep-level currents, transferred massive amounts of heat around the planet, and that those currents were vital for nutrient cycles. And we know that as the Slow happened, the whole system was thrown into chaos. But these days there must be all kinds of new currents, carrying warm water towards the Coldside and then bringing colder water back the other way, maybe deeper.'

'Granted.'

'But I don't think there's anyone at Environment studying the new long-term currents that we'll have. Why not? Because they can't imagine getting beyond the coastline, because of the closures and the shore defences. Nobody's taken the measure of the new currents, despite the fact that they could determine whether we have any hope of long-term survival. And because the satellite system's collapsed, we won't be able to, unless we get out there. It's sheer stupidity.' She had spoken so urgently she could feel her heart beating faster than normal. She couldn't remember the last time she'd said this much to a tutor.

'And you don't think we could do with someone studying these new currents?'

'I can't change the syllabus, and our last tutor thought there was no point.'

'That all sounds rather more important than a syllabus. And your last tutor sounds like a fool. What would you do?'

She hesitated, then thought: *he can only say no.* 'I did some reading last year. The system they used to measure currents before satellites was imperfect and labour intensive, but it did get some results. They used these things called drifters.' She remembered she had a drawing of one in her notebook, fumbled for it and showed him the page. 'I want to build some new ones. Some at the surface, some hundreds of metres down. They drift along with the currents, and if you track them, they can tell you how the ocean's moving. I think I could rig one up to send radio signals back giving us a rough idea of their movements.'

'Why didn't you suggest this to anyone else?'

'I did. I told our previous tutor. He said it wouldn't work.'

'Do you think he was right?'

'No.'

'Do you think his authority invalidated your opinions?'

'No.'

'Do you want another person's poor teaching to be your academic epitaph?'

'I suppose not.'

'Well then, that sounds like a prospect. Wouldn't you agree?'

'I don't know.'

'I'd like you to compose a preliminary paper on longer-term prospects for oceanic study for this time next week. If you haven't left us, of course.'

She was confused. He had listened; had told her there might be something in her idea; had taken her seriously. Now he was looking at her, smiling, offering her control of the situation. She thought for one irrational moment of her father, patiently showing her how to operate the long-distance radio. But she did not quite want to agree – not yet – so she shrugged one shoulder, and said:

'I'll think about it.'

'I hope you do, Miss Hopper. Good morning.'

16

Hopper had just missed a bus, so started walking to Camberwell instead. It would help her think: about Thorne, about why he had summoned her here, about what he had wanted her to find.

Waterloo was dingy after Embankment Gardens. Forty or fifty train services ran from the station each day, but freight took priority. The passenger trains that did run were hopelessly crowded. Many were armed: travel between cities was dangerous.

And living in the spaces between cities, of course, were the woodsmen.

They were a combination of outcasts, escapees and exiles, voluntary and forced. The men outnumbered the women, she remembered reading that much. The only thing they had in common was the woods. Some were outlaws who had never been sent to the Breadbasket, for whatever reason. A few had been exiled by soft-hearted towns, too sentimental to send their sons and daughters across the Channel; others had escaped in transit.

They weren't far away, either. The police networks were so degraded these days that a man might live a completely new life just fifty miles from his previous home. To survive, the woodsmen foraged, stole livestock, raised their own scratchy crops outside the big farming belts. Occasionally they grew bold enough to move into towns, attacking badly defended places for their canned goods. Some had supposedly built whole villages that didn't appear on maps, a network of fragile settlements in the wooded spaces between towns. Like a tumour, a new kind of tissue pushing outwards and testing the limits of the host body.

Sometimes they were swept out: during a land reclamation, or if the thefts grew too audacious. When they were arrested, the thin, bearded men, the shaven-headed women clutching mewling bundles of rags, the filthy saucer-eyed children were paraded through the streets of their local towns before being dispatched to the Breadbasket or executed.

Hopper shivered. Here was Lambeth. The old War Museum stood here, the gates padlocked, the site ostensibly deserted. The rusted howitzers still sat at the front gates, and between them was the husk of an APC, burnt out by vandals and looking like a monstrous beetle. But the grounds were planted with crops behind the barbed-wire fencing, and she saw figures moving slowly back and forth at the windows.

The area got poorer as she moved south. Past the crumbling plastic blocks at Elephant and Castle; down Walworth, a long high street of near-empty shops and youths idly scuffling over footballs.

It took her two abortive attempts to find the street where Thorne's old friend Chandler lived. Eventually she found it and pushed open the protesting gate of number 45, a two-storey house halfway along the terrace. The front garden was a hopeless tangle; fallen leaves lay everywhere, in various states of decomposition. Between them she saw lilyweed, ragwort and knotweed, huge loops and tangles of tendrils occasionally arcing above the soil like sea monsters before plunging back down to devour the foundations in peace.

She knocked. After thirty seconds the door opened a crack, on a double chain. In the darkness beyond she could see only a slice of a figure, smaller than her.

'Yes?'

'Mr Chandler?'

'Who are you?' The voice was quavering, high and thin with age.

'My name's Ellen Hopper. I'm calling about Dr Edward Thorne.'

'Thorne?'

'Yes. I believe you used to work for him.'

The figure made no movement.

'I was wondering if I could speak to you about him.'

'Who are you?'

'I'm from *The Times*.'

The line had occurred to her as she walked through Waterloo, but she was surprised to hear the facility with which she offered it now. First Jessica Hayward outside Thorne's house yesterday, and now this. When had she become such a good liar?

'Why do you want to speak about him?'

'I'm afraid he's dead, Mr Chandler.'

'Thorne?' The figure repeated the name forlornly.

'I'm part of the obituary team. I'm sorry, I didn't mean to break the news like that, I—'

'How did you find out about me?'

'Your name was on our list. Our other writer, Harry Markham, may have phoned you, some years ago?'

'Why didn't you ring? The phone works.'

'I live nearby. They let me leave the office early.'

Chandler still did not move.

'It needn't take long. I'm sure ten minutes would do it. But if you're not free, I can always go.' Hopper smiled reassuringly.

Another long pause. Then he slowly shut the door.

She had ruined it. And she hadn't even come up with a false name to give him. What if he reported her visit? Stupid, stupid.

A second later, she heard the rattle of the chain against the door, and he opened it to let her in. 'You can't stay for long.'

'Thank you. I won't take much of your time.'

It was uncomfortably warm inside the house – the cooling system must be broken – and dark, too, the semi-dark of a home without proper blackouts. Most people who lacked the luxury of underground darkness just thickened the curtains in their bedrooms or taped them at the edges. Some daylight always made it through, though: it prised its way in, testing every seam it found.

In the hall, her eyes adjusted to the gloom. The man before her was at least eighty. His eyes were small, a little clouded. He wore loose, shabby trousers and a jumper stained with egg. Beneath the jumper his shirt was far too large for him, and billowed briefly out before being tucked in at his waist. On his feet were worn slippers emblazoned with some smiling figure from a child's cartoon. He looked at her with hostility.

'What's your name again?'

'Ellen Hopper.' Too late to lie now.

He nodded, and turned along the long, wood-lined corridor to the back of the house. There was a heavy smell here, a tang both sharp and sour, and the air grew thicker as they moved.

The first room they passed was open to the hall. The shutters were sealed, but it was lit nonetheless, by an image projected onto a large, yellowed canvas sheet hanging at the back of the room. It was the sun, tinted red, pushing up from the horizon while a little voice burbled about the beauty of dawn. The only occupant of the room was a hunched figure sitting before the screen in a chair, facing away from them. In the corner was a single bed and a cabinet covered with medicine bottles.

'My wife,' Chandler muttered. He leant into the room and spoke up. 'It's someone from the paper, Miriam. They want to talk to me. I won't be long.' The figure in the chair gave no sign of having heard.

He walked on, into a second parlour at the back of the house, decorated with dark floral wallpaper and Victorian furniture, and gestured to a chair. 'Will you wait in here?'

'Thank you.'

'Would you like anything to eat, or drink? Tea?'

She nodded. 'Tea, thank you.'

He nodded. 'Was it the *Mail* you said you were from?'

'*The Times*.'

'Ah. I misremembered. Back in a minute.'

He shuffled out of the room, carefully closing the door behind him. She heard a kettle click on, and then the sound of laborious footsteps on the stairs.

She got up, and looked around the room. This side of the house was the darker one – north-westerly, so it would have got little enough sunlight even when it was built. On one wall hung two bronze snakes with candles sticking from the tops of their heads, on either side of a mantelpiece. Below it, a huge stack of old paper tottered in the blackened fireplace.

The faint burbling still came from the recorded voice in the front room, through the thin wall. Faint sounds of wildlife accompanied the voiceover now: birds with strange calls, the screams of primates.

While television broadcasts lasted, it had been official government policy to show sunrise and sunset on public screens at the beginning and end of the day. The practice was supposedly calculated to help the population adjust.

She had first heard of the custom aged about ten, and it had seemed childish even then, a spasm of magical thinking intended to trick oneself into believing the world had not changed. Her own father had had no patience with it: 'Most of these people paid no attention whatsoever to the sunrise when they had it, so for them to start now is absurd.' He had drummed disbelief into her, hardening her against the world.

And yet, when he had fallen ill with pneumonia in her twelfth year, in the few days when his survival was uncertain, he had admitted to her shamefacedly that he would love to see a sunrise and sunset once again. Too tactful to point out this recantation, she had scrounged a projector from a school friend and set it up in his room. He had cried almost instantly at the picture on the screen, and she had too, although she could not say whether it was for him or the sun.

After a few years, the government had ended the practice, whether in tacit acknowledgement that it did no good, or in impatience with the sentimental streak it betrayed among the British people. She had had no idea it still happened. She wondered how many sunsets and sunrises the old woman in the front room sat through each day.

The stairs creaked again. After a minute the door opened and Chandler entered, carrying a tray. 'I wasn't sure what you wanted,' he said, in his high, querulous voice, 'so I've just done it straight.' He was probably trying to save milk. She took the mug and sipped the steaming, bitter tea.

He sat opposite her, breathing hard, and reached over to the tray for his own drink. He looked at her, sharp little eyes staring out from a pale, etched face. 'So. What do you want to know?'

She pulled her notebook from her bag. Thank God she had brought it. 'Really I'm just trying to find out as much as I can about Dr Thorne's career. We've spoken to some of his relatives, but obviously his work was such a large part of his life ...' She remembered reading somewhere that the liar supplied too many details, and tried instead to allow silence to fill the room. Panic rose in her throat. *What am I doing here?* 'We really just want to know what it was like working with him.'

Chandler let the silence hang for ten full seconds. Hopper forced herself to wait, to stay calm. Then he spoke. 'We first worked together soon before the Stop. You don't remember the time before the Stop, do you?'

'Not quite.'

'You're lucky.'

She said nothing.

He carried on. 'I always think it must have been better to be Cain than Adam. No memory of paradise. Just yourself and the new state of affairs.' He lapsed into silence, and as she wondered whether to prompt him again, he began speaking, slowly.

'I was at Cambridge when I met Edward. I was a sort of assistant to lots of the dons. Passed all my exams and never got around to leaving. Thankfully they liked having me around, so I got a job as a factotum of sorts and they let me stay.'

'What was he like?'

'He was brilliant, of course. Quite brilliant. Younger than me. I couldn't teach him anything after his first term. He just went straight up the tree. Eventually I became his laboratory assistant. We worked on crop strains together.'

'Which ones?' Her curiosity had got the better of her, and he glanced at her.

'Plenty. Will your readers know or care about rice varieties?'

'Perhaps not. I'm sorry. Please carry on.'

'Eventually I became Edward's personal secretary. He came to rely on me, I think.' Even at this distance, Chandler was flattered by his small importance in the life of a significant man. 'When he left Cambridge, I followed him to Harvard.'

'What was he like personally? To you, I mean?'

'I don't think I knew him very closely. I don't think anyone did. He was only interested in the work. He barely even mentioned his own son.'

Hopper interrupted in spite of herself. 'A son?'

'Yes.' Chandler looked at her sharply. 'I'm surprised none of the family you've spoken to mentioned he had a son.'

She forced herself to speak slowly. 'They weren't close relatives I spoke to.' Chandler nodded vaguely, and she allowed herself to breathe again.

'A boy. Joshua, that was his name. He came to the office a few times.' He lapsed into silence again.

'Is he still alive?'

'No. He was in the army. Died young, like his mother before him. Thorne never spoke to us about any of that.'

'And when you worked with Dr Thorne … what were you working on?'

'As I said, initially on the crop programmes. This was several years before the Slow began, of course. Then he went off into the army and came back, and moved into government. He was promoted. Then when the Slow happened and Davenport came in, he was promoted again. I went with him.'

'When did you stop working with Dr Thorne?'

'When he left. Fifteen years ago.'

'I see. Can you tell me any more about that?'

He looked at her sharply again. 'I don't think I should.'

'It would be very helpful. Obviously I won't put anything in the obituary ...' Hopper let herself tail off, leaving the words unspoken: *that would harm you.*

A thin cry came from the next room, repeated after a few seconds, pitiful in the silence of the house. Chandler stood. 'Excuse me.' He shuffled once more from the room. After a long pause, the cries stopped. She heard him speaking muffled words. After several minutes, he returned and sat again.

'I'm sorry,' she said. 'I didn't mean to pry. But it would be helpful to know.'

He sighed. 'It's not a secret. We were all sacked unceremoniously. It was very unpleasant. We worked together for many years, you know.'

'When you say "we" ...'

'All of us. The heads of several departments under him, and their assistants. When he went, we went. He'd been in charge of so much. He was responsible for agriculture, yes, but his operation was doing far more than that. They were reorganising the hospitals, re-planning the cities, starting the population programme ... More or less everything that wasn't direct state security was Edward Thorne. They had to hire four people to replace him.'

'Why sack you all?' Chandler glanced at her, and she realised she was risking the lie, knew that an obituarist from *The Times* would be more careful than this, but she had to know. 'Did they give a reason?'

'He was working on something he shouldn't have been. With Thomas Gethin. One of our other bright young things back then, Thomas Gethin. Always the golden one. They became inseparable. They wouldn't shut up talking. Until I walked into the room. They were doing something all right.' His voice was bitter, and his mouth made little chewing motions.

'Do you know what it was?'

'I never managed to find out. Some projects are clearly too important to share with the help.'

'But you were all let go?'

He nodded. 'All of us. I think some of the top team were *really* let go. If you know what I mean. All of them bar one.'

She felt a prickle on her forearm. 'Who stayed?'

'Need you ask? Gethin.'

'Surely the department couldn't survive if you—'

He waved his hand. 'They had replacements lined up for the top officials. But not Gethin, of course. Not the boy wonder.'

'What happened to him?'

'Why do you want to know?' He was sharp again now, veering between indiscreet and secretive.

'Professional habit.' She leant forward. 'I won't write any of this up.'

'He was sacked originally. He cleared his desk with us. I thought they'd got rid of him the same way they did us.'

'Then how do you know he stayed?'

'I saw him again. About three years ago, I was walking through Whitehall – and I saw him. He was going into one of the ministries – Internal Security, it was. I watched. He walked right on through the reception; he wasn't visiting. I rang later, and they said there was nobody of that surname in the department.'

He plucked a lump of sugar from the bowl and dropped it into his now lukewarm tea. Then he spoke again.

'Why've you come here?'

Hopper blinked. His memory must be unreliable. 'I'm an obituary writer from *The Times*, Mr Chandler, I—'

'You're not from *The Times*.'

'I'm sorry?'

His milky eyes remained unfocused, looking past her, as he spoke.

'I don't think *The Times* would be writing about the way Edward left, or the reasons why. I think they'd be too careful for that. And *Times* journalists have cards, they have credentials.' He spoke with venomous satisfaction and his eyes flicked to her. 'So you're not from *The Times*, are you?'

'I don't know what you mean,' Hopper managed to say. 'If you like, you can ring my editor. He'll tell you. Thorne died in hospital yesterday, we're writing his—'

'Are you from Security?'

'No, I'm not, I ...'

The cry came from the next room once more – higher, more insistent.

He ignored it. 'No, you're not. If you were from Security, you'd probably have said so. So you're not from *The Times* and you're not from Security.'

The cry rose to a wail. He shouted past her at the wall, his high, thin voice ragged with anger: 'Shut *up*, will you?' The noise subsided.

'I think I'd better go,' Hopper said.

'I think you're right.'

She stood, gripping her notebook, and walked along the dark corridor with its burning smell, past the door from which the keening cry had come. But as she reached the front door, a strong, claw-like hand gripped her arm. Chandler was close to her now.

'My life was ruined when we were got rid of. Ruined. And it was his fault.'

'I have to go. The piece will appear in . . .' Her sentence got lost as she stumbled out into the garden. Then, without knowing what she was doing, she started to run, past the swirl of dead leaves, back through the rubble and weeds to the crumbling brickwork of the gate, away from the decaying house and its two wretched occupants.

17

She was out on the street, breathing deeply; she was out and hardly knew where she was. Her heart was hammering at her chest. Even London's tarry air felt clean in her lungs compared with the foulness of Chandler's house.

What had he said? Thorne had been sacked along with all his colleagues, except the man Thomas Gethin.

What else did she know? Thorne had written to her telling her he had something to show her. His house had been burgled on the day of his death. He had been anxious in the hospital, worried about her safety even as he died. And his final words to her: *My house*.

She had to go back to Hampstead.

As she walked back towards the main road, she heard a foot-fall, and glanced round to see two men about twenty metres behind her. One was rotund and bald, halfway through mopping his brow. The other was taller and leaner, and walked with a bony, angular gait. Both men wore long grey coats, unsuitable in this heat.

She had to struggle not to walk faster. It was unlikely they were following her. Impossible. Why would she be of interest?

Two hundred metres later, they were behind her still, a little further back. But when she looked around again, they were not talking, and their attention was focused on her. For a second her eyes met those of the taller man.

There was a café up ahead. She ducked in, ordered a cup of tea from the proprietor, and waited for the men to pass by. A minute later, they did so. The shorter one glanced inside as they went.

She was the only customer in the place. It was dingy, the glass counter thick with dust, the few cakes behind it looking like museum pieces. She sat at the counter with her cracked china mug, blowing on the tea to cool it, thinking only about the men. The news bulletin came to her as if through a fog. Another bomb, this one in a shopping centre in Canterbury. Sixteen dead so far. The manageress loudly predicted the guilty parties, and looked sourly at the radio as though it had to take its share of the blame. Hopper didn't respond, and eventually the woman moved off to sit in a little room behind the counter.

After a quarter of an hour, Hopper paid, and walked over to the window, glancing out to her left as idly as she could.

The men were lingering a little way down the road. The taller one stood scuffing the ground, smoking. The shorter, balder one gazed abstractedly back towards the café. She could see a little curl of smoke from the taller one's cigarette. They weren't even bothering to hide.

Panic flooded her. She picked up her bag and, not knowing quite what she was doing, walked slowly out of the café, towards the men – as though by keeping to her original route she might deflect their attention. They moved off, ambling ahead of her, occasionally looking back. She kept moving. They must know she had noticed them. Their proximity was almost insulting.

She was nearly at the bus stop. Would they stop there? Would they get the same bus?

At that moment, an alley opened up at her side, a little path between two houses. Her feet moved before she had even decided to take it, and she slipped along it as quietly as she could. Behind the houses the alley turned onto a narrow walled path, the sides shaded and sprouting with bushes, and she broke into a run, her arms lashed by overgrown nettles, her feet dodging the stones that strewed the ground. No shout followed her, no footsteps.

She passed what she was sure was the back of Chandler's house, looking as innocuous as any of its neighbours. How many other houses on this street were cages for people scratching at each other in miserable, hollow lives, waiting for relief that never came?

After several hundred metres the alley opened onto the main road; she crossed and plunged back into the same alley on the other side. She realised now that the bricks on her right were a raised railway line above her head.

The alley emerged, finally, onto another street. Where was she? Somewhere between Camberwell and Elephant. The square she was in had once been pretty – it looked Georgian. It was bisected by the railway line she had been following, which dragged its way across, twenty metres off the ground, cauterising the houses on either side as it passed through. One of the brick embankments over the road had collapsed, or been partially demolished, and several of the houses were covered in thick-growing ivy that thrived on their shady fronts.

She realised how hard she was breathing. She leant against a wall under the railway arch, taking advantage of the cooler air. Who were the men? Who had sent them? Were they with Warwick? They must be.

She resolved to walk up to Waterloo and travel to Thorne's house from there. At least it was overcast. It was just after five in the afternoon. The air was closer, but she would walk the first mile even if she sweated. There were a lot more storms these days than before the Slow. The air was stirring in strange new patterns, drawn onto the land and bringing the sea with it. It was just as well – without rain, the only way to grow a crop would be indoors. Even the big indoor factory farms couldn't feed forty million people.

North it was, then, back across the river, to Thorne's house.

The streets grew a little busier as she approached the centre of town. She found a bus at Waterloo heading in the right direction; realised with surprise it was the same route she'd taken yesterday. Was it only yesterday? Eventually it dropped her at the same stop in Hampstead, by the little Korean grocery, and as she approached the house she saw with relief that no policeman stood outside. The street was quiet.

Before Hopper reached the gate, she remembered the house across the road from Thorne's, where yesterday the figure had stood in the window, watching her leave. On an unexamined impulse she moved closer, ducked the thick tangle of brambles hanging over the porch, and rang the bell.

It was answered quickly, by a woman older than Hopper; perhaps in her forties. She had a hard mouth, punctuated at one end by twin points of scar tissue, and she wore a grey dressing gown a little too large for her. She held a baby against her shoulder, and gently jogged it up and down as she spoke.

'Yes?'

'Hello. I'm just here because … The house over the road …'

'What about it?'

'It was burgled yesterday.'

'So?'

'I'm just wondering if you saw anything.'

'You police?' Her voice was quiet, low, accusatory, and she shifted the baby protectively to her other side.

'No. I know the man who lived there.'

'He seemed nice. Gave me his spare clothing tokens.'

Hopper nodded. 'I think … there might have been something strange happening. Can you tell me?'

'Why should I?'

'He was my friend. I think he might have been in trouble.' It was close enough to the truth. Hopper tried to make herself as friendly, as harmless as possible.

'The police were outside all afternoon.'

'Did you see anything that wasn't the police?'

'Couple of fellers in grey coats.'

'When?'

'Just after the police turned up. They walked right past them and went in.'

Hopper thought of the two grey coats who had followed her from Chandler's home. 'I see. Thank you.'

'Except ...' The woman looked down, tracing an invisible pattern on the floor with her toe, suddenly childlike.

'Yes?'

'Except they came by in the morning as well, before the police arrived.'

Hopper stared at the woman, at her dingy dressing gown, her scarred mouth. 'Sorry?'

'They were here before the police.'

She thought back to the words of the policeman standing outside the house yesterday. *We were called out this afternoon*, he'd said. *There's been a burglary*. The woman was staring at her warily, as if waiting for something. Ridicule, perhaps. Hopper tried to disguise her interest.

'Can I just check – you mean they arrived in the afternoon, and the police let them into the house ...'

'That's right.'

'And yet they had already been here several hours before?'

'Yeah.'

'You're sure it was the same two men?'

The woman gave a little gesture of irritation. 'Course I'm sure. Two blokes. One bald fat feller, one thin one. Grey coats. They was here at six in the morning. I was up with him,' she added, gesturing to the baby. 'We have a little balcony. They didn't see me, though. I was just sitting out. They didn't have a car. Or if they had a car, they left it a long way off.'

'What happened when they arrived?'

The woman looked at Hopper as if she was dealing with an idiot. 'They went through the gate, and I didn't see 'em after that. You can't see his front door from the balcony. But I never heard it shut. And it shuts loud.'

'Did they stay long?'

'I don't know. I was out there for another fifteen minutes, then I had to get him back into his cot. It's none of my business what people do. But I didn't hear the door in the next hour.'

'Had you seen them before, ever?'

'No.'

'Was there anyone else with them?'

'No.'

'What did you think they were here for?'

'Visiting the old man.'

'But he was in hospital.'

'I thought maybe he'd come back. I didn't think about them too much.' The woman was haughty suddenly, as though affronted at the suggestion that she spent her day idly observing her neighbours.

'All right. Thank you. I think that's everything.'

'You're welcome.' The woman looked at her. 'What happened to the old man, then?'

'He died.'

'Shame. I liked him.' She paused. 'Well, good luck with it, whatever it is.' She cocked her head to one side, and moved her free hand in a strange, abortive gesture of friendliness. Then she turned and closed the door behind her.

Hopper looked at Thorne's house across the road. As she approached it, she felt herself observed.

This street was not what it had once been. The area had been fashionable before the Stop, but so much of London had been left to fend for itself. The really successful people these days – the manufacturing chiefs and the senior politicians and the rest of Davenport's gang – lived on private estates outside the city, powered by a private stash of fossil fuels. Davenport himself spent almost half the year in his Cotswolds dacha, supposedly stuffed with loot requisitioned after the Stop. There were rumours he had the Elgin Marbles there: they certainly weren't in the British Museum, famous today only for its acres of smashed glass.

Thorne's house loomed before her. It seemed deserted. The garden at the front was cool and shaded – the huge hedges behind the wall saw to that – and a vine was growing rampant across a trellis over the central path. Beneath it, the soil was dry. A little central water feature was discoloured with rust and moss.

The place was even more impressive than it had seemed yesterday. The ancient, faded brickwork was studded intermittently with black blocks, and large bow windows bulged out beyond the rest of the structure. But the impression of grandeur crumbled on close inspection. There were tiles missing from the little turret in the front. The paint of the woodwork had chipped away, and the windows were stained and smeared, with dark, furry mould round their frames.

Hopper didn't want to try to enter without having first ascertained whether anyone was at home – perhaps some police officer left to do their work in quiet. She reached out and let the iron knocker crash down onto its plate; it was in the shape of a sun, grey swirling rays shooting out of it. One of Thorne's little jokes.

The knock echoed through the house.

After a minute or so of waiting, watching a blackbird fussing for insects among the dry leaves, she guessed it was safe to go in. The front door was locked, but there was a path to her right, and a low gate barely tethered at the side of the house. At the other end of the cool passageway, rampant with nettles, the back garden opened up. It was worse than the front: the lawn was yellow, the paving slabs monstrous with algae. The trees at the garden's edge were hardy varieties, but even they had wilted. The whole place smelt of decay.

She tested the back door. A stroke of luck: it was unlocked, and let her in with no more protest than a low squeak. She moved through into a little study crammed with bookshelves and armchairs. As a final precaution she said, in a voice designed to hide her unease, 'Hello?'

In the corner, a black shadow unfurled and moved towards her.

For a second she recoiled, horrified, imagining the men from Chandler's house – then laughed. The only animal disturbed by her presence was a cat.

It followed her as she moved, butting against her legs. Barring the room she had arrived in, the ground floor was grand and abandoned. She found a kitchen lined with an enormous range, a dining table bearing just one forlorn place mat. She headed into the main hall and moved upstairs. The cat stayed on the ground floor and stared at her as she went. The staircase was broad; halfway up was a little landing with a door off to a bathroom. At the top were four more doors. She picked one, opened it, and gasped.

The room was large and high: huge windows ran from floor to ceiling. It must have been beautiful before it had been torn apart. The wallpaper had been slashed, the carpet ripped up and hacked to pieces. The long cream curtains lay heaped in a corner. The pictures had been pulled from the faded walls and were piled carelessly on the curtains, their backs torn off. A bookcase had disgorged its contents over a quarter of the room – the books had been left open, spines protesting at the unnatural poses they had been left in. *This wasn't a burglary*. The thought occurred to her as though whispered in her ear. *It was a search*.

A desk against one wall was piled with papers, weighed down by a telephone. She picked it up and dialled 0, groping in her pocket for a pen. After a few seconds a bored female voice spoke.

'Operator.'

'This is North 3 – 74 Harlesden Road.' She looked at the phone. 'Uh, 4489. I was just wondering – do you have a list of calls made from this number, please? I'm trying to track down a shop I was talking to and I've stupidly lost the details.'

'We're really not supposed to.'

Hopper pictured the operator, sitting in one of the telecoms centres, cigarette in her ashtray, patching calls to bridge the gaps left when the old exchanges had fallen apart. The woman was probably Hopper's age, spending her life saying 'Operator' a thousand times a day. She put on as subservient a voice as she could manage.

'Please. It's for my father – I'm trying to get him a gift, and I've completely forgotten the shop I identified as just the place. If there's anything at all you could do, I'd be hugely grateful.'

There was a sigh from the other end of the line. 'I need the date the calls were made. I can't look up more than a few days at a time.'

'Oh, of course. It's …' She fished in her jacket for the hospital notes, found the date of Thorne's admission. 'Just before the ninth of June, please. Any time up until the ninth.'

'Just a moment.'

Hopper looked around the room as the operator searched the record. An armchair in the corner was lying crazily upside down, pockets of its stuffing bursting through slash marks in the lining like a plant sprouting through a seed case.

The voice at the other end of the phone returned. 'Hello?'

'I'm here.'

Just as bored, the operator spoke again. 'Here they are.' She rattled off a list of numbers, so fast Hopper had to ask her to repeat a couple. There was a doctor, a few local food shops, the local regional committee. No Gethins.

The operator paused. 'What about this: Central 12, Fisher. A bookshop. Was the number phoned a few times?'

'Er … yes. Yes, I'm pretty sure I rang more than once.'

'I'd give that a go if I were you. It's one of the only ones you rang more than once. You rang that three times on the morning of the eighth.'

'Thank you so much. Yes, that must be it.'

'There's one more number. This one you rang twice the night before the ninth. Could that be it?'

'Possibly,' Hopper said, reluctant to pass up the opportunity. 'Could you tell me the details, please?'

'Oh, no, sorry. It wouldn't be that. It's Westerly 12. One of the Atlantic rigs. I don't think you'd be going there for a birthday present, would you?'

Hopper leant against the table. 'I ... No, I don't think I would. Did those calls get through, please?'

'Looks like they did, yes. Two calls, two minutes and four minutes.'

'Did he ... I mean, was that rig phoned before that at all?'

'Not in the previous week, dear. That's as far back as my records go.' Her voice had softened. 'Anything else?'

'That's everything. Thank you.'

'Not at all. And by the way ... if it's a man, and he's cheating on you, punch him in the eye from me.' The line went dead.

Hopper exhaled, slowly, trying to remove the sudden knot of tension from her throat. Thorne had phoned the rig as well as writing. Why? And who had answered the call? The main phone was in Schwimmer's office. She never used it. There was nobody on the mainland she had needed to talk to. Had Schwimmer deliberately not told her of Thorne's call?

She looked at her list of numbers, rang the operator again, and got through to the number that had been called three times the day before Thorne had gone into hospital. It purred, metallic, and was snatched up.

'Fisher's Books.' A man's voice.

'Hello. Can you tell me your address, please?'

He sounded like he was breathing heavily. Perhaps he had run for the phone. 'We're in Cecil Court, madam, just off the Charing Cross Road. Number 28.'

'Thank you. I'll try to come by tomorrow.'

She rang off, and resumed looking through the room. To one side there was a tiny pile of papers, notable for their neatness amid the chaos. Whoever had been searching up here must have preserved them. She rummaged through the pile: mostly financial statements, none especially interesting. There was also a collection of correspondence with a lawyer called Stephanie Clayford. She noted the address – in the lawyers' labyrinth at Temple – then moved on to the rest of the first floor.

Two of the other rooms up here had had the same treatment. But the final room – a bedroom, undoubtedly Thorne's – had only been torn half apart. The other half was still neat – pristine, in fact. And in the middle of the room was a tool bag, left open.

The search, or whatever it was, had been left unfinished.

Hopper surveyed the rest of the room. Where would Thorne hide something? She looked between the floorboards, but found none that lifted out. The wardrobe had no inner parts, as far as she could tell, and the small chest of drawers opposite it had already been ripped apart. She searched fruitlessly for twenty minutes, then sat back on the bed.

On top of one of the exploded bedside tables was a photo frame, facing downwards and with its back ripped open. She turned it over: a lopsided picture of Thorne and a woman, holding a small boy up between them. All three were smiling. The glass was cracked. And then she noticed it: a tiny corrugation at the side of the photo, a little lump of adhesive.

She pulled the photograph out, and looked closer. It felt thicker in places; it had been altered somehow. She held it up, held it perpendicular to her eye, and there, catching her eye, she saw. There was a diagonal seam right across the front of it, almost invisible unless you looked in the right light. She scrabbled for something sharp. One of the shards of glass from the frame. That would do. She levered it out, held it carefully, and made a small incision in the corner. As soon as she had done so, the rest of the picture yawned open, Thorne swinging away from his wife and child. The photo had been bisected with a scalpel at some point, across its front. She folded it out. Inside the picture of Thorne and his family, there was another photograph.

It was a group of people gathered in a loose semicircle, facing the camera, in a half-posed, half-awkward framing. They stood in a nondescript office of tiled ceilings and thin-carpeted floors. Outside one window was the tower of Big Ben. She recognised Thorne immediately. He was accompanied by three men and two women, all in suits. Names were written on the back: *Hollis, Lee, Drabble, Symons, Gethin*, and in the corner, *Nov. '43*. Less than a year before she had met him for the first time. The first four names were crossed out, with little annotated dates. The dates were close together, she noticed: all around a year after the picture was taken.

Gethin was standing at Thorne's right hand and was wearing a suit, but must have been no more than thirty to Thorne's sixty.

He looked lawyerly, saturnine. His features were sharply defined, his little round glasses tied with a knot of tape and resting on a slender, patrician nose.

The group were assembled behind something. In the foreground of the picture was a small white oblong box. On the side were three semicircular indentations, all the same size; on the top a long groove was scored along the whole length of the box. What was it?

At that moment, she heard voices outside, and footsteps approaching the house up the broad gravel drive.

She ran to the window and glanced out, almost too quickly to tell anything. Two figures – they looked like the men who had been following her at Chandler's house. How had they found her here? No time to think about that now. She grabbed the photo of Thorne and his colleagues and shoved it into her bra, threw the photo frame back facing downwards. She shouldered her bag, ran back onto the first-floor landing, moved to the stairs – if she could just get downstairs, she could slip out of the house at the back – and froze as she heard a key twist in the front door. They were in the hall.

'Want a drink before we finish the bedroom?'

'Yeah. Whatever's in the cupboard.'

One set of footsteps started climbing the stairs. Hopper moved back into the first room she had seen. The footsteps arrived on the landing, turned right into the bedroom she had just been in. She risked a glance. The door was angled: she wouldn't be seen if she moved to the head of the staircase. But if she ran into the other one as he came up the stairs … She would have to take the chance.

As gently as she could, she slipped out of the study, across to the stairs, and descended, hardly breathing. She stopped and flattened herself against the wall as a voice came from downstairs, loud and coarse:

'You want ice?'

The man in the bedroom responded: 'Is there any?'

'There should be.'

'Yeah, go on then. Not too much.'

She kept moving. She was halfway down now, on the little landing between the two flights, by the doorway to the bathroom. Before she could move again, the voice came from downstairs:

'The freezer's on the fritz. Have to have it without.' She heard footsteps moving towards the hall, about to reach the stairs. She eased back into the bathroom and closed the door behind her, sliding the bolt shut.

The glass in the door was frosted. Anyone passing by would see there was someone in here. She moved back and sat on the closed lavatory as she heard the footsteps approach up the stairs. They paused for one awful second, then passed her. The second man was continuing up. He must have seen her and thought she was his colleague. In a few seconds she would have a chance to slip out. And then, as he passed, he shouted back, towards the bathroom door: 'Hope you like your whisky neat.'

A second's pause. Then a voice came back from the bedroom. 'No problem.'

In that pause, she could almost hear the second man turning back to the bathroom. And before he had the chance to move, she unbolted the door, heaved it open, and ran. She barely saw the man, still holding a tray with two glasses on it, staring at her.

She ran down the stairs, heard a smash she later realised was the tray landing on the ground. She crossed the hall, heaved open the heavy front door, heard footsteps clumping behind her, gaining. She was on the path, running between the weeds towards the gate.

And just as she reached the gate, already planning her route back to the main road, to anywhere, she ran straight into the back of the police officer stationed once again at the front of the house.

18

It had been too hot for a fortnight. Nobody was sleeping, and people were starting to lose their tempers. Most people, that is, but not Thorne, who smiled as Hopper entered his office, flustered and late.

'Take your time. No rush.' Then, once she had settled herself, he said, rather more sharply: 'All right, then. Showpiece day. This had better be worth a month's work.'

'It is. I swear it.' She dug the folder out of her satchel and handed it to him. 'I phoned the Department of the Environment and told them what I was studying. They told me they're only focused on coastal waters. There are no expeditions planned for more than ten miles from the coast, barring naval activity.'

'Wait a second. Before I even start to read, how does all this' – he waved the document – 'help your colleagues trying to get an extra annual crop out of a cabbage field in Lincolnshire? That's what people will want to know.'

'It makes all the difference.'

'Go on.'

She breathed in. 'As I said last time, we know the water will have cooled dramatically on the other side. Much of it may have frozen over already. And the oceans here will have warmed dramatically. But there will be new currents established by now, replacing the old ones. Much of the churn will be around the edge of the Coldside, but there should be some bigger currents too: warm surface water flowing outwards from the Hotzone, and colder water flowing in the other way from the Coldside, probably beneath it. But we've got almost no information about any possible new current systems.'

'Granted.'

'All anyone's focused on is more crops, and getting soil-free as fast as possible. But the currents are the way to do that. If we don't know about them, we don't know where's going to be most habitable.'

'Go on.'

Time to go for it. Don't fuck up. 'I think Europe's in the path of one of those colder currents. I think it might be cooling the whole continent as it goes, making places like Britain – especially Britain – more habitable. It seems very possible, but because of the coastal blockades, nobody's being allowed near it or allowed to study it.

'So' – *please don't let him laugh at me* – 'you remember those drifter devices I mentioned?'

'Yes.'

'I wrote to a friend from home who's in the navy, and asked him to drop a few prototypes I made off his ship as he goes. He's in the Irish Sea. They should be able to measure the currents. They're wired to automatically radio the signals back to me. You can see the results there.'

He stared. 'Did you really do that?'

'It's in the file I've given you.'

He thumbed his way to the right page.

'I hope it's not too obvious. Or treason, for that matter.'

He ran a hand over his jaw as he read, back and forth. 'Well, it's not too obvious. Almost certainly treason, though, interfering with the workings of Britannia's navy. How did you rig these devices up to send the results?'

'A little blip. I found a wavelength I can receive the locations on and calculate the movements. A friend in Scotland's going to help me triangulate. We're using a broadcasting set I picked up.'

'Those aren't allowed, Ellen.'

'I know. I'm sorry. But the prototypes weren't hard to build, and a lot of the wavelength is going to waste. I just had to know.'

'You really did this?'

'Yes.'

'And the results?'

'My friend is still on his way. I think – if it works, if we roll it out – we could discover all sorts of new currents. If the navy agree. There's nobody else in this hemisphere with the ships to do it. The more we know, the greater the chance of survival.'

'This is … yes, I think it's fair to say this is worth a term's work.' He pinched the bridge of his nose. 'This might have an impact.'

He flicked the pages back and forth once more, slowly, pausing to look at the diagrams of the drifter she'd built. 'Your parents were scientists, you said before.'

God, he was going to mention them again. Last time she'd felt furious and manipulated. She wouldn't be this time. 'Mum was a doctor, not in research. But yes. Both scientifically minded.'

'I wish you could have shown them this, Ellen. I can't pretend to have known them, of course, but I think they'd be impressed.'

There was a lump in her throat. 'Thank you.'

As she crossed the quad back to her room, between the huge, crumpled college buildings, she couldn't help grinning. He had seen her work. Thorne, the great man of government, had found her idea impressive. She'd thought of something nobody else was doing. The scientific wings of government had been cut so brutally and chaotically that there must be almost nobody left to think about the long term.

It embarrassed her a little that her mind had been changed so quickly about staying at university. He had returned her first essay the same day she had submitted it, torn to shreds in the margins, with a reading list appended. A week later he had secured her a special permission for the university library's Rare Books collection, with instructions to spend as long as possible working on her next one.

They had met twice a week since then, and had talked about plankton, whales, tidal collapse, everything. He was relentless. From the quad she often saw his office light still on behind his curtains long into the hours of curfew, faint against the sunlight but still gleaming. She could see why he had been successful in government. And there *was* something of her father about him. The dedication, the drive. Back in her spartan room, she wondered what her parents would have thought of him.

Yet in all their tutorials over that term, he never referred to the years – the decades – before he had come to Oxford. It was as though they had never happened, except for one or two moments when she could have sworn that, at the brink of saying something, he'd stopped himself speaking and changed the subject.

And she could not help noticing that there were times when he became completely lost in abstraction, and a curious kind of depression. Mid conversation, he would bring a session to an end, and request that they carry on next week. After she left, she would look back across the quad and see his curtains twitch closed. When they met the following week, no mention would be made of it.

These moments were irregular, and not wholly predictable. Even so, it was not beyond her attention that these strange lapses of Thorne's tended to come whenever she mentioned the southern coast, and particularly when she referred to the rusting jaws of the Tidal Defence Zone.

19

The back of the police car was unshaded and overheated. Hopper's wrists were handcuffed to the back of the seat in front of her, shackled in a patch of sunlight. She could feel her skin pinkening.

Harv had once told her the security services in London used the sun to their advantage. On cloudless days, prisoners would be moved to the roof, placed in glass-capped cells with walls of polished steel, and left without water until they were delirious. You might be there for days, crimsoning and blackening in the heat, your only companion a distorted reflection of your own burning body. Maybe that was where she was going now.

She had been knocked to the ground by the officer at the gate. He had picked her up and wrestled her back into the house, assisted by the men in coats. At one point she had jerked her head back and made satisfying contact with the policeman's nose, hearing a little crunch and feeling a dribble of wetness on the back of her scalp.

She'd been seated on one of Thorne's armchairs. The policeman had left again and the two men had stood there, the shorter one panting angrily, furious that he'd been forced to humble himself by breaking into a run. The taller one, who seemed the older of the two, had asked her name. She had said nothing. His colleague, red-faced, had slapped her, putting as much weight as he could into it. When she moved her jaw, experimentally, little tendrils of pain arced all the way to her ear.

The older one had sighed, and asked his colleague to go and make a phone call, then sat with her, reading a book of verse Thorne had owned and humming a little tune. Within ten minutes, an unmarked car had pulled up outside, and she was pushed into it, her wrists bound with the gate policeman's borrowed handcuffs. He had looked embarrassed putting them on her, with his nose swollen and scarlet. Outside the room, she had heard him telling the two men about her visit to the house yesterday.

As they had pulled away, she had looked across the street. In the first-floor window she saw the woman with her baby, dispassionately observing the scene.

The car swung round the corner to the main road and started heading south. The shorter man turned in his seat, grinning at the coincidence that had brought her back into their orbit so soon after she had fallen out of it.

'You ever been arrested before?' His ear had been malformed by some violence, she noticed.

She did not answer. She felt frightened yet elated; as though this journey could not help but bring her closer to whatever they were searching for, to what had pushed Thorne out of government in the first place.

She had been arrested before, just once. After her mother had died.

It was six years after the Stop. She had been ten years old. Her mother had been in northern Europe, working with the human wreckage after the collapse of the Hotzone. She had been away for a month. Hopper had spoken to her just once in that time, on a crackling phone line, noises of distress and chaos in the background. She couldn't remember her exact words, just the sense of standing in their family hall, clutching a phone to her ear, thinking how strange it was to hear people suffering a hundred miles away. Her father had spoken to her mother next, and after he had put the phone down, he said to Hopper and her brother: 'It's all right. She's found a ship. She's coming back. And she won't leave again.'

The ship, so her father later related, was the *Elpis*, a Greek-flagged vessel. It had two thousand people on board, miraculous survivors of the remains of the Middle East. Some deal had been struck to allow the residents passage; some payment, whether in gold or guns or food, had been weighed and found adequate. The phone call her mother had made was to say she had secured a berth, that she would be home within two days.

She never arrived. Enquiries to the authorities were useless, met with hostility or a blank wall of ignorance. And a few days later, reports began to spread of the major new security system established by General Richard Davenport, guaranteed to protect Britain's shores from chaos, and the positive results it was already yielding in the Channel.

Two weeks after her mother's disappearance, walking through London, still stricken by the grief swelling within her, she had wormed free of her father's grip and thrown a stone at a police officer outside the Admiralty buildings. It amazed her now to think that furious child had once been her. She had been plucked from her father and thrown into a van, one of her skinny ribs broken in the process. She had been released within a day, thank God, thanks to some bribe or intercession by her father. The *Elpis* never appeared. But for months afterwards, bodies had washed up along the south coast with their few possessions. An empty dinghy. A sodden Red Cross ration sack. A doll.

The car was making its leisurely way through the evening traffic. They were coming down through Bloomsbury. Pretty squares rolled past the window. They would be beautiful on their upper storeys if one could ignore the human wreckage lower down.

Thorne had phoned her on the rig just before he went into hospital, although Warwick had claimed he had not asked for her until the day before his death. Perhaps that was why she had been summoned with such urgency on Thorne's final day: Warwick and her colleagues were convinced he would tell her some information they wanted to know. But he'd been too careful for that.

And now she knew about the bookshop he had phoned, and the name of his lawyer, Clayford. And tucked under her clothes she had the picture of Thorne and his colleagues around that strange box. What had it been?

The car made its way along the north bank of the Thames, westbound, until the concrete tower of New Scotland Yard rose up before them. They drove through two discreet black gates, into a little asphalt car park abutting two buildings: one tall tower and one longer, lower block. They parked at the end of a row of similar cars; the lean man got out and pulled open her door.

'Out you get.'

Hopper was signed in, briefly patted for any weapons by a gangly female officer, and taken through into a large, airless chamber at the base of the taller building. The men had taken her bag with them.

'Wait here.'

It was a long, rectangular room, lined with three wooden benches. The only door was dark metal, complete with sliding hatches. The sole decorations were a row of faded posters on the right-hand wall. The prime minister's sorrowful, heroic countenance, discreetly touched up. A grotesque cartoon squirrel holding a sack and saying, *If You Don't Save Up Your Rations, You're Nuts!* Another encouraging the public to register as donors: to give blood for the troops, labour for the farms. Everyone wanted something from you these days.

There were fifteen or twenty other people in there, sitting along the uncushioned benches. An enormous bearded man, rough-faced and scarred, slept fitfully, shifting around in a futile search for a comfortable position. Three bored women in tight skirts sat together, picking at their nails and muttering to each other.

Hopper sat as far as she could from anyone – two spaces from a small, mild-looking woman in a thick brown coat. The woman looked up as she approached, then back down again immediately. She was knotting and unknotting her hands, wrestling with her knuckles one by one as if they were rosary beads.

She spoke as Hopper sat. 'What have they arrested you for then?'

'I'm not sure yet. They'll tell me soon enough. What about you?'

'Ration fraud.' The woman's voice was soft, embarrassed. 'It wasn't my fault.'

'I'm sure it wasn't.' Hopper had practically forgotten about ration cards. She'd been on government food for three years.

'I got three kids. They only give us two lots of rations. I told them again and again, we need an extra ration. They told us no, that we should put our eldest in the army. But he doesn't want to go. He's only fifteen.' Her eyes were watering behind her glasses. 'He can't go and fight.'

'I'm sure it won't come to that.' Hopper wished she sounded more convincing.

The woman looked back at her lap. 'They keep telling us we got to do better. We're doing our best, but they don't believe us.' She kept manipulating her knuckles.

It was the same story everywhere these days, Hopper knew. Shortage, shortage, shortage; shortages of food, of water, of fuel, of sleep, of levity, of decency. The shelves in shops were a carousel of shifting produce depending on which supply chains had collapsed or – more seldom – been re-established. On the rig, they had charted the fortunes of the mainland by the state of the supply boats.

Eighteen months ago, the shipment had been half its normal size. Schwimmer had phoned headquarters, confident of some mistake, that another shipment would be on its way already – only to find an exhausted official explaining that for the next two months, rations were halved. The crowning insult was that three of the rice sacks had been shot full of larvae.

The meals – never generous – had become pitiful. The soldiers had grown thin, their muscles shrunken. Deck duty had been cut back. Iceberg crews were similarly pruned, almost disastrously so. When the next supply shipment bore the same paltry cargo, the rig troops had accused the crew of stealing their food. If the supply boat's crew had not been as etiolated as the troops, they might have been attacked.

Eventually the food supply had recovered, and these days it was as regular as it had been before the interruption. Occasionally there were new stocks, new lines opened, the sudden shock of a forgotten flavour re-established. Nevertheless, the direction of travel was unmistakable. The list of foods available shrank monthly. Hopper wondered when the last human would taste pepper, or coriander, or an orange.

'You should send him into the army,' she said. She was surprised at herself. The woman looked up, just as surprised. 'He might receive an easy posting. I'm on one of the rigs in the North Atlantic. It's not a bad life out there.'

'The rigs? You've been out then?' The woman's voice had risen a little.

'Yes.'

'Is it true about the Breadbasket?'

'Is what true?'

'They keep them working eighteen hours a day, the convicts. The locals too. And if they don't work, they get shot. That's what I heard. And when they die, they get fed to the soil, to grow the crops they've been picking.'

'I don't know about that. I'm not on the Breadbasket. I'm on the rigs.' Clearly, the difference between one foreign environment and another had not impressed itself on the woman.

'My husband's out there. Breadbasket.'

'I'm sorry.'

She smiled. 'Don't be. He was a bad lot. Deserter. Did this to me.' She pulled down her collar and gestured to a pink, puckered burn mark at the base of her neck. 'Fertiliser's all he's good for.'

They were interrupted by the door opening at the end of the room. A new officer, burly and ill-kempt, looked down at his clipboard and spoke in a broad West Country accent.

'Selkirk.'

A red-headed young man got up and shuffled towards the far end of the room.

'Wharton.' Nobody moved. He repeated the name, louder, and the huge sleeping man jolted awake, and heaved himself up and after the boy.

'Hopper.'

She stood and spoke to her neighbour. 'Good luck.'

The woman looked up at her, eyes narrowed. 'Don't tell them anything.' She seemed, for a second, totally in control of herself, not the pitiful creature of a moment ago, and Hopper wondered which was her true self.

She was roughly escorted from the room by the new officer, her arms still tethered in front of her. The pleasant thought occurred to her that if the policeman outside Thorne's house needed to handcuff anyone, he wouldn't be able to.

They walked down a long corridor, lit only by bulbs whose electric scent gave the air a harsh, burnt quality. The carpet underfoot was frayed, and after about fifty yards it stopped completely, replaced by hard brown squares of linoleum. Then, through another door, they were in a translucent plastic tunnel, gridded with steel on the outside.

She knew they were leaving the headquarters of the civilian police. Although the police today had guns and tear gas and frequently full riot kit, they were still the people who investigated burglaries, assaults, ration cheats. But the long, low building adjacent to New Scotland Yard, she knew, was reserved for Internal Security. At the other end of the tunnel, they passed through two more doors and her escort signed a form.

They climbed three floors. For a second Hopper thought they were taking her to the fabled rooftop cells, but they turned off onto another almost featureless corridor, studded with pairs of doors along one side. As she moved, she considered the body of evidence suggested by her behaviour.

Her notebook – with the notes from her conversation with Chandler inside it – was in her bag, doubtless being pawed through already. She should have left it in Thorne's house, in a heap where they'd never look for it. Too late now. What else did it contain? The notes on Thorne's obituary, written by Harry. Oh God.

But the photograph of Thorne in front of the strange device: she had put that down her bra just before she had run. She could feel it there now. What *was* that box Thorne and his colleagues had been standing in front of?

What else did they know? They knew she'd shown up at Thorne's house the day before and lied about her name. They knew she'd been to see Chandler. They would know where she was staying. And the bookshop. They'd be able to tell she had phoned up.

They had arrived outside a pair of doors, indistinguishable from the others. The officer escorting her opened the left-hand one, gestured her into a room furnished with a desk and four chairs, then asked her to sit, checked her handcuffs and left. A second after the door closed, a set of bolts clicked shut behind him.

The room was windowless, grey. The only light came from a fluorescent tube overhead, a couple of flies lying on their backs inside. Darkness: usually the preserve of the rich, and here it was being dished out to dangerous criminal suspects. Funny. The inevitable mirror lined the wall to her left.

She was not afraid; not yet. She felt even a little distant from the whole situation. It was so absurd. She had been cut off from the world ever since her marriage ended. All she had been doing since was observing the seas, trying unsuccessfully to make sense of this dying world. And now here she was being treated like a criminal. What would they use against her? They could hardly threaten people she was close to. Apart from Mark, and David, and perhaps Harv, she had few friends.

Once they found Harry's obituary notes, would they call at *The Times*? She couldn't bear the thought of costing David his job.

Footsteps approached along the corridor – more than one set. She heard the door to the adjacent room opening and closing. A few minutes passed and then it opened again, followed by the door to her own cell. In the doorway stood Ruth Warwick.

'Hello, Dr Hopper.' She moved lightly into the room. Behind her, the man who had accompanied her on the rig, Blake, came in, closing the door gently behind him. The pair sat opposite her.

Today, Warwick was wearing another ensemble reminiscent of an old film: a double-breasted houndstooth jacket and matching skirt, too heavy for this weather. She was smiling softly. As she fussed with some papers and received a glass of water from an officer, Hopper took the chance to observe the man, Blake, more closely. He was sparsely built, legs and arms long, his hands out-sized and bulbous, his grey-mottled hair scraped back from his high forehead and plastered down with grease. His skin was dry, and two thick lines ran from the corners of his mouth down to his chin, giving him the look of a dummy. He wore the same grey suit he had done on the rig.

'I'm sorry we have to meet again under these circumstances, Dr Hopper.'

'I'm sure you're not wholly surprised.'

'Not wholly. Well ...' Warwick opened the file in front of her, 'you've been busy since we last met. You remember Inspector Blake here, of course.'

'Why have I been arrested?'

'You broke into Dr Thorne's house. The laws of England still apply in this case, Dr Hopper, even if the victim of the offence is in no position to do anything about it.'

'His house had already been broken into. I was trying to find—'

'Find? Find what?'

That had been a mistake. 'The house was unlocked. I wanted to see if his family were there, offer my condolences.'

'It's customary to phone, Doctor, or to write. Not to ransack the home of the deceased. Why did you take his medical notes from the hospital?'

'I needed to know his address.' They had her bag; there was no possible benefit to be gained from lying here. *Save up the lies.* The line popped into her head, from her schooldays, when she had been caught stealing from the kitchens. The absurd congruity between the two situations – being hectored, in both cases, by a well-spoken woman determined to seem disappointed rather than angry – made her grin suddenly. Blake looked momentarily surprised, then cast his eyes down at his knuckles where they rested on the table.

'Why did you go to Thorne's house?'

'I've told you. I wanted to offer my condolences. There might have been family I didn't know about.' The lie sounded thin, even to her.

'Why not ask the officer who was waiting outside on your first visit?'

'I wanted to see for myself.'

'Why lie about your name to him, then? That's hardly how most mourners behave.'

'It's none of his business who I am.'

'Dr Hopper – Ellen – you had no right to be there.'

'Neither did you. I didn't see any badges on the two men you had searching the place.'

'Sometimes, Doctor, a little discretion is necessary in the prosecution of the law. The fact remains that you are under suspicion of breaking and entering. The penalty for this crime – after trial, of course – is transportation.'

Hopper knew what kind of trial Warwick was referring to. Soon after the Stop, the British judicial system had been reformed with little protest into an administrative arm of the state's labour policy. She had read once that before the Slow, some trials had taken weeks. These days they lasted ten minutes; some took five. Acquittal was almost non-existent, the idea of a jury as archaic as a horse-drawn plough.

'So what do you want to know?'

'We know you went to visit one of Thorne's colleagues. Graham Chandler.'

'What makes you think that?'

'He rang us, not long after you arrived.'

She thought back to the creaking stairs in Chandler's house, after he had gone to make the tea.

'Thorne had mentioned him to me in the past. I wanted to break the news of Thorne's death to him personally.'

'With some cock-and-bull story about being from the newspapers?'

'I lied to him. I wanted to know more about Thorne.' Hopper put her elbows on the table. 'So transport me.'

'I don't want to. It would be a shame. And your record of service to the state' – Warwick gestured at the thin file she had brought in with her – 'is something to be very proud of. We're just trying to solve this little matter to everyone's satisfaction.' She moved her mouth into a smile. 'So why were you there?'

Hopper paused. 'I've already told you.'

'Come along.'

'I'm serious. I took Thorne's medical notes because I wanted to visit his house and see it for myself. That's it.' *Stop talking; the liar is condemned by her need to embroider. Each extra lie is a new strand in the rope they will use to hang you.*

'Your association with him goes back some years, I believe.'

'He taught me at university. I haven't seen him since I left.'

'Then why did he want to see you?'

'I don't know.'

Warwick leant forward. 'Dr Hopper. I know our acquaintance hasn't been smooth so far. Nobody wants you to be in this cell. I want you to succeed, and I want this country to be made safe from harm. Thorne was not a healthy man. It's in our interest and yours to find out the truth about his activities in his later years. So I ask you, from that simple position, trusting you will do the right thing: what did he try to give you?' She moistened her lips as she breathed.

'I don't know what you mean. I hadn't heard from him since I left university: that was fifteen years ago. He didn't try to give me anything then or now.'

Warwick looked at her and sighed, a disappointed teacher once again. She opened the file in front of her and pulled a paper out. 'As you wish, Doctor. If you are determined to be unhelpful ...'

'I'm not being unhelpful. I'm telling you the truth.'

Warwick spoke over her. ' ... we will give you more time to think. Lots more time.' She signed the piece of paper in front of her. 'Your employment on the Westerly 12 rig is terminated, immediately.'

'What?'

'Your belongings will be sent back here. Your results will be—'

'You can't just do that. I don't work for your department.'

'You're not working for anyone any more, Doctor.'

'But ...' Hopper was panicking now, 'my work. My work on the currents. It's important.'

'Only to you. Perhaps others will take it on, if anyone with sufficient interest can be found. And I can guarantee you won't ever find another job in science. Perhaps you can work on the solar farms. They always need new labourers.'

Warwick paused, and licked her lips again. Hopper was fighting for breath.

'You might make your way back to the rig, of course. If you remembered anything else about your time with Dr Thorne.'

And there it was. The offer of safety if she helped them. She could go back to the rig. She would see Harv again, could stay studying the currents and living on her island, semi-detached from this crumbling world.

She could feel the photograph inside her bra, scratching her skin. With surprise, she realised she didn't want to go back if it meant giving it up. Whatever it was.

'I've told you everything I can. You're just wasting your time.'

Warwick took a little watch from her top pocket and consulted it. 'As you wish. Other work calls me away. We'll speak again. But for the time being, I will leave you with Inspector Blake.' She stood, picked up her glass of water, and drained it. 'A shame.' She walked to the door and knocked. The bolts slid back, and unknown hands pulled it open.

Before leaving, Warwick looked back into the room. The strip light behind her head in the corridor gave her a sickly yellow halo. 'I hope you remember, Doctor, why we do the things we do. We are making this nation whole again. And we will succeed. Don't forget that.'

As she moved away, the door closed and the bolts slid home again. Immediately, with a fluid grace, Blake stood, slid the table aside, and punched Hopper hard in the stomach.

The force of the blow propelled her from the chair, and she landed awkwardly on her shoulder, hands still bound before her, unable to break her fall. Her shoulder took the brunt of it, but her head still landed hard on the concrete. For a few seconds she was dazed, too muzzy to register anything except an incipient wetness on her cheek. Then, as the pain started to flood her torso, Blake hauled her off the floor, righted the chair, placed her back in it, and returned to his own. She sat, slumped, still struggling for her breath.

'What did you take? Where did you hide it?'

She tried to speak. Anything that would defer the next blow until she could ready herself.

'I ... I didn't take anything. You can search my bag. I haven't got anything—'

He was already upright again. This time she readied her stomach muscles. But instead of punching her, he placed his foot on her chair, between her legs, and gave it a violent thrust. She shot back. The chair hit the wall first, followed by her head, and once again she fell sideways, on the same side as last time. There was a thin rivulet of blood making its way down her temple. She could taste blood too; she must have bitten her tongue. She thought she heard muffled laughter from behind the mirror.

Again the abrupt pull from the floor; again the replacement of her chair beneath her. Blake moved around and leant on the back of his own chair. He repeated the question.

'What did you take, and where did you hide it?' He was furious, this man. He was itching to hit her again, would probably do so even if she told him what he wanted to hear.

'I didn't ... take anything.' It was an effort to talk. Her tongue was thick; her stomach was on fire. She was still recovering her breath from the first blow. She focused on a little bead of yellow paint on the floor, studied its contours. 'I didn't hide anything.'

Blake looked at the mirror and smiled, the paper-thin skin around his mouth stretching. His lips were cracked. He reached into his pocket, pulled out a little brass device with three finger holes, and placed it delicately on the table. 'Come along now. Or I'll use this for a bit. And after that we'll start working on those hands of yours.'

'Please. I don't understand what I'm supposed to know.' She tried to hide the tiny things she had learnt in the back of her mind, Thorne's letter, and the man Gethin and the bookshop and the photograph, but it was no good, she could feel them swelling in her mind, and she knew that one or two more blows and the surface might crack.

'I'm sorry. I told Warwick everything. That's it.' She felt herself beginning to believe her own story. Better. It was so close to the truth, it could surely hold. She focused again on the little dab of yellow paint on the floor.

Blake stood and pulled the brass ring over his fingers. 'Your choice.' He began moving towards her – then stopped at three loud knocks on the door. He moved across to open it, leant out of the room. Another voice spoke, low and urgent. Blake looked back at her, regret commingling with dislike. 'Be seeing you,' he said, and slipped from the room.

20

Her brother was waiting outside, standing by his car and smoking. He was holding her bag. As he saw her, he started; she wondered how bad she must look.

'Jesus. Ellie.' He dropped his cigarette, forgot to stub it out.

'Hi, Mark.'

He gave her a small, tentative embrace, which hurt her bruised ribs so much she grimaced. Her wrists still chafed with the marks of the handcuffs.

After Blake had left, two guards from the next room had taken her from the cell to a little medical chamber at the end of the corridor; it held a hospital bed, a huge array of bottles, and a cheerful, matronly orderly, who smiled brightly and chatted as she cleaned the cut on Hopper's head. She wondered what other horrors had passed through that room, whether the orderly ever lost her composure.

'What happened? Where did they put you? Jesus, I was worried. What the fuck happened?'

She had lost track of time; it was late evening, she saw from his wristwatch. The clouds had cleared; the sun was gradually warming up the cars again.

'I'm fine, Mark. I'm just tired.' She pulled open the passenger door and sat inside. He opened his door and sat beside her.

'Seriously, Ellie, what the fuck happened? Did you get in a fight?'

She couldn't help smiling. 'Yeah, Mark. I got in a fight. But to give the other guys a chance, I let them tie my hands first.'

'But—'

'Let's just go, can we? Or I'll walk, and take my chances with the night wagons.'

He started the engine and pulled out of the car park onto the Embankment, towards the bridge.

The bank of the Thames rolled past her window. Every so often they would pass a bored-looking guard, slowly waving through the afternoon traffic. It must be better being bored in London than being one of the poor bastards patrolling the Highlands. She'd heard that when the insurgents up there caught a soldier, they would wire the corpse to a mine. Most units didn't have minesweepers, or enough expertise to defuse them, so you had to watch your colleagues rot on every patrol.

'We'll be home in about ten minutes, I'd say.'

'OK.' *Home.* She didn't have a home. She had had a little monkish cell at the rig, and now she didn't even have that. Christ,

Warwick had taken her job. Fifteen years of work, studying the currents, trying to make sense of the chaos, and it had been taken away in a second. How would she live? How would she eat?

The streets were thick with people; the crowds around Brixton as busy as they had been when she arrived. Hopper shrank in her seat as they drove, embarrassed by the luxury of a car.

When they reached the house, Mark reversed into the drive, and sat back in his seat. The front gate slid shut behind him automatically.

'Ellie, what is going on?'

'I don't want to talk about it.'

'When you didn't come home this evening, I asked a friend to look up any possible admissions: hospitals, police stations. You came in to Scotland Yard about twenty minutes before he started searching. It's lucky I had a friend on the desk. Christ, it's lucky I knew who to call. You could have ...' He was breathing hard. His hands reflexively gripped the steering wheel, and let go.

'Could have what, Mark? Could have been killed, by your colleagues?'

'For pity's sake. We don't kill people. I don't.'

'You know Warwick, don't you?'

He reddened. 'We've met four or five times. Seminars, functions, that sort of thing. She's senior to me, El. She's senior to the whole department.'

'Well, next time, maybe you should let her know her pet goon beat me up. He was about to do much worse when you arrived.'

'Christ. It shouldn't have happened. They probably didn't know who you were.'

'They knew exactly who I was. That's why that woman came to question me.'

'Well …' He looked out to the right awkwardly.

'Well what?'

He'd clearly mastered his discomfort, because he said it anyway. 'Why were you in that house in the first place?'

'I'm not going to talk about it.'

'Why did you run?'

'Mark, I'm not going to tell you anything.' Her wrist was throbbing from where she had hit the floor; she was very tired suddenly. The tide of adrenaline of Thorne's house, of the station, even of Blake's blows, seemed to have receded all at once. 'And if I did, I'd have to report you to Warwick so she could beat it out of you.'

'Oh, for God's sake.' He pulled the keys from the ignition, petulant. 'I've told them to leave you alone.'

'That's gracious.'

'But I want you to stop whatever you're doing. Promise me.'

Hopper's whole body hurt. She couldn't even let her head loll back against the seat, because of the hen's-egg bruise at the back of her skull. She sighed. 'Yes, Mark. I promise.'

He looked relieved. 'Thank you. I'll pass that on.'

As well as being a bad liar, the lovely thing about Mark was that he never knew when he was being lied to.

Inside the house, the older of Mark's children, Tom, was still up.

'Auntie Ellie! Auntie Ellie!' He threw himself at her, and surveyed her gravely. 'Did you fall over?'

She smiled. 'I did. Very silly of me.'

He leant closer, conspiratorial, and whispered in her ear: 'Daddy fell over in the garden and he said a bad word and I heard it.'

'Really? Oh dear. Well, I hope you haven't remembered it.'

He squirmed with glee. 'I have.'

Laura walked in. 'Come on, darling, time for bed,' she said, and then caught sight of Hopper. She visibly blanched; Hopper had to restrain a laugh. 'Ellie. Christ. Are you all right?'

'I'm fine. I'm sure Mark will tell you all about it.' She felt a little bad for enjoying her sister-in-law's evident discomfort quite as much as she did.

'You should … Well, Mark's looking after you. There's food on the hob. Mark, do you have a moment?' Laura withdrew, taking Tom with her, and Mark followed.

Hopper ate alone.

As she was finishing the meal – some sort of vegetable hash; clearly they weren't quite wealthy enough to eat meat every single day – Mark walked into the kitchen. He allowed himself the luxury of stepping up and down a couple of times, a kind of physical throat-clearing to gather his audience's fullest attention.

'Ellie, if you're mixed up in something, I can help. We can arrange for you to be moved, or … we can bring other people in if needs be. I can pull all sorts of strings. My point is, you're not alone.' Her instinctive thought rebuked him: *I am, I am.*

But he looked so grave, so sincere, that she nearly told him Thorne had wanted to show her something before his death. And then, just as quickly, a gate in her mind closed against him.

'Mark, it's been a busy day. I just want to sleep.'

She saw him swallow a tiny flash of irritation – really, it was amazing he had got anywhere in Security with such transparent features. 'Fine, fine. Sleep on it. But I want to ask you again in the morning. We can get you back to the rig.'

'Too late for that.'

'What do you mean?'

'Warwick. She fired me.'

'Oh.' He looked deflated for a moment. 'But maybe that'll be in your favour. If there were people on the rig who were—'

'Leading me astray? It's mostly soldiers and nuclear physicists there. When was the last time soldiers overthrew a democratic government for their own ends? Present circumstances excepted, of course.'

That did it. 'That's the kind of talk to get you in trouble, Ellie. I'll let you get some rest. You know what I think and you've told me you'll leave it alone.' He said the words as though speaking for an invisible audience. The possibility crossed her mind that he might have bugged his own kitchen.

'Goodnight, Mark.' Hopper left him alone and withdrew upstairs. It was quiet up here: now was a good time to hide the photo of Thorne and his colleagues. She retrieved it from her clothes and looked around the room. There was nowhere good enough. She went back out onto the landing, where there was a little side table bearing a few ornaments. At the back, there was a gap between two pieces of wood just big enough to jam the photo into. It was a risk leaving it out here; then again, it felt like a bigger risk to leave it in her room, or carry it on her. She retreated to bed feeling oddly vulnerable now the photo wasn't on her person.

Twenty minutes later, she realised she was thirsty, and padded back downstairs. Her brother had not come up yet. The only light on the ground floor came from under a heavy oak door, a room she remembered as a small second parlour. On placing her ear to it, she heard the murmur of Mark's voice, too indistinct to make out any words, and she silently moved upstairs again and tried to sleep.

After half an hour of wakefulness, her mind still too over-whelmed for sleep, she opened the shutters in her room, and looked out at the bright night. Somewhere, an exhausted blackbird sang. Barring that, it was quiet.

They wouldn't know she had the photo. And there was some-thing else: the lawyer's card she had spotted at Thorne's house. Stephanie Clayford, that was her name. Tomorrow morning she would visit her, and then go over to that bookshop, Fisher's. It wasn't as if she had anywhere else to go now.

Eventually, she slept, and found herself at the bow of the boat she had discovered two days ago, moving across a black-ened, charred ocean. From the front came a crunching noise. She looked ahead, and saw: the sea was not water. It was a dark, glis-tening carapace, ground by the boat's motion into thousands of glittering shards like insects' shells. From the closed hatch behind her there came the sounds of movement. There were hundreds of people down there, the dead, demanding her attention. And she knew too that her mother was somewhere among them: already one of their number, already beyond help.

She turned, and walked towards the hatch, wanting to hold it down, knowing the people down there would overwhelm the boat as they emerged from its innards. It was no good: she saw the door rising like treacle against her will, saw desperate hands beginning to claw out of it, the nails on the fingers shredded, the skin like parchment tearing on the rough deck. She woke, and stared at the ceiling, dry-eyed, a knot in her throat.

21

Hopper woke shortly before seven, her alarm jerking her from a dream she couldn't remember. Her body was aching. She could hardly move her shoulder as she dressed, and a patch of her cheek was sore and swollen. She startled herself in the mirror; her skin was pale through tiredness unmended by sleep, one eye unexpectedly reddened. She washed, and to cover her bruises applied make-up inexpertly, long out of practice.

Before going to bed last night, she had gone through her bag. It was in no greater disarray than usual: her envelope of money was intact, her papers in place. Even the little amulet she'd taken from the hold of the fishing boat was still there, upside down between a tub of sunblock and an unopened compact. It still had a little dirt on it, and she wiped it off before she could consider whether it was organic.

Once dressed, she padded downstairs, shoes held in her hand. The door to Mark and Laura's room was closed as she passed it. She tiptoed through the hall, unbolted the door and slipped from the house. She left no note.

She wondered if she was to be followed this morning; casually, she walked up and down, a hundred metres each side of the house, looking behind the wheels of parked cars, but saw nobody. The street was boiling. The night had clearly been cloudless, and the morning was too. As she walked to the bus, she felt the first prickle of sweat under her arms.

The buses were running already, and she boarded one bound for Temple. The queuing crowds were poor: Europeans, mostly, muttering in little cliques. French, German, Spanish; the pitiable survivors of the continent's collapse, tolerated as serfs and kept uncertain about their status.

She wondered sometimes how bad it must be on the continent to prompt so many people from those areas to stay in Britain, living cramped and miserable lives of constant work without prospect of respite. Those permitted to stay were here on sufferance, as though the host nation was granting them the enormous favour of letting them work fourteen-hour days in solar fields or fertiliser pits. Nor were they secure. All it would take was a tweak of bureaucracy and the guarantees of the past would vanish like the foam lapping at the country's shores.

She remembered the arrival of the Swiss. The constant sunlight had melted their glaciers within a few years. Some thirty thousand of them had come – unlike the vast majority of other arrivals, they had been welcome, an orderly people queuing for entry, trusted partners, practically pre-assimilated. It had all been arranged in advance with Davenport's government, on terms unknown. Guns, probably.

Hopper had seen the convoy from her posting on the east coast. They had filed ashore in Felixstowe looking unwell – a landlocked people relieved to be off the water. They had been filtered through the huge steel gates like krill through a whale's teeth, sorted by the leviathan machine of the state into separate channels, channels for security and registration and pathogen sprays, and they had meekly submitted to it, exhausted and dirty.

A few doubtless remained sweating in the high Alps, hunting the few poor livestock that were left and regressing to itinerant scrapers of the soil. Their children would be illiterate, their grand-children half dumb; a few generations from now, they might be little better than hunter-gatherers.

The Americans had it bad too these days, of course. Stories of privation and war had reached even the rig. The children of the old southern counties' original residents had been taught to hate the people they blamed for the Southern Clearances; frequent attacks with nasty little bombs were launched against the inter-lopers from the west. The Americans were constantly recruiting for their defences: men, women, young, old. On the rare occa-sions Hopper had met any, there was a huge sadness about them. The land that had birthed them was now rejecting them.

Two women behind her were talking in low voices. Hopper stared out of the window, straining her ears.

'I heard the Fifth are losing the north badly. They lost an entire company last month. Got drawn right into a gully and slaughtered.'

'I heard that. My sister sends cards sometimes. They censor them but they can't disguise the strain. Her writing's hardly legible.'

'You noticed they widened the bands again? They lowered the training age to thirteen last month. *Thirteen*. Jesus. My nephew's thirteen, he can hardly tie his laces.'

Her stop was approaching. At the door, she turned and looked: the women wore coats, but beneath one she saw camouflage colours. For a moment she panicked, thinking she was being followed; but after the bus had pulled away, she waited in a doorway, and everyone else who had disembarked dispersed. Of yesterday's men there was no sign.

Temple's buildings had remained smart. The area had been – still was – rich in lawyers. The street Hopper needed was tucked away somewhere in the little warren below the main road; but it was still only just before eight. She settled into a café, ordered breakfast, and sat smoking and reading *The Times*, turning the pages awkwardly with her less painful arm. Progress on New Tower Bridge was brisk; a new cross-border force would cooperate with the Americans to stamp out terrorism; a new feed factory would help double livestock numbers within four years.

Outside, sirens rose and fell. Her thoughts drifted away from the paper. Was the photograph hidden back at her brother's house the thing Thorne had wanted to show her? And if so, why was it so important? Where had he left the box in the picture? If she was lucky, the lawyer, Stephanie Clayford, would know.

Soon after nine, she paid and left. Again she perused the street, walked a circuitous route. She noticed nothing. If she was being followed, it was being done more subtly than yesterday. Maybe Mark really had intervened, helped call Warwick and Blake off.

She found the street where Thorne's lawyer had her office; had misremembered the number but nonetheless found a little pennant with *Clayford* written on it in thick copperplate. She rang the bell and a voice answered:

'Yes?' It was a female voice, guarded.

'Hello. I'm a friend of one of your clients. I'm hoping to—'

'Name?'

'I'd prefer not to say.'

A pause, to convey irritation, then: 'First floor.' The door buzzed.

Stephanie Clayford's office was up a flight of creaking, uneven stairs, the walls lined with murky brown watercolours. Hopper knocked. After thirty seconds she knocked again, and a pretty young woman answered the door.

'Yes?' The woman looked startled before mastering herself; she even made a little involuntary movement to close the door. Hopper had forgotten her appearance.

'I'm here to see Ms Clayford.'

'Do you have an appointment?'

'I'm afraid not.'

'Will she know what it's about?'

'I'd rather talk to her directly.'

'Wait here, please.'

She closed the door. Within a second, she had reopened it. 'She won't see you without a name.'

'Tell her it's about Edward Thorne.'

Back she went. After another little wait she opened the door again. 'Ms Clayford will see you in a minute. Please wait here.' She gestured to a small, hard sofa.

No matter how dingy the stairwell, the office spoke of affluence. In one corner of the high-ceilinged room was a small desk, scrupulously neat; in another was a large wall-to-ceiling cupboard holding hundreds of files, spines delicately pencilled with names. Two sofas for clients; a long, low coffee table. Near the secretary's desk, a tall, dark door led to what was presumably Clayford's private office.

She was clearly affluent, this woman; one of the last survivors of an endangered species, the wealthy lawyer. Most lawyers these days made their money in property. After the Stop, the mess of forced requisitions, reallocations, inheritances and entailments had provided fertile soil for anyone willing to toe the government's line as necessary.

One of the prime minister's boasts was that the law of England had survived unscathed; and if you looked at it from the right angle, that was almost true. Most lawyers dealt with property and death; working out how to parcel out the goods of the dead and preserve the land of the living.

Hopper tried to make conversation. 'Busy morning?'

Clayford's secretary was polite and uninterested. 'It will be. Ms Clayford will be free in a minute.'

And sure enough, a little buzzer on her desk crackled shortly, and the secretary took Hopper through. Another high ceiling, another ornate desk.

Edward Thorne's lawyer was a tall woman, perhaps fifty years old, dressed in a pale grey suit. She moved around the desk as Hopper entered, shook her hand, and gestured to two chairs in the corner.

'Have you been offered a drink?'

'Thank you, I'm fine.'

She nodded. 'A coffee for me, please, Natalie.' The secretary bobbed and left; Clayford surveyed her blandly as she went, then turned her attention back to Hopper.

'So. You need a lawyer.'

'Not exactly.'

She smiled. 'A leading question. Forgive me. Why don't I let you start?'

'Thank you. A friend of mine' – Hopper hated using the word, but it was the easiest way of putting it – 'has just died. I think you represented him.' Clayford had been smiling slightly; now the smile faded into a smooth mask of polite, blank attention. 'Edward Thorne.'

The mask remained still. 'I see.'

'Did you represent him?'

Another pause. 'I did. How did you know him?'

'He taught me at university. We lost touch. And yesterday …' She gave the basics only: the hospital, the house. She didn't mention the photograph, or Thorne's dying words – in fact, she said nothing Warwick didn't know already, in case Clayford repeated their conversation at a later date. As she spoke, Natalie moved in, placed a coffee at Clayford's elbow, and left wordlessly. As she reached the door, she turned and gave the lawyer a look; Clayford shook her head a fraction.

Eventually Hopper finished her truncated version of events, and added, nervously, 'I'm just trying to find out anything more I can about him. I hope you understand.'

Clayford pulled over a pad, slowly drawing her fountain pen across the cream of the paper, and spoke as she did so.

'Dr Hopper. I remain Edward Thorne's lawyer until the final execution of his will. As such, the estate of Edward Thorne is my only interest, and my sole duty is to carry out his wishes in accordance with that will. I cannot tell you anything else about him. He is my client; you are not. I hope you understand.'

She slid the pad across the desk. On it she had written, in a looping cursive hand, *Wait on the stairs*. Hopper looked up and Clayford held a finger to her lips, before adding: 'You seem disappointed, but please remember: I am simply doing my job. If you ever have a lawyer, you will be grateful if they are as discreet with your affairs as I have been with those of my own client. Is there anything else?' She shook her head at Hopper, who replied in a voice quite unlike her own:

'No. I see. Sorry to have troubled you today, Ms Clayford.'

'I'll ask Natalie to show you to the door. Goodbye.' Clayford pressed the buzzer, then walked to the mantelpiece and opened a cigarette case. As Hopper rose, the lawyer pulled out a cigarette, and gestured to her once more, mouthing: *One minute*.

Hopper waited on the stairs, staring at a dingy landscape of an underfed horse. After a minute, Clayford joined her there, and nodded at the picture.

'Miserable, isn't it? These all belong to the landlord. I'd cheerfully chop them up for kindling.' She dragged on the cigarette and offered Hopper one.

Hopper could only stare at her.

'Sorry about that. All I can say is that I assure you, Thorne's house is not the only place they have been looking.'

'Here?'

Clayford nodded. 'I come in at about seven each morning. When I arrived yesterday, the lock was damaged. So Natalie and I have been conducting a little survey.'

'How do you know it was Thorne they were interested in?'

'The little that did go – it was on my desk – related to him. They made a silly effort to conceal it, took some other files, but it was pretty obvious. Anyway, the good news is that they didn't find his personal file.'

'Why not?'

She smiled. 'I happen to have taken it home to read last night. I was informed of his death by the hospital and wanted to familiarise myself with his will. I admired him.'

'Why did they want it?'

Clayford shrugged. 'I work with clients who require delicacy. They may have unknown second families, trusts for children their new wives never learnt about … Most importantly, I help people with their assets – sometimes undeclared ones. It's helpful to have a parcel of land for one's old age.'

'Did Thorne have anything like that?'

Clayford looked up at the ceiling. 'How do I know you're not from Internal Security?'

'If I am, then this is the most pleasant way I'd get it out of you.'

'And if you're not, I'm jeopardising my practice and my liberty when they catch up with you. From the look of you, they already have.'

She blew smoke out above their heads, then looked back at Hopper. 'Why tell you anything?'

'I just want to know what they're looking for, and it occurred to me that Thorne might have entrusted you with something for safekeeping. Was there anything?'

Clayford shook her head. 'He was almost unique among my clients in that whatever he had to hide, he was happier not telling me about it. I wouldn't be surprised if he hired me simply as a front, so his records appeared in perfect order.'

'What are you going to do about his will?'

'I'm going to leave it on my desk, and if the police call, fully aid them with any enquiries they may have.' Clayford looked back at the painting. 'And then, after a week or so vocally establishing my innocence in that office, I'll get an electrician in to tell me if I've had any undeclared attendees at my meetings.'

Hopper decided to take a risk. 'Thorne had something he wanted me to have. If he did – if I'm right – is there anything else you can think of?

'He once asked about our security arrangements for storing small objects. But when I told him, he didn't take up our offer.'

'When was that?'

'Fifteen years ago.'

Hopper had already known what the answer would be. That was around the time of his sacking. She thought about the box again. Maybe he'd considered leaving it here. 'Thank you for your help with all this.'

Clayford made to go, then turned back. 'I won't give you my card. I'm sure you understand. Good luck.'

And with that she loped off upstairs, two at a time, her long legs moving like pistons.

Hopper was back on the street. Leaving the office building was like hitting a wall of warmth; the external door handle was almost uncomfortably hot to touch. It was busy, too; the streets were thronged.

She made her way back to the café she had sat in earlier, a cheerful place of orange walls and an elegant curved glass counter, and sat with a coffee. She couldn't concentrate.

She offered money to the café manager: again was permitted the use of a phone, and rang *The Times*.

'David?'

'Yes?' He was terse.

'Do you have a minute?'

'Yes. But we've just finished conference. I have a lot to do.'

'Sorry to bother you. Is the line safe?'

'Nothing's perfect. But it's pretty reliable.'

'I need you to search for one other person.'

'Go on.'

'His name's Thomas Gethin. He was in Home Affairs, Thorne's old department. Then he moved to Security. But that was fifteen years ago.'

'Anything else?'

'He must be about forty-five now. He was one of Thorne's assistants. Everyone else was sacked with Thorne; he's the only one who wasn't. I think he might be able to help.'

'They take rather a dim view of us ringing up and asking for the employment history of senior government officials. I'll start with general population records. Then I guess I can start hunting elsewhere.'

'Thank you. Anything you can find. Why are you so busy, anyway?'

'Oh, everything. There's a big push happening in the Midlands. And there's all sorts going on with the Americans. Davenport's visited three times in the last month. And Harry's missing.'

Her stomach lurched. 'Missing?' She had had Harry's notes for Thorne's obituary in her bag when they searched it. He must have been arrested because of that. Oh Christ. *Christ.*

David continued. 'He's not at work, and his wife hasn't seen him. He's never done anything like this before. So we're fucked for obituaries.' He sounded worried.

'Will he be all right?'

He must have heard the distress in her voice. 'What do you mean?'

She couldn't say it over the phone. It had been stupid even mentioning Gethin.

'Can we meet?'

'There's so much to do here.'

'Please, David. This is important.'

A pause.

'All right. Meet me in Regent's Park.' He gave her a time, a little gruffly, and rang off.

After a tussle with the operator over making a call outside the country, she managed to get through to the rig. Schwimmer answered. She asked for Harv, embarrassed at having to make the request to the senior officer. Coolly amused, he sent someone to fetch Harv from the deck.

'Hello, Hop. What's new?'

She told him about the burglary at Thorne's house and her arrest, glossing over the beating. Harv whistled.

'Jesus. Get back here, won't you?'

'No, I'm staying.'

'Why?'

'I just am. For a few more days.' She didn't want to tell him yet that she'd lost her job. She didn't really want to believe it herself. 'But I have a question. Are you alone in the office?'

'Yeah. Schwimmer's wandered off somewhere.'

'Can you see the duty logs from where you are?'

'Let's see …' She pictured him reaching up to the high shelf where Schwimmer kept the logs. 'Yes. They're here.'

'Can you check a date? Tell me who was on duty then?'

'Sure.' She told him the time and day Thorne had phoned the rig. 'On duty that morning was … let's see … it was Schwimmer himself.'

'Then he's the one who stopped Thorne getting through to me when he phoned.'

'Why?'

'I don't know. And I don't know why this woman Warwick would let me see Thorne if they'd previously stopped him contacting me. It doesn't make sense.' She leant her head against the wall.

'In the nicest way, Hop, just come home. Keep doing your work. Whatever this is, it's not worth the risk to you.' She heard the strain in his voice and felt touched. If she ever made it back to the rig, after this was all over, she would take him – take their relationship – more seriously.

'I can't explain, Harv. I just have to stay here.'

'What are you going to do next?'

She paused. 'I don't know.' She didn't say what she thought: that she couldn't tell him, even though she wanted to, in case they had intercepted the rig's incoming line.

'Sure.' She heard a scuff on the receiver. 'Hey, Schwimmer's coming back. I'd better go.'

'Thanks, Harv. For everything.'

'Look after yourself.' The phone clicked.

There was a lump in her throat. She pictured some listener along the line taking note of her weakness: *Seemed emotional.* Outside, London's rush hour was dying down. She felt tired suddenly. She had no home, no job, nowhere to retreat to. She was dominated by powers far superior to her own, and with only one small clue to what Thorne had wanted her to see.

Unless she could track down Thorne's old colleague, Thomas Gethin.

It was only ten thirty. Time to visit the bookshop Thorne had phoned on his last day of freedom, before he went into hospital. There was a chance the owner, Fisher, could help her somehow. She left the café and moved cautiously back into the street, looking around for familiar faces.

22

Her route to Fisher's bookshop was erratic; she went too far west along the Strand, and had reached Trafalgar Square before she knew where she was. She looked over it again, just as she had on her first day here. The top of the square was lined with stalls selling all manner of plastic junk from the last century: the detritus of another world, now missold as useful in this one. Above the stalls, the amputated column met no reflection in the fountains below. They were left unfilled except on state days, when a few inches of water were pumped in. The fourth plinth with its statue of Britannia looked far too new; jokers said it resembled Davenport.

Hopper rather liked the column. She had never known the original, which had been cut off – some bomb or something – in the year of her birth. Davenport had made noises about restoring

it, just as he had claimed the old Ferris wheel would be disman-
tled from its current spot, grotesquely folded and trailing into
the Thames. Nothing had been done about either. Part of her
suspected he liked these vistas of decay; that the thought of presiding over the last nation on earth held a romantic appeal for him
just as strong as the idea of reconstruction.

The area north of the old hotel at Charing Cross had hardly
changed. The streets were narrow and tall; the stones were
bleached on the sunny side and dark on the other, mosses and
algae petering out as they approached the light. Here, behind
the old theatres, a thriving little world had built up that shrank
just as emphatically from the sunlight. She had heard that under
these streets there lived men and women so averse to the sun
they remained pale even now. They grew mushrooms in the base-
ments of abandoned buildings, and slept in a subterranean maze
of tunnels and old utility shafts.

Hopper found the entrance to Cecil Court, and walked past
it, nonchalant. It looked abandoned. She stepped into the quiet
street. Halfway along, she glanced back. Nobody was standing
on the main road looking in: no Blake slipping a brass ring over
his fingers, no tweed-clad Warwick smiling artificially. And there
was the shop she was looking for – Fisher's Books. It had a dim-
painted wooden frontage, and a sign carved in the shape of a fish
– the ichthus symbol.

She paused a moment, taking a breath. Stephanie Clayford
had told her that Thorne had not entrusted her with an object or
a secret to keep safe. Maybe Fisher's Books would yield more.
Maybe the box in Thorne's photograph was somewhere in the

building. She remembered Thorne's words – *you always wanted the truth* – and pushed the door.

Her entrance rang a bell above her. The shop's interior was dark, and full, the air heavy with unfamiliar scents. The books ran from floor to ceiling, three deep on the shelves, crammed between cases in whatever gaps could be found. Even the plate-glass windows were blockaded above her height with more piles.

The few small areas of free floor space were hemmed by stacks of volumes; some climbing the cases that supported them like muscular ivy, some teetering and precarious. At the back, an open doorway led to a passageway disappearing into murk. The ceiling had sallowed until it was almost the same colour as the stalagmites of yellow paper rising from the floor.

Nobody had arrived in response to the bell, and the desk at the front was abandoned, finger-deep in more papers and studded with half-full mugs of tea. The milk in the mugs had coalesced at their surfaces, drifting across them like a pale algal bloom.

How did Fisher make his living? Some people must come for paperbacks from before the Stop. And there were a couple of hundred new novels printed each year – various combinations of adventure, romance and propaganda. A few positioned themselves squarely amid the Stop, and based their action around that. Most ignored it, setting themselves in prelapsarian versions of the past that only a diminishing number of readers would even remember.

She moved through the shop towards the back. Halfway along – she realised now that it was a clumsily converted house – stairs sprouted upwards, narrow and unlit. She continued to the rear of the building. After the corridor, the place opened into what must have once been a back parlour.

The books changed here. Where the front had held fiction, this room was full of books about – she looked up at the sign, one corner torn off – *Lifestyle*. Books about houses, how to build one's own home or buy one better than the one you had. How to improve one's relationship, how to love oneself, how to be thin, how to be rich.

One corner was exclusively given over to books of recipes, stuffed with ingredients nobody could acquire any more, manners of eating that must have seemed like a calculated insult in the days of famine. The cuisines were alien, the names those of places discussed by adults in her childhood. Lebanon. The Philippines. Vietnam. Here was the lifestyle the world had been forced to abandon, gradually ceded as privation had folded into catastrophe. Here was the biography of the world that had died.

Still no signs of life. Hopper moved back towards the front. At the foot of the stairs, she hesitated. A sign read: *PRIVATE: MANAGEMENT*. She called softly up the stairs: 'Hello?' No reply came.

She moved up. As she climbed, the air grew even warmer than on the ground floor. Her skin prickled, and her thick shirt – so useful on the rig – rubbed at her, heavy with her sweat.

At the top of the stairs there were two doors. The first was ajar, and led to a kitchenette, a cramped and mouldy room with a fridge unit, a freezer and a few low cupboards. The freezer door hung open. On the far side of the room, shielded by a thin curtain, was a bathroom hardly worth the name, consisting mostly of a toilet and a sink. The carpet ran out before it reached them, frayed and blackened at its edge. The patch of tiled floor also held a drain, a bucket and a cake of soap, which might have served as a shower.

Hopper returned to the top of the stairs, to the second door. It was closed, seemingly dark inside – no light came through the cracks onto the dim stairwell. She knocked, and when no reply came, tried the handle. The door moved a little, but sprang back when she stopped pushing. Something heavy was blocking it from the other side. She looked down and saw a tidemark of dark liquid creeping to the edge of the landing carpet, and realised with a lurch of horror what lay behind the door.

Eventually, after a lot of pushing, she was able to squeeze around and into the room. The confirmation of her suspicion made no difference to the wave of nausea it provoked. She had been pushing at the outstretched hand of a man's prone body, which had become wedged under the door as she tried to open it. As she closed it, the hand remained depressed, no blood returning to the pale fingers.

He was sprawled out facing the door, lying on his front. His clothes were unexceptional: slack brown trousers and a casual jacket. Below him there was a dark pool of blood, still sticky. Hopper forced herself to kneel and push the corpse over onto its side. He had been large. After a few seconds of struggling to gain purchase without touching him too much, she abandoned the attempt to give him dignity and rolled him, heaving him onto his back, his left arm folded under him. She sat back, looked for the first time at his face, and had to twist her head away, tasting bile in her throat.

He was – had been – bearded, his scalp thinning and greyed. The left half of his face remained unharmed – the intact cheek was yellowed, puffy, and the eye stared out and up towards the ceiling. The rest of his head was almost unrecognisable. His shirt was soaked in blood. Moving him had disturbed a small throng of flies, which had been walking in the remains of his head, and they buzzed, irked, for a few seconds before settling back down to feed. Hopper really did feel sick now. She groped her way over to the shutters across the window and threw them open, pulled the sash open too, and leant out.

The light and air revived her somewhat. She stayed looking outwards, trying to avoid the man on the floor. This must be the man she had spoken to on the phone yesterday afternoon. Fisher. She remembered a strained quality in his voice. Had she interrupted him after he had first heard someone in the shop? Or had she interrupted the killing? The possibility that the killing had been prompted by her phone call, that the men in Thorne's house had checked the phone records and come straight here, was so distasteful she hardly let it into her mind.

After another minute surveying the bricks opposite her, she turned to look at the rest of the room. It had been an office-cum-bedroom, lined with shelves; a desk and chair sat in one corner, and opposite them was a single mattress on a low frame. Between the desk and the bed were huge cardboard cartons, full of books.

Her gaze was drawn back to the body again and again. Had he been surprised, or greeted by someone he knew? Her mind twitched to Blake, his skin stretched tightly over his skull, itching to use his brass knuckle, and she felt certain it had been him. She thought she could detect his individual brand of violence on Fisher's corpse. Had Warwick been here too? It was hard to envisage her committing violence – but easier, since yesterday, to imagine her requesting it.

She realised there was a long smear of blood on the floor, leading almost to her feet and thickening as it neared the corpse. He had been struck in the chair, still alive, and had crawled towards the door.

Wait. No. The blood curved round to the right. He had been crawling, but not towards the door. He had been aiming at something else.

As the door opened into the room, it skirted three low shelves in a little corner. The bow of blood arced darkly round towards them – he must have collapsed back onto the door with his last movement. She moved over to the shelves and squatted, her gorge rising as her foot brushed Fisher's hand. The body, rolled over from the door to let her in, was now too close to her, and she pushed it – him – back into its original position. His jacket stuck to the flesh beneath.

She had a few square feet to move in now. The books on the shelves were almost all on a single theme. There were a few outliers at the top left – a poetry anthology, a few classic works of fiction – but most were geopolitical tomes, dealing predominantly with the Coldside. *Winter in America. The Next Ice Age. Longitudes of Conflict.* One by one she pulled them down and looked inside.

All were marked *AF* inside the front cover, and annotated in the same hand. Nothing struck her as special; no notes fluttered out as she leafed through them. When they were all out, piled along the floor under the window, she looked at the shelves themselves. The case was not fixed to the wall, but was cut out at its base to fit neatly above the high skirting board. She shoved the pile of books away, and removed the shelving unit from its place.

Behind it, the wall was smooth and intact, the floor solid. There was nothing there of interest – no crack in the floorboards that might be exploited, no safe built into the wall. And then she saw. At the junction between the floor and the wall, a tiny loop of fabric stuck out from the edge of the high skirting board.

She pulled it. A section of the board some two feet long came out from the wall, cracking as it reached the corner. She leant forward – her torso still protesting after yesterday's encounter with Blake – and looked inside. There was something in there. She reached in, dislodging a couple of spiders, and her hand found a long, low metal case. Her breathing was suddenly shallow.

It was a dull tin case, locked. She looked around, found no key, searched in the desk, found a chisel. She inserted it in the tiny gap available to her, gained a little purchase, repositioned the chisel, *pushed* ... and felt the lock crack.

Inside was a smaller box. Not the box from Thorne's photograph, though. This was a radio. It wasn't like the radios they had been issued on the rig – this one had dials she had not seen before, and a small microphone with wires. It was a transmit radio. Outside the armed forces and security services, their ownership was illegal. Hopper extended the radio's aerial, pressed the largest button on its front, careful not to twist the frequency dials, and after a few seconds, music filled the air.

It was an old tune, one of the European classicals. She had heard it once before; it swayed, skipping up and down, leaping up scales, sliding back, surprising and soothing in equal measure. She sat back against the wall, facing the dead man and letting the music surround her. After a minute, the piece ended. A woman's voice filled the air.

'This is Radio Albion. That was Brahms' Fifth Hungarian Dance, performed by the English Symphony Orchestra. The news again: a military engagement outside Harrogate has destroyed a consignment of Trojan tanks being escorted north for the pacification of the Borders. With government forces already pushed from the Hebridean Islands, and stretched tight across Scotland, this means ...'

There followed more news of supply lines intercepted, consignments firebombed, the blundering army harried. Then more music. Hopper had heard of these illegal radio stations. They sheltered on wavelengths inaccessible to the average citizen, broadcasting to almost nobody. Or at least nobody admitted listening to them. The penalty, for listening or broadcasting, was transportation. She snapped the music off. As the room fell into silence, she smelt once again the musty, sharp tang of decay – as though the music had temporarily cleaned the air.

So Fisher had been one of the small, deluded band devoted to bringing down the government. The label 'resistance' hardly applied. Assorted democratists, monarchists and separatists had devoted themselves to the idea of reclaiming the country from the government almost since the Stop. There was little popular appetite for it, then or now. Most people today were too exhausted by survival, never mind rebellion.

Then again, if they were losing troops even in the prosperous north now ... No, for Christ's sake. The upset and misery in the country was not cohesive, was not the sort that would ever swell into the ugly fruit of a popular revolt. It was nothing but the delayed violence of the Slow, the daily wounds engendered by food shortages, and a freshly stoked hatred of anything foreign. The element of foreigner hatred was the least palatable, to Hopper at any rate, perhaps because her parents had both been killed in their own ways by their inability to relinquish their attachments to people unlike themselves.

She looked at the microphone attached to the radio. Had Fisher been a broadcaster? Had he sat up here reporting London's failures, the bombs and the riots and the shortages even in the capital? Was this why he had crawled across the floor in agony, half dead? Was it why Thorne had contacted him in the first place?

On the back of the radio there was a switch: RECEIVE/ TRANSMIT, it said, in small, precise lettering. She pressed it, extended the antenna, and turned the set to the front. Where was the wavelength he had been broadcasting to? Next to one of the dials on the front was a tiny groove, carved into the plastic by a human hand.

She pictured the signal radiating outwards. Was it being caught and filtered along the way? The fact of Fisher's death made it likelier. Then again, they hadn't found his radio.

She tapped the microphone and one of the dials spiked. So the sound was going through. Still she did not trust it. She tapped the microphone again, using the first Morse code message that came into her head. She'd learnt Morse on the rig, during a bored afternoon, and she and Harv would sometimes make each other laugh by tapping messages on the desks during briefings from Schwimmer.

F-I-S-H-E-R-K.

The 'K' was 'over'. She remembered that, God knew from where. Then she switched to Receive, and waited. After thirty seconds, she sent the message again.

F-I-S-H-E-R-K.

And then, from the speaker, there came a voice.

'Who's there?'

The voice was rich, and male, and American. So, as well as listening to banned British stations, Fisher had been in contact with the Americans somehow. She didn't know whether she should speak.

'Fisher? Is that you?'

Hopper realised that whoever these people were, they had been friends of Fisher's. And Fisher had been a friend of Thorne's. So she spoke.

'Fisher's dead. I'm sorry. I found his radio.'

'Dead? Jesus. Who are you?'

'I was coming to see him. I thought he could help me with something. We had a friend in common.'

'How did he die?'

'He was stabbed, I think. Or clubbed.' Her voice was trembling, and she didn't look behind her at the bulk on the floor. 'Who is this?'

'I'm Fisher's receiver in the American Zone.'

'You're in the American Zone? Now?'

'We are.' The voice didn't clarify how many 'we' meant, and Hopper had thought of another question.

'Who was Fisher to you?'

'He was one of our London representatives, although I'm sure you've already guessed that. Who are you?'

'My name's Ellen.'

The voice sounded mistrustful for a second. 'And how do I know you didn't kill Fisher, Ellen?'

'You can't know that. But I didn't. I just found him here.'

The voice paused. 'All right. I guess I'm inclined to believe you, for want of anything else to believe. Are you his contact? Did he give you anything to send?' The voice had an edge to it as it spoke those questions – a kind of strain. A burst of coughing came through the speakers, harsh and wet.

Hopper looked around her at the miserable room. 'I'm afraid I'm not. I just knew someone he was in touch with. There's nothing obvious around here. Even if he had something, they might have taken it after they ...' She gestured to the bulk on the floor, forgetting for a moment that the voice wouldn't see.

'Are you sure there's nothing there? Are you positive? He said there was something big coming when we last spoke. But we've been waiting a long time and it never came through.'

'I think ...' She didn't know why she believed this voice. Something in it – the tired quality, the frustration – made her think it could be trusted. 'I think I'm looking for the same thing.'

'We don't have long, Ellen.'

'No.'

'I'm serious. The conditions here … We need help. Can you keep hold of the transmitter in case you think of a way of helping us?'

'They're not legal on this side.'

'From the sound of your voice it sounds like you're already involved. Legal doesn't matter any more. Or it won't in a few days. Please. Keep hold of it.'

'I'll think about it. Listen.' She'd never had the chance to speak to an American before. 'What's it like where you are?'

'Where we are?' The voice laughed a little, thinly. 'Not so good, Ellen. I'm sure it's no picnic where you are either. But we're really in it right now.' Another cough, and the voice spoke again. 'I need to report this upwards right now. Will you keep the radio? In case?'

'All right. Yes, I will.'

'Thanks, Ellen. Good luck to you.'

'What's your name?'

She spoke too late; the signal had clicked off. She put the radio back in its tin box and looked at it for a second. It would be an unpleasant risk carrying it with her. But she'd taken enough risks already that one more made little difference. And she had said she would. That counted for something. She shoved it into her satchel, before pushing the false panel back into place and returning the books to the shelf.

As she stood and turned to face the door, she noticed a photograph. It was of a graduating Cambridge college, the 2003 year. The young men and women stood locked there in their gowns, clutching their mortarboards and smiling, wholly unaware of the cataclysm to come.

There he was. Two rows from the back, a slender young man with a gentle smile. Adam Fisher. Thorne had graduated in 2004. Fisher would have been a year older, not in Thorne's league academically, but nonetheless, they must have known each other. She turned and looked back into the room. There was no sign she had been present.

She wondered if anyone would find the body. The shop had been left casually open, as though nobody ever came in. Eventually, she supposed, even thieves would take all the flimsy paperbacks they desired. The remaining books would rot or soak, and the time before the Slow would take one more step towards its inevitable final position: a myth.

At the bottom of the stairs, she picked up her jacket and left the shop, turning towards St Martin's Lane. Not long until noon. Her steps carried her south, and she moved past the site of the old opera house – now a community of tent-dwellers, slowly moving around in the gloom inside. Still a few hours before she had to meet David. The sky was overcast, the city descending from blazing sunlight to a prickly, heavy heat.

She found a bench overlooking the top of Trafalgar Square, tore a page from her notebook so she could discard it once it was clear in her mind, and began to write a chronology.

T ill – realises seriously. Writes to EH. Then tries to phone EH on rig. Call blocked. Why?

Internal Security bring EH over to see Thorne, then follow EH's movements. Why bring EH over in first place if T's call blocked?

T contacts Fisher – unsuccessful. Fisher's contact expected something – did not receive. Americans looking too. T in hospital soon after contacting Fisher.

The Last Day

When EH visits, T suggests something in his house she should see.

T's house burgled, then his lawyer.

T may have considered stowing something with lawyer. Did not.

Was picture what T wanted to pass on? Or box? Where did box from picture go?

T's contact Gethin most important person to speak to next. Still working? Why kept on?

Fisher dead.

In the square below, the gulls pecked at each other, occasionally hopping to the edge of the dry fountain and looking in, waiting for water they distantly remembered might one day reappear. She crossed out *dead* after Fisher's name, and substituted it with the proper word: *killed*.

23

'All this work, Ellen ... it's very good. But you're never going to make progress unless you can get out there.'

They were sitting side by side on a bench in Oxford's University Parks, overlooking the river. The river was sitting higher than usual in the muddy groove of its bed: there had been heavy rains to the north and west five days ago. It was March.

'I know. But the department isn't recruiting. They said to come back in two years.' Hopper sighed. 'It's all taking too long.'

Thorne smiled at her, broad and knowing, and she noticed afresh how his smile changed the whole cast of his face, how charming he looked. 'Good thing I've told someone about you, then.'

'Someone? What do you mean, someone?'

Thorne carried on, evenly. 'I've phoned an ex-colleague and told her there's a student she might be interested in, one who's absolutely worth recruiting over the summer.'

'But aren't you ...'

'Aren't I what?'

'In disgrace?'

He gave her a sidelong glance – so long she started to worry she had insulted him – and then laughed. 'I suppose I am. But the fact that I left in a hurry doesn't mean I've lost all my contacts in the building. Write to my friend Hannah – here.' He handed Hopper a card. 'Send her your ideas. She wants to see you.'

The thought of other eyes reading her work panicked her. And now more than ever she realised how much her work here tied up with him; the discomfiting extent to which it was done to win his approval. 'Edward ... this is very kind. Why are you helping me with all this?'

'You'd be a dead loss in the army.'

'Seriously.'

He looked out at the river, oozing past like treacle, and his smile faded.

'You're bright. You ask the right questions. There are enough people learning the ropes of crop science, hydroponics, land work, but we left the sea to the navy. It was stupid. There's almost nobody dealing with the oceans in Environment at the moment. They need ideas. And you have ideas. You could change the whole map of this country. What an achievement for a scientist.'

She felt her face redden. 'Really?'

'Really. I haven't taught for a while, but as far as I can remember I've never had a student like you.'

They sat silent for a few minutes. She couldn't believe he meant it. And she felt something else too: fear. She wasn't going to have Thorne's advice during her summer away. She would be working for people who didn't care whether she succeeded or failed, who only wanted her ideas. Or maybe they wouldn't even want those. They might laugh at her. Eventually, Thorne spoke again.

'Although frankly there's every chance we won't last the century, so it's a pretty big task you're setting yourself.'

'You really think not?'

'Well, it's hard to know, isn't it? Let's take it point by point.' He started counting on his fingers. 'The whole planet's magnetic field is much weaker these days, so we think the atmosphere may be eroding. We think there's a growing hole above the Middle East already, although nobody knows how fast it's expanding and in general we don't know nearly enough about that. Then there's biomass. We don't know the state of vegetation around this side of the planet, never mind the Coldside, so it's hard to make predictions about the oxygen levels. The only thing we do know from the Wojtek expedition is that the desert's still advancing towards us on this side.'

'What do you think we should do?'

Thorne looked at his fingers. 'Well, if by "we" you mean this country, I think we should enact your data-gathering plans for the ocean. There's no harm in knowing as much as we can.' He smiled again. 'And for the rest of it, we wait, and we see if the oxygen in the air declines, and by how much. If it declines by more than a few percentage points, it won't matter much either way after a few decades.'

'So what's the point?'

He shrugged. 'We might have enough oxygen after all. Maybe the world's vegetation is thriving in places we haven't visited. Maybe the atmosphere is hardier than we thought. And then you'd feel foolish at having given up, wouldn't you?'

'You're so optimistic, Edward. I wish I was.' Hopper paused. 'You know, I think I'm going to find it difficult going from here straight to a government department.'

'There's nothing to worry about. Your work is solid.'

'Yes, but ... it's different being here. You're very supportive.'

'Only because your work is good.'

She felt a little affronted suddenly. Here she was, trying to explain – to hint – how much he mattered to her, and he was just turning it into another discussion about work.

'But what if they laugh at me? What if they've already rejected all my ideas for a good reason I haven't thought of yet?'

'They won't. They're sensible people.'

Hopper had resolved to ask Thorne about his work in this week's meeting. Ever since she'd first heard that he'd been fired, she couldn't help wondering why he had left government, why he had been exiled here. And this felt like her opportunity. She took a deep breath. 'You know, I think I'd feel better if I just knew a bit more about what it's like in these departments. Can you give me an example? Something you worked on?'

He gestured, vaguely. 'I'm more interested in your future. My past has little bearing on the breakthroughs I think you can make.'

'I think it would be helpful to me. Maybe there's something you're proud of. Maybe something from your time working with the prime—'

He cut her off. 'The future you're trying to make can't be worse than the past, Ellen. It can't be.' His voice was a little louder and his cheeks a little pinker than usual. 'So we have to make it better. You're one of the few people who can have any effect on it. So let's talk about how you do that instead of dredging up these old matters. This country has been through enough.'

She was angry now. At their first meeting she had told him about her past, her parents. He knew all about her, things she'd never told even her few friends here. And now he was keeping her out. It wasn't a fair exchange.

She spoke again. 'I don't know why you say "this country". Other countries had it much worse than this one. And we're the ones who shut them out. We let the world die.'

His voice was really loud now, loud and ragged. 'We're not talking about this, Ellen. We're here to discuss the ocean. I think your time today would be better spent reading. And I have just the book for you. Here.'

As he leant over from the bench to dig the volume out of his bag, she noticed that his hand was shaking.

The walk to Regent's Park took longer than Hopper had expected. Every couple of hundred metres she ducked into a shop, took an unexpected turn, turned back on herself: all the while scanning vehicles, drivers, faces. She saw nobody familiar. The other pedestrians, the tired shopkeepers lingering in their doorways, the rickshaw boys touting for trade: all gazed impassively back at her, if they met her gaze at all.

Fisher had been in contact with the Americans. And Thorne had been on the brink of getting information to Fisher. So what had Thorne wanted to tell the Americans?

Either way, their efforts had come to almost nothing. Thorne was dead. Fisher was dead. Thorne's home, his lawyer's office, had not yielded whatever Warwick and her men were looking for. The loop was almost closed now. There was no link between the world Thorne had lived in, with whatever secret he had been trying to pass on, and this world.

No link, at least, except Hopper herself.

She arrived with only ten minutes to spare, and noted with pleasure that Regent's Park was largely unchanged since the last time she had been here. The most southerly part of the gardens was still maintained and green, and the large playing fields to the north were still dry scrubland, a world away from the unnatural lushness of the park's lower half.

She and David had often met in Regent's Park when they had first been going out, at the central water fountain, two thirds of the way up the wide boulevard between the city and the biodiversity gardens. They had had an enjoyable little game, finding the largest possible place and developing a shorthand for it. 'Waterloo' had meant not the clock, but the station's north-west steps. 'Paddington' had been the noodle stand at the base of the station's first platform. 'Regent's Park' had meant this spot. A few months ago, she had tried to start a similar game with Harv, but had felt a preposterous sense of semi-adultery and had instantly abandoned it.

The fountain was beautiful – an elegant bit of Victorian absurdity, a rearing edifice of marble and bronze far more ornate and two tons heavier than its function necessitated. It must have felt right at the time: a fountain fit for the gilded capital of a nation that owned a quarter of the earth, the natural centre of gravity for plunder from lesser realms. Marble belonged here; so too statues, friezes, jewellery. And now people from the same lands as the marble, and the statues, and the friezes, toiled in the fields for the right to survive, cringing to make themselves useful enough to avoid eviction. Clearly the nation's old slaving spirit survived.

She used to think the fountain was a folly. Nonetheless, it was a shock, as she walked up the wide boulevard, to see that it wasn't there any more. The marble structure had been torn up like a dead tree, and tarmac hastily poured over the surface, blotchy and uneven.

Hopper retreated to one side, sitting on one of the benches that remained around the edge of the little plaza, surveying the mutilation. It was still hot, clouded but nevertheless uncomfortable. When would the rain come? Two policemen approached, walking slowly, one glancing at her then saying something to his colleague. Her muscles tightened, and she looked south to see David approaching, scarcely looking at the police as he passed them. As he neared, she remembered with a start the last time they had met here. It had been near the end of their marriage – a crisis meeting, held on a tranche of neutral turf they had discovered together.

What a marriage it had been. Always stimulating, founded on love, but doomed to failure by ... by what? Perhaps by her own resistance to proximity, she thought now. Towards the end she had loved solitude more than her husband. Perhaps it was a reaction against the death of two parents, her brother's remoteness. Then again, she had friends from her student days who had been orphaned and who were happily settled now, their spouses civil servants, farm administrators, solar planters. Not like her own existence, clinging to a bit of metal flung out into the cold sea, hunting for patterns in black waves interrupted only by lumps of ice and floating coffins.

She could not ignore, of course, the influence of Thorne, the man who had let her down so thoroughly. It felt cowardly to blame another, but her preference for her own company, and her inability to trust others, also felt connected to him and their final, dreadful parting.

During the marriage itself, of course, the main problem had been children. In many ways, their attitudes to the idea of parenthood had served as microcosms of their whole feeling about their place in the world. Despite the nature of her work, she had seen no purpose in continuing the species; despite the cyclical native of David's work, it was all he wanted. Once that had been established, it had only been a matter of time before one or the other left.

As David came nearer, his smile dropped.

'Jesus, Ellie. What happened?'

She hadn't seen herself in a mirror since the morning – her bruises might have developed by now, flowering into purples and yellows. She should have put on more make-up. 'Promise you'll hear me out.'

'I promise anything. Just tell me.'

She told him about going to Thorne's house, and about her arrest and release – just that. She left out – for the moment – the photo, and the part about Warwick and Blake taking her bag, with Harry's notes.

When she had finished, he looked away for a few seconds, out across the gardens. 'You have to stop this. This is madness. You'll end up in the Breadbasket, or worse.'

'I'm fine.' She saw him visibly suppressing a comment to the effect that she clearly wasn't. To distract him, she asked him a question, one that had been on her mind since she had heard how stressed he was at the office:

'What's going on at the paper?'

David frowned. 'Big news. Really big. Davenport's getting his victory.'

'What?'

'It's our lead tomorrow. Christ, it's going to be our lead for the next six months.' He pulled a thin sheaf of paper from his pocket and read aloud. '"Prime Minister Richard Davenport will this week welcome to Downing Street a delegation from the American government to finalise plans for a new Bill of National Unity. Mr Davenport announced that the time was right for America to acknowledge its increased debt to Britain, and that a true union between the United States and Britain would benefit both nations while acknowledging this debt.

'"If passed, the American legislators will be granted limited representation in the House of Commons" – which means nothing, let's not forget – "in exchange for prospecting rights, and the formal union of the British and American armed forces. The American people will be naturalised and receive the protection of the British state, and the assets of the American and British nations will be combined."'

Hopper felt dazed. 'Meaning?'

David sighed. 'The Americans are caving, at last. They must be starving. We guessed they were pretty hungry for a few years, but it must be much worse than we thought. Either way, it's huge. No more Divided Kingdom. They'll get citizenship, the border into the American Zone will come down, the whole thing.' He paused. 'Don't you see? Davenport's getting the lot. A massive glut of manpower, whether for the fields or the army, all that land … He's been wanting this for years, and it looks like the Americans are finally willing to accept it. It also means he's got something to threaten the Scandis with, and the Russians. Christ, he'll be able to blow up half the planet when he gets his hands on the nukes.'

'Do you think he'll use them?'

'Hard to say. We've known for years how much he wants them. But maybe just having them is enough.' He turned to her, his face flushed. 'All right, your turn. What do you think Thorne was sending you to find?'

'Actually, I think I found it.' She took a breath. Here she was, about to trust her most significant find to someone else. Some deep-buried part of her couldn't stop her blurting out, 'This is all secret, you understand.'

'No shit, Ellie.' He smiled.

'All right. Well, when I was at Thorne's house, I found a photo.' She told him about the picture frame, and the family picture with the seam across its front, and what the photo showed: the mysterious box, the names on the back: Hollis, Lee, Drabble, Symons, Gethin. Only one of them not crossed out.

'So that's why you wanted to track down this Gethin man.'

'Yes.'

'Do you have the photo here?'

'No. I've hidden it.'

'Shame. I would have liked to see it. Do you think that's what he wanted you to find?'

'Maybe. Or perhaps he wanted me to find the box in the picture. I'm pretty sure that the people who picked me up, Warwick and Blake, are looking for either the box or the photo. So that's why I need Gethin. I think he could tell me more. Did you track him down?'

'I did.'

'Where is he?'

'You might not like the answer …'

'Just tell me, David.'

'He died fourteen years ago.'

Hopper felt a knot in the pit of her stomach.

'That's not possible.'

'I checked, El. He's dead.'

'I don't believe you.'

'There's an obituary. We ran it, for Christ's sake. I have it here.' He fumbled in his pocket, brought out a piece of paper. She looked at the copy of an obituary. The headline read, *Talented scientist dead at 36*. The picture at the top was of the same man as in the photo.

David spoke again. 'Why's it not possible?'

She remembered Chandler's words when she had spoken to him. *I was walking through Whitehall – and I saw him. He was going into one of the ministries – Internal Security, it was.* She fumbled in her notebook, and found the note. 'Look. He was alive three years ago. Chandler – Thorne's ex-colleague – saw him. He was certain about it.'

'He may have misidentified him.'

'No.' Yet even as she spoke she felt a bubble of doubt in her gut – felt the protestations she was making were defensive, the rearguard action of someone incapable of accepting they were wrong. 'He can't be dead.'

David sighed. 'Have it your way, Ellie. I just looked him up.'

'I know. I'm sorry.' She felt tears, involuntary and stupid, pricking at the back of her eyes. She hadn't slept enough for the last couple of nights. She missed the rig and its simplicity. She took a breath. 'There's something else.'

She told him about Fisher's bookshop, and about the discovery of the body, and the transmitter, and the American at the other end of the line who'd been waiting to hear the news. She told him about the radio she'd taken, the one in her bag now. As she spoke, David placed his head in his hands briefly, then sat staring across the park. She concluded: 'So Thorne was trying to get something across to Fisher, who would have sent it to the Americans. It looks like that was an insurance policy that didn't pay out. I must have been the other one.'

David looked at her and said nothing. She carried on. 'But I think this American news – what you're saying about the deal – must have something to do with all this. Whatever's in Thorne's box, or whatever the photo shows, it must have a bearing on the deal with the Americans. They're connected. Don't you think?'

David shook his head a little and spoke for the first time. 'Ellie, what the hell are you doing?' His voice was harsh.

'I'm just trying to work out what we do from here. How we get that box back, whatever it is.'

'No. I just mean ...' He gestured, his palms upturned. 'People are dying, and you're running around in the middle of it without a clue.'

'I know that, David. I'm not stupid. I know there's a risk.' She pointed to her bruised cheek.

'I don't think you do. Jesus, can't you ever take advice from anyone? No, of course you can't.' He was breathing deeply. 'Because you have no idea how dangerous these people are. They're mad. And if you try to resist, they'll kill you. They won't beat you up again. They'll just shoot you and leave you somewhere. And nobody will know.'

He was red now, embarrassed by his own anger. But he carried on. 'I'll miss you, of course, and maybe your other friends will, if you've got any left, but even as I miss you, I won't be surprised. This is important to these people, whatever the fuck it is. You should go back to the rig, you should keep working there, and you should let this whole thing drop.'

'I'm surprised to hear you speaking like that, David. I remember you caring about whether stories were news or not.' She shouldn't have said that. His cheeks flushed a deeper scarlet.

'Very wise, Ellie, coming from someone who ran away from the entire country to live in the middle of the fucking Atlantic. You don't know what it's like seeing colleagues disappear overnight. You don't know what it's like having to check yourself in meetings with your oldest friends, in case they shop you for a single unguarded comment. This whole sick island is a madhouse, and everyone I know is fighting two wars, because nobody knows who's on whose side any more, and here you come, just wandering into the middle of it explaining how perfectly *simple* it all is.'

The police were walking back through the park, and she and David fell silent as they passed the bench. One of them examined her, had clearly spotted the bruise on her face, and she tried as hard as she could to seem calm, happy, normal. She even smiled at David, hoping the officer would see.

By the time they had passed by, the tension had dissipated. David spoke first.

'I'm sorry.'

'No, I am. That was unfair of me.'

'Well, if it's any consolation, I'm only angry because I suspect you're right. Harry's still not turned up.'

She felt sick, but spoke anyway. 'I think I might know why that is, David.'

'Why?'

'I had the notes in my bag. Thorne's obituary notes that Harry gave us. They had his initials on and when the men picked me up at Thorne's place they took my bag away. Do you think that's the reason?'

David sighed. 'I wondered whether something like that had happened. It might be because of that. Yes.'

Hopper's mouth felt dry. 'Why didn't they go for you too? They must know we were married.'

'I don't know. It's possible they saw Harry's obituary in your bag and just went straight to him.'

'Where do you think he is now?'

'He could be halfway to the Breadbasket. Or in a ditch somewhere. Some journalist I am, eh? I can't even find my own colleagues.'

'Christ.' Poor David. He looked miserable. Poor Harry. 'Will it affect you?'

'I spoke to that assistant of his, Charlie. He doesn't know where Harry is either. I managed to persuade him not to mention our visit. Jesus. I promised him Harry's job if he didn't. I don't know if it'll work. But it might. Harry was the one he didn't like. And now I'm giving his job away to save my own skin. He shouldn't have helped us. We shouldn't have asked.'

He wiped his eye with the back of his hand, and she pretended not to notice it. After a pause she hoped was long enough, she asked: 'What are you going to do about all this?'

He breathed deeply. 'I'm going to help you.'

Their eyes met, and she felt a strange happiness within her, a sense of security despite all the horrors of the last three days. 'You really mean it?'

'I mean it.'

'What happened to "it's not worth getting yourself killed over"?' She gave him a small smile. He met it with his own, then frowned.

'It's not easy, Ellie.'

'I know.'

'But you're right. I've been playing along with the whole thing for too long. And that idea of yours about the Americans isn't bad.'

'You think it's connected? Your story and mine?'

'I think it could be. And if it is, it's clearly something pretty big. So. What do we need to know?'

'I need to find Gethin. He's alive. I know it.'

'Well, let's think about it,' David said. 'Let's say, for the sake of argument, he is. What's the next step?'

'Isn't there anywhere else to look?'

'From fourteen years ago? No. He's government, so unless his family buried him, he'd have been cremated.'

'Hospital records?'

'Seems unlikely after so long. Most hospitals trash them one year after death.'

Hopper was about to criticise him for being unhelpful, before seeing his gaze, unfocused and distant, and realising he was thinking about it properly for the first time.

'They'd have had to keep him on under another name,' he said slowly. These people are obsessed with paperwork.'

'So we're looking for a different name. Any random surname. That sounds impossible.'

'Well, it would be. But the advantage is, we'd know the time his employment began. They'd let Gethin die, then hire the new man. They couldn't have him alive under both names at the same time, so let's say we're looking in the following six months. Now, we *can* track government workers by the date of first employment. So we've got Gethin's death date' – he pointed to the piece in the newspaper – 'meaning we know roughly when our man should have started. Or rather, when he should have started under a new name.'

'We'll never find him if we don't know what name they put him under.'

'You're right. Except that Gethin's new name will be linked to a photo in a separate register.' He smiled, and pointed to the photo in the obituary. 'And we know what the man we're trying to find looks like. So that's something.'

'Do you have access to the photo register?'

'No. But I know someone who does.'

'When can we see them?'

He looked at his watch. 'If I hurry, before the close of play this afternoon. Want to come along?'

'Where?'

'Downriver.'

The journey was a short one by car – in Hopper's case, a filthy old taxi she'd found idling at the edge of the park. David had provided the address and she had insisted they travel separately. It had seemed paranoid even as she said it: she had seen none of her pursuers all morning. Perhaps her brother's influence was worth something after all.

It was a shame she and Mark had never been close, she thought now. Even as motherless teenagers, shuttled between their father and their aunt, they had been more like travelling companions than siblings. Their confidences had been limited; their interests almost wholly separate.

She wondered how Mark viewed her now. His errant sister, suddenly having to be scooped out of police stations, being beaten – probably her own fault. He had always been obedient to the marrow.

The taxi slowed. Here was the old Docklands. This area was rougher by some degree than the centre of town, and far less pleasant than Brixton. The buildings – mostly warehouses – were low off the ground. The scent of tar in the cab was slowly replaced by the stink of the river, of mud either left to bake or softened by the foul water of the lower Thames.

The cab dropped her off on a side road; she had arrived first. To the north was a high tower, rare this far east: an abortive skyscraper, abandoned halfway through its construction. 'Abandoned' was the wrong word. The tower had been deserted only by its builders: on every floor, blankets and pennants signalled the presence of residents. Today it was a slum built up into the sky. She could picture the interior now: the stairwells full of filth, the concrete cells subdivided by plastic sheeting, the conditions worsening as you climbed. The poorest would live furthest up: these days, ground floors were reserved for the wealthy, and the cool and dark of a basement for the wealthiest of all.

She heard footsteps: David approaching along the street. It was quiet in this part of town.

'Is this the actual place?'

'No. That was just for the taxi. It's a little way from here.' He turned and set off.

They walked together for several hundred metres, leaving the main road, down towards the riverbank. The traffic of London's roads receded behind them as they approached the water. This had been a thriving port once. No longer: a few Scandinavian-flagged barges were making their way laboriously up the empty river, their decks almost bare.

Further down sat a cargo ship, ground into the river mud, its decks covered only in the rubbish of opened containers. It had been built for a crowded world, a world with sea lanes full each day. And now here it was, a dead island of rust. She thought once again of the boat they had found near the rig, and the bodies on board, and wondered where they had been running from. How bad life in the south must be to make this place worth risking it all for. She could feel the child's amulet, still in her jacket pocket, still cold to the touch.

The streets were almost empty. It was unsettling, yet at the same time gave Hopper a pleasant thrill: it was a treat to avoid for a while the crowds of hungry-looking strangers thronging the centre of London.

'Where are we going?'

'To meet someone who might be able to help us.' David gestured right, to a gap in the wall filled by a high iron gate, and they crossed the road.

The place, whatever it was, was well defended: the gate was thick-barred, with a gap of only a few inches between it and the concrete lintel above it. Even that gap had been stuffed untidily with barbed wire. At the side was a box with buttons; David pressed one.

After a few seconds, a woman's voice spoke: 'Museum.'

'Good morning. I'm here for a quick look at the exhibits.'

'Are you a member?'

'Yes. David Gamble.' He waved at a small camera on the wall Hopper hadn't noticed until now.

Unseen bolts in the gate clicked back, and he pushed at it. On the other side was a dark alley of old brick some thirty metres long, leading to a courtyard. On the wall a scrawled paper sign read: *SHUT THE GATE, or we'll feed you to Sally.*

As they walked along the brick corridor, she asked, 'Who's Sally?'

'Who?' It took David a few seconds to realise what she meant. 'Oh, that. Sally was the dog. Died a few years ago. Harmless old Labrador.'

'What is this place, David?'

'You'll see.' His voice was high. In his throat, Hopper saw his pulse butterflying faster than usual. For a moment she felt painfully tender towards him, remembering his clumsily feigned nonchalance on their first dates, seeing just the same flutter in his neck then, the manifestation of a desire he was unable to hide.

At the end of the alley was a small courtyard, two storeys high, lined almost completely with plants. Ferns and creepers snaked up the shady side, and on the sunny side grew a plant she did not recognise, a Jurassic-looking thing with thick roots and huge flat leaves. Lizards sat high on the furthest, sunny wall, and scattered at their approach.

In the centre of the sunlit wall was another metal door, light blue, its paint chipped and peeling. David walked straight across and knocked.

It clicked, just like the gate at the front, and he swung it open onto a large space beyond, pitch black after the courtyard. As they stepped in, Hopper's eyes slowly began to adjust. It was a huge, long chamber, cavernous and gloomy. A warehouse, crammed with a vast array of glass cabinets, cupboards, cases, wardrobes, trunks, running around the walls, forming irregular passageways, leaning on each other for support. Above the ground floor, a narrow gantry ran around the edge; the far end was divided into two layers by an iron platform, supported by erratic metal piles. The upper stack looked as full as the cluttered ground floor.

Hopper looked at the nearest case. Through the grime she could see a box of puppets, half disgorged across the floor on the inside – regal figures dressed in sumptuous cloths. Above them was a label: *Indonesian Collection. 384*, then a string of letters. She turned, and opposite her was a collection of musical instruments, harmoniums and accordions and other squeezeboxes, their ridges full of dust.

David was watching her.

'What is this place?'

'It's from the early days of the Slow. A collection of culture, history, archaeology, sociology. Everything you might want to see from the places that were going to end up Coldside.' It sounded dimly familiar, now she thought about it. 'The museums combined their strength after the land requisitions. They needed somewhere safe, somewhere to escape the looting. Some went to the countryside, but there was still a huge amount needing storage, so ...'

A voice spoke, gruff and sharp through the cool air: 'So we came here.'

A figure stood on the gantry. It stumped over to a set of stairs close overhead and made its way laboriously down – a muffled clump, then a sharp bang, repeated.

As the figure approached, Hopper realised it was a woman. She was short – little over five feet tall – and plump, her body swollen by the several layers of cloth she was swaddled in. She had just one eye, the other socket a little dark void, and leant on a crutch.

'Hello, Hetty.'

'Hello, David. Who's this you've brought?'

'This is Ellen Hopper. She's a friend of mine.'

'Hello, Miss Ellen.' Hetty spoke with a faint accent, hard to define: half mid European, half from further afield. Her skin, olive-coloured, gave no clue. Her clothes were eccentric: a long skirt ringed with concentric blues and reds, and a leather jerkin on her upper body, over several other miscellaneous garments. Peeping out beneath her skirt were two odd shoes – one trainer, one leather boot. She must have been at least seventy. 'What do you think of my place?'

'I think it's wonderful.'

'Wonderful, she says! She can stay, David. Now, what am I standing down here for instead of in my nice cool office?'

'We have a favour to ask. A records favour.'

'What sort of thing?'

'Employment.'

'Oh, David, you know it's a risk to me.'

'I wouldn't ask if there was any other way, Hetty.'

'You can pay?'

'I can pay.' He patted his pocket.

Hetty reached to her lapel and pulled up an old-fashioned watch, the kind nurses used to have.

'We better be quick. I got a group coming in. Wait here. I'll go and set up.'

She stumped over to the stairs, her crutch pushing up under her arm. As she climbed, Hopper's eyeline was level for a few moments with her shoes. She saw for a second that the leg in the trainer was artificial; a thin metal pole protruded beneath the skirts and speared the shoe. Hetty made her way slowly up and into a side room.

'Is it just her?'

David murmured, 'It is now. But she's doing just fine. Everyone looks out for Hetty.'

'How does she support herself?'

'People bring things for her. Rations, money, food. They're grateful to her for keeping the place running.'

'What about the police?'

He shrugged. 'A mad old woman with a warehouse full of junk? Who cares? As long as she's not actively breaking the law, I think they're happy to let her be.'

'What about when she is breaking the law?'

'She pays them off and they shut up.'

A door clanged open. Hetty leant over the stairwell. 'I got it, Gamble. Come on up here.'

David shouted back: 'Both of us?'

She shook her head. 'Nobody comes upstairs on the first visit, Davey. Just like with my boyfriends.' She cackled and turned back.

David looked at Hopper. 'Do you mind waiting down here for a few minutes? We won't be long.'

Hopper shrugged.

'Thanks, Ellie. Don't break anything.' He smiled, before vaulting up the stairs two at a time, and disappearing off into the side room, whose door closed with a heavy metal thud. She was left alone in the huge warehouse.

The cabinets were full of the artefacts of a hundred different places she'd heard of, and some she hadn't, all labelled in the same old-fashioned handwriting. Japanese theatre masks. Strange metal spoons perforated with holes at the tip. A selection of nasty curved knives with bone handles, their blades glinting darkly in the uneven light of the lamps above. A row of shrunken heads sitting on wooden rods: their texture leathery and waxy, their minuscule mouths sealed with firm jagged stitches. An oboe.

She wondered whether David was managing to trace Gethin upstairs. If not – if he really was dead – there was nowhere else to go. From there, inexplicably, she found her thoughts sliding to the question of why David and his second wife, Pamela, had split up. She had attended their wedding, just a year after the divorce and shortly before she had walled herself up in the rig. She had gone almost as a protest against the expectations of her few remaining friends that she should mind attending. It had been an attempt to show that the human emotions provoked by a divorce should not bother anyone living through this time in history.

It had been a mistake; she had been surprised by the depth of her feelings, had hardly made it through the ceremony without crying. Even if she hadn't had her experience with Thorne, she suspected now that the day had prompted her to resolve, at some level, not to engage too closely with anyone again. That was probably the source of her affair with Harv too, although even there she had started to feel her heart contracting a little at the thought of him lately.

The door buzzer went off behind her, making her jump. After a brief pause she heard a squawk from upstairs, and an answering comment from outside. The door clicked; an elderly man pushed his way through, let it clang shut behind him, grinned at her, then shuffled down the long warehouse. He looked as if he was from South America. Not many had arrived from there in the initial wave – too far for most. A few had come; others, chasing the European dream, had gone to the south of the continent, and had been driven from there as rapidly as everyone else.

More people arrived, the doorbell buzzing each time, and made their way through. Hopper followed them, drifting towards the back of the warehouse, where a door opened onto another courtyard. This one was larger, roofed with corrugated iron with patches of sun leaking through. It held a hundred or so seats, arranged in concentric rings describing an approximate semi-circle, and in the middle was a rough pit lined with blocky stones, with ashes at its centre.

She hovered just inside the warehouse, watching the figures move into the courtyard, not wanting to interrupt their preparations. Some were conversing quietly, others moved back and forward, unloading bags, changing their clothes, lighting incense, placing a book by each seat. Three started building a fire in the pit.

The garments they were putting on were wraps of cloth, brightly coloured, the rings of dye interspersed with odd, boxy figures of animals real and imaginary. In the centre of London these people would be servants, perhaps commuting in each day from outside the barriers, working and cleaning, receiving small rations: Britain's new slave caste. Here, they were different. The air started to take on the scent of metal, and of earthenware warmed by the sun.

The courtyard was full now; the chairs were all occupied, and more visitors stood round the edges behind them. The front row had produced drums from the rough cloth sacks and old sports bags shoved under their seats.

The group seemed to have assessed its own size, decided it had reached quorum, and the space fell silent. One figure rose, from the front row, skirted the fire so it was between him and the audience, and began to speak in a language Hopper did not know. His voice was matched by a gentle drumming that echoed round the courtyard.

She recognised the rhythm of the words from somewhere, though the exact meaning escaped her. Beyond the drums and the speech there was only the crackling of the central fire. The speaker's voice varied – for a few seconds loud as a blare of trumpets, then sinking to a murmur. And as he spoke, the drum matched him, rising and falling with his words.

She could not tell who was leading, the speaker or the drummer. Maybe they were following each other. Tendrils of incense smoke curled around the courtyard. Every so often the speaker made an expectant call, and the whole room sighed a response, breathed and ecstatic, astonishing in its intimacy. She knew this ceremony; had been taken to it by her aunt in childhood. What was it?

'Hello.' David had arrived at her side, so close to her she jumped.

'Did you get it? Gethin? Did you find him?'

He smiled, the movement of his mouth pushing up the tired, tanned creases around his eyes. The drum and speaker were urgent, their muffled beat garbling David's words. 'Want me to tell you now or later?'

The vision of Thorne filled her head, dead before he could tell anyone what he had known; Fisher, killed because of his connection to Thorne; Chandler, sweating in fear, reporting visitors to the police before anyone could report him. 'Now.'

The drum had kept going, *tap-tap-tap*, steadily louder, and still the space swayed and echoed with the voices of the congregation. They were all speaking now, all together, and Hopper felt a sense of belonging just by watching them.

David spoke again. 'You were right. Gethin's still alive. He's still working.'

She grabbed his arm. 'You really mean it? Still working?'

'He's there, Ellie. He's real. And he's got a government pass.'

She breathed out. There was a link, a living link to Thorne. Someone who might know why that picture she had found was so important.

And in the centre of the yard, the first of the congregation knelt before the speaker to receive a circle of wafer on his tongue.

26

They were alone: Hopper, Hetty and David. They were sitting in the courtyard, three of the chairs pulled close to each other. The air still smelt of incense, sweat and dust.

The group had dispersed soon after the end of the ceremony, the alchemy of the congregation suddenly reversed: their chatter had died into individual comments, the bonds between them kicked over until the next time. As they had left, Hetty had said nothing. She had just raked the sand, scattered water on the fire, and stacked the chairs laboriously back against the wall.

Hopper spoke first. 'How did you find him?'

'We looked through the new employee records,' David said. 'That's what Hetty has up there. It's not, ah, widely known that she has them. We have everyone up to a few months ago.'

'How did you get hold of them?'

Hetty said, slowly, 'Through someone putting himself at risk.' She glared enough with her single eye to discourage further questions. Hopper reached to David for the sheet, and he spoke as he handed it to her.

'A month after Gethin's death – supposed death – another new employee joined, a Stephen Mulvaney. But the identity's fake. Almost insultingly so. The record of previous jobs was slim, and very familiar. Basically their boilerplate stuff for when they want to reassign someone: two years in Transport, three years in Home. I'm surprised they even bothered changing the dates. And the photo of him is basically unchanged from Gethin's old one. Guess they thought nobody would be looking.'

'So how do we speak to him?'

'We'll come to that.'

'David, you got payment?' Hetty said suddenly.

David reached into his pocket, pulled out an envelope, and passed it over. Hetty opened it and rifled through, counting the crumpled notes.

'Where these from?'

'All over. Like usual. Not traceable.'

'Promise?'

'Hetty, when have I ever given you bad notes?' She grunted, kept counting. 'There's extra in there, in case you're wondering. We know it's difficult.' She reached some number in her head, fanned out the remaining notes, and murmured to herself before folding them into one of her sleeves.

'Who were those people?' Hopper asked.

'They're Shuar. From South America, if you never heard of them.' There was a little challenge in Hetty's words, an assumption that Hopper, with her British accent, would be ignorant of other cultures. Hopper wished the older woman was wrong.

'What is this place?'

Hetty shrugged. 'Just a museum.'

'I've never seen anything like that ceremony in a museum before.'

'Maybe you should go to more museums.' Hetty's eye was staring at her with dislike.

David interrupted quickly. 'The whole museum is for anyone to keep whatever traditions they had – have – alive. Some groups don't want to attract any more attention than necessary. Hetty, can I use your phone? I need to check in with the office.'

'Use the wall one in there. Halfway along.'

He got up and left the two of them sitting there. Hetty was still holding the rake she'd used to level the sand. She moved it idly back and forth, making little rings in the ground around her metal foot, crooning a song. She stopped as soon as Hopper spoke.

'How many people know about this place?'

'Enough.'

'Why do you do it?'

Hetty took a deep breath, and let it out slowly, considering her answer. 'Everyone lost something, even here. But these people, they lost everything. Seems like they should have some place they can go, at least. Not much to ask.'

'What about you? Where are you from?'

'Belgium. Breadbasket, now. But it used to be Belgium.'

'When did you leave?'

'When your country arrived.'

Hopper ignored the slight. 'How did you live after you got here?'

'Got lucky. Got a job as a servant. Working in a rich man's house, looking after him. He had no family. When he died, he left me the house. That was before Law 12.' That was the law that allowed the government to requisition property and banned the foreign-born from inheriting it. 'That was twenty years ago. Then I sold the house and came here.' Hetty paused, then rubbed her eye.

'Your home. What was it like before?'

'Like everywhere. It was just like here was before the Stop. Not now, though. Now it's ...' She shrugged. 'Like hell.'

'How do you know?'

'My husband, Tomas. When you came ... when your people came, he was still in our town. Ghent, it was called. We arranged I'd come here, and he got me on one of the last boats. Told me I had to find a home, wait for him. A couple of years later he got a letter over to me. Told me what it was like.

'Everyone said I was crazy, trying to get back into that place. And I was. I got in, though. I got to see him again. They told me he was dying, and he was. And then, when he was dead, I got back out. Lost this doing it, though.' She tapped her false leg. The ring on her finger gave a sharp clink against the metal under the cloth. 'That was a few years ago now.'

'I'm sorry.'

Hetty shrugged. 'Not your fault. But makes me want to make some kind of space for everyone here. Everyone who's not you.'

'I can understand that.'

Hetty shifted her weight and changed the subject. 'So, what's this man you're trying to find? What's special about him?'

'I can't tell you, really. We haven't found out yet. But we think it's important.'

'Something to damage these people we got running the place now?'

'I hope so.'

'Then you got my support.' She crooned a little more, then broke off. 'Yes, anything you do to damage these people wins my un-am-biguous support.'

They lapsed into silence. Eventually Hetty spoke again, looking up at the iron ceiling of the little yard.

'You and David together then?'

'No. Not any more.'

'Shame. I think he likes you.' Hetty smiled at her, and Hopper was irritated to find herself blushing.

The buzzer sounded, harsh and surprising in the court-yard. Hopper looked up and saw where the noise was coming from, a squat grey box bolted to the ceiling. A few seconds later, it buzzed again, twice this time, and as it did, they heard running footsteps. David arrived back in the courtyard. He was breathless.

'Hetty, I can't tell for sure, but outside … I think it's police. Plain clothes. Three at least. I saw them on the monitor by the phone.'

Distantly, from the other end of the warehouse, they heard someone beating on the metal door, clanging and resonant. The hammering ended, and after a few seconds of silence, a dull thud sounded – a rich, heavy noise, like a gong being luxuriously struck. After five seconds of echo, the reverberations were cut off by another blow, ringing the length of the warehouse.

'They're knocking the door in.'

Hetty stood. One of the slats of light streaming from the roof caught her leg, making it gleam. 'There's a door in that wall. Leads to the street. Quiet that way. Your best chance. Go.'

'But—'

'Go.'

David grabbed Hopper's arm and pulled her to one side. As she moved, she saw a flicker of daylight from the other end of the warehouse as the far door crumpled under the force of the battering ram. Hetty was moving smoothly along the warehouse wall, inconspicuous in her dark jerkin.

The door at the side of the courtyard was old and rusted over, almost completely invisible in the darkness of the wall. It opened out, hatefully noisily, at David's leaning, into a filthy, abandoned alley, lined with weeds and stinking of decay.

He pushed the door closed behind him, and found a thick iron grille lying on the ground in the alley, covered in the soft remains of dead invertebrates and rotting fungus. He wedged it in front of the door to stop it being opened.

Hopper pushed ahead of him, only to hear him say, 'Not that way. They'll be in the street.' She moved back in the other direction. As they moved, the sharp pang of a gunshot came from the warehouse, followed by the tinkle of shattered glass.

David jumped. 'Jesus.'

Two more shots followed, and then the boom of a larger gun, a shotgun. A volley of shots answered it.

A few metres along was another doorway, barely visible in the gloom, and just as old as the one they had come through. There were others all along the alley but David placed his hands to this one, hammered and hauled, to no avail. Behind them Hopper could hear voices growing louder from inside the warehouse, approaching the courtyard. One of them was high and imperious. A woman's voice. Warwick.

They were in the courtyard now, and Hopper could hear them shoving at the alley door. She looked to the next door along, beyond the one they stood at now. But she could see it was padlocked shut from the outside, and the next one was too far away, and at the other end, a matchstick of sunlight marked the street, where there were doubtless more officers waiting.

She looked around for a weapon. Nothing. And then two low flat blows sounded on the other side of the door David had been struggling to open. He stepped back. It opened outwards, and they tumbled inside.

The space beyond was pitch black. They were shoved to one side by unknown hands – one person, two? – as the door was pulled shut. She heard the clatter from the alley as the police finally blundered through the door from the warehouse: heard their steps suddenly irresolute, faced with choice. Two sets moved away; two others approached, and hammered on the door they had come through.

They stood in the dark, close enough to feel each other, side by side. David found her hand and squeezed it, briefly and urgently. And then a third figure, the one who had pulled them inside, moved sideways and opened a tiny grille in the door to the alleyway at eye height. Hopper shrank away as a beam shone in, illuminating a slice of their rescuer's face. All she saw was a high cheekbone, and one unblinking eye.

'Has anyone been here? Anyone approached this building?' It was a man's voice. She thought it sounded like Blake.

'Nobody. This is a plague house. Quarantine.' She heard the man on the other side step back a pace.

'Hear anybody come by?'

'Nothing.'

'If you hear anything, contact the police immediately. Failing to comply is an offence.'

'Thank you, officer. I understand.' And then the grille closed abruptly, leaving them in the dark, silent and trembling.

27

In the close darkness of the plague house, they heard footsteps moving away smartly up the alley, hammering on the next door, then the next, into nothing. Perhaps two minutes passed. Hopper could hear David's breathing, her own pulse thudding. From the stranger there was no noise, apart from a tiny rustle of fabric. Eventually, after an unknown spell floating in the blackness, they heard the voice again. 'All right. Let's see you.' There was a click, and the space they were in was suffused with a sickly grey light.

They were in another courtyard, shaped like the one they had left, but arranged differently. The roof was bricked over, allowing no light in. The only furniture consisted of twin iron benches, chained down, flanking the entrance to the building.

The man before them was slim, well over six foot tall, his head shaved and polished, his nose aquiline. His bare head gleamed, reflecting the weak strip light overhead, and he wore a grey, formless robe, folded and refolded around his limbs.

'Where are we?' Hopper asked.

'This is a hospital for incurables.' His voice was deep – speaking what used to be called the King's English – and as smooth as the rest of him. His hands were almost all bone: long, slim fingers unencumbered by flesh. His eyes were low-lidded and grey.

David spoke next. 'The police ... they want us. Not for a good reason. We're innocent.'

'You don't need to tell me any more.'

'Can we stay a few hours?'

'Yes. We'll find you a space.'

'Is it safe to be here? With the ... incurables?'

'Not very. But there's no danger from us. We're the doctors.' The man moved to the other side of the courtyard, opened a door, and gestured for them to follow him.

Inside, they climbed a gantry to a long, tall gallery. Below them, beneath clear plastic sheeting stretched taut over metal frames, they saw the main hall of the hospital.

The ward ran the whole length of the warehouse. It consisted of twin rows of broad beds, white against the dark grey of the floor. There must have been fifty on each side, recessed into shallow alcoves in the breeze-block walls. A few were tented off with thick, billowing plastic.

Each of the open beds held two human forms, so close they almost touched. The bodies at this end, furthest from the main entrance, were shrunken and hunched. As Hopper walked slowly along the upper gallery, towards the light windows at the other end, the bodies grew, until those nearest the main door were full, stretching the length of the bed, close to upright. Flanking each bed were two little tables, with a bucket beneath them on each side.

Many of the patients were old, the sinews of their necks standing out against the receded flesh, their white hair floating wild on the pillows as they lay staring at nothing. A few looked like children, from their size. It was quiet. Between the beds, a few taller figures moved, as bald as their host and clad in the same grey robes.

'Who pays for all this?' Hopper asked, thinking of Thorne in his hospital bed.

'City authorities. We have to take people in when they're brought to us. If there are diseases they don't want spread, they become our responsibility. We try and keep them comfortable as long as we can.'

'Is this everyone in the hospital?'

'No. We have people in the basement too. Worse cases.'

'How do you look after them if they're contagious?'

'We have isolation rooms. This' – their guide gestured at the hall below – 'is for those who aren't contagious. Just incurable.'

'Why would anyone volunteer to work here?' Hopper hadn't meant to ask the question, but their guide took no offence.

'Staff are convicts. It's an easier life than on the continent. Most people there would trade, given the chance. You might live longer here too, if you have immunities.'

'And if not?'

'Most last about six months.' As if he could sense their next question, he said, 'I've been here three years. I've done the longest of anyone here.'

'Why did you let us in?'

'Police aren't always right. Lots of us are in here because of the police. Undeservedly.'

'You?'

'No, I would say I deserved it.' He let the sentence hang. In the hall below, the grey robes of the orderlies swished on the flagstones.

'How long until we can leave?'

'You should wait a couple of hours. We can get you out in one of our ambulances, and drive you where you need to go. Doesn't matter how late. Curfew doesn't apply to us.'

Hopper's limbs ached. She looked at her watch – it was still only just after seven in the evening. It seemed impossible. This day alone: the lawyer, the bookshop, the park, the museum, and now here.

'Where can we wait?' The long gallery they stood in was scrubbed and bare, but for another grey-clad figure sweeping the stones at the far end.

'We have a room, a bit like a priest's hole. Although we're not priests.'

'You could have fooled me.'

The warder-cum-doctor did not smile, the death's-head line of his mouth undisturbed by the joke. 'This way.'

The Last Day

They had been deposited in an ersatz hermit's cell at the top of the building, a heavy-doored room lined with breeze blocks and unrelieved by a window. The ventilation system was an antiquated monster, noisy and ineffectual, so they left it off and sweated. The only furniture was a medicine trolley, a bookshelf, and a single bed, which they sat on with their backs to the wall.

The shelf next to Hopper had a dozen ancient, yellowed diagnostic works on it. She leafed through one. Most of the medicines listed – perhaps three quarters of them – were crossed out in thick black pen. Next to each, various hands had written dates. Inside the front cover, someone had scrawled: *November '34. God help you.*

David looked sideways at her, and spoke first: 'Want to leave?'

'I don't know.'

'Can we trust him?'

'If he was going to hand us over, he would have done it when they knocked, wouldn't he?'

'Probably.'

'All right then. I say we stay, and take their offer of a lift.'

'All right.'

'Do you think Hetty—'

'I don't know, Ellie. I don't know. She's been raided before, I know that. I don't think they ever started firing guns before.' He stared at the ceiling for a few seconds, then looked at his watch, and slowly placed his hands over his eyes. 'Fuck.'

Hopper reached into her pocket, feeling the bruises on her ribs once again, and offered him one of her last two cigarettes.

He took it, and bent to the light she held out. 'I think my job's gone.'

'Surely nobody saw you in the warehouse.'

'It doesn't matter. I can't stay at *The Times* any more, not now they've taken Harry. Stupid not to see it before really, but I was doing well, and the success turned my head.' He drew on the cigarette, still sitting against the wall, knees high, looking like a dropped puppet. 'Anyway, if that little shit of an assistant of Harry's shops me, it's arrest I need to worry about, not my job.'

Hopper tried to think of something else to say. 'I didn't mean to get you in all this trouble.'

'Not your fault,' David said, but he didn't look at her.

'Slightly my fault, I think.' She looked up at the strings of smoke dissipating above them.

He sighed. 'You were always the one who wanted risk, Ellie. It's what I liked about you in the first place. I've missed it.'

Ordinarily, she would have steered the conversation away at this point, made clear that David's new life was his own. Looking at him now, the streaks of grey at his temples, something in her wanted to know more. 'Will you miss the work?'

'Of course.' He shook his head, grimacing. 'I know what you think. You think I was an idiot for going along with it until now.' She started to protest, and he waved it away. 'No, no. I know it. I don't think you're wrong. All I will say is, it's hard to tell at first, when you get given a little gold chain. You put it on, you think it's a reward. Then you get another. And then suddenly you're wearing thirty and you can't move your neck any more.'

'No risk of that for me.'

He nodded. 'Lucky old you.'

'I'm sure there's lots about me you don't miss.'

'Oh, I don't know.' He looked at her, along the side of the bed, and she felt abashed suddenly. 'Do you know the funny thing? Here it is, you'll love it: Pam and I split up because she wanted children.'

At first she thought she'd misheard him. 'But David, *you* want children. Or you did. That was why we broke up. Wasn't it?'

He shrugged. 'Seems like I've come round to your way of thinking.'

'That's pretty big news.' She had always liked the fact that he had wanted children, even if she didn't. He had always been the optimistic one, finding a way to the future, working out the route. And now here he was, telling her the main obstacle that had forced them apart had dissolved, that he thought there was no future worth making. 'I'm very surprised.'

'You and me both. Clearly your arguments took a few years to penetrate, but they got through in the end.'

'What changed?'

'In case you hadn't noticed, it's horrible here. Jesus, I've got a good job, or I did have. I'm lucky. But it gets worse every day.'

He looked so forlorn she couldn't resist some encouragement. 'The whole place is surviving, though, isn't it?'

'With respect, you've been on a rig in the middle of the North fucking Atlantic. You don't know.'

He puffed out his cheeks and exhaled, scattering the thin ropes of smoke above him into mush. The grey cement of the wall behind him had leached the pink from his cheeks.

'About four years ago – soon after you left, actually – I went to a Breadbasket farm. Actually in the zone, it was, somewhere in Normandy. I was on features at the time. They'd just had their fifth crop of the year, had worked out how to squeeze an extra one in. Some genetic modification they'd done. Something clever. And they wanted to show us how well it was working.

'So we were all there, four from *The Times*, four from the *Mail*, two from the *Post* – this was about three months before the *Post* got the chop. They sent us on a bus together, along with a few press officers. Tried to keep it light, only two guards on the bus. Most of us hadn't left London for months. It was a treat just to see a full sky for once. Stayed overnight in Portsmouth – decent hotel, lots of drink, all on Dickie Davenport. A real jolly.

'The next morning they stick us on the old ferry. Eventually we arrive, and it's ... nice. You know, surprisingly so. A few farmers in their smartest clothes. Chickens around the place – scrawny but, Jesus, alive. And the farmers seemed genuinely proud of what they'd done.

'The government had laid on a few people from the GM division to come along, talk us through the science. And the whole thing was ... working. Obviously you know it's all laid on for you, you know it's not the whole story, but for about half an hour, I really thought ... maybe this is how we start the road back. And I get to thinking about all those lands beyond the Breadbasket, and how maybe we'll begin farming them one day, or how we might get those huge solar works we were promised thirty years ago, free power for everyone. Maybe there'll be enough land to go round, so the guys up north and out west stop the bombs. Maybe even the continentals start to get back on their feet.

'Anyway, we're heading back to the bus. The press officers are a bit behind us, talking to the farmers, probably dishing out some extra cash to thank them for such a convincing show. And there, just by the stables as we reach the bus, sitting on the ground, there's this ... kid. Must be no more than five years old. Half naked. Starving. Little belly poking out. So thin you can't tell if it's a boy or a girl. We all just slow to a halt, looking at it. We must have stood there for ten seconds, but it felt like an hour. And it didn't say anything. It looked exhausted. Like it could be eighty years old.

'And then its mother arrives round the corner, looks at us all frightened, picks the kid up sharply, takes it back indoors. She was in even worse shape herself, from the brief look we got at her. Nobody says anything. And a few seconds later our handlers come round the corner. They don't know what we just saw.

'None of us said very much on the bus back. But it made the whole thing clear. If even the kids on the show farms look like that, firstly, where the fuck is the grain going, and secondly, what's it like everywhere else? I know that was when things were bad, but honestly, even if it's a lot better than that, it's still pretty fucking awful out there.'

Between his fingers, David's cigarette burnt unnoticed. He rubbed his jaw.

'I still wrote the piece, though. Because if you don't write the piece you get sacked. And if you're sacked, you really can't do anything. Then again, if you're not doing anything anyway, you might as well get yourself sacked, but then some other bastard will have the decent job and the perks. So you don't do anything and you hope the person who'd replace you would do it worse. Writing that piece was pretty much the end of journalism for me. Everything since then has been propaganda. Until you showed up.'

She leant over and patted him on the shoulder, clumsily, and he gave a little nod to acknowledge the gesture, but he kept staring straight ahead, the smoke from his cigarette curling upwards.

'It might be all right in the cities, Ellie, but it's a lot worse further out. Everyone's got a reason to hate this lot, and things aren't getting any calmer. The army keep losing convoys, having to switch routes at the last minute, worrying about driving over fucking fortified bridges that haven't been dangerous since the days of the collapse.

'I keep telling myself it's going to end at some point, but then things might get even worse, because the lunatics will have won and there won't even be a mismanaged country. But Davenport and his gang keep trying to prove it's fine, to shove in more splints, carry on. Because they have no plan to leave. As soon as he tries to go he'll be shot. So they're probably just doing what I'm doing, keeping going for fear that what comes after them will be worse.'

He nodded again. 'No, I don't think I could bring a child into a place like this.'

Now or never, she thought. No more lies. He doesn't deserve them. 'You nearly did, you know. We nearly did.' She had to force herself to say it.

He gave her a long look. Here it was, the last secret she'd kept from him. She met his gaze. Finally the end of their marriage was making sense to him as it did to her.

'When?'

'About six months before I left.'

He nodded slowly. 'How did it end?'

'Naturally. I miscarried at eight weeks. There was only a short while when I even knew about it before it was over.'

He looked exhausted suddenly. 'Why didn't you tell me at the time?'

For a moment she sensed, vividly, the space in the middle of herself where the baby had been. Her muscles contracted, and she felt a matching pang in her throat. 'I felt so guilty. I felt like losing the ... baby was a sort of punishment, for not wanting it in the first place. It was my fault.'

'Why didn't you tell me afterwards?'

'Because I'd be responsible for your grief. I didn't want you to know about it because I thought it would feel even worse for you. It was something you'd wanted for so long, and all I could have told you was that I'd lost it. So I said nothing.'

'Jesus. You're saying that you ... that we ...'

'Yes.'

'Well ... what a world, where I can hear something like that and think, *that's probably for the best*. What a world.'

They sat in silence for several minutes. David's cigarette burnt out, and he left it where it was. Eventually he spoke again.

'Maybe this plan of Davenport's, this alliance with the Americans to get the nukes – maybe it is connected somehow with the radio you found, with Thorne's attempt to tell the Americans something. Maybe it's a proper story you've dragged me into.'

'Maybe.'

'Fingers crossed I remember what one of those is, eh?' He smiled.

'What if we do find whatever it is? What if it's enough to bring down Davenport?'

'I don't know. Don't get me wrong. He deserves everything he gets. But it's a long road back to anywhere near normal.'

He stretched out along the bed. She stayed sitting at the foot, staring at the wall opposite, trying to work out why she *was* doing all this, what had given her this feeling that things suddenly mattered once again. But it was hard to get under the surface of her mind, especially feeling as tired as she did.

Eventually she must have slept too, sitting upright, as the next thing she knew was a soft tap at the door. She swung her legs off the bed and shook David gently by the shoulder. 'Our lift is here.'

28

Downstairs, in the evening's brightness, an ambulance was waiting at the front of the warehouse, its squat rear wedged into the doors. Two patients had just been brought in; as the ambulance received a cursory clean, their benefactor shook Hopper's hand, and David's.

Hopper found herself thanking the doctor in oddly formal terms, as though stiff language could erase the unwanted intimacy created by his having rescued them.

He nodded. 'I hope whatever you were looking for in our neighbour's home is worth it.' He turned and walked away, his long grey robe gently brushing the floor as he stalked between the beds.

Hopper and David were invited to sit on the trolleys clipped into the vehicle's floor, and driven through streets emptying for curfew by a woman as lean and bald as their host.

David spoke first. 'What are you going to do?'

'I'll find a way of getting close to Gethin. He's the only person in Thorne's past who we know is alive, and he's in the photo.'

'So you're just going to visit this Gethin man. And what will you do *after* you're arrested?'

'My brother—'

'Your brother's already bailed you out once, Ellie: And after a certain point he'll give you up. He's got kids. Will you promise me you'll just go home tonight until we work it out? Together?'

'Yes. Of course. Sorry.'

They sat in silence until the ambulance was approaching Queensway. The driver pulled off the main road, meandered until they were a couple of streets from David's house, and turned the engine off.

Hopper broke the silence. 'I'll take care, David, I promise. And when I do talk to Gethin, I'll let you know.'

'All right. I'll go in to the paper tomorrow as usual. They'll already have worked out you and I were married, I know that. But short of running away, I don't see what else I can do.'

'Good luck.'

He smiled, then turned, and without looking back hopped down to the street, pushed the large door shut behind him, and began the short walk home.

The driver spoke for the first time. 'Where next?'

'Bethnal Green.' She gave the address of Gethin's house, the one she had memorised from the sheet Hetty had shown her, and the driver nodded, and pulled away.

The journey didn't take long. The traffic always thinned just before curfew.

She hadn't fully worked out what she was going to do. She only knew she had to ask Gethin about the photo, and the box. Everything else – whether he would call the police, what story she would use – was fog.

The ambulance swung onto Gethin's street, slowing a little, but as they neared the right house, it did not stop or slow. Instead, it maintained its speed, cruising easily by. She saw a light on in the building, thought she even saw shapes of people moving around downstairs, and yearned for a crazy moment to wrench the wheel from the driver.

'What are you doing?' she asked, her voice strained.

'Did you not see?'

'See what?'

'Three of them. In three cars. Waiting for you.'

Hopper looked in the mirror.

'No. Stop. Pull over. We have to go back. I have to speak to the man in that house. It's urgent.'

The driver shook her head. 'If you get out now, you'll be arrested. Whatever you're trying to do, you need another way.'

Then, as they cruised along the street, Hopper saw two police officers, waiting around the first corner they came to, leaning against a wall. They straightened up to observe the ambulance, and she was suddenly grateful for the smoked windows.

'I'm not letting you out here,' the driver said.

'I have to get to him.'

'Worth your life?'

'Yes.'

'Not true. Meet him another time. I can't let that happen to you.' As she spoke the driver hitched up her left sleeve, revealing a long, ugly scar along the top of her arm, studded with welts. 'See him some other time,' she repeated firmly. 'It's not worth your life. Nothing is.'

Hopper sat back, and stared out of the window as the ambulance carried her away from the last lead she thought she had.

29

'Come in, come in.' Thorne's room was messier than she had ever seen it before. The bookshelves were half empty, their contents spilling out of boxes interspersed with papers. On his desk, the ancient computer was alive and flickering.

'Having a clear-out?' Hopper moved a heap off one of the armchairs and sat.

'In a manner of speaking. So? How did the exams go?'

'I think bioengineering was the worst. I really do think I failed.'

'I'd be surprised. You've got a pretty strong internal critic, Ellen. Any word on the placement?'

She had been keeping this from him for two weeks, waiting for it to be properly confirmed. She supposed there could be no harm in telling him now. 'I was accepted. I leave for Skye in two weeks.'

'Oh, Ellen. Congratulations! And you thought it wouldn't happen.' She had been interviewed by a panel of three, had been almost deliberately brusque with them, unsure whether she really wanted to go, convinced they would laugh her out. But they had not. They had been interested.

'I know. I think it'll be all right. Thanks for helping me with the application.' She smiled. He smiled back, expansively.

'Your parents would be proud, Ellen. If they could see you now.'

For a few seconds she was unable to speak. Eventually she managed to nod.

'I couldn't have done it without your help.'

'Nonsense. Just needed someone to light the fuse. You made all the running yourself.' He smiled. But as he did, she noticed for the first time the heavy bags under his eyes, and his skin, pale with exhaustion.

'Is everything all right, Edward?'

'Yes, absolutely. But as it happens, I may well beat you out of the building. I'm leaving too. At the end of this month.'

'What? Why?'

'University politics. Not hugely different from the real sort, it turns out. There have been interventions made on behalf of the college by some of its more reputationally minded members. They're worried my presence affects its standing.'

Hopper felt a stab of indignation. 'That's shit. What standing?'

'Come now. The warden has been told by the rest of the council that my presence makes funding bids harder. They informed her that my teaching is outweighed by the – what was the phrase? – ah, yes, the "negative associative freight" I bring.'

'I don't believe it.'

'It doesn't matter. Caroline did her best, but the tide's running against her. Nothing she can do about it. She and you are the only two I will miss. One of my oldest friends and my newest one.'

There was a lump in Hopper's throat. 'It won't be the same without you.'

'Of course it will. That's the whole point of Oxford. You told me when we first met that it never changed.' He smiled.

'You really can't stay?' She couldn't imagine spending another year studying here without his guidance.

He shrugged. 'It's not fair on anyone I've worked with here to taint their careers through association with me. Not that their careers are worth very much, but they're acting rationally, guided by self-interest. It's all one can expect. That's what Richard always used to say.' Hopper was surprised. He had never referred to Davenport in her hearing before.

She looked at him, gripping the back of his chair as he stood behind it. 'I was only ever a scientist for many years, and then ... then I became involved in politics. But the change tarnishes one, Ellen.' He glanced at her. 'Politics tarnishes what you did before.'

She said nothing.

'Everyone says they're opposite endeavours, politics and science; that one deals with truth and the other with perception. It's not really true. Science doesn't change with perception, of course. Photosynthesis doesn't alter based on public opinion. That much is true. But what we think possible, what is ... acceptable to believe: that is another matter. Whether we explore this sea or that, whether we think we can support a hundred million people or only fifty: these are matters where perception counts.' Hopper wanted to interrupt, but he was speaking distantly, only half to her.

'What about things that are true but unacceptable? Do we accept them? Of course we don't. We are rational agents, acting with self-interest. That was what Richard – excuse me, the prime minster – always said to me. It was his mantra. And once you've persuaded people their self-interest aligns with yours, they'll follow you like a river to the sea.

'If Richard can persuade enough people their self-interest is best maintained by living in the world he's built, he'll stay. But there are two ways of doing that. To persuade them their world is bright and good – that's the first. But to persuade them the alternative is catastrophe – that's even more powerful. Do people want to live like the poor bloody slaves on the continent? No. So they'll support him. Even if he's wrong.'

'Is he wrong?'

After a long pause Thorne looked up, his abstraction dissipated. 'Probably not. Anyway. You'll be back in the autumn, I hope?'

'I hope so. What will you do?'

'I'll start by going home, to London. After that, who knows. I'll read a lot, I dare say.'

'Why did they make you leave the government, Edward? Last year, before you came here?'

She had never asked him outright before. He looked at her, and laughed. 'That's a pretty big question from nowhere, Ellen.'

'I'm sorry, I didn't mean—'

He waved his hand. 'Don't worry about it.'

'I didn't mean to ask just like that, but I ...' Her face was burning. So many times she'd pictured herself asking him, being let into his confidence, and she had blurted it out like a child. And now she was angry too, her question disregarded with such ease because of a little social awkwardness.

'I can't tell you.'

'I see.' She was frosty now.

He sighed. 'Just differences of opinion, that's all. Working so closely with someone is rather like a marriage. Eventually the differences grow so broad you can't remember quite how you found yourself in bed with these people in the first place, and once you've realised that, it's time to leave.' He looked at his watch. 'Goodness. I had better be going. I'm visiting the warden to plan my leaving drinks, and I want her to feel so guilty that she doesn't mind me drinking some of the bottles she's saving for her own retirement dinner.'

She noticed the way he moved effortlessly off the question, hated him for a moment, then felt suddenly sad once again. 'I don't want you to go.'

'Thank you, Ellen. I don't want to go either. I'll miss you.' He smiled at her, and the pause stretched unnaturally. After a few seconds, he picked up his jacket, and lowered the blinds, plunging the room into darkness. Then he saw her out, closed the door behind him, and turned at the end of the corridor to cross the quad.

She waited in the archway for a full minute, to ensure he wasn't coming back. Then she moved back along the corridor, tested the handle, and slipped back into his office.

30

Like all the others on the road, her brother's house was closed for curfew – the shutters ranked against the sun, narrow white slats rebuffing the constant heat.

The streets were quiet: curfew was observed faithfully, for the most part. It was another of Davenport's innovations: much easier to govern if you could recreate the hours of darkness and re-establish control over your cities while the lawful slept. Ambulances were exempt, as Hopper's driver had explained. And, of course, the police still kept their curfew wagons out, even though these days most of their victims were no more criminal than teenage partygoers or furtive adulterers.

The hall of Mark's house was dark, the only light coming from a lamp in the living room. Laura called it the 'drawing room': one of the little tics of propriety that convinced Hopper her sister-in-law would have been much happier in the 1940s than now.

Hopper hung up her coat, and moved to the living room to switch the lamp off. As she entered, she noticed a large bulk in the chair in the far corner, a form that suddenly pushed up into the room towards her. She jumped, her pulse racking up.

'It's me, Ellie.'

Her brother walked over to the hall door, closed it, snapped the main light on. He looked dishevelled: eyes crusted, shirt untucked.

'Where have you been?'

'Visiting a friend.'

'Bollocks. Where did you go?'

'You can't push me around, Mark. I'm not a child.'

'I thought you'd been arrested again. I've been ringing round police stations all evening. Do you know how worried I've been? I've been completely losing it since you didn't come back. I shouted at the kids ...'

She suppressed a smile at the magical transformation of his bad parenting into her fault. 'I'm sorry.'

'Of course you're not. I know you don't give a toss about any of us, but it would be nice if you could just confirm you're not dead of an evening. Some of us have jobs. Do you want a drink?'

This was another of Mark's curious features: the ability to switch in midstream from anger to pleasantries, with no acknowledgement and sometimes no change in his tone of voice.

Hopper nodded, and he moved to the sideboard, poured two whiskies, and handed one over.

She looked at the tumbler, a heavy crystal thing ornamented with a hundred delicate cuts. 'These were Mum's, weren't they?'

'That's right. Used to take two everywhere in that little padded case. You remember?'

'I do.' This had been on their first trip, before their mother had sent them home. The heat of the desert around them, living in a tent from night to night, guarded by those tall young brothers armed with rifles. And all the time, trudging from one rest station to the next, the column. The people walking under her mother's care were among the last to leave, the ones who had stayed through stubbornness or lack of choice. And so now they trudged through a hot, dead landscape, a landscape unrelieved by cool or dark, along a path the vehicles had fled.

When people collapsed, her mother's teams tried to intercede, but there were too many collapsing and not enough helpers. The escort tried to take them in their pitifully few jeeps to little improvised hospitals along the route. They had started in Kenya, she remembered, northern Kenya, and the air had been thick with a horrible sharp tang for hundreds of miles in every direction. After a few days, they reached the cities, where the transport became mechanised, and where one stood a better chance of getting out, but only one in ten made it there. And even then, Britain's borders had already been shut to those without passports.

She drank the whisky. It tasted good, that delicious burn sliding down her throat and settling with a dull warmth in her stomach.

'Funny, really. Mum spent all that time trying to help people getting out of the Hotzone, and I work for the people who devoted themselves to keeping the same people out of Britain. Wonder if she'd see the funny side.' He was looking down into his own tumbler. She wondered how many drinks he'd had before she got back, sitting in a dim house, his family disordered, his colleagues growing suspicious of the man with the seditious sister.

'Yeah. Pretty funny.'

'What are you doing, Ellie? I'm sure you're working on something terribly clever. You always are. But I don't want them to kill you, and I'm afraid, if they want to, they will. So, indulge me. What is it?'

'I'm sorry. I can't say.'

'Thought you wouldn't. But it's about that man Thorne.'

'That's where I started.'

'Take my advice. Leave it alone, and go back to your rig. You've got a man there, haven't you?'

'Sort of.'

'That's you, Ellie. The queen of the sort-of.' He was definitely drunk, Hopper could tell. The words were thick on his tongue. But he had always been the type of drunk to keep his eloquence longer than his inhibitions. 'You're going to stay in the sort-of all your life if you're not careful. But it's better than what my colleagues will do if you don't pack it in. So take my advice, and leave it.'

'I can't.'

He snorted at that, and a little fleck of saliva stayed at the corner of his mouth. 'You don't understand, do you? You don't get the things people have to do in this life, just to survive. It's not anybody's fault, sis. It's the planet. It would be lovely to treat each other well. But that's not the world we've got.'

'I don't want to bother you any more. I should leave.'

'Where would you go?'

'I'd stay with a friend.'

'You have friends still, do you? Someone from school? Or university? Or maybe one of the many, many friends you've made in your job?'

'Mark, I don't want to talk about it any more. I'd just like to sleep.'

He stood. In his absence she never remembered how big he was; some inner smallness in him mitigated against it. But he was five inches taller than her, over six foot, and broad. On his wedding day, she remembered, his suit had hardly fitted, the jacket stretching in broad lines across his back. He put his hands on her shoulders, gently. 'Ellie. Go home. Go back to the rig. You can't do anyone any good if they put you in the Breadbast-Breadbasket.'

He moved past her to the door. Before he pulled it open, his hand resting on the handle, he said, looking down, 'I won't help you. If they come again, I won't help. I'm sorry.'

He left the room, closing the door behind him, and she reflected that he had probably been waiting all night, drinking, to build up the courage to tell her something she already knew.

31

His heavy tread disappeared upstairs, and she heard the door of the bathroom open and close behind him. A few minutes later, it opened again, and the bedroom door opened and shut. The ceiling above her creaked for a few seconds, and then was still.

You've got a man there, haven't you? That was what Mark had said. But she had never told him about Harv, had told him nothing about her life on the rig. Perhaps he had just been guessing. But it hadn't sounded like it.

Hopper waited another ten minutes, sitting on the leather couch, trying not to make it squeak. Then she stood, crossed the hall, and tested the door of the ground-floor room where she had heard Mark speaking last night. It was locked. It must be some private study of his.

At least she could guess where the keys might be. When they had lived together in her third year at Oxford, Mark had put his keys in the hall cupboard, at the top. She moved to the front of the hall, quietly, and opened a few cupboards until she found them, high up, and pulled them out, gripping them tightly to stop them jangling.

Standing in the dark hall, she was painfully aware of each noise she made. Every rustle of her clothes sounded magnified, every movement grew in her ear. The first key didn't work, and neither did the second. There were only two left for this sort of lock. The third didn't work either, and she began to panic. What if he kept the key for this room elsewhere? What if the door had sensors on, triggered an alarm that would sound in his room?

The fourth key worked, and no alarm sounded as Hopper opened the door.

The room was as dark as the hall, the shutters firmly closed, and the light switch snapped horribly loud as she turned it on. The place was as neat as she had imagined it would be: one wall of books, a filing cabinet opposite, between them a desk, which lay under the window overlooking the neighbouring house. The carpet was thicker in here. Odd: she had not had her brother down as a household elitist.

What was she looking for? She wasn't sure. Better start with the filing cabinet. It was easily opened; the small metal key took little finding on the bunch. The topmost drawer contained brown folders, arranged alphabetically. In front of them was a folder marked *INDEX*. She pulled out the first file. Inside, in Mark's crabbed, neat hand, too cautious even to take up the entire height of a line on the page, was a contents list:

1. Acro. 2. Adelman. 3. Anderby. 4. Arnos. 5. Astro. 6. Avis. And so on, down the page. She turned to 'Arnos'. *Information summary for three males suspected of plotting to detonate an explosive device in central London. Suspects observed by Nautilus for three weeks. Grounds for further observation warranted.* Then, a few paragraphs down, *Recommend search and arrest.* At the bottom of the page was a note in larger, less formal writing. *Conclusions: house raided. Three suspects returned fire; shot dead. Presented to Featherby in end-of-year summary.*

She leafed through the rest of the folder. Each code name seemed to link to a real person who had been placed under surveillance for whatever reason. The details were always capped by her brother's observations at the side in dark ink. They seemed like private observations, too: he would occasionally write *blunder*, or once, *sackable blunder here*. Occasionally the text was adorned with a tick. She turned to the front folder, the index, and found it consisted of a key, a long list of the code names and the real names of the surveillance targets they matched up to. Neither Gethin nor Thorne appeared.

The next drawer down had another alphabetically arranged rack of files hanging in it. At first, she couldn't tell why the files had been placed in different drawers. And then, on the front of the top drawer, in tiny capital letters, she spotted the words *BRITAIN CENTRAL (2046-)*. The next drawer down was *BRITAIN NORTHERN*. It contained another batch of files covering the same span, the last thirteen years. After that, *BRITAIN SOUTHERN*. The bottom drawer was marked *OFFSHORE*. She knelt on the rich carpet, opened it, and pulled out the index file.

This one was slimmer. Fewer people were living offshore to be spied on, she supposed. She ran her finger down the list of surnames, by this point not really expecting to see Thorne or Gethin. But immediately one name jumped out at her:

Cromwell = Hopper

If she hadn't already been kneeling, she would have sat down abruptly. Her ribs ached suddenly, the blood rushing to her muscles.

Neither of the first two folders contained the name Cromwell.

The third did. It was several entries back, thicker than most of the others in the file. She felt her fingers grow clumsy as she turned to it, rifling the paper, deaf to the noise it made.

Subject entered Westerly 12 rig (LB4) 26/03/56. Rig representative has kept her under observation through close professional contact. That must be Schwimmer. She had been wrong to assume the CO wouldn't spy.

And then she read on: *Rig operative has entered an intimate relationship with subject; does not believe himself suspected. Subject emotionally self-contained and mistrustful. Hard to persuade with financial inducements: best means of approach uncertain. If approach is ever necessary, suggest appeal to patriotism.* Hopper's heart grew thick in her chest.

Behind this were crabbed notes of correspondence, signed by her brother.

Intimate relationship. Not Schwimmer, then. Harv. The man she had lain with, exchanging confidences on those small metal bunks; had played music for, an ancient tape deck balanced between them. Harv had slept with her, and submitted notes on her, and her brother had requested them or stolen them in his turn.

She sat back on her heels. So that was why Warwick and Blake had come for her. Thorne had almost got the letter to her without interception; but Harv had found it, had opened and read it before carefully resealing it, and letting it reach her. She tried to remember what else she had told Harv, until she realised it didn't really matter. It was all too late. At the very end of the folder, in darker ink, in her brother's writing, were the words: *Subject released after initial arrest, pending second arrest.* The third-person writing was as wounding as anything else.

She closed the file, returned it to the drawer, locked the cabinet once again, and moved back to the door, scuffing the carpet to remove the indentations of her footprints. Before she left, she looked back, surveying the room, seeing nothing out of place, and turned the lights off behind her, before slipping out and relocking the door.

Upstairs, she noticed the door of her own room was slightly ajar. She was certain she had closed it before leaving the house in the morning: remembered the thunk of the oak against the white-painted frame. On the rig she had got into the habit of pressing doors shut: unclosed ones could lash around. So someone had been into her room. Perhaps Mark had waited for her in here at first. She pushed at the door and flicked the switch inside.

The first impression she received was of an odd transference to Thorne's house, as though a door in this building opened onto a room in that. Her room had been shredded. Her clothes were piled at the foot of the bed, the sheets torn off. The mattress was at an angle, one corner hanging weakly over the edge like a tongue from an exhausted mouth. The bedside tables were miniature volcanoes, their contents spilling over the floor. The carpet was slashed.

In the centre of the bed was an unsealed envelope – a strange formality. It contained a single piece of card, bearing four short words: *We will find it.* The card was unsigned.

This was why Mark had sat up waiting for her. He hadn't been worried: it had been his way of forewarning her of the scene upstairs, a scene he had eventually lacked the courage to describe. Perhaps he thought letting it happen was helpful, that it would show her what these people were like. As if she did not already know. As though he had not seen the state of her outside Scotland Yard.

The photo. Had they found it? She moved to the door of the room and onto the landing, pristine by comparison. She edged the side table out and groped behind it. For a moment she felt nothing. Then her finger just grazed the edge of it in its cubbyhole, and she pulled it out by her nails. Thank God she had left it out here.

She moved back into her room. Perhaps Mark had tried to dissuade them from tearing her things apart; perhaps he had called them in the first place. It didn't matter either way. She had to leave.

She made her way over to the window and opened the thick black curtains, lifting them as she did to prevent the brass rings scraping on the rail. She leant over to the white shutters and shifted one slat up, very slowly.

The road was lined with cars: all empty, as far as she could tell. A flicker of movement caught her eye: a bird, scratching in the ground of the front garden.

For several minutes she stood and stared: first to her left, then to her right, towards the station. And then she saw it. A tiny shift under the windshield. One of the cars parked three doors along was occupied.

She looked intently through the almost-closed shutter, saw nothing, looked so long her eyes began to blur, thought perhaps she had imagined it, until finally she saw it again: a little movement of an arm. And when she saw that, the rest of the shapes inside the car resolved themselves, like one of those pictures you had to squint at to see the meaning inside, and she made out a human figure in the passenger seat.

It must be Security. It was exactly the car they would pick to look unofficial – a dark green family saloon, roomy but harmless. It looked a little too clean, considering how infrequently most cars were driven these days.

Around her, the house felt unconscious, even though Mark and Laura slept just two rooms away. Laura was the only risk; Mark would be dead to the world. She reached up to the top of the open wardrobe, found a yellow sports bag. She gathered a few clothes from the pile on the floor: not too many. She moved to avoid making any noise, only taking items that would not disturb the papers on the floor.

She added her notebook, her wallet, a few toiletries, and transferred the transmitter from Fisher's shop, still in its iron box, over from her satchel. She looked at the heap of her possessions for some souvenir of her life so far, some object with sentimental value, and found nothing. The contents of the bag would be better anonymous. The only things she took that had any meaning were the transmitter, the photo of Thorne with the box-like object, now safely tucked into her wallet, and the amulet she had salvaged from the boat. It reminded her of her mother now.

And then, as an afterthought, she looked under the bed and found what she half remembered had been there the last time she had visited: a short, blunt rod of hard wood, half of an old pool cue, lined with brass at one end. She jammed it into the top of her bag.

She moved to the doorway and looked back. She wondered who would come into the room next – Mark, thick-headed and remorseful the next morning, or Laura, horrified by the anarchy wrought by her sister-in-law. Before she closed the door, a thought occurred to her. She moved back and found a pen in the detritus of the desk, turned Warwick's note over, and wrote on it, in thick block capitals: *TELL HARV TO GO FUCK HIMSELF*. Then she turned the light off and made her way out and down the stairs, trying to remember which ones creaked.

Downstairs, she retrieved her jacket, moved into the kitchen, opened the thick curtains blocking the back door, and for a minute looked out for some sign of surveillance. She found none. Eventually, satisfied there was nobody observing from this angle, she undid the bolts, and slipped out into the burning light of the garden beyond.

32

It was a hot night, too bright to hide anywhere. Clouds had massed to the north like a high, distant mountain range. The garden was a riot of scents, fresh soil mingling with the sweet honeysuckle on the house's back wall. Beyond Laura's vegetable patch was a thin stretch of lawn, lined by laburnum, forsythia, even a couple of fuchsias sheltering along the shaded side. It was impressive, Hopper thought, what you could do with enough water.

A few apple trees stood further down the garden, their trunks gnarling out of the ground, thick with bark. A handful of apples, unpicked and shrunken, clung to their upper boughs. Mark had called the trees 'the orchard', ironically at first, and over time the joke had been forgotten and the orchard was what it was, sliding somehow from a joke to a boast. For the sunny side of the house Laura had bred plants that would survive well in constant sunlight

– most people had by now. Untended patches of common ground had become tiny, scrubby deserts, a reminder of the dry land in southern Europe pushing its way gradually north.

Hopper was grateful for the orchard now. The trees should shelter her from any observers, unless they were stationed in the houses on either side. Even then they might find it difficult to notice her as she was currently dressed, in jeans and a long-sleeved top with her black jacket over it. Mark and Laura's bedroom looked out on the garden, but their shutters were closed.

And yet she felt her heart beat tighter in her chest, her breathing shallower and less controlled than usual.

Barring a few birds muttering to themselves in the shaded branches of the trees, and the rustle of the leaves, the garden was silent. She walked to the far end. It was less luxurious up close. The soil down here was drier; the sunlit plants had browned and wilted, unrelieved by rain.

At the back of the garden the soil formed a handy ramp, making the fence on the right easier to climb. There were just three gardens between here and the side street. From there she might be able to make her way along back routes, might just avoid meeting any police. It would be surprising to see anyone on the roads apart from one of the curfew vans, but it would take only one neighbour looking out of their window, insomniac or patriotic, to call the police. It would take only one car to deliver her back to Warwick and Blake.

The side fence was her height, sturdy, supported by staves Mark had placed on this side. She reached over, deposited her bag, and pulled herself up, treading on one of the crossbeams for support. It creaked, but held, and she was over, in the next garden, her hands reddening where the wooden fence had bitten in.

This garden was longer than Mark's. Here there was long-dead mulch on the ground, and the lawn had been dug into vegetable patches, quartered by thin paving slabs. Hopper moved across, surveying the house warily, and found herself at the next fence. It was rickety. She threw her bag over and climbed up, reaching one hand to a tree branch to support herself as she did. It wasn't enough. As she hauled herself up, a section of the fence gave way, and she fell, clawing at the air. The jagged upright edge scraped the inside of her wrist, and some protuberance ripped her jacket sleeve. She slithered over into the next garden, dropping to the hard earth with a grunt.

She hauled herself up, sitting behind one of the shrubs at the end of the garden and waiting to see if anyone had heard her. Mercifully, the wood of the fence was rotten enough not to have made a loud crack as it snapped. After a minute, no window had opened, no head had poked out. Perhaps she had been mistaken for a fox.

She inspected her wrist. The top layer of skin had been scraped away, droplets of blood starting to ooze out. Could have been worse. She looked around. This garden was more affluent. Although still dug for vegetables, it had a small pagoda at this end, the white-painted window frames flecked with algae.

The third fence was as weak as the second. She found an alternative – the low branches of the oak that overhung it. She swung her bag over, scrabbled up the tree to a convenient fork, and dropped six feet or so into the final garden before the street. Just one more fence to go – taller, this one, and sturdier.

As she crossed the garden, she saw movement at the other end and froze.

A dog. A big one. It had been lying in a small, shaded kennel abutting the house, and emerged from it slowly. It looked like a Dobermann – she had seen them straining on the arms of the police, barely restrained from violence by their handlers' grips. This one moved forward, looking at her, padding slowly into sunlight. She could hear it growling from here.

Very slowly and carefully, she started to walk towards the far fence, looking down. Wasn't that the thing to do? Avoid eye contact, make yourself unthreatening?

When she was halfway across, the dog broke into a bark and a run. Hopper ran too, the final fence high in front of her, the barking so loud it would surely wake up half the street. She pitched her bag awkwardly over, and jumped onto the lower struts of the fence. The dog was almost on her as she scrabbled upwards, not feeling the pain in her arm or her ribs, and she kicked blindly backwards, making contact and hearing a bark turn into a yelp.

And then she was over, tumbling onto the other side of the fence, landing on top of her bag. This was a narrow side road, houses only on one side, and she was mercifully shielded from view by a parked van. She waited there, hearing the dog on the other side of the fence, leaping up again and again, shaking the panels. Its bark was enormous, street-filling.

A window swung open behind her. 'Shut that dog up!' someone shouted. She heard the click of another latch, and an answering

'Get fucked! Monty, shut up, will you?' The dog left off barking, and its panting receded.

Hopper's hands were raw from the final fence, and her ankle was burning. It felt like she'd twisted it. She manoeuvred into a better position, and the pain abated a little.

Sitting on the hot pavement, she pulled her bag from under her; there were painkillers in one of the pockets. She took two, forcing them down her gullet dry. She had to swallow a few more times and stayed crouched on the narrow pavement between the fence and the van, waiting for an engine, for approaching footsteps, for the car outside her brother's house to nose round the corner and spill out officers.

But the street remained silent. After a few minutes, feeling the warmth of the pavement beneath her, the pain in her ankle had become a dull throb. She stood, leaning on the fence for support, careful not to move it in case the dog came back, and tried walking, taking a few steps up and down in the concealed space behind the van. Her ankle was sore but the pain was manageable. She checked the bag: four aspirin left. She would take a couple more in a little while.

Moving through the streets during curfew was dangerous; then again, so was staying in one place. It would make more sense to find a quiet alley and wait there, maybe snatch a few hours of sleep before moving. There were still – she checked her watch – six hours left before curfew was lifted.

But staying around here had risks too. Her brother might wake, drunk and remorseful, go to her room, find her missing, raise the alarm.

The treacherous thought of turning back also occurred to her. She had pushed it away several times, sitting on the pavement with torn clothes and bruised palms, but now she thought again: she could do it. March into the street, approach the front door, and ring the bell. Before the policeman in his car could arrest her, someone would have come down; she would be back on her brother's property, safe for a few more hours.

Except she would have to sleep in that ruined room, taking Mark's hospitality, knowing it was worth nothing. Given what she had read in Mark's files, it seemed likelier he would welcome the police in. Hopper pulled herself upright, stretched her legs, and began to walk.

She'd made her decision. From here it couldn't be more than four miles to where she needed to be, five with the zigzag of the streets. She could do it in a couple of hours, even limping. She would keep the sun at her back as she walked, so knew she was heading north-west – first to the end of one residential road, then right onto a broader one for fifty yards before she could duck back onto a side street.

There were a few foxes around, filthy, mangy beasts, un-adapted to life in daylight, snatching what food they could. Some people, she had heard, had resorted to eating them a few years ago, when the shortages were very bad. Their numbers had recovered since then, though many people still thought of them as a mobile larder for the next time it happened. She had no doubt there would be a next time.

She kept thinking of Harv. She remembered lying with him, play-acting a proper relationship, talking for hours, gradually letting him into her confidence. And all that time he had been listening, then going back to his room to take notes. Was she his sole charge? Was he taking notes on Schwimmer, on the other soldiers? Probably. But she was the one he had become closest to. Had he written in his notes the precise occasions they had slept together? Had he been instructed to, or simply taken her body as an optional extra?

Her thoughts were interrupted as she approached one of the main roads that lay between her and the river. There weren't too many security cameras around, as far as she could see – still more than enough to spot her, of course, but the widespread rumour was that they weren't monitored any more, and stayed on the streets simply to intimidate, sightless eyes long cut off from an atrophied brain. She would find out now.

The road was deserted. No engines disturbed the air as Hopper crossed. In the middle, she slowed to a stop, looked up and down, held her arms out, for a moment giddy with the sheer space around her. Even on the rig, even up on the deck in the dead of night, there were soldiers in the lookout towers. Not here. She could be the last woman alive.

She lowered her arms, self-consciousness reasserting itself, and walked back into the warren of side streets, thinking of Harv and of Warwick and of David and of Thorne, and around her the world lay dead and silent, dazed by the curfew and by the sun.

The landscape was opening out now, broadening as she came to the jumble of low buildings and larger roads that marked the river's edge. She must have walked two miles, and her foot was starting to protest above the painkillers. She swallowed more, and kept going.

Vauxhall Bridge loomed before her, its narrow barriers hemmed in further by concrete devices. It was exposed, of course, but all the bridges would be exposed. Travelling further down would take her into the path of the old Parliament buildings; crossing further upriver solved no problems. She would go through into Pimlico, west onto the main roads, which had plenty of side roads to duck into and where you could hear a car coming a mile off, then eventually north. Just once she was over the river.

She started to cross.

Below her, the banks of the Thames were thicker than ever. Viewed from above, it must look almost artistic: two plateaus of white-flecked brown sandwiching the turgid waters.

The shores were steeped in detritus – old shopping trolleys half exposed like the skeletons of miniature dragons. Gulls hopped around, pecking at the eyeless worms they found amid the debris. At the water's edge a dining chair sat upright, its cushions torn, the carved spiralling wood of the legs almost completely hidden beneath a thick layer of river scum. *This is the world we have made*, she thought, and the image of Fisher's corpse, one eye smashed, rose unbidden to the surface of her mind, like a monstrous creature slowly becoming clear through the deep.

She was almost halfway across. The smell of river mud was thickest here. The barges anchored in the middle of the water were filthy, rusty, but still occupied: she could see frayed curtains lining the inside of the boats, closed against the sun. Again she thought of the boat now at the bottom of the Atlantic, and the pitiful bodies inside.

She paused. Carried to her on the motionless air, she heard a little sound behind her. Then nothing. She resumed walking. There it was again. An engine. She did not look around but stayed moving briskly, pretending everything was normal, moderating her limp as best she could. It could be another vehicle trying to avoid detection.

But then, as the sound swelled, she risked a look back, and saw it turning onto the bridge: one of the police pick-up vans. That was it, then. There was no use running now. She turned and watched it approach. It halted twenty feet ahead of her, and a man opened the passenger door and got out.

33

He was bulky, his shirt tight over his frame; a body over-developed through exercise and too much food. Hopper could see thick patches of sweat inside his armpits, turning the shirt from beige to a sickly mahogany. Like the policeman outside Thorne's house, he was young, could not have been more than twenty-three. Unlike that policeman, he wore a look of pleasure and disdain, his little eyes creasing with the expectation of sport. 'Good evening, madam.'

'Good evening.'

'You're out late.'

'I know. I'm sorry.' *I'm sorry.* What a weak thing to say. 'I was visiting a boyfriend; we had a terrible argument, and I had to leave. For my safety.' She had been preparing this line, implausible as it was.

'Even knowing the penalty?' The penalty was transportation.

'I know.' She attempted a smile. 'I tried to tell him that, and he said he didn't care. How's that for charming?' She held up her hands to him, showing the red of her palms, her ripped sleeve. 'See?'

'Well, you'll have to go in the van. We'll take you to the station, get you checked in. If your story's true, you should be out by tomorrow night.'

'Please. I'm just trying to get home. That's all I want.'

'ID card?'

She shook her head. 'They're still at his house. My wallet, everything, it's all with him.'

'Why don't we go back, then? He won't bother you if we're there.'

'I can't. I just want to go home. Please.' She wondered about the cudgel in her bag. If she moved fast, if he faced away from her, if his attention dropped for a moment … assuming it was just him in the van. She started moving her hand towards the zip of the bag, trying to picture where the pool cue was, how to swing it properly as she pulled it out.

She stopped as the other door of the van opened and closed, and she heard footsteps moving round – slow, halting. The man who appeared beside the bonnet of the van was older, larger, dressed in the same beige shirt as his colleague. He had a lopsided, unshaven face, a doughy complexion with his eyes studded in too far down. He leant on the van as he looked at her.

'Who's this then?'

The younger man spoke. 'Says she had a fight with her boy-friend and he kicked her out. Doesn't want to go back to his place.' He turned to her, and smiled unpleasantly, unseen by his colleague. 'No ID card, either.'

'What's your name, miss?'

'Jackie.' Hopper could feel herself beginning to shake. Maybe if she went with them she'd get lost in the system; maybe Warwick wouldn't track her to whatever police station she was held in. *Fat chance*, her brain whispered.

The older man looked at her again. From inside the van, there was a muffled thump against one of the walls, then another.

'We should take her in to the station,' the younger one said.

'Go and check on the others.' The thudding was insistent now.

'But she's clearly—'

'Shut up, Eric. Just do it.'

The younger man strutted to the back of the van and squeezed himself through a little door. A few seconds later, the thudding stopped. The second man looked at Hopper again, still leaning on the bonnet. She could run, she thought, but her ankle was starting to ache again, and she wouldn't make it to the end of the bridge before they caught up. And then he would definitely take her in.

'Why are you really out?'

'I already told your colleague. My boyfriend. If I hadn't got out tonight he'd have killed me.'

'What's in the bag?'

'A few clothes.'

'Anything else?'

'Yes. A stick. In case he followed me.'

'I should arrest you.' But Hopper noticed he did not look pleased about the prospect.

'Look. I can't go back. And if he picks me up from the police station, he'll kill me. He said he would. I need your help.' She was doing her utmost to seem vulnerable, but beneath the surface she felt as hard as concrete.

He sighed again. 'All right, Jackie. I'm clearly going soft. Where do you need to get to?'

She tried to hide her excitement. 'Queensway. I have a cousin there.' He looked at his watch, and made a face. 'Or anywhere. But not back to Brixton.'

'No, that's all right. Queensway it is. We should be there in about fifteen minutes, I'd say, unless we see anyone else on the way.'

'Thank you.'

'Not at all. Nice to have someone calm to talk to. Get in.'

She moved to the passenger side, boosted her bag up before her. He pressed a button. 'We're moving off, Eric. Stay tight for the moment.' He flicked a switch, and Eric's voice shrank into a tiny, high-pitched burble, and then to nothing.

Hopper jerked her head backwards. 'Who's in tonight?'

'Nobody exciting. Few drunks. Kid with a knife. Probably just needs a talking-to. But my colleague is very assiduous.'

She was surprised. She'd heard the night wagons and the men who drove them were uncompromising, brutal. It was disorienting to be chatted to like this. 'Why didn't you arrest me?'

'You're sober, you're not acting erratically – just stupidly, being out here. And I believe your story.'

'Thank you.'

'Or at least, I believe that whatever lie you're telling me, it's probably not a cover for something worse.'

She wondered what he would think if she told him the truth: *Actually, I'm trying to trace a body of evidence that could collapse the government.* The engine groaned as he switched up a gear. They were moving faster now, the bridge disappearing from the mirrors as he swung west. His little eyes surveyed the road, and occasionally he glanced sideways at her.

'What's your line, anyway?'

'My line?' Oh Christ. He knew she was lying.

'Of work.'

'Oh.' She suddenly wanted to tell him the truth, or at least something as close to the truth as she could manage. 'I work on one of the rigs. Government ones.'

'What do you do out there?'

'Study the ocean. Work out which way it's going. See how many fish are left. Which way *they're* going. That sort of thing.'

'Scientist, then?'

'Yes.'

'Well, you can tell me then.' He kept his eyes on the road, talking as casually as if he was discussing a football match. 'How long do we have?'

'Until what?'

'Until the air runs out.'

'You mean the oxygen?'

'Whatever. Till we can't breathe.'

'A few hundred years. Or just one hundred. Or maybe never.'

'Why never?'

'It depends. There might be more algae in the ocean than there used to be; they make half the oxygen. So it may not matter if there aren't as many trees producing oxygen.'

'What do you think?'

Hopper sighed and rubbed her eyes. 'I think it'll decline. Even if it doesn't, I think this country won't last much longer. Not in its current form. There are too many ...' She couldn't find the word. 'It's like a machine that's jerking itself to pieces.'

'And yet, look at them all.' He gestured towards the building site lining the road. A billboard outside declared: *NEW HOMES FOR FAMILIES. COMING SOON.* 'They keep going. Why do they do it?'

'Ask a priest,' Hopper said, and the driver laughed shortly. 'Why do *you* do it?'

He didn't answer immediately. She heard a muffled shout from the back of the van as they turned a corner sharply, and then he spoke. 'I keep having the same dream, over and over again. It's night. I'm with my wife. We're away, somewhere. I can't work out where. Somewhere in Europe. And we're on a little terrace, overlooking the sea. It's not even a dream, really. It's like a snapshot. We're both just there, happy with each other. I think I keep going so I keep having that dream.'

Hopper didn't want to ask what had happened to his wife.

'You have kids?'

She shook her head.

'Lot of people thinking like you, it seems.' He pointed through the windscreen. 'We're nearly there.' The streets here were familiar, reminding her of the past, of moving in here with David in a van about this size.

They drove in silence until they were interrupted by a burst of static from the radio: 'Vehicle 19, please report.'

The driver briefly pressed his finger to his lips before flicking a switch. 'Just making my way to Queensway. One of the people we picked up reported a gathering round there earlier tonight.'

'Cancel that. Move to Hammersmith. Resident's phoned in a report of movement in the streets. Coordinates coming to your ticker.'

'Right you are.' He flicked the switch again. 'Better drop you here then. That OK with you?'

'More than. Won't your colleague report you?'

'I don't think so.'

'Why not?'

'Last month I caught him nicking a ration book off a dead man. I imagine he'll want to keep that quiet.' He looked at her shrewdly. 'Good luck getting home, or wherever you said you were going. Obviously, stay off the main roads.'

Within seconds, Hopper was on the sunlit street again, her bag heavy at her side as the van moved off. She was just a short walk away from her old home. David's current home. She turned down a side road, her footsteps unnaturally loud in her ears. It was just before two in the morning.

She could not approach David's house yet. If she knocked on the door mid curfew, his neighbours might spot her and report him. So she had to spend three hours out here, in the sleeping, sunlit world.

There was one place she knew she'd be safe, a little park a few streets over. She turned towards it. As she rounded the corner, she recoiled. Facing away from her, near the park's entrance, was a guard. Her heart tightened. They knew she was here. She should hand herself in now, plead ignorance, hope for clemency.

After a few seconds of panic, she calmed down. Lots of places were guarded at night. Curfew was designed to stop people gathering in precisely these sorts of spots. Of course there was a guard.

He stood, unaware of her presence, shifting his weight a little from one foot to the other. Around the back of his head she saw wisps of smoke curling upwards. She decided to take the risk, moving quietly between the cars lining the road outside the park, then crossing, following the curve of the road out of his sightline to a point halfway between two gates.

She hauled herself over the railings and fell to the ground on the other side – remembering too late the last time she had landed on her ankle. Pain shot through her leg, and despite herself, a small cry escaped her lips. She grabbed her bag and crawled between two hedges, shaded by an oak, waiting, trembling.

After a couple of minutes, she guessed nobody had heard her, and wondered whether to move to somewhere safer. But the hedges were full and rich and muffled the outside world. Her thoughts slid and overlapped and were nowhere, barring one jagged thought, an important one, which made her want to wake. But it was too late for that.

Unheard by her, the air stirred the leaves, and the songbirds chirruped softly as they rooted in the soil. All that was visible of her was a single trainer poking through the undergrowth.

34

It was almost half past five when she woke. Just a few more minutes until the world began again. Her face was pressed to the soft dirt, the rest of her body twisted around behind her. Her foot felt worse, and her ribs too. She did not want to risk taking her shoe off, worrying it might not fit back on, but the top of her ankle looked reddened and furious. She prayed she hadn't broken anything.

She limped towards the gate, concealed under the shade of the trees, and looked for the guard. He had left his post; the gate was open.

It was time to get to David's, if she wanted to catch him soon after the end of curfew. She started walking, gingerly, keeping the weight off her ankle.

The noise hit her as she walked. She heard the klaxons approaching from a distance, blossoming one after another into the slow, miserable sound, a heaped and confused dirge, one block out of time with another and then a third overlaid on that until the entire area was a bank of murky noise, lapping and over-lapping and pushing against the ears.

She kept walking, briskly, for a full minute, while the sound swirled around her like dirty water in a bath. And just as sud-denly, it was over, the sound receding in the opposite direction. Had she been observed? She did not risk a look to either side. A few doors ahead of her, a door opened, and a suited man stepped out, case in hand. An insomniac, perhaps, or a workaholic. As he passed her, his eyes slid onto her for a second, before moving away again, cool and expressionless.

It didn't matter. She was almost there now. She turned right onto the road, marking the differences since she'd been away. The garden that had held ranks of hollyhocks was now bare. The paint marking the centre of the road had been redone. The aban-doned house halfway along, its windows boarded up with card daubed with apocalyptic signs, had been refurbished, was now fresh-painted and shuttered. Shame.

And here was the house she and David had shared. Fearing a loss of nerve, Hopper forced herself to walk up the drive, and knocked on the door.

He probably wasn't up yet. A house call at this hour would alarm him, especially given yesterday's events, but there was no other way. After half a minute she knocked again, and peered through the frosted glass to see a shape descending the stairs. He opened the door slowly, his expression wary, and when he saw it was her, his face sagged in relief.

'Can I come in?'

'Yes, but ... yes. Of course.'

The hall was completely different. The tiles on the floor had been covered by a thick rug. The table had changed, the art, everything. There was a grandfather clock taking up far too much of the available space, crammed in at the bottom of the stairs, and ticking aggravatingly slowly.

David was unshaven, in a dressing gown, his hair at odd angles, his eyes crusted and reddened behind his glasses.

She gestured. 'Is this still the living room?'

'Yes.'

She moved around him, avoided the ridiculous clock, and stepped into the front room. This was unexpected too: unwelcome new furniture. How absurd to be thinking about the decor at a time like this.

She sank into the sofa, feeling momentarily ridiculous as the cushions puffed up around her. 'Do you have ice?'

'Ice? What for?'

'My foot. Twisted my ankle.'

He left, clattered, returned with a tall tumbler full of cubes. As she slowly levered the shoe from her foot and began rubbing her ankle with the ice, he stood across the room from her, leaning on the mantelpiece, his arms folded.

'What happened? Did they find you after you went home?'

She told him, briefly, about her visit to Gethin's house, her brother, the secret room. When she told him that Mark's colleagues had been spying on her, David interjected.

'They were observing you even on the rig? How?'

'Through Harvey. He was someone I was close to. A . . . friend. Or someone I thought was.'

David nodded, tactful, and she was grateful for his circumspection. She told him the rest: the garden, the bridge, the van.

'And you're sure they haven't followed you here?'

'I wouldn't be here if they had. I don't think they want to talk any more. They just want to bring me in.'

David looked towards the window, where the slats were shut against the world, as if expecting them to be kicked in at any moment. 'All right. Let's think about what we've got.'

'Well, the first thing – I suppose the only thing, now we know there's no way of getting close to Gethin – is the photo of Thorne and his colleagues. I retrieved it from my brother's place before I left.' She pulled it from her pocket and handed it over.

He looked at it as she continued. 'I think the box in front there is the thing he wants me to find, and that's what Warwick and her colleagues are looking for. But it wasn't at Fisher's place as far as I could tell. It seems to have disappeared.'

David pointed at the box. 'Ellie, you do know what this is, don't you?'

She looked at him blankly. 'No. Do you?'

'Of course I do. It's a satellite.'

'What?'

'A satellite. It's not a typical-looking one, but I'm sure of it. Look at this line here. These little gaps; they're instruments. I'm certain of it. I've seen it before.'

Hopper couldn't believe it. 'But . . . I know what satellites look like, and that looks nothing like one. And anyway, they don't exist any more. The whole network collapsed. I learnt that at university.'

'That's not true.' He smiled. 'One of the advantages of working for *The Times* is that the government sometimes tell you about things they don't want you to print. But to do that, they have to tell you exactly the information you're not allowed to know about. And when I became news editor, I got a briefing on a few topics that were strictly off limits. They only give you the vaguest information, nothing more than an outline really, but I know for a fact that this is what a satellite looks like these days.'

She felt euphoric. 'David, you genius.'

He grinned. 'Never thought it would come in handy.'

'So Thorne made one. Maybe he sent it up. And saw something he shouldn't have done. Some evidence of what Davenport's doing, or something in the Breadbasket.' Hopper's heart was racing. If only she'd brought the photo a day earlier.

'Exactly. And that tallies with what we know about Thorne's career. It's not surprising that he might have been working on a satellite. His department covered almost everything non-military right before he was fired. Why not a satellite?'

'All right, so this is what we're looking for.'

David frowned. 'The only question is what we can do based on that. It's not like we can go and retrieve it. If he even managed to get this one into orbit.' He jabbed at the box in the photograph.

'Actually, I think I know where we have to go.'

'Where?'

'Oxford.' The idea had come to her in the park, just at the edge of sleep.

'Oxford? What for?'

'Warwick and her men have been through Thorne's home. His only other contact we know of was Fisher, and he didn't get through to Fisher. There was nobody else in his life he trusted, apart from one person. Caroline Heathcote, the warden of my college. She's the one who took him in when he needed it. He once said to me that she and I were the two people he was closest to. So my guess is that he left it with her.'

'Didn't the warden force him out?'

'The whole college did. The warden couldn't resist. Better for her to stay in power, still able to do him a favour.'

'Sounds plausible enough. All right, Oxford then. You'll need company, though. I'm not missing out on this.'

'Are you sure?'

She had meant it kindly, had meant to imply she didn't want to burden him further, but he looked a little affronted as he spoke. 'Ellie, I've made my choice to do this with you. I'm as tired of these people as you are. I was there with you yesterday in the warehouse. I'm here today. I trust you. I'd like you to do the same with me.'

She looked at him, and he met her gaze, and for the first time in years, she felt something less than alone.

'What about your work?'

'Fuck work. I decided for sure last night. I'm not going back. Not after Harry.'

'Do you have a car?'

'I can borrow one.'

'When?'

He looked at his watch. 'I'll phone my friend now. He's only ten minutes away.'

'Is it safe to phone?'

He shook his head. 'Guess not. I'll go round. Let me dress.'

He left the room. Outside, the sun had vanished behind cloud. Hopper turned to her side; there was a radio there. She turned it on, and after a few seconds of crackle found the right line.

David came back in, dressed. She left the radio on for him to hear the headlines – more news on the American deal – before twisting it off.

'That's going to be all we hear about for the next year.'

'When shall we head off? Now?' Hopper asked, aware that waves of tiredness were hitting her. 'If you go and borrow the car, we can leave in twenty minutes.'

He shook his head. 'We'll be less conspicuous in a few hours. And without wanting to be rude, you look exhausted. I'll get the car while you rest.'

Hopper started to protest for a moment, lacked the strength, and nodded.

'Good. The bed's made up in the spare room.'

'Which is that?'

'Your old study.'

She got up, knocked over the tumbler of ice in the process, made it to the door. At the top of the stairs, she glimpsed herself in the full-length mirror on the landing. There were bits of leaf stuck in her hair. Her eyes were bloodshot, her forehead bruised, and her jacket had a torn sleeve. On her feet, she had only one shoe, the other discarded downstairs, and her ankle was a livid red, streaked with white. She was being reduced; boiled down from a scientist, to a citizen, to a woman, to a moving body with only one destination.

Her study had indeed been turned into a bedroom; it had a soft bed, and she found it, methodically took off her clothes, and slept.

35

She was sitting quite still when Thorne arrived back in his office. It was dark – she had not touched the thick blackout blind, and the only light in the room came from the desk lamp she had read by. The air smelt of burnt dust.

She had been sitting here for over an hour. She had crept back in on a whim, and then she had looked through his desk, and now she was not sure whether she should stay or go, whether to confront him or simply leave and never speak to him again.

It was not intentional, she kept telling herself; she had not meant to learn what she had learnt. As though she need feel any guilt compared with what he'd done.

She had entered the room almost innocently, convinced she was doing nothing wrong – hardly doing anything at all. Why was she doing this? Because she needed the truth. Because he had been evasive for the whole year about why he had left government, and because she had never quite believed his suggestions that he had been uninvolved with important matters of state.

One of the drawers in his desk had been half open, and she had idly pulled it, still pretending to herself she might just be looking for one of her old essays, that this was accidental. Near the bottom, a string of words caught her eye: *Interior Ministry Confined Reports*. It was a plain burgundy folder, wound with a string tie. The date on the front was the year before Thorne had left office.

There were lots of reports inside the file, each taking no more than ten densely typed pages. One report from each department, according to a contents page at the front: Farming (subdivided into Arable and Livestock), Fishing, Energy, Security, Defence, Policing.

The rest of the drawer held more folders full of reports. She picked out the earliest one – from nine years ago, Davenport's first year in office – and looked at the contents. They were identical, but for one extra category at the end of the list.

English Channel: Emergency Response.

She opened it and began to read.

An hour later, Thorne returned, edging through the door with a stack of books in his arms. 'Hello, Ellen. This is a strange time to see you here.' Beyond that, he made no other comment on her presence, nor on the fact that she was behind his desk. Afterwards, she thought that in some way he must have known what she was about to say.

She looked at him and had to breathe in and out so her voice wouldn't shake when she spoke. 'You gave the order to sink all those ships. All the ones that came after the Stop. That was you.' She gestured at the pages in front of her.

In the dim light of the lamp, Thorne seemed to age before her. He put the books down on a table, ignoring one that fell to the ground, and moved over, taking a place in the armchair she normally sat in.

His voice, when he spoke, was quiet, unlike his usual tone. 'Yes. That was my responsibility.'

'You wrote this.' She picked up a piece of paper she had found in the file. It dated from a month after Davenport's takeover – his true takeover, six years after the Stop, when the second collapse was under way – and was headlined *Channel Closure and Instructions to the Fleet*. It suggested the requisitioning of all civilian boats around the coast for the duration of the 'Immigration Emergency', and that the navy fit any seaworthy vessel with guns. And it proposed that the newly engorged Royal Navy should sink any foreign vessels that entered within a ten-mile zone, irrespective of the nature of the boat. Civilian, military, industrial, trafficker, refugee. Everything. Including any boats flying colours of allies, and any non-military British ships.

At the end of the document, a thin line of black stated: *There can be no exceptions to this declaration*, as though that was not clear already. The lazy loops of Thorne's signature as Chief Scientific Officer at the Ministry of Defence were the same three twirls she had seen at the end of her essays. Across the page, the second signature, that of Richard Davenport, granted permission to change the diseased plan into law. The letters of his name were faded black spikes, jutting like iron railings.

A separate document – same author, same co-author – gave orders, using the RAF, the USAF, and the thousands of rockets prised from the US military, to simultaneously attack hundreds of ports across northern Europe, to demolish as many boats as possible. The big ones – Rotterdam, Zeebrugge, Antwerp – were to be treated especially heavily, but countless smaller ports would be smashed, reducing the continent's escape route to matchwood. The same methods were to be employed across northern Africa, to 'degrade as far as possible' all ports and all boats over a certain size. The attack was ordered to take place over three consecutive days, to minimise the number of vessels that would survive. No warnings were to be given to civilians in advance of the raids.

This document bore Thorne's signature too.

'Why?'

'I had no choice.'

'You could have said no.'

He breathed out, long and slow. 'The prime minister asked me for a solution, and I provided it.'

'Everyone said it was Davenport's decision. That's why he won the election; people thought he was the one who'd seal us off, and he did.'

'He was in overall command. But he wanted me to come up with the method. He liked to ensure people shared responsibility for ugly or unpleasant decisions.'

The blood pounded in her ears. 'This wasn't an unpleasant decision. This was genocide.'

'It was ... security.'

'Do you know how many died?'

He didn't answer her question. 'Some people were returned to France if their ship was close enough to shore and seaworthy. The majority ... were not. Those who offered resistance or refused to leave their ships to be returned had their vessel sunk.' His chin was almost on his chest. 'Later, it became necessary to sink on sight. Too many traffickers were escaping and returning.'

'How many?'

'I don't know.

'Yes you do. What was the final total?'

'Perhaps ten million.'

'Ten million. Jesus.' She voiced the thought that had been occurring to her from the moment she had read the document. 'My mother was on one of those boats.'

He didn't say anything.

She was dimly aware she was crying. 'You used my mother's memory to get me to stay here. And you were the one who killed her.' He made no movement. 'Why did he ... why did you order this?'

'The country was on the brink of collapse. Right on the brink. For six months it seemed probable we would be totally overrun. What do you do if you're in a full lifeboat and there are thousands more in the water?'

'It wasn't a lifeboat. It's a country. We could have taken more people.'

'I'm sorry, Ellen. I really am. But people were starving. It was the only way. If we had failed to act, the whole country would have collapsed.'

'And this is success? Scratching from hand to mouth, two decades of rationing? People screaming in the streets? Living in the woods like animals?'

'I didn't know what Davenport would become, but I knew what we ran the risk of becoming. A dictatorship is better than a wasteland. We truly believed – I believed – those were the only two options. Barbarity or collapse. He chose barbarity. And I joined him.' Through her tears, Hopper could see he was knotting his hands before him.

'You murdered . . . you don't even know how many millions of people whose deaths you ordered, one of whom was my mother. And you can't even admit it to yourself.'

'I can, Ellen.' She felt momentarily revolted at his use of her name. 'I can admit it. I cannot change what I have done. The fact that someone else would have signed it if I had not is irrelevant. I signed it.'

'This is why he kept you on in government?'

'It's one reason.'

'How can you live? Knowing this?'

'I don't know.' From this angle, his head low, his eye sockets were hollow, and she saw a shadow of the skull beneath the skin. 'I have tried to find ways to atone.'

'What could possibly atone for this?'

'Nothing, I know. Nothing.' He was hardly audible.

'Why would anyone go along with this?'

331

He raised his head. 'Do you think there aren't thousands of people who remember this? The mobilisation alone ...' He waved his hands. 'Everyone knew what was being done on their behalf. It was a matter of survival.'

Hopper took a breath. 'What if I started telling people, the people who don't know about this? People my age?'

'I have caused enough deaths, Ellen. I wouldn't like to cause yours.'

'Does this still happen?'

He shook his head a little. 'The Breadbasket has obviated the need for it. And almost nobody comes to Britain now, anyway.'

'I have to tell someone.'

'You would only be telling them what they already suspect.'

'Why did Davenport force you out? If this became open knowledge ...'

'Ellen, it practically is. People don't want to know exactly what happened. They want to know they'll have bread to eat tomorrow, and next year, and they'll support anyone who gives it to them. If this was on the front page of tomorrow's *Times*, Davenport would say he had sorrowfully done the right thing to protect our nation.'

'Why did you leave the government then? Knowing what you know, why did Davenport get rid of you?'

Thorne looked away from her again, to the side. 'I can't tell you.'

'Bullshit.'

'It's true, Ellen. I'm sorry. I'm not as brave as I should be. Not any more. Not with more of other people's lives.'

'Sure.' She picked up her bag.

'Ellen. Please stay.'

She did not wish to hear any more explanations. She could not bear any more of this. The door was in front of her and she pulled it stiffly open. As she turned back for a moment, she had a sense of him, still crumpled in the armchair, but she averted her eyes and walked out to the hot, close air of the quad below.

She left Oxford that afternoon, changed her address two days later, failed to take her placement in Skye over the summer. By the time she returned in October, he was gone. He had left three letters in the porters' lodge for her, which she tore in two and burnt, unread.

36

Hopper was awake again, looking at the ceiling of her study. No, not the study, the spare bedroom. Her former study. It was clean, barring the pile of her clothes in the middle of the floor, almost denuded of personality.

The mattress under her was thick, luxurious; she wondered when it had been made, and where. The only mattresses she had slept on in the last few years were military issue: clotted with lumps and hardly thick enough to stretch a bed sheet tight. The rest of the furniture consisted of a little desk and chair, a wardrobe and a bookshelf. In the corner was an ottoman she recognised, an old carved thing so heavy and impractical it would probably never leave this room again.

This one folded open, and was designed to store bed linen. She opened it, its hinges groaning at the unaccustomed exercise.

In the base, resting on a pile of cotton sheets – so, he had kept it – was a child's mobile, now a tangle of wires and wood knotted almost past redemption. She pulled it out. It had birds dangling on it, studding each wire: little painted toucans and puffins carved from pine. He had bought it for her as a sort of joke when they had first talked about having children, and before she had said no. But the joke had had a little tang of meaning at its heart that reminded her of some supposed deficiency within herself, and she had been wounded.

And later she had left him, had taken the job on the rig, formed a near-perfect barrier between herself and the world. The barrier felt pretty flimsy now.

She found a towel beneath the sheets, replaced the mobile, and made her way into the bathroom. She tried the shower, standing gingerly to avoid putting weight on her twisted ankle. The water was warm – better than warm: hot. It scalded her bruised forehead, her bruised ribs, her scarlet ankle, unknotted her muscles.

On her way back from the bathroom, she noticed that her bag had been placed outside the bedroom door as she slept. She changed her clothes, crammed the old ones into a corner of the bag, and made her way downstairs. David was standing in the kitchen in front of a pan. In the corner, a radio burbled at the edge of hearing.

'You've had a decent rest. Hope the shower was warm enough. I heard it going, started some breakfast.' She felt a sudden prickle of self-consciousness at her wet hair, tangled and cold, and started to thumb the knots out of it.

'What's the time?'

'Coming up to eleven.'

'Shouldn't we have left already?'

'We can be in Oxford in a couple of hours. You need food.' He served up the contents of the pan, a hash of mushrooms and scrambled eggs and garlic. She realised she had missed a couple of meals yesterday, and ate, hungrily.

As she finished, he jerked a thumb at the radio. 'You should hear what's started in your absence.'

'The Americans?'

'Yeah. Sounds like it's an unconditional rolling-over. They want a pact based on recognised mutual interests.'

'What does that mean?'

'Not much, bluntly. They need our food, that much is clear. We just didn't realise how badly they need it. In return for the weapons, they'll get access to our resources, a cut of the Breadbasket. It makes them much likelier to survive. And Davenport's won the final thing he wanted. He'll have the whole country restored, lots of new manpower, and all the military might of the last superpower. Albion is reborn.'

'They can do that? Just give up?'

'They've had a rough thirty years, El. If you ask me, it's a miracle they lasted as long as they did.'

'You don't sound happy about it.'

'Not especially. I always hoped they'd be all right or that their sector might survive if this one fell apart.' He paused. 'I can't believe Thorne sent up a satellite. I can't stop thinking about why he did it.'

'The warden will know. If anyone will know, she will.'

His head bobbed. 'Before we go, Ellie, is there anything else to it?'

'What do you mean?'

He sighed. 'El, in all our time together' – he swallowed, suddenly nervous – 'you mentioned Thorne a couple of times at most, and you were pretty strange about it when you did. Anyone else would talk about the fact that they had been tutored by practically the father of the nation. But whenever I asked about it, you shut down the conversation immediately. I always assumed something happened between you. Well, to be blunt, I thought you and he ... had had an affair or something.'

'Oh God, David, no. Nothing like that. I admired him for a long time, and then ... well.' She could either tell him now or not at all. So she told him about her last meeting with Thorne.

When she had finished, he whistled. 'Christ, Ellie. That's ... I mean, everyone sort of knew. But you're saying you had proof? You saw it, in his office?'

'Yes.'

'Why didn't you take it? Think of what could have been done with it. Jesus, we could have got rid of Davenport. Even he couldn't have survived proper evidence of a blanket attack on civilians.'

'I was nineteen, David. I was terrified. And Thorne told me there was no possible benefit in telling anyone, and that I'd be killed if I tried.' Her eyes were prickling.

'You've carried round that knowledge for such a long time. Come here, Ellie.' He crossed the room and hugged her. Maybe it was the physical contact, or the relief of telling him something she hadn't even in their marriage. Whatever it was, she felt herself crying. She had hardly been touched since she arrived in London. Her brother had hugged her welcome, Harv had hugged her goodbye, and David was the only one of the three who had not let her down.

Eventually he stepped back.

'When I came over as he was dying, I thought he was going to tell me something about all that. That's the only reason I came.'

'Do you still think it's about that?'

'I think it could be. Maybe it's the proof of the sinkings. Maybe he wanted to publish during his lifetime but he was too scared. But I don't see how it could damage Davenport.'

'Either way, we need to go to Oxford.'

'Yes.'

'All right then. Well, at least we shouldn't be stopped leaving London. They normally don't check people leaving, not at this time of day. I've put some of Pam's paperwork in the car; you can use that if required.'

It didn't take long to pack the car: the same bag Hopper had taken from Mark's place, a little food and drink for the journey, sandwiches in an old biscuit tin with pictures of a bucolic harvest scene around the edges. She remembered it from their marriage.

As they were about to leave, David said, 'Just a second,' and darted into the house. He was back within a minute, and as he got in, he leant over and carefully placed a heavy object, wrapped in a handkerchief, into the glove compartment.

'What's that?'

'Nothing. Something I borrowed from a friend.'

She opened the compartment and twitched the handkerchief aside.

'A gun? A fucking gun, David?'

'Not a good one.'

'I'm glad I'm not your defence lawyer. Look at this thing. It's practically antique.'

'I know. I'm not intending to use it.'

'Does it work?'

'I don't know.'

'I suppose you could lecture someone about it until they died of boredom.'

He laughed, and started the car.

The sky to the west was dark as they drove out through Notting Hill, up onto the old flyover, where the sky broadened out and the west of London opened before them, mile after mile of bland suburb. There was a large smear of charcoal in the sky ahead. The forecasts had been right: rain was coming.

The roads were quiet. Most private cars didn't make long journeys these days, and the less they were used, the fewer cars proved roadworthy the next time their owners did need to travel.

Hopper always wondered, when she saw the blank faces in other cars, what desire or crisis or secret hope had prompted their journey. Today, as always, the faces of the drivers they passed revealed nothing. They overtook a military convoy, six trucks with half-open backs hauling along the slow lane. Young men and women were visible inside, their tanned faces obscured by the gloom of the trucks.

Within half an hour they were out of London. The barrier was easily crossed, with only a cursory glance at David's papers. He had been right: the queue into the city was long, but nobody was leaving.

After the suburbs had receded behind them, he spoke. 'Can you smell that?'

'What?'

'Not-London.'

He was right. The tarry stink of the city had faded from Hopper's nose. She lowered the window and stuck her head out a little, just to smell the clean air.

When she pulled back in, David spoke again. 'How will we find the Warden?'

'She'll be there. I know it.'

Hopper knew the warden was still in post – had been two months ago, anyway. Her birthday had been listed in the *Times* passed around the rig's canteen. It wasn't surprising: the job was not taxing, and Hopper could well imagine her being pliant enough to avoid being dislodged in favour of a younger candidate. The real surprise was that she had risked her reputation by offering Thorne a position in the first place. They must have been truly close.

Hopper's memory of Heathcote was of a stout, crafty woman, intelligent and waspish, leaning to one side to better hear her guests along the top table at dinner. Like a lot of women her age, conscription and conflict around the time of the Stop had left her half deaf.

'What if she refuses to see us?'

'I don't think she will.' She tapped the glove compartment and grinned. 'I'm armed and dangerous, after all.'

The Chiltern Gap loomed ahead of them, a huge hollow in the hills through which the road had been cut. It was the pinch point – in Hopper's mind – dividing Oxford from London. The beauty of it pressed them temporarily into silence. It was jungly, the chalk of the hillside barely visible through the thick dark leaves. As she looked, there was a little flutter of brighter green – two parakeets, one pursuing the other, flitting over the road. The only sign of humanity was a rusted, abandoned guard's hut.

And there, before them, Oxfordshire opened out, a patchwork of greens and browns and yellows, the pale grey artery of the road diminishing to invisibility in the distance. Hopper had always loved this moment, and this time found little enough changed – at this distance, anyway – to preserve her sense of the county's beauty.

They carried on for a few miles, descending into the broad low plain of the Thames Valley, past abandoned road signs she had seen before, had been passing since the first time she came for her interview. *CALLAGHAN HAULAGE. MACHINES MOVED. RING NOW* read one, followed by a number for a phone network that no longer existed. They were comforting, these signs, faint implications that the world might one day begin again.

David was silent beside her. She nearly spoke to him, but was conscious he was in the middle of his own thoughts, and felt a sudden tenderness, a desire to protect him there for a while.

They drifted off the motorway at the right junction, onto one of the tiny capillary roads that served Oxford. Up ahead, a queue of cars blocked the road. Hopper could just see, in front of them, a corrugated iron structure topped with a Union Jack, and the red and black of a road barrier grinding down. A checkpoint. She swore under her breath.

'Can you come off? Or reverse?'

'No.' The embankment of the road was high – probably why they had placed the checkpoint here. Even past the embankment, the road was lined with thick trees. And there were already more cars approaching behind, boxing them in.

They halted about six cars from the front. Two figures were manning the checkpoint, in the uniform of the army, not the police. One was in a roadside booth, the other was at the side of the foremost car.

Hopper felt sick. 'What do we do?'

'Pick up Pam's papers in the front there. There's no photo on them, so you can pretend they're old ones and your new ones are in the post. Do you think they'll know you're missing yet? Will there be a description out?'

'Maybe not.'

'Sure?'

'No.' It was nearly one in the afternoon. Her bedroom door had been shut behind her. It was possible that her brother had left for work, that Laura wouldn't have pushed the door open. If Mark had realised she was missing, would he have reported it by now? Or would he have granted her a few hours' grace?

The soldier running the booth was rotund, unsmiling. He waved the car ahead of them through, and David slowed to a halt in front of him, winding down his window as the man approached.

The soldier was reddened, his skin livid under the sun. The sides of his neck and the backs of his hands were raw and cracked. They shone, too, and as he leant briefly on the edge of the car window, his knuckles pressed a faint oily slick in eight fat lines on the edge. They still looked raw. Some people had never adapted to the sun. Hopper wondered how long it would take them to die out.

'What's the purpose of your travel today?'

'Visiting family,' David said.

'Where?'

'Oxford.'

The soldier lowered himself awkwardly, inspected Hopper in the passenger seat, and grunted. 'Papers?'

'Yes, of course.' They handed them over, David fumbling as he did so. He was easily flustered. Hopper remembered a time when she'd found it endearing, and felt a pang of it now, even through her mounting panic.

'I'm sorry,' she said. 'These are expired but there have been problems with the new ones.'

The man stood, flicking through the papers, so all they could see of him was an expansive stomach, a curl of thick black hair poking out between the buttons on his shirt front.

'Wait here.' He turned and lumbered back towards the booth. After the door clanged behind him, Hopper looked at David.

'What if he arrests us?'

'I suppose you should try to get out on your side, get away. If I open the door quickly on him I could slow him down, maybe, surprise him ...' David tailed off. It was obvious to him, and to her, that they were no match even for a fat, bored guard at a road-block armed with a rusting pistol.

Even so, her feet tingled, and as the door of the booth swung open again, her hand rested lightly on the door handle, while the other eased off her seat belt.

As the soldier made his way out, one of the cars behind them risked a couple of blasts on its horn, the noise startling birds from nearby trees, and he shot a baleful glance towards it. He leant down into the car and looked at Hopper for a second. As she was preparing to hurl herself out, to try and make it into the trees at the side of the road, he simply said, 'Drive safe.' He ditched the documents into David's lap and stood once again, already waiting for the next car, as the red-and-black barrier ground upwards.

David released the clutch and the car sprang forward, nearly stalling as he pulled away. Neither of them spoke until the booth had disappeared behind them around a curve in the road. He pointed ahead: 'Good thing we didn't just drive through.' Before them, parked at the side of the road, was an armoured vehicle, three soldiers sitting in it. One straddled a gun mounted in the back.

They had the road to themselves once again.

David spoke. 'Do you want to stop before we arrive?'

'No.' She had answered without thinking about it. Her hand was shaking. She sat on it, squashing it beneath her leg. Her breathing felt short. 'How much further to go?'

'We'll be there before two.'

After a mile, the hedgerow widened and jerked away from the road. They saw the slow-down signs next, followed by the village sign welcoming them to Bicklehampton, beneath a painted image of a hare and a fox chasing each other in a circle, an idealised rural ouroboros. It sparked a memory in her, but before she could catch hold of it, it was gone, whipped away by the movement of the car.

Bicklehampton was nearly abandoned. David slowed the car as they went, but from the look of the outskirts – houses choked with weeds, an old community hall with a moss-stained door – there seemed little reason to do so.

Before they reached the dilapidated heart of the village, they passed the human flotsam on its edges: two young women sitting in a rusty corrugated-iron bus shelter, one pushing a pram back and forth, the other smoking. A little way along, two children were kicking a football against a wall. Both pairs followed the car's movement with their eyes as they passed. A hundred yards beyond was Bicklehampton proper: houses, a dark-timbered pub, and a parade of shops, showing more chipboard on the ground floor than plate glass.

'We've been here before.'

He was right. She'd had a feeling since seeing the sign as they entered, a feeling now punctured by the banality of the truth – it was just memory, after all. They had stayed here for a night.

It had been some sort of driving holiday, a few months after their wedding. Her idea: she had just taken possession of a car, an ancient but lovingly patched Ford. She had wanted to show it off, and so for two weeks they had travelled across the country, staying in little bed and breakfasts as they went.

They had been happy. David had been granted an extended break from his work, and her first job was not due to start for another month, so away they had gone. David had called it 'The Great Patriotic Tour', making fun of some propaganda campaign running at the time.

They had stayed in cheap establishments run by proprietors keen to earn a bit of extra money, many of them elderly people who remembered life before the Slow and had tried to recreate it in small ways. One woman in a little family hotel in Wiltshire had rigged up a region of her garden with hanging sheets to give the impression of 'evening sun', as she called it. A retired army officer who had seemed perfectly normal at first showed them the earthen cellars he had dug out beneath the foundations of his now tottering home. It had sent everyone a bit mad, the Slow, in different ways.

As they passed out of the village, Hopper thought about the women at the bus stop, and wondered where they were going. People's borders had shrunk. Even fifteen years ago this sort of journey, sixty miles or so from London, would have been normal, worth making to see family. You could get anywhere in the country in a couple of days. But as the petrol shortages had tightened, everyone's mental boundaries had been circumscribed, degree by degree.

David spoke. 'Why leave him alive?'

'Who?'

'Thorne. He launches a satellite unannounced, and without approval, and discovers something he shouldn't have. The department is disbanded. Everyone else – barring Gethin, who must have proved his loyalty somehow – gets the chop. Why not just kill Thorne?'

'Maybe they thought he had arrangements in place and that he'd pass the information on remotely if they killed him. We don't even know if they ever got the satellite up.' She sighed. 'I'm just guessing.'

Outside the car, on her right, a huge span of long, boxy buildings denoted a farm, one of the new four-tier hydroponic places. 'I'm not sure how much longer I can do this, David. It feels like asking the questions, visiting people, is causing them to die. First Thorne, then Fisher. And Harry, whatever happened to him.'

He shook his head. 'You're just following the story, Ellie. But one thing to think about is: what are we going to do when we find what Thorne saw on the satellite?'

She shrugged. 'Try to tell people. Somehow.'

David leant over and, unexpectedly, gripped her hand. They stayed like that for a minute or two, and then he pulled away to change gear as Oxford rose before them.

On the eastern horizon, a pall of smoke hung in the sky, a light grey that stood out against the dark clouds stretching from one horizon to another. The bruise of smoke crawled across the cloud as they moved: some chemical process, Hopper guessed, or factory wastage being incinerated. Perhaps it was just the aftermath of a village on fire. That happened these days.

They were coming in from the south-east, past Headington. The old car factory in Cowley was used by the army now, she remembered, making munitions. The Oxfordshire zone was proud of its munitions.

Her wedding aside, Hopper had not been in Oxford since her graduation, a day of threadbare pomp and quiet desperation about the future. She and her cohort had been given a speech about the benefits of the education they had received, she remembered that. Parts of the day's addresses had been delivered in Latin, an archaism even before the Slow and a total absurdity now that Rome was smouldering and abandoned.

The university's vice chancellor, a well-padded man just beginning to shrink into old age, his skin loosening as food shortages bit, had offered some feeble justification for the dead language. His arguments, if she remembered right, were that this world might learn something of a noble death from the old one, and that their new educations would help them keep this world alive. Nobody had pointed out the contradiction. The speech was greeted with a silence more tolerant than attentive. Even from her seat near the back she had seen the deep, dark lines on the speaker's salmon-coloured face, heard the lack of conviction in his voice.

They were at the Cowley roundabout. Headington and Cowley looked the same; even some of the bars she had visited were still there, which pleased her. The sites piled up in her head as they passed them – the bridge over the Isis, chained punts nudging the bed of the shrunken river beneath; the botanical gardens; the high walls of Magdalen covered in creepers; the threadbare, bleached high street. It was less changed than she had feared.

Traffic was light; these were the dog days between terms, when the city was at its emptiest. They turned right off the main road and made their way round the narrow back streets to her old college.

Outside, David parked on the quietest street possible. It felt uncanny to be here, a substantial place of brick and stone, not the half-imagined, half-real place she had been recalling over the last few days. Hopper felt as though she had woken from a dream, only to find herself in the landscape in which her dream had been set.

'Let's go,' she said, getting out and slamming the door. They walked back up towards the porters' lodge. Half of her expected cars to pull up as they approached, or Warwick to sprout from the slender oak door, Blake at her heels. She squeezed David's shoulder, only half consciously. She didn't know what they would do if they failed here.

Little had changed at the college. The gates, still huge and wooden, with a small cut-out door on black iron hinges closed during the hours of curfew; the cool flagstones in the vaulted archway beneath the inner and outer walls of the college; the tightly defended lodge itself. It was a tiny, perfect facsimile of the whole country. David stayed outside while she ducked her head through into the lodge, crammed with pigeonholes and notice-boards and a glass-screened office in which the porters sat.

The porter was new. This one looked about forty, sallow-faced and bony in his chair, strands of greying brown plastered over the top of his scalp.

'Hello there. Is Fred in?'

'Fred's retired, madam. Five years ago.'

'Oh, I'm sorry to hear that. My name is Ellen Hopper. I used to study here.'

He nodded. 'Can I help with anything, madam?'

'Yes please. I'm here to see Professor Heathcote.'

There was a moment's pause, and for a second she thought: *Jesus, not her too*. They might have picked her up. They might have realised where Hopper was heading. They could have arrested Heathcote days ago, if Thorne had tried to contact her as he had Fisher. But the porter simply picked up the phone and said, bored, 'What time's your appointment?'

The clock behind him read ten past two. She swallowed and said, 'Two fifteen. Can you tell her the subject of the meeting's changed? It's about Edward Thorne. That's important.'

He pressed a button on the phone, and passed the information to a secretary. After thirty seconds of waiting – she tried to look around the lodge instead of staring at the phone held by the porter's ear – she heard a little squeak and he looked back at her. 'She can see you at half past.'

'Her residence?'

'That's right.'

'Thank you.'

'Feel free to look around the college. You'll know your way around, I suppose. Since you're an alumna.'

David was standing at the edge of the shaded area, looking over the quad. The lawn was still unfeasibly green. 'Well?'

'She'll see me. Us.'

'Good.' They turned and began to walk around the quad. The sky was as close to darkness as it ever got. Heavy banks of cloud sat across the sun's spot, with further, darker heaps piling up to the west. She wondered whether the dye in the lawn had to be reapplied after rain. In the corner, she saw Thorne's old room, and felt momentarily sick.

Halfway round the second side came the chapel. 'Want to go in?'

'Not especially.'

'Come on. You don't know when we'll be here again.'

They had been married in here. The chapel was absurd really, a nineteenth-century monstrosity kitted out in high Victorian Gothic style, crammed with elaborate brickwork, tapestries, enormous stained-glass windows, ornate tiling, benches of carved oak. A couple of major works by minor artists hung unvisited in a side chapel.

The choice of venue for the wedding had been hers, more by default than anything else. It had been a poor choice. Her friends from college had mostly left; David's friends from different points of his life were variously in London and Scotland. Oxford was a point of almost mutual inconvenience for all attendees. But by then it was too late, and David had been pleased by the archaism of the religious element. He had been amused, too, to have the ceremony conducted by the college chaplain, a young man whose carefully assumed aura of gravitas could not wholly conceal his pleasure at officiating at what must have been one of his first weddings.

The guests had huddled at the front, barely filling the first three rows. The ceremony had been conducted with vigour by the young chaplain, his Adam's apple bobbing in the light of the candles along the front rail.

And yet she had been happy; happy even in the partial knowledge of the gap between herself and David, assuming it might one day be bridged, that a few years' ageing might change things. The truth – that she had found her resistance to motherhood hardening rather than eroding as the years passed by – was a surprise neither had expected, but still, there it had been, the gap broadening until the other bridges between them had collapsed.

David pushed at the door. It was heavy but unlocked, and slowly gathered momentum before crashing into the wall. Hopper picked up a hymnbook – it was clean, where she had expected dust. The air was lemon-scented, and the flagstones underfoot still bore the final imprints of a mop.

'Want to go again?' He was grinning, enjoying himself. He had always enjoyed teasing her. He moved up the aisle away from her, laughing, and she felt the lump of tension in her throat dissolve a little, appreciating his idiocy, forgot temporarily the pain in her ankle and ribs. He sat in the front row and looked forward, his shoulders still moving, and yet as she approached him, she realised with a start that he was no longer laughing. He had slipped somehow into crying, clawing his glasses off his face and masking his eyes with his hand, fat tears rolling down his face as he breathed and sobbed and spoke all at the same time.

He was saying the same phrase, over and over again: 'What am I going to do?' It took a few attempts to make the words out.

'You're going to be all right. We're going to find out—'

'I've always had work, El. I've always done the right thing. And now I'm out.' He spoke in a whisper, but the high ceiling above them magnified his words. 'I don't think I realised before. It's just shock.' He was almost hiccuping with the effort of suppressing tears. She remembered the panic she had felt the last time she had seen him cry: in a restaurant in London, two days before she had left.

And yet here there was nothing to panic about. 'We're going to be all right, David. We are. We're going to be fine. You're going to be fine. I'm here. I'm not going anywhere.' She spoke in low tones, as one would to a child, and she could not help but reach out and put her hand on his back, and from there it was a short step to putting her other arm around him, tucking her chin over his shoulder. They sat like that for some time, oblivious to the quiet movements of the birds that had made their roost in the roof beams high above them.

It took a while for his breathing to slow, but it did, and he moved so his arm could be around her as hers were around him. She shifted, pushing her head to one side on his shoulder, looking to the front of the chapel. To her this new pose felt more normal, more like the pose any couple might adopt. *Any couple*, she thought, and wondered whether they now were.

'I'm sorry,' she said.

'It's all right. If it had happened to me I'd probably have dragged you in too, to be honest.'

'That's what you get for being so useful.' She felt his jaw muscles tighten in a grin.

'Were you happy? With her?' Hopper spoke without thinking.

'I don't think it matters now. We weren't very happy. That's certainly true. But it was better than being without anyone.'

'You're not without anyone.'

His arm tightened around her. From where they were sitting it would take hardly any movement for them to kiss.

It was only after a few minutes sitting like this that she heard the chapel bell ringing, and realised it was time to meet the warden.

A thin drizzle of rain had started to fall while they were inside the chapel. Little gusts of wind whipped discarded leaves into spirals along their path.

The warden's residence was in a corner of the second quad, a large detached house somehow transplanted into the college. Hopper found the doorbell – a discreet pad with security camera, sitting beside an ostentatious Victorian bell-pull that hung polished and abandoned. Eventually the door opened a few inches, on a chain, and a suspicious eye observed them through the gap.

'Warden's residence.'

'We have an appointment.'

'Under what name?'

'Hopper.'

The door closed and opened again, without the chain. Before them stood a woman of about forty, dressed in a severe skirt and a ribbed bottle-green polo neck with pearls peeking out from beneath. Her face was lined and exhausted. Hopper remembered this woman, had seen her sitting beside the Warden at dinners. Back then she had been in her middle twenties, glamorous but bored; now she seemed simply bored, and the glamour lent to her for her youth had been recalled, bestowed just as unfairly on some other young woman who would lose it in turn.

'Are you Professor Heathcote's daughter?'

'I am.' She gestured with one hand; Hopper could smell the nail polish on it. 'Please will you wait in here.' It was an instruction, not a question. As they moved into the room she had pointed out, she began to draw herself up the stairs, haltingly and painfully.

The Last Day

The room was light; huge windows at one end, shutters half opened. It was a library: the two long walls were filled with enormous bookcases, groaning with volumes and each fitted with a mobile set of stairs mounted on a rail. One was interrupted by a fireplace, a huge stone monstrosity clearly still used, with tarnished brass tools sitting inside a wire screen. The room's far end held an array of open glass cases, stuffed with artefacts, antiques, bits of flotsam from the time before the Slow. It reminded Hopper of Hetty's warehouse. She gingerly picked up a small red-and-black vase and turned it upside down.

'What do you think?'

Caroline Heathcote – the warden – was standing at the door, her hand resting lightly on the handle. David, who had been examining the bookcases, jumped. Hopper spoke first.

'Very beautiful.'

'Very pointless.' Heathcote shuffled into the room. 'But part of me found all those things beautiful once, I suppose. A lot of them I collected before the process of slowing even started.' She moved cautiously, staying close to the edge of the bookcase, and holding a discreet railing placed at hip height, until she reached one of the red leather armchairs.

Professor Heathcote had always been short, but now her spine had begun to curl over. She must be at least seventy-five, Hopper thought, maybe even eighty.

'If they're pointless, why do you keep them?'

'You never know. Someone else might find them beautiful. I must confess – please, sit down – I have a little fantasy that this might be one of the last rooms to survive. That it will be boarded up after my death, and discovered one day, to puzzle archaeologists.' Heathcote sighed. 'Then again, once I'm dead, I suspect the next warden will have different tastes and give it all away. I imagine there will be at least a couple more wardens before everything comes to an end.'

Heathcote paused as she examined Hopper, then David. 'I hope my daughter wasn't too abrupt with you. A disappointing life, I think, sitting around in a big house you know you'll have to leave when the old woman dies. But there are worse fates, of course.' She smiled. Hopper's slight and instinctive dislike of her gained substance.

'I'm Ellen Hopper.'

'I know who you are. I remember you.'

'And this is David Gamble. He's a friend of mine. We're here about Edward Thorne.'

Heathcote nodded. 'Yes. You've caused quite a fuss.'

'For you?'

'For me.'

'What sort of fuss?'

'Let's just say I was aware I might meet you before you turned up at the lodge this afternoon.'

Hopper spotted the deflection of her question, and as she looked at Heathcote, became aware of the intelligence behind her slow speech: another creature, squatting inside the decrepit frame, watching her through the hooded eyes.

'We have a photograph of Thorne and what we think is a satellite.'

Heathcote looked at Hopper, more sharply this time, then at David, standing by the mantelpiece and still holding the book he'd taken from the shelf.

'Yes?'

'We think it might be important.'

Heathcote sighed. 'I knew about the satellite.' Hopper glanced at David, euphoric for a second, until the older woman continued. 'But I'm afraid he never told me what he found.'

'Why not?'

Another pause, this one embarrassed. 'I never asked.' Hopper's look of incredulity must have betrayed her, because Heathcote continued: 'I think he might have said something to me, if I had done. But it's not always proper for people to tell each other everything. This way, if I had been questioned I could quite happily tell the officers from the security services I had no idea what Edward's satellite was designed to observe. I was confident he would confide in me if it was important to him to do so.'

'Why did he tell you about it in the first place?'

'We were close, Miss Hopper.' As she said 'Miss', her eyes slid to David and then back again to her. 'I took Edward in here, you know, when nobody else wanted to have anything to do with him. It cost me a lot.'

'You sacked him too, though, didn't you?'

She nodded. 'I loved Edward. But he felt his continued presence here was causing the college problems. And it was. I wish I hadn't had to choose between him and the college. But I did. And this place is more important than any one of us.'

'It doesn't sound like it was a difficult decision.'

From his spot beside the fireplace, David coughed: a little warning not to provoke too far. Hopper was irritated that he was right, and spoke again. 'I'm sure you did everything you could for him.'

'It wasn't enough, I fear. I barely heard from him after he left. But you're not interested in his post-university career. You want to know what brought him here.' She was clearly determined to milk this little moment of celebrity for all the attention it was worth. 'You know, someone else came to see me on this very matter, just yesterday. A woman called Warwick.'

'What did she want?'

'She wanted to know if Edward had left any papers here. Any parcels, perhaps something in a college safe. Something academic.'

Hopper took a sharp breath. Warwick and Blake were still looking, then. And they were a day ahead. 'And what did you tell her?'

'I told her the truth. That I was aware of no such object.'

So that was it. Whatever Thorne had discovered, he had destroyed. There was nowhere else: everything that had led her here had been for nothing. Her career and David's, Harry's and Fisher's lives, all thrown away chasing the same phantom.

Then Heathcote spoke again. 'I did not, of course, mention anywhere I suspected such an object might be found.'

'I'm sorry?'

'Everyone signs a declaration of assets when they arrive at the college. It details everything they own. And when they leave, they sign a similar document. When he arrived at the college,

Edward signed a declaration, like any other; it included a small house in a village nearby.' Heathcote smiled, clearly enjoying the sense of an audience paying court.

Hopper leant forward. 'And?'

'When he left the college, he signed a similar document. The cottage had disappeared from the register. Out of curiosity, I dug out the original form and looked up the address.' *Curiosity indeed*, Hopper thought. Heathcote had been intrigued by her friend's secret bolthole and was too vain to admit it. 'And then I ensured the original form was destroyed.'

'Why are you telling us this? Why us and not Warwick?'

Heathcote sighed. 'Because I should never have betrayed my friend.' And there, miraculously, the shabby, attention-seeking role fell away from her. 'Edward was a talented scientist. Very talented. His work shouldn't be destroyed, whatever it says, and whatever its consequences. I would not want it falling into the hands of a woman like Ruth Warwick.'

'What makes you so confident we won't destroy it ourselves?'

'I remember you were one of his students, Ms Hopper, and I remember how highly he spoke of you.' She shrugged. 'Let's just say I'm playing the balance of probabilities.' And with that, she crossed the room to her desk, pulled out a pad of paper, and wrote two words on it in a faltering hand.

The rain was coming down harder now, pooling in the gravel of the first quad, swirling above the half-blocked drains on the street outside.

They had left the Warden in her residence. She had walked with them, slowly, to the door. On the threshold, she had offered neither a handshake nor encouragement. Hopper had said something about their gratitude, and Heathcote had simply said, 'Don't get caught.'

The last thing Hopper saw, as the door swung shut, was the Warden's daughter, standing on the stairs and staring at her, interest and disdain mingled on her face.

As they walked out of the college, David was silent. Back in the car, the thud of the Ford's door shutting the world out, he said: 'We can be there and back before curfew. Or stay out. They don't really have curfew out in the sticks.'

'Do you want to go? I can go by myself if you prefer.'

It was raining harder on the windscreen now, blattering on the long bonnet in front of them. He looked at her. 'Ellie, you keep asking me if I want to stay with you. If I'm sure about driving you here, if I want to go home yet, if I wouldn't rather curl up back in London, go back to Pamela, keep writing propaganda. So for the last time, I don't want to go home. I don't wish I was in London. I want to be here. With you.'

'Sorry. Force of habit, I think.' She felt abashed, realising how much she'd been testing him. 'I guess I'm just a bit surprised, that's all.'

'That's all right. I'm as surprised as you are.' He grinned, and started the engine.

They pulled onto the main road, then turned again, onto the Banbury road, heading north, towards the village Heathcote had written on the paper.

There was a map book in the glove compartment, a crinkled and well-thumbed volume, pages browned by old spilt coffee. The village they were headed for was on the edge between two pages, hardly visible. Alnford. Hopper directed David through the outskirts of Oxford, the houses slowly getting larger and grander. They passed Summertown – she and her friends had come here to escape the university during revision for their finals, sitting in the same grimy café all evening, nursing a single drink before curfew.

Before long, they passed the edge of her memory. They turned north again after the ring road. After a few miles of double-lane road, the track fell into disrepair, until they were creeping along it at fifteen miles an hour, dodging potholes. They were leaving farming country, heading into one of the thick, unconquered belts of forest spreading across England's middle.

As they drove, the trees approached the road on either side. At first they were twenty yards away, but the gap slowly closed until the tall roots above the ground started taking little bites out of the road, testing the strength of the tarmac, forcing their tendrils into the fissures. Overhead, the trees knitted their branches together, until the road stopped being a road, and became a chute of a hundred whispering greens along which they were funnelled.

Hopper looked at her watch. It was just after four in the afternoon. Her brother wouldn't have got home, but even if Mark had missed her absence in the morning, Laura must have notified him by now. Was there a chance it would not be reported? In the rearview mirror came no sign, no car carrying Warwick and her gaunt friend to arrest them.

The sky darkened. It was still raining, now even harder than at the college. Hopper remembered a perky radio broadcast predicting it when she was last on the rig. When had that been? God, it was only a few days ago. It felt like a month. She and Harv had listened together in his room, and she had – in an unguarded moment – let herself feel that life on the rig might not be so bad, that she might establish some kind of home there.

The woods had closed in completely now. The windscreen wiper moved slowly, dragging across at half speed. The blotches of rain that fell on the window stayed for several seconds, fragmenting the road ahead.

'Can you see where we are on the page?'

She looked at the map. 'There should be a church.'

And sure enough, there it was, on their left after a few more minutes of creeping.

'Do you want to shelter inside until the worst passes?'

'How much further?'

'Perhaps four miles.'

'Let's carry on.'

She looked at the church as they passed. Its decay was well advanced, its walls hidden by sheets of ivy running rampant up the shady side. The tower was only visible by its shape. A few more years and it would perhaps have ceased to be a church at all, would simply be a sleeping leviathan by an abandoned path.

The cemetery outside was full of saplings. She pictured what must be happening beneath the ground – roots pushing urgently through the skulls of the dead, tombstones providing only holds for creeping shoots. She said, hardly listening to herself: 'We're not coming back, are we?'

But David did not hear her, and even if he had, she could not have said what she meant by the question.

London: the heaving city, so full of people, would grow empty. The world would die and not be replaced, and there was no indication of what would follow, if anything, on the tiny ring of the earth remaining habitable.

'Look. There.' He was pointing. At the side of the road there was a large creature, picking at the foliage. They slowed to a halt twenty metres from it, and it looked briefly up before carrying on grazing. 'What is that?'

She had never seen one before, but she recognised it from pictures. 'I think it's a wallaby.'

'What's it doing here?'

'It must have escaped from the ARK project. I think it was based somewhere around here.'

'That was over thirty years ago.'

'I know.'

After a minute, the creature half walked, half hopped away, through the undergrowth. David started the car, and they rolled gently onward. Some minutes later, she asked again: 'Much further?'

'Not too far.' He nodded abstractedly. It was so shady under the trees and in the clouds that he flicked the car's headlights on, and they sputtered haltingly into life.

Just a few seconds after the lights went on – as though they had summoned him – a man stepped into the road. He was waving at them, gesturing frantically away and up the road ahead.

There was no time, they had to decide whether to stop now, and Hopper was alarmed to see David's hand automatically go to the gearstick, feel the car slowing down. Afterwards, she wondered how they would have reacted in London, and reasoned that maybe they'd stopped because they were in the countryside. You could trust people in the countryside.

The man could have been anywhere between thirty and fifty, his brown hair matted and streaked with grey. Hair sprouted on the upper reaches of his cheeks so only his eyes were left staring out from the no-man's-land between his low brow and his beard. He wore a long grey coat that fell nearly to his knees and was covered in pockets with plastic bags sprouting from the edges. His shoes, once perhaps light brown, were now covered almost completely in mud.

'Please,' he was shouting. 'Please. You must help us. My wife.' He gestured up the road, and as the car rolled to a stop, he ran around to David's door, leant down, was shouting and jabbering through it. David did not open the window. The man kept bellowing, not giving David time to reply.

'Ask him what's wrong,' Hopper said. 'Ask him what's going on,' but her voice was half drowned by the shouting and the banging, and she knew as she said it that they should have kept driving.

David turned to her and looked first at, then past her, and as his eyes widened, she turned to see other men, two of them, just metres away, moving fast, carrying something between them. They were too close for David to pull away again, and she screamed at him to drive.

It was too late. The men were past the front of the car, dropping the heavy log they held between them, and as David shoved the car into reverse and looked over his shoulder, they felt a thump behind the wheels. They were boxed in, the wheels grinding uselessly against some second obstacle. And then a blow shattered the window and hands were dragging at her, disorienting her, making her feel she was being pulled in two. Something struck the side of her head and she saw nothing, only heard the noise of shouts and the grinding of the car's engine and the smash of the window on David's side.

She found one of the hands gripping her, dislodged it and grabbed, bit down on two of the fingers. She heard a scream and the hand withdrew sharply, giving her space to release her seat belt, and she managed to push out at the car door with a foot. It swung, shoving one of the men outside into the other. As she got out, David was wrestling with the man on his side, had grabbed him by the collar. The two of them were half in and half out of the car door.

The rain was falling in sheets around them. One of the men facing her was bleeding from the hand – she had done that, she thought – but the other was back on his feet, staring at her. And she had no weapon. Too late, she remembered the gun that had been right in front of her in the glove compartment. If she turned to try to get it out, they would be on her.

The second man rushed at her. Hopper tried to pull away to the side, remembering confused fragments of self-defence she hadn't tried for fifteen years. But he was taller than her, stronger, avoided her parrying arms and simply shouldered her to the ground, slithering down with her into the mud as the rain fell around them. Her head struck the bottom of the car's frame, just where Blake's blow had knocked her into the wall, and it felt like a seam at the back of her skull had come open. The second man pulled back and scrambled to his feet, breathing hard, and turned to his colleague, grinning.

From her position on the ground, she turned, half falling into the car's footwell. She had felt something metal in there as they drove. She groped for it and it came to her hand – long, heavy – and just as the second man started to pull at her legs, she closed her fist around it and swung backwards, narrowly missing herself as she turned. It bit into something, making a horrible wet crunch, and the man's grip slackened as he fell to the ground.

The Last Day

She wiped the rain from her eyes as she levered around and stood. The other man was waiting there, looking from her to his fallen friend and back again. She kept the long spanner in her hand, waiting for him to approach her. As soon as he did, she would swing for his head as hard as she could. The back of her scalp was sticky. There was a sound of ragged breathing coming from the prone man on the ground, and the hammering of rain on the windshield behind her.

The standing man inched forward, putting his hands out ahead of him, one still dripping flecks of blood onto the ground. She remembered what she wanted, how close to it she was, and she held the heavy spanner tighter and waited for him, ready to strike.

He stood, breathing hard, glancing at the car and yearning for whatever luxuries he imagined were inside. For a long moment, their eyes met. Then he turned and ran, stumbled away, still clutching his injured hand, lopsided and halting, until the green of his coat was lost among the trees.

She turned and moved around the front of the car, half falling, slipping on the bonnet. There was a man on the ground, not moving, and for a terrible second she thought it was David. But it was not. It was the man who had first approached them, the one – she reproached herself for thinking of his lie – the one with the wife.

David was sitting with his back to the car. He was bleeding above his eye, the left half of his face already puffy. He spoke in a voice barely audible above the rain. 'I stabbed him. He had a knife and I got it off him.' Beneath the man, she saw a dark patch spread over the mulchy ground. She saw, too, that David had thrown up, and the tang of his vomit reached her nostrils.

'We have to get back in the car now, David. One of them ran off. He might come back.'

David looked up at her, then nodded and stood.

'We have to move these.' The two of them shifted the log at the front of the car out of the way, slowly and painfully. There were two long hand-made wedges deposited behind the back wheels, heavy lumps of wood coated with pitch. She and David must have been distracted by the first man – the one now lying on his front – for longer than she had realised.

On the ground, he seemed shorter than he had at first. His head was to one side, and the visible side of his face had already relaxed in death, under its grey-streaked beard. He had goggles above his eyes, the double effect making him look like an insect. The first fly landed on him as she looked.

She moved back around. Her one – the one she had hit – was being washed clean by the rain. He could not have been more than about seventeen. The wound she had inflicted with the spanner must be at the back of his head. His coat had fallen open, exposing a wooden club inside. He reminded her of the children on the rig, or the fresh-faced police officers in London: interchangeable youths, their lives blighted from the beginning, not given the chance to become anything before they were seized into the service of this dying world.

And then the body at her feet groaned, and coughed.

Hopper made her way back to where David was dragging the second wedge out of the way.

'The one I hit. He's alive. I didn't realise.'

'So what?'

'So we should …'

'What?'

'I don't know.'

'What do you want to do, take him with us?'

'No.'

'Want to take him back to his friends?'

'But just leaving him …' She felt the absurdity even as she said it. 'Should we try to help him?'

'No. We have to keep going.'

She moved round to her door, and gave the boy a long look. Then she and David slowly clambered back into the car and left the scene, accelerating through the heavy splotches of rain towards their final destination.

40

Perhaps that would be how it ended, she thought. The cities would fall apart, everyone would make their way into the woods, and the towns would be left populated only by the police and the army, running out of bullets, raiding the country-side around them.

David's face had swollen, and his eyelid was already being levered shut. He asked Hopper for a cigarette and she retrieved one from the glovebox, lit it for him and passed it to his free hand.

There were still two miles to the village. He drove quickly, nervously, hugging the middle of the road so he could get an extra few miles an hour without the risk of hitting the frequent potholes, speeding up whenever he found twenty metres of clear tarmac. He checked the mirrors every few seconds. So did she.

But no obstacles detained them further and the trees gradually relented as they arrived in the village of Alnford.

It was abandoned. Doors hung open on hinges; the gardens grew wild. The only life that disturbed the street was a pair of crows, which flapped from one roof to another above them as they drove. The rain on the car's roof was deafening.

'This must be one of the Protected Villages,' David shouted, above the noise of the rain. These were trial areas, cleared soon after the end of the Slow in a vain effort to assist places with high numbers of vulnerable individuals. The populations had been sluiced towards larger cities. Only a couple of hundred villages had been cleared that way before the idea had been abandoned. Fifteen years ago, Thorne could not have sold the home to anyone if he had tried – either that, or he had deliberately acquired a property in an abandoned hamlet.

The house itself took five minutes to find. Twice David had to slow and turn the car around, and both times became fearful, swivelling his head back and forth so his good eye could survey as many houses as possible. It was only on the third pass, right on the outskirts of the village, that Hopper spotted the second word the warden had written, painted on a slate tile hanging outside a gate. *Lambsfoot*. It was almost the furthest house out. Across the road from it stood the treeline, silent and menacing.

'Don't leave the car right outside,' she said.

David nodded, although the tiny subterfuge could hardly do them any good, and parked a little along the road. Hopper left her bag – with the transmitter and the photograph – on the back seat.

By the time they had reached the house's porch, they were soaked; it took effort, once in from the rain, to leave the shelter and walk the outside of the house, inspecting it for signs of life. It was a perfectly ordinary double-fronted brick home, two storeys high. The front garden was scrubby and pebble-strewn. Behind the house, the forest had grown up to the door, and above the rain she heard branches scraping the windows in the breeze. There was nothing visible through the trees. As they moved round, David smiled lopsidedly. 'Nobody home.'

Back at the front door, Hopper had to resist the urge to knock. One of the front windows had been smashed by weather or vandals, and she gingerly placed her hand through the glass, reached around to the latch, and eased the door open.

The house had been closed up in good order. The ground floor held the hall, a kitchen, two small parlours, and a locked room. In one parlour, the furniture was half covered in dust sheets, but they stopped halfway across, as if the placer had been distracted mid departure.

'I'll look upstairs,' David said. 'Check there's definitely nobody home.'

The locked room had the key still in the door. Hopper turned it with difficulty, and it opened onto a low-ceilinged study, its height reduced further in places by heavy wooden beams. Unlike the rest of this floor, it had no dust sheets. It was simply furnished, with a desk, a chair, a filing cabinet and a large empty bookcase, but it looked as though it could have been closed up just yesterday. An image occurred to her: that of a burial chamber, the last resting place of a long-dead king.

The Last Day

The surface of the desk was bare, except for a heavy brass stapler, oddly shiny in the dull house. She looked through the cabinet; it was empty. The desk was not. The first drawer contained a handful of paper litter. The second held another few discarded letters.

The only other objects in the whole desk were in the second drawer down on the right-hand side: a hard block wrapped in black plastic, and a yellowed envelope bearing the words *Joshua. 02.09.44.*

'David?'

He appeared within a few seconds. 'Nothing upstairs. The roof's gone in one room, it smells completely ...' He fell silent as she gestured at the envelope. 'Joshua?'

'His son. But he was long dead by the time this was written.' She opened the note, dry as parchment, almost fallen into three pieces along the folds, and began to read.

Dear Joshua,
You are a more than worthy son to an inadequate father. The generation above yours was a failure. We found no answers. I suspect there were none to be found. And yet the ways in which we failed were our choices, so they are now our responsibility.

You have been born in the shadow of a great misery. Your own survival means everything to me. None of this is just as well; none of it is for the best. Good luck.
Your father

'What was the date again?'

'September 2044.'

He gestured. 'Let's see it.'

It was heavy, the block, and sealed all the way round with black binding tape, too thick to tear.

'Keys.'

He dug in a pocket and pulled out his keys, handing her a sharp one. For a second, she saw the men in the woods approaching her, not thinking they needed a weapon.

She nicked the edge of the packaging, ran the sharp key steadily along one edge. 'Careful.' She couldn't tell if he'd said it or she had. Inside, there was paper, sandwiched between two thick sheets of balsa wood. There must have been three hundred sheets. She lifted off the top layer of wood and read the title: *Report of the first operational flight of the JAT satellite, dispatched 19/06/44*.

She breathed out, slowly. 'Jesus. We were right, David.'

The title was followed by an elegant line drawing of the satellite, the same one the group had been posing in front of in the photo she had found in Thorne's house.

There were pages of technical specifications at first, dozens of them. Then a little passage dealing with the project objectives. (He had once said to her: 'Never a mission. Always a project. Missionaries take their own beliefs with them. The Spanish Armada was a mission. Darwin's voyage on the *Beagle* was a project.')

Objective. To lay the foundation for a new satellite network for governmental use. The JAT will be the first of a projected fifteen satellites, beginning to replace the GPS networks of the century's early decades. The potential rewards are enormous.

The Last Day

This project is an internal matter for the Department of the Interior and as such should be reported nowhere else. The aim is to secure civilian benefits before military ones. If the department of Internal Security were notified, the JAT's use might spread beyond the initial planned applications in ways disadvantageous to the successful completion of the project. This lies within the department's budget and remit, and there is no specific duty to report it. Only six senior members have worked on this: Hollis, Drabble, Lee, Gethin, Symons and the author.'

'So it was a secret from everyone. Even from the rest of the department. And definitely from Davenport.' David was reading by her side, their backs to the window.

'Looks like it.'

'Why?'

She shrugged. 'Davenport couldn't strap a weapon onto it if Thorne had already sent it up.' She read on, passing him each page as she finished.

Launches. The first unsuccessful launch – of three – took place on 22/04/44. The launch point was sited on the Suffolk coast, in an area sufficiently remote to avoid detection. The forest just inland from the Walberswick marshlands proved an adequate site, but the vertical trajectory had been misprogrammed, and after ascending to a height of approximately 2,800 feet, the rocket levelled and crashed into the sea.

The next launch took place in the same location and suffered its own different malfunctions, failing on the platform (necessitating hasty removal and disposal). The third launch made it into orbit, but a failure of communications halfway through the launch procedure rendered it useless. The final, successful launch did not occur until 19/06.

There were more details, pages of numbers, ballistics information, solar radiation defence strategies, mapped and rejected trajectories.

By the time of the fourth attempt, official interest had been piqued by those who had observed the two launches to leave the ground. Internal Security reports were looking for the parties responsible – then suspected to be separatists planning an attack of some kind – and secrecy was of the utmost importance.

The final site for a launch was in North Wales, close to the coast. The coastal location was, as usual, to help with possible disposal in the event of an urgent need to destroy evidence.

Hopper pictured the men and women in Thorne's photo standing on the hills near the sea, constructing their rudimentary tower under cover of woodland, unloading the meagre supply of bartered and stolen fuel for the attempted launch of this one small box.

The launch was successful. The solar battery Drabble installed should last several decades; the decryption key at the front of this document is what allowed me to decipher the satellite's data and print this report.

She flicked to the first page and saw it: a long string of letters and numbers. 'It's still up there, David. It could still be working now.'

Observations

Once successfully launched, the first pass of the JAT revealed nothing unexpected. It orbited almost in line with the Greenwich

Meridian, along a path that took it directly over Britain, south through France and down over Africa, before it eventually plunged into darkness on the other side of the earth. Thankfully, it survived its first pass, and then made its way around the earth, sending information as it did so to a secure receiver in our department.

The JAT moved slowly across the planet taking photographs at twelve-second intervals, which allowed us to assess the whole planet's surface without any gaps.

The images of our surviving side of the earth, transmitted from the satellite, were expected but nevertheless extraordinary. The spread of the Sahara Desert south and west had been even faster than we had projected. Across the lower half of Africa, vast swathes of formerly tropical area had died off completely. Curiously, there had been some resilience at the southern edge, and forests had grown across the Kalahari region. Huge algal blooms have arisen in the South Atlantic: the implications for oxygen supply are dealt with elsewhere. These observations were of interest, but they are nothing compared to what was found on the cold side of the earth.

As the JAT moved east across the former United States, it took a series of photos that revealed human activity. It is not easy to write these words. We counted twelve areas, scattered across the region, and eight larger sites in Asia, all appearing to sustain human life.

For a second Hopper could not quite support her weight, and would have crumpled had she not been leaning against Thorne's desk. She read the paragraph again, a third time, almost held back from understanding by the scale of the idea. She passed it to David. 'This can't be.'

As he read it, his eyes widened, and he looked to her. 'It's not possible. There's no way they could have survived. They can't have.' He looked appalled.

She turned the page, and there, against a black background, was a photo – a filigree of lights, spread out across the entire page. There were dozens of images of the various sites, taken at different times and from different angles, some from a distance, some zoomed in close enough that the bulbs had flared into miniature stars. But all showed the same thing. Lights. Life.

She turned to the next page of text and read on.

These settlements were the only ones with lights appearing visible to our satellite. It is possible that others survive in subterranean environments, with no indications above the surface of the earth.

In the years of the Slow, the United States of America was one of the few nations equipped with the resources to salvage a small core of population internally, while simultaneously arranging the largest planned migration in human history. One of the others was China. Both countries would naturally have made alternative arrangements should all the planned evacuations have failed in their mission. In the early years of the Slow, the USA retained the organisational ability required to keep this project secret, and the enormous manpower to make its new sites a reality. China's own remarkable infrastructural abilities would have provided that nation with a substantial advantage too.

On receiving these first images, the satellite's course was altered from the ground to make further passes and analyse these areas more closely. It was possible that these lights might have

remained on after the inhabitants of the city had been evacuated –
in short, that the lights had survived and the inhabitants had not.
Later analysis of the photos showed the pattern had changed sub-
stantially between batches of photographs being taken. The heat
signatures the satellite detected moved in patterns too unpredict-
able to be a dead system. This was, and is, human habitation.

There were more pages after that, more close-up photographs,
detailed annotations suggesting possible functions, circles around
possible power sources or waste outputs. Then another compos-
ite shot of the whole Coldside from the air, a dark orb spotted
with gleaming lights, looking like a constellation of stars hanging
alone in the night sky.

Hopper turned to the chapter's final page.

Based on pre-Slow city estimates (accrued from photos of
night climates and approximate populations), I would estimate
the conurbations hold some tens of millions of individuals. Obvi-
ously, if they go underground (as the author suspects they would,
for reasons of heat preservation), the populations might be sub-
stantially higher.

Hopper remembered the bodies on the boat, and wondered
afresh where they were from. Had they been making their way
from the darkness to the light?

'It can't be. It can't. How would they eat?' David said.

'We don't know what kind of supplies they had on that side.
Or built up. There must be something there ... I don't know, tidal
power, nuclear power, they could generate heat, grow hydropon-
ically ...' Hopper tailed off.

'So this means ...'

'There are survivors. Jesus, David, there are …' She looked at the papers blurrily. 'Christ, there are people out there. And they're alive. Or they were fifteen years ago. They might well still be.' It felt suddenly far too warm in the room. Her throat was dry. The rain hammered and hammered on the window.

'But why wouldn't they make contact?'

'We don't know they didn't try.'

'Are they still alive?'

She shrugged. 'If there were millions alive fifteen years after the Stop, why not?'

'Why didn't Davenport just have Thorne killed?'

'Look.'

She had been leafing as they spoke. At the back was a sheet of paper in a different size, and not typed – handwritten.

Teddy, my friend,

I feel great sorrow that we will not be able to complete our task together. But you will understand your position is untenable. A rift has opened in the trust between us now, and I will have to continue alone. But I have happy memories of the work we did together. Your efforts will not go to waste.

This place, this wonderful island, this precious stone, is the world's last hope, and the best. All I need is a little more time, as I think you know. But if you upset the scale now, our whole mission here could fail. And I know I can make it succeed – with a few more years of toil, with the mission we have been blessed to complete.

This is the only place that can survive. And I confess, Teddy, it could not cope with the images you have sent me. So I repeat: let me do my work, and keep the things you value safe.

With fondest love,

RD

'So that's why he was sacked,' David said. 'And why he couldn't tell anyone.'

'Maybe he bought Davenport's line,' Hopper said. 'Or maybe he couldn't bring himself to carry out a course that might tear the country apart.'

She remembered Thorne's face in the hospital bed, just a few days ago, and how relieved he had been to see her, and she realised how alone he must have been, and how unsure of himself. He had spent fifteen years not telling anyone, through fear, or misplaced loyalty. But he had realised what he ought to do, almost at the very end, and tried to pass it on. And when Fisher had failed him, he had turned to her.

David picked up the pile of papers again, leafed through the documents. 'Heat signatures ... theories on how they feed themselves ...' He held up one full-page photo and squinted closely at it, then placed it back.

'Wait.' A possibility was dawning in Hopper's mind. 'I think this makes sense of what you were talking about yesterday. Davenport's plan for the Americans.'

David looked up. 'You mean the deal?'

'Yes. You said it would involve Davenport gaining the American ...' she could hardly say the words, 'their nuclear weapons.'

'You think ...'

'Why else would he want them? You said it yourself. As soon as he gets them, he could use them, or as many as he needs to. On the Coldside.'

'He wouldn't. He'd have to be mad.'

'Why not? He carried out one genocide thirty years ago. He must have been negotiating to get these weapons for decades. He must spend all his time worrying that the survivors on that side will arrive over here, or the truth will come out somehow.'

'And this way there would be nobody left to arrive.'

'Exactly. And once the Americans are folded in here, he can begin the process of expanding back onto their continent, if he wants. What's to stop him? They must have enough natural resources to keep this place going for centuries.'

'Jesus.' David looked sick. She felt it, could taste a knot of bile rising in her own throat. He went on. 'What do we do?'

'What if this was published?' Hopper said.

'That there are cities alive on the Coldside, surviving? That the American government colluded with the British to abandon millions of their own people? Jesus, that parts of *China* survived? And that these people might be still alive now? Still surviving?'

'Yes. What would happen? To Davenport? His cabinet?'

'The Americans would riot. They'd never hand over the nukes. The merger would fall apart. And Davenport ... I don't know. The whole Davenport project is based on the idea that we're the world's last hope; that's why we'll put up with everything. And now ... we're not.'

Hopper looked at the thick parcel of papers, spilling out of the shiny plastic encasing it, and felt a sudden, crazy pang of tenderness for it. She leant over and smoothed down a corner. 'It feels like the whole country would go up if this came out. Who would replace him?'

'I don't know.'

'It's still worth doing.'

'I'm not saying it's not.'

Hopper looked down at the bundle, and remembered Thorne's words to her, fifteen years ago: *I have tried to find ways to atone.* But he hadn't acted on them until he was on his deathbed. 'Could you print this?'

'Of course not.' David laughed. 'I couldn't get more than five words out without being arrested. But this is the story of the century. They survived, Ellie. There are people out there, and they've spent years and years surviving after they were abandoned. For years we've been lied to, told we were all that remained. And now you're saying Davenport wants them wiped out. How do we handle this?'

The thought had already occurred to her as he spoke. 'I know where we can take this. Fisher. The man Thorne was in contact with, the one who owned the bookshop. I have his radio. We could contact the people running that station, tell them everything, and make our way to the American Zone.'

'But what happens after the news comes out?'

'Who cares, David? This is the only thing that matters. If we get it to the Americans, we could stop Davenport's deal going through. We could stop this happening.'

At the edge of her hearing, the rumble of a car's motor swelled and just as quickly died. Next, the gate gave a tiny creak, inaudible beneath the rain battering the roof. The first noise she heard clearly was the growl of a second, much larger engine, abruptly cut off, and by that point it was too late. Running to the hall, she looked through the grimy window and saw three people walking towards the house. Ruth Warwick, accompanied at her right hand by her colleague Blake, and on her other side by Hopper's brother, Mark.

41

Hopper's shock at seeing her brother made her pause for an extra second before she spoke.

'We have to leave.'

David was already at the back of the house. 'No, Ellie. There are more outside. Soldiers. Hide the papers.'

There was nowhere to put them except the study. She rushed through, crammed the file back into its plastic wrapping and into the desk, then left the room, standing in the hall like a nervous host about to greet a dignitary.

One of the party knocked on the door in a little rhythm. *Rat-a-tat-tat*. Blake, she thought, imagining those big hands of his making a game of the situation. He didn't wait for Hopper to open it: he reached through the broken window and did it himself. Warwick came through first, brushing the rain from her shoulders, her inch-high heels clacking on the hall floor.

'Good afternoon, Dr Hopper, Mr Gamble. Please: let's go through and sit down.' *Go through*. She sounded like she was having them round for tea.

They moved to the front parlour, a few battered old couches sitting under clouds of drifting dust. The ceiling was stained and bowed: the room upstairs must be the one where the roof had collapsed. Blake stood at the door. He had a new injury under his eye, still crimson, not yet sliding into the purples and greens of a bruise. Perhaps he had got it at Fisher's bookshop, Hopper thought.

'First things first, Doctor: there is a lorryload of soldiers outside. Don't think about trying to run away. It won't do you any good.' Hopper heard them now: shouts and footsteps over the battering of the rain.

'Please. Sit.' Warwick took the one armchair, which allowed her to sit upright. Hopper and David sat on a collapsed sofa, which tipped them sideways and together in a strange little moment of low comedy. Mark stood by the fireplace and looked down as though hoping to be anywhere but here. He hadn't met Hopper's eye yet.

She gestured at him. 'Why is he here?'

'He's here to talk some sense into you. In case you fail to realise the gravity of the situation.'

'Given that he's been spying on me since I got here, I'm afraid he's not going to be very useful to you,' Hopper said. 'Do you think that's fair, Mark?'

Mark continued to look down, saying nothing.

'We're very relieved to see you again,' Warwick continued. 'Some of my colleagues wanted you arrested as soon as we had the chance – in the warehouse, for example. After we missed you there, we were very concerned we might have lost you.' She paused. 'But thankfully, once you'd made your way back to your brother's home, I was able to persuade my colleagues we could afford to show a bit of patience.'

'Why?'

'We thought you had a reasonable chance of finding out where Thorne's little legacy had been hidden. So we left you to your own devices. And look where you have brought us.'

Hopper felt sick. 'How did you find us here?'

'It wasn't so difficult. We reached Mr Gamble's home too late to find you, which concerned us. But then one of our sources phoned to inform us you had arrived in Oxford. I don't suppose you remember Professor Heathcote's daughter?'

Hopper thought of the woman in the warden's lodging, her face twisted by some unknown bitterness, and understood.

'We guessed that you might receive help from inside the college, but fortunately Miss Heathcote feels the same way as we do about the importance of good governance. So here we are.' Warwick smiled. 'And now we have a chance of finishing our work.'

'Yes. I suppose we do.'

'Dr Hopper. We know what you're looking for. Where is it?'

Hopper was a better liar than her brother – or, at least, she had thought she was, until going through his filing cabinet – but not good enough to sound convincing. 'We haven't found anything. There's nothing here.'

Blake leant out into the corridor and murmured a few words. Two sets of boots clumped in, and moved to the other side of the house – not the study, the other front room. Hopper heard the noise of furniture being noisily pulled apart. If the soldiers had any interest in their work, it wouldn't take them long to find the papers.

Warwick sighed. Her stern aspect lapsed into disappointment, and just for a second, in between the two expressions, Hopper noticed how curiously blank she looked. She thought of Thorne on his deathbed, and how terrified he had seemed, and she wanted not to think of him, so she forced her attention back into the room.

' … exactly did you hope to find?' Warwick was looking at her expectantly.

'I'm sorry?'

'I said, Doctor, that I'm curious as to what exactly you were expecting.'

'There are people alive on the Coldside.'

David had said it, not her. Mark looked at him sharply. Warwick's attention switched to him, and for a moment a little spasm of dislike took control of her mouth. The only person who didn't react was Blake, who stood at the door, his eyes following whoever spoke.

'Don't be so stupid, Mr Gamble.'

'Millions of people. Maybe tens of millions. Thorne sent up a satellite before he was sacked. And there are reports. There's proof.'

'Your story is a fiction, a pointless attempt to harm this country's interests. Britain is the only nation that survives as it did before.'

Hopper wondered if Warwick really had been ignorant of what she was trying to find, whether she had been instructed simply to track it down; or whether she knew but did not care.

'It doesn't matter what you believe,' she said, steadying her breath. 'What you told people – what Davenport told people, that there was no hope for that side of the world – it wasn't true.'

'It was and it still is,' Warwick said. 'Those people in the former America are – were – just a few million more who were in the wrong place. They'll be dead soon, if they aren't already. It's for the best.' So she did know about them, Hopper thought.

'I'm not talking about then. I'm talking about now. Davenport's not willing to tell anyone these people exist because it destroys the point of his government. If the Americans find out their families are still alive, they'll riot. The deal will fall apart and Davenport won't get his nuclear weapons.'

David addressed Warwick. 'Do the Americans know?'

'That there are people living on the Coldside? Fewer than ten insiders. And those few understand what sacrifices have to be made for the survival of the group.'

Hopper interrupted. 'What about the nuclear weapons? Is Davenport going to use them against the Coldside?'

A slight spasm crossed Warwick's face, and it occurred to Hopper that she was almost as frightened by the prospect as they were.

'Whatever decision he makes will be the right one,' she said.

David put his head in his hands. 'Jesus. He's really going to do it. And if the Americans don't know about the survivors, they'll let him.'

'So you're happy for millions of people to be killed off for your own benefit?'

'I'm afraid so, Doctor. After all, that's what we did with the rest of the world.'

Hopper allowed herself a moment's uncomplicated hatred. 'Why did Davenport let Thorne live?'

'Some fatuous clemency on his part. I would have done it differently,' Warwick said. 'But we didn't know what arrangements he had in place to publish the document. If only we'd known sooner that he had none, we could have avoided all this difficulty.'

'What about Gethin?'

'Ah, yes. We know how badly you wanted to speak to him. He runs the government's satellite operation now. Using the descendants of Thorne's prototype. He was able to prove his loyalty. He's the one who informed us about Thorne's satellite in the first place, although Thorne was paranoid enough to keep the location of its findings even from him. The new models are coming in very handy these days.' Warwick smiled. 'And once the American deal goes through and Britain is whole once more, we'll be able to press on. Expand the Breadbasket further south. Plant new forests, push the desert back. Make this planet healthy again.'

'Unless word gets out that half the Americans have family still alive. Family their government and yours left to die.'

Warwick sighed. 'Well, if you insist on spreading such a preposterous fabrication, Doctor, there is no reason why we should not kill you now. Is there?'

Hopper attempted one last lie. 'There are others who know. And they have been told to broadcast if they don't hear from us. By tomorrow.'

Warwick cocked her head. 'I doubt that. What would be the point of you coming here if you already had proof? I think we will have to take the chance. Blake.'

Blake stepped forward, reaching a hand into his pocket.

Mark spoke for the first time. 'Wait.'

Blake stopped halfway across the floor, looking to Warwick.

'Ruth, you said it wouldn't be … you said this wouldn't happen.'

'I understand it's not always pleasant for the squeamish to see the consequences of their actions, Mr Hopper, but we don't have much time. Donald, please take Mr Gamble into the garden.'

Blake stepped forward, and was standing above David before Hopper heard herself speak. 'No. There's no need for that.'

'And why not?'

'I'll show you where it is. What Thorne hid. It's the proof. You can have it. If you don't hurt him.'

That moment lasted unnaturally. The motes drifting lazily through the air in the rain-soaked light; the white patch on the wall bleached by the sun's position, surrounded by dirty yellow. A bird was chirruping in the eaves, above the noise of the rain.

Eventually Warwick spoke. 'Well, that's better. Please. Lead the way.'

As they stood, Hopper considered her options. She could try to run, to grab the paper and get out, but that would leave David in the room, and she would be shot anyway. She could try to grab Blake's gun: they would all be shot. She could tear the paper in two, pretending there were more copies, and she would not be believed, and they would all be shot, and they would have the papers anyway. She could change her mind now, leave the soldiers hunting the house, and eventually they would find the brick of paper, and it would be burnt, and they would be shot.

All she had known, as Blake approached David, was that she would rather die herself than see him harmed on her behalf. The feeling thrilled her even as it frightened her.

So, without a better plan, she made her way to the door, Warwick after her, then David, then Mark, and finally Blake.

In the hall, two soldiers stood in the doorway facing into the house, replacing the two who were making a thorough search of the kitchen. They were older than the usual teenagers you saw in uniform these days, and they looked tougher. Outside the window she could see a troop lorry, one of the armoured ones they used in the city, capable of holding thirty bodies, and a few soldiers standing outside it dressed in black. Some had blunt-snouted masks on. Not regular troops.

The journey along the corridor was short, but Hopper noticed everything on it. A butterfly case hanging on the wall, a gossamer creature pinned inside, still here thirty years after the world's end. A pencil mark on the paintwork. A missing tile in the floor.

David muttered to her, almost inaudible. 'What are you doing, Ellie?'

'I don't know.'

She took them into the study. They filed in behind her, and Blake closed the door. It was a little small for five to stand. Hopper had her back to the desk, and she noticed again the solid-looking metal stapler on its surface next to her.

Her brother spoke first. 'You did say you wouldn't hurt them. Just now, in the van, you said that.'

'As the brother of a terrorist, Mr Hopper, you are in no position to negotiate.' Warwick's neck was flushed, Hopper noticed, and her hands too, a stinging-looking redness that betrayed her pleasure.

'You promised. You said she wouldn't be harmed once you had what you wanted.' Mark was almost pleading.

Warwick stood still, her eyes resting on Mark. She spoke gently. 'I gave no such guarantee, Mr Hopper. I said we would do our work in the interest of the country, on the highest authority. You know how important it is that these papers remain in responsible hands.'

Hopper noticed Blake's hand moving from his belt as he waited for what might come next. She looked at David, and then to Mark. If the three of them rushed Blake … it wouldn't make any difference.

'Mark, this isn't what you want,' she said, desperately. 'You don't have to side with them.'

He said out loud, 'Ellie, for Christ's sake, just give them what they're asking for. Then I can take you home.' But she saw his hands flexing nervously by his sides.

'Give us the papers, Doctor. Or Inspector Blake here will hurt your companion.'

She couldn't see how to escape, and handing over the papers was the only thing that could buy them a little more time, but she couldn't do it. She wouldn't.

Mark spoke again. 'It doesn't matter if she gives them to you. You've already decided they're not leaving this house.'

'I've had enough of this. Blake.'

Blake moved across to Hopper and struck her, hard, in the stomach. She fell to the ground, trying to hold on to him as she did so. He reached to hit her again, but was obstructed by something. Mark had tried to pull him away, pushing him off balance, but the older man grunted and elbowed sharply backwards, striking him on the side of the head, and he fell back instantly.

They remained there for a second in tableau. Hopper, winded and on the floor, her back to the desk; Mark sitting against the wall, dazed and bleeding; Blake standing above him, the brass ring conjured from nowhere over his fist; Warwick, now red-faced, still trying to seem calm, despite the deep flush in her cheeks and neck. Hopper looked over and saw why nobody was moving.

'Stop. Stop stop stop.' David had produced the pistol – he must have removed it from the car without her noticing, she thought vaguely through the pain in her torso – and was pointing it at Blake. 'Move back, please. Back to the wall.'

Hopper couldn't take her eyes off the gun. It looked like it hadn't been fired in decades. David raised a hand, made sure the safety catch was off, steadied his right hand with his left. Blake stepped back.

'Put it down, Gamble. You don't have to die in this house. None of you do. You can still do the work you are meant to do. I can take you back to London. All of you, if you like. We can decide what to do with these papers. I can save your job. If you fire that gun, you die here.' Warwick was speaking, low and urgent. She took a step towards him.

Hopper saw the gun waving between Blake and Warwick.

'Shoot her, David. For Christ's sake,' Hopper said.

'You can't win. Think of all the soldiers outside. If I scream, they'll come in. If you fire the gun, they'll come in. Nobody needs to do anything drastic here.'

Again Hopper saw David wavering. Warwick was close to him now. Another few steps and she would be able to push the gun down from his hand.

From beyond the house, they heard the crack of a gunshot. Then another. Then two more, from the other side of the house, and answering shots from further away, and a dull roar that made the remaining windows rattle in their panes. In the corridor, Hopper heard running feet, and the back door opening and slamming shut.

Warwick's voice was higher now. 'Nobody is to move. Nobody is to move an inch.'

'I'm sorry, Ellie,' David said. But he did not put the gun down. He swung and pulled the trigger. Blake fell. And Hopper, rising from her prone position, grabbed the heavy brass stapler from the desk and hit Warwick as hard as she could across the back of the head. Warwick fell too, landing awkwardly, and did not move.

'Mark?'

'I'm OK.' His face was grey, and blood was still streaming from his temple where Blake had hit him. She could see a vein pulsating in his neck, a tremolo back and forth under the scarlet rivulet of blood.

They pulled open the study door and looked out into the hall. One of the two soldiers who had been standing there had gone. The other was slumped just outside on the porch, taking sobbing breaths, a dark patch beneath him spreading across the yellow-bleached boards.

The scene at the front of the house was chaotic. The rain was coming down even harder than it had been when they arrived. The armoured lorry Hopper had seen from inside was on its side in the middle of the road, a gaping hole in the side that faced upwards, the cab full of flames and the windshield smashed in. What kind of firepower could have pushed a lorry that size over?

Several soldiers were lying immobile on the ground. Others were finding shelter behind the upturned lorry, hauling ammunition cases open, firing out into the woods, reloading with shaking fingers. One was pulling himself behind the vehicle, his leg broken, until a shot found him and he slumped. Another, crouched behind the gate, fell backwards, wounded by some missile from the treeline. She saw then what was happening. The men of the woods had returned.

Four huge iron plates were sitting on the ground inside the treeline, repurposed riot barriers she remembered seeing in

London. The fronts had been spray-painted with obscenities, cartoons, colours far brighter than the surrounding woodland. One by one the plates were being hauled up and shoved forwards, a few feet at a time, each receiving a volley of shots as they did so. But they were gradually advancing, and as they moved, unseen assailants from the other side fired inwards.

Lots of the woodsmen didn't care whether they lived or not, Hopper had once heard. They simply charged, taking the bullets they received as a blessing, as their permission to die. It must have been either a mistake or a lie, for there was no sign of that here. The men behind the shields clearly wanted to live, to harvest the soldiers' equipment, their ammunition, their food. Beyond the plates she thought she recognised one of the men who had attacked their car earlier, the one who had run off. He was clutching a large tube he must have fired at the lorry, and shouting directions.

There were perhaps a dozen soldiers left upright, and ten more scattered around the ground, both crawling and still. But David's car looked unscathed. Thank Christ they had parked along the street. If they could cross the garden, and get over the low wall, they would be at it. To its right was the soldiers' lorry, the troops huddled behind it.

'There's no way we can get to the car,' she said.

'Yes there is.' Mark had grabbed the rifle from the soldier slumped inside the doorway.

'Wait. We can't go yet.' She ran back into the house, into the little study. Blake and Warwick were still on the floor, not moving. Blake sat half upright, his back against the wall; Warwick was facing downwards, blood oozing slowly from the wound on the back of her head. Hopper stepped over her, pulled the bottom drawer of the desk open, found the brick of paperwork inside and pushed it tight inside her jacket, swaddling it against her front.

As she turned to go, she looked over at Blake. He was still breathing, just about, with bubbles at the corner of his mouth and his shirt almost black with blood. His eyes rested on her, half conscious, until another bang shook the windows in their panes and she ran out, along the corridor and back to the front door, where David and Mark were waiting.

Even in the minute since she had left the scene, the troops' situation had deteriorated. A soldier who had been sheltering in the smashed cab pushed open the door at the top and tried to haul himself out over the hot metal, then fell back as a bullet found him. And still the metal shields pressed inwards. The closest was nearly at the lorry.

'I'm going to get to the garden wall,' Mark said, pointing. 'When I start firing, run to the wall nearest the car. Once you're there, stop. When I start firing again, get into the car. You have the keys?'

'Mark, this is stupid. Let's go together.'

'I'll leave through the back once you're clear. But none of us will get out with the three of us running like chickens. Wait for me to say go.' He pulled at the door, grunting with the effort as it pushed against the soldier's body, and slipped onto the stone porch and across the garden.

Hopper turned to David. He looked grey and half vacant, flinching at every new round of gunfire, and she remembered how shocked he'd been after he'd killed the woodsman. She grabbed his jaw, focused his eyes on her.

'David. We have to leave. We're going to get to the wall. Do you have the keys?' He fished in his pocket, pulled them out as though he'd never seen them before. She spoke again. 'When Mark says to go, we have to move.' He nodded.

There were just eight or nine soldiers left behind the lorry now. They were gathering to the vehicle's right-hand side, perhaps to outflank the woodsmen. From where they were, the men behind the shields could not see them. Half the soldiers began to run, the others leaning out from the lorry and firing to cover them, and at that point Mark opened up with the rifle, the bullets clanging off the shield closest to the car. Hopper grabbed David and pulled him across the garden, the short ten metres to the wall.

She glanced across at Mark. *Come with us*, she thought she shouted, but she could not tell for sure whether she said it, or if he could even hear her above the gunfire. He did not acknowledge her, just chopped his hand through the air, telling them to leave, and started firing again. They jumped the low wall as his bullets clanged on the nearest shield, and after another ten metres of slow, slow open ground, every step agony on her ankle, David pulled the car door open and fell in first, scrambling over so she could get in beside him.

The back left window of the car exploded, and she could not work out how the woodsmen had hit it from the wrong side. She turned, slowly, and saw Warwick stumbling from the house with a pistol in her hand – she must have taken it from Blake – and firing it at Mark, still facing the other way. Her first shot missed and hit the wall he was sheltering behind, and Mark began to swivel around towards her, too slowly.

Warwick fired once more and Mark's body arced and fell. She fired again, hitting him where he lay. Then she turned to her right and fired two more rounds, which clanged harmlessly off the metal shield closest to her, and no more, for by that time the men of the woods had moved from either side and descended on her.

And with that the scene disappeared from view, as David shifted up through the gears and accelerated away as fast as he could.

42

After ten minutes, nobody had appeared behind them, and David started driving a little slower along the battered road. Hopper had been looking back all that time.

David spoke first. 'Are you all right?'

She nodded. 'I'm fine. What about you?'

'My shoulder hurts.' He gestured with his head.

There was a rent at the top of his jacket and a puddle of dark wetness inside it, smaller than a fist. She reached back, grabbed a shirt from her bag, and pressed it as hard as she could onto the wound. He winced, and the car veered, but he pulled it back into the centre of the decaying road.

'It's all right. It's very small. We can get this treated somewhere.'

'What happened to Mark?' He glanced at her, and she shook her head.

Neither of them spoke for a few minutes. Mark, dead. It didn't feel real. Her last family, her last connection to this old world. She thought of Laura, and the children, now fatherless, not knowing it yet. She felt a pang of grief, painful and unexpected, for her brother.

Tentatively, despite the shock, despite Mark, she smiled at David, and he caught a glimpse of her expression and smiled – just a little – himself. They were approaching a turning.

'Which way?'

She thought for a second. This road would eventually lead onto the one that would take them to London. 'Go right when you can. We won't go back into London.'

'Where are we heading?' He had said it not quite to ask for information, not quite for confirmation of what he already knew, but somewhere in between, an idea that both of them saw growing slowly distinct. Like a mountain looming in the distance, or the slow approach of dawn.

'South-west. American Zone.'

'It's not a sanctuary there, you know. We don't even know who we're looking for.'

Hopper remembered the man on the radio in Fisher's bookshop.

'That's not quite true, David. I know who we're looking for.'

'There might be more roadblocks,' David said. 'They'll know before long that their plan hasn't worked out. We need to tell someone as soon as possible.'

Hopper twisted around in her seat, reached back for her bag, and heaved it towards her. She rummaged through it and took out the transmitter. 'Pull over. Anywhere that looks quiet.'

The Last Day

They crunched to a stop in the mouth of a little lane, so shaded by trees and overhanging bushes that anyone not looking closely would think the car had been abandoned. They got out. Hopper assembled the radio, erected the aerial, and found the notch on the front, the bandwidth Fisher had been transmitting to.

She sent a few pulses to wake up whoever might be receiving. There was no answer. Had they said they were shutting this loop down? Were they even monitoring this wavelength any more? She sent three more pulses, then three more, her fingers shaking, willing the signals onwards, hoping there was someone at the other end to hear.

For ten agonising seconds, the radio made no response. Then there was a crackle, and they heard the same voice she had heard in the bookshop: warm, rich, American. 'Hello?'

Hopper sagged in relief. 'It's me again. Ellen. From Fisher's place. I kept his radio.'

'I remember.' The voice was wary.

'I have a message for you. Something important. I think it's what Fisher was trying to get hold of. Are you ready to take this down?'

'Wait a second … OK. I'm receiving you.'

She spoke for ten minutes, passing the pages over to David when she had read each one. After she finished, there was a long pause.

'I can't believe this.' The voice cracked. 'I can't believe it.'

'It's all here. Proof.' The word sounded luxurious in her ears. *Proof.* She had it, at last. 'And the satellite is still up there, and still working. You have receivers, don't you?'

'All sorts.'

'Then as long as you can find the signal, this is how you can access it.' She read out the satellite's frequency, then the long string of digits at the front of the document, the decryption key that would allow them to access its data. She read it twice, to be sure. And as she finished the second time, she felt something else passing over the waves, something intangible and precious. It felt like hope.

The voice spoke again. 'OK, I've got that copied. We'll check it out today.'

'There's one other thing,' Hopper said. 'We can't stay on this side of the border. Not now.'

'No,' the voice said. 'I'm inclined to agree. I think you'd better come and see us. There's a place where we can get people across without anyone noticing.' He gave directions, which Hopper wrote down. Then she packed up the radio, and they clambered slowly back into the car.

David turned the key, and they crunched out onto the road. 'What about after we get to the American Zone?'

'I'm going to go on.'

He laughed. 'What? To actual America?'

'Yes.'

'You're mad.'

'We can do it, David.'

'I'm not saying we can't.' He paused. 'What will we do there?'

'Whatever we decide.'

'Well, then.' He gunned the engine a little, and shifted up a gear. 'South-west it is.'

'Give me your hand,' she said. He freed one hand from the wheel and Hopper took it in her own, her other still pressing on his injured shoulder.

He smiled at her again, more broadly. 'Do you think we can do this?'

'I do.'

'Still sure about the future?'

'I'd say it's a little more open than it used to be.' And she smiled back at him.

They drove under a lightening sky until the rain was behind them. Up ahead were patches of blue, the clouds scudding lightly across. Above the car, they heard birds that had made their homes in unfamiliar branches, parrots and cockatiels and mynahs, and the trees coming through the lower reaches of the forest floor were thicker and wilder, displacing the older trunks to take their place in the light of the sun.

The car turned west at the next junction, and began to make its way, driving once again careful and slow, towards the American Zone.

Acknowledgements

A lot of people have helped this book see the light of day.

My literary agent Peter Straus has been a patient guide ever since I wandered into his office and told him an unlikely-sounding idea for a book; and once it was ready, he knew just who might like to read it. My sincere thanks to him and to all his colleagues at RCW.

At Penguin Random House, I have been very lucky to work with Selina Walker, a superb editor who has helped shape and improve the book beyond measure. Jane Selley's assiduous proofreading caught numerous blunders before they made it to print – and Stephanie Heathcote created the beautiful cover. Fergus Edmondson on marketing and Klara Zak on PR were responsible for anyone actually finding out about the book. Thanks too to Susan Sandon, for taking a punt on a story like this in the first place, and the whole team at PRH, who made the process of publishing a debut novel far more enjoyable than I had anticipated.

The scientific advisers Rob Blake, Matt Loxham, and Harry Bryden gave their time and provided knowledgeable direction about the state of the heavens and the oceans. On the astrophysics side, the advice of Josephine Peterson (PhD) was vital in dragging the planet to a halt.

Early readers Palomi Kotecha, Caroline Lord and Heather McRobie generously lent their time and advice. The earliest reader of all, Maisie Glazebrook, gave tremendous feedback (it *was* too long). And Katherine Rundell saw potential in the idea in the first place and recommended I keep going when I was considering giving up.

Personal thanks are due to my colleagues at *QI* and *Private Eye*, who have been hearing about this idea for a few years now, and to my parents, who let me read throughout my entire childhood, even at meals.

My final thanks go to Molly Lyne, whose support and encouragement have been unfailing throughout. A lifetime spent facing you will be no hardship.